The
Next Best
Fling

The Next Best Fling

GABRIELLA GAMEZ

FOREVER

New York Boston

Copyright © 2024 by Gabriella Gamez
Reading group guide copyright © 2024 by Gabriella Gamez and Hachette Book Group, Inc.

Cover design by Daniela Medina
Cover illustration by Leni Kauffman
Cover copyright © 2024 by Hachette Book Group, Inc.

Forever
Hachette Book Group
1290 Avenue of the Americas, New York, NY 10104
read-forever.com
@readforeverpub

First Edition: July 2024

Forever is an imprint of Grand Central Publishing. The Forever name and logo are trademarks of Hachette Book Group, Inc.

The publisher is not responsible for websites (or their content) that are not owned by the publisher.

The Hachette Speakers Bureau provides a wide range of authors for speaking events. To find out more, go to hachettespeakersbureau.com or email HachetteSpeakers@hbgusa.com.

Forever books may be purchased in bulk for business, educational, or promotional use. For information, please contact your local bookseller or the Hachette Book Group Special Markets Department at special.markets@hbgusa.com.

Library of Congress Cataloging-in-Publication Data
Names: Gamez, Gabriella, author.
Title: The next best fling / Gabriella Gamez.
Description: First edition. | New York : Forever, 2024. | Series: Librarians in love
Identifiers: LCCN 2023049630 | ISBN 9781538726631 (trade paperback) | ISBN 9781538726648 (ebook)
Subjects: LCGFT: Romance fiction. | Novels.
Classification: LCC PS3607.A436 N49 2024 | DDC 813/.6—dc23/eng/20231030
LC record available at https://lccn.loc.gov/2023049630

ISBN: 9781538726631 (trade paperback), 9781538726648 (ebook)

Printed in the United States of America

LSC

Printing 3, 2024

For all the readers, educators, and librarians fighting the good fight to get diverse books into the hands of those who need them the most.

I hope we win.

One

A little black box sits in his outstretched hand.

The shape is so recognizable, my breath catches. It could be earrings, I think wildly. His smile is shy, hazel eyes shining with hope at the unspoken question between us. Adrenaline surges in my veins, keeping me at attention. My heart thumps so hard my ears fill with the sound of rushing blood until it's all I can hear. *Thump. Thump. Thump.* When he opens the box, I let out a gasp.

Definitely not earrings.

The ring nestled inside is modest and delicate, the diamond elegantly set in a gold band surrounded by a cluster of smaller stones. My mouth opens as if to speak, but all that comes out is a muted noise from the back of my throat. The ring is stunning, but that's hardly the most important aspect of this moment. His eyes stay trained on my face, analyzing for any clue he can. I hold out my hand for a closer look, and he deposits the box into it.

Dread settles in my stomach as I realize what this means,

but I try not to show my emotions on my face. I've learned to become good at that when it comes to Ben Young.

"Well?" he asks, no longer able to contain himself. Then, the question that threatens to undo me completely—

"Do you think she'll like it?"

The chatter of the restaurant dulls to a low register. We're surrounded on all sides by the early lunch crowd, but I can't hear a single sound. He means Alice Cho, his girlfriend of eight years and future recipient of this engagement ring. I don't care how long they've been dating or what anyone else has to say about it, but twenty-seven is far too young to be thinking about marriage. But then again, *anyone else* would argue that I'm just bitter the man I'm pining over is legally binding himself to someone else until death do they part. And maybe I am, despite how close our friendship still is after all these years. I want him to be happy regardless of my feelings. Not that anyone aside from Angela, my other best friend, knows about these feelings.

I haven't been close with Alice in years so I can't say if the ring is to her taste, but the style is hardly what matters. It's the love between them that does, and for all my years of pining, I've never been able to question *that*. I glance across the table at Ben, meeting his hopeful eyes. My mouth turns up into a smile I don't feel, but it fools him anyway. Hiding your true feelings is easy when the person you're hiding from has never really seen you to begin with.

"It's perfect," I tell him, because it is. The lasagna primavera I just scarfed down churns in my stomach. I swallow hard past a wave of nausea. I can't tell if it's nerves or acid reflux making me queasy, or maybe just the diamond staring up at me. Taunting. When I can no longer stand to look at the thing, I shut the tiny box with a loud *snap* and hastily hand it back to him. He's too preoccupied to note any sign of agitation on my end.

"You really think so?" Ben asks, guarding the box close to his chest. A lock of light brown hair falls over his brow, making him look boyish and fragile. He glances down at the object his hands are cradling with a wary expression, like he's looking down at his heart instead. And I suppose, to him, he is. There are enough metaphors out there to make the two synonymous.

"Are you kidding?" I ask with forced cheer, but it comes out so smooth you'd never know that internally I'm quaking. He visibly brightens at my tone. "She'd be a fool to say no."

His tense shoulders deflate immediately, the edges of his mouth turning up as he returns my fake smile with one that is undeniably real. He flashes a full row of straight, shiny white teeth, and the sight makes me smile brighter. A hint of real amid the plaster because his happiness is ultimately what I want most for him. Even if it's at the expense of mine.

"You really think so, Marcela?" he asks.

"She's going to love it," I say with as much assurance as I can muster. If I ever had another chance with Ben, that time is long gone, and has been for a while. Years, probably, if I'm being honest. Still, I'm ashamed to admit just how much time I've spent holding out hope that one day he'll see that he was an idiot to ever say we were better off as just friends. God, it should feel like a lifetime ago, but our freshman year at the University of Texas at San Antonio still feels like just yesterday.

Wishful thinking.

Now, with the engagement ring between us, I'm struck by just how long it's been. The years wear on me all at once, a wave of exhaustion crashing over me.

"Stop worrying," I tell him, reforming my supportive-friend facade. "When are you gonna pop the question?"

"I was thinking this weekend. I have a reservation at Whiskey Cake on Friday night. I'm just not sure if I should ask during dinner or wait until after when we're alone."

"Whatever you choose, just *please*, for the love of God, don't put it in her wineglass." He laughs, probably thinking of the way she'd downed shots throughout college. We all went pretty hard back then, but Alice could drink us all to shame. The girl can chug a full keg of beer without thinking twice. "Otherwise, y'all will be celebrating the rest of the night in the emergency room."

"You might have a point." He smiles, his eyes lighting up with unbridled happiness. "I can't believe this is really happening."

You and me both.

"Well, believe it!" I exclaim with feigned enthusiasm. "And tell me all about it on Monday. I wanna hear every detail."

I most certainly do *not*, but what else can I possibly say? The truth I haven't once dared to utter out loud? Doubtful. We spend the rest of lunch chatting about all possible outcomes, how his parents will respond to the news when (he says "if," but I already know it's a forgone conclusion) she says yes, until the check arrives and we part ways in the parking lot.

Once I'm safely tucked away in my car, I allow the emotions I've been holding off to finally crash over me. I had no idea until today what Ben's been planning. That he and Alice have talked about building a more permanent life together. Tears sting my eyes, but I'm too stubborn to let them fall. *So stupid.*

This shouldn't have been a surprise to me. They've been together since they were *nineteen*. Nearly a decade. It'd be weird if marriage wasn't on their minds. But even still, *this*, an honest-to-God engagement ring, is a gut punch I never saw coming.

I've known for a while now that I have to get over this silly crush, but today was a wake-up call. If Ben and I were ever going to happen for real, it would've happened already. Now I can move on. After a pumpkin empanada or six.

Friday night, I arrive back at my apartment from work with my second box of pan dulce this week to drown my feelings in. Stress-eating is my time-honored tradition, and pumpkin empanadas are my kryptonite. Consequence of having a Mexican mother with an all-powerful sweet-tooth gene. I'll feel guilty in the morning but will do nothing about it until Sunday, when my best friend, Angela Gutierrez, comes over for our weekly morning walk on the trail outside my building. It's the only exercise we get since neither of us can afford gym memberships with our salaries. Not that I would ever step foot inside a gym willingly.

My two-bedroom apartment is tiny, but it's all I need. A plush, heather-gray couch is pushed in the corner of the living room facing a small black TV stand, where my twenty-inch smart TV resides. I'm not even sure my apartment comes with cable, but there's no need for it when a good chunk of my paycheck is divided among three different streaming sites. The living room and kitchen are separated by this weird half wall that transitions into the dining bar past the couch. I keep most of my library books along the half wall, as well as on the antique entrance table by the front door. If I keep them with the books I already own, they'll never get returned and I'll be the first librarian to ever get their library card permanently confiscated.

My best friend arrives moments after I do, announcing herself by ringing the doorbell five more times than necessary. When I let her in, she's carrying a familiar, nondescript white paper bag I immediately recognize from our favorite panadería downtown. *Bless her.*

"Oh, shit, you beat me!" Angela exclaims when she spots the equally nondescript white box sitting on my coffee table. "How are you already here when I got off an hour before you?"

"Erica let me go early. Apparently, I've been nothing but useless to myself and others all day." Those weren't her exact words, but I wouldn't have blamed her for saying them. My boss was much nicer when she sent me home, telling me to sleep off my "mind fog" when the third person I'd checked out left the building to the blaring sound of alarm bells. There's a reason we bump the books before handing them off to patrons, and three is too many times to forget in one day. Angela was buried in shelving all day, so I'm not surprised she didn't notice.

"It was a slow day, anyway."

"You need to get out of this funk, Marcela," Angela says. Then she holds out her hand. "All right, let's see it."

I hand over my phone with a dramatic groan. Her expression turns contemplative as she reads over the profile I've just updated. Underneath my name and age—Marcela Ortiz, 27—is my job title and a list of my favorite authors, quotes, and drinks. Her eyes narrow the longer she reads, until finally she shakes her head in disapproval.

"No." She hands me my phone back. "Absolutely unacceptable."

"Oh, come on! I thought I did a pretty good job this time."

"You *cannot* put an obscure quote from *An Ember in the Ashes* in your Tinder bio." She rolls her eyes at my pout. "Read the room, Marcela."

"What? I thought it was fitting, considering the circumstances."

She rolls her eyes again so hard that I'm surprised she doesn't get brain damage on the spot. "Your subliminal messaging is positively uncanny."

I look down at my phone and read over the quote in my bio.

"There are two kinds of guilt: the kind that drowns you until you're useless, and the kind that fires your soul to purpose."

It had been Angela's idea to revive my dating accounts when I told her all about my painful lunch with Ben. She wasn't nearly as surprised as I was to learn that Ben was taking the next big step in his relationship with Alice, which only shows how far removed from reality my own feelings have made me. Loving someone you can't have is exhausting. But loving someone who's in a committed relationship crushes you under a thousand-pound weight of guilt and shame until it bleeds you dry. Living under that weight isn't just unsustainable, it's also lonely and heartbreaking and unbearable and I can't do it for a second longer.

So, in choosing Tinder, I'm choosing the latter. Fire my soul to purpose, baby.

"Sabaa Tahir is too wise for this world," I say, almost wistfully. Then I glance over my shoulder at my friend with an innocent look. "Too deep for Tinder?"

"I really don't think I need to answer that."

She snatches the phone out of my hand before I can blink, fingers darting across the keyboard to rewrite a half hours' worth of thoughtful consideration. Angela finishes typing in under two minutes, and when she hands my phone back to me, I guffaw as my eyes trail down the screen. Apparently, I live for spontaneous adventure and am NOT looking for anything serious. She even changed two of my three profile pictures, and my teen librarian title is gone.

"*Casual*." My brain sticks on the word, refusing to make sense of it. "I really don't think I'm a 'casual' kind of girl."

"No better time to start than now. You should be using Tinder for what it's intended for." Her curly hair bounces off her shoulders as she leans forward to grab a bright yellow concha from the box on the coffee table. "One-night stands."

Angela, ever the commitment-phobe. She has her pick of romantic interests, being beautiful, willowy, and tall, with gorgeous hazel eyes and olive-toned skin. Although she's quick to dole out relationship advice, she's never actually had one of her own. Not even a fling, for as long as I've known her. The girl can expertly flirt her way to free drinks for an entire table, but she rejects every single advance that comes her way. I've always wondered if there was a reason for that.

"When have *you* ever used Tinder for a one-night stand?" I shoot back, raising my brows at her.

"I've never used dating apps in general. I have no interest in them." I've always suspected as much, but I'm still a bit surprised by the confirmation. "My time will come when it comes. But you"—she shakes a bony finger at me—"you need all the help you can get."

I heave a sigh. She's not wrong about that.

"I still don't think a one-night stand is the answer."

"Not according to every rom-com out there," she insists, voice slightly garbled around a mouthful of pan. Once she swallows, her expression turns serious. "They've been together a long time, Marcela. You can't keep doing this to yourself." I look away from her, not wanting to go down this rabbit hole again. "I know it's tough, but you should've done this a long time ago."

"It's not like I haven't tried. I don't like the idea of random hookups. It all seems too nerve-racking."

I've been on a string of failed first dates, enough talking phases to test my sanity, and exactly two relationships (if you could call them that, given that both fell apart almost as quickly as they came) since Ben. Maybe if any part of me found dating exciting, I wouldn't have so much trouble. As it is, my body confidence is in constant fluctuation depending on the day and dating only adds more pressure to that. Sure, when I'm feeling particularly confident, I can appreciate the hourglass figure my soft curves form—a large bust that dips into a slightly tapered waist before widening into rounded hips and thick thighs. My butt, however, is surprisingly flat. Of all the departments to fall short in, it *would* be the one area I wish a little more fat would travel to.

But I never know how the men I date, and potentially become intimate with, will react when they see my body. I've been burned before, the few times I actively participated in hookup culture. And that was with men I spent time getting to know, only for them to turn around and treat me like crap in bed. They got what they wanted from me, but what did I get? Certainly not what I'd (ahem, *didn't*) come for. Not decency, not respect. Not even a call or text back after, though the ghosts were almost preferable to the ones who'd attempted to let me down easy directly after sex. As if telling someone you'd just been inside that you never wanted to see them again wasn't gross enough, there aren't enough showers in the world to wash off the shame of hearing I wasn't their "usual type," or even worse, that they weren't attracted to me.

That one was a head scratcher until I realized it was a coded way of saying what they were too afraid to.

Score one for fatphobia, followed by another point for every time I internalized that shit. Which is why until now, I've practically given up on dating entirely. I'm able to love my body so much more when I'm not bombarded with the reminder that there are plenty of men who don't. I'm not interested in putting myself in that position again.

"Okay, then how 'bout a fling?" Angela suggests instead, brows waggling suggestively. "Get to know the guy a little bit before jumping into his pants, and then never speak to him again."

I scrunch up my face. "That sounds mean."

"Or let him loose gently into the wind for the next girl to find," she amends. "Happy?"

"Not particularly." I let out a sigh, knowing I don't have much of a choice if I'm serious about getting over Ben. "But I guess it wouldn't hurt to try."

Angela finds the vodka stashed on top of my refrigerator as I swipe left and right with no real meaning. I take a shot when I get my first match, and then another when the guy never responds to my message. When the bottle is halfway gone, Angela takes my phone and sticks it with hers inside the lock case under my TV stand. The two of us have too many shared secrets not to secure our phones somewhere far, *far* away when the booze comes out.

By midnight, we're both trashed and laughing for no reason. It's the best I've felt all day, which I drunkenly gush to her.

"This is how I know it's time to cut you off." She snatches the bottle out of my hand. When I pout, she says, "Pobrecita. You'll get over it." I'm not sure if she's talking about the vodka or Ben. Either way, I don't believe her.

She crashes onto my bed right beside me, fast asleep as soon as her head hits the pillow. Her soft snores fill the bedroom, keeping me up. I lie awake next to her, my head swimming with thoughts of diamond rings and randomized Tinder profiles.

The next morning, after retrieving my phone from the lock case, my first text message of the day is from Ben.

She said yes!!!

I type out a quick reply, "**Knew she would!**" and roll over with a loud groan. Angela remains fast asleep, and I envy her. My head is pounding from last night, and my heart is pounding for reasons too early in the day to abuse myself with. But what's done is done. Yet another outcome I can't change.

Two

Please Join Us For an
Engagement Party
In Honor of

Ben Young and Alice Cho

Saturday, September 30th
At Seven O'clock in the Evening

look down at the gold foil, the afternoon sunlight bouncing off the lettering as dread sinks low in my stomach. Reality settles over me for the second time, as if knowing I'd willfully overlook it the first. *He's getting married.* It's real now, as real as the embossing beneath my fingertips.

Surprisingly, Alice was the one who came over to hand-deliver the invitation. She's wearing light-wash jeans and a cream mock-neck sweater that hugs her frame in all the right ways. I envied her that, when she first started dating

Ben. Her straight black hair falls sleekly past her shoulders, her light brown eyes narrowed slightly, as if she can see right through me. There's no malice in her expression, but it's always unnerved me how keen her gaze is. How naturally inquisitive. I've never breathed a word of my feelings for her boyfriend—fiancé now—to anyone besides Angela, but I can never quite shake the feeling that she *knows*. Not that she's ever breathed as much, either.

Maybe it's just paranoia.

Her smile is warm despite the knowledge shining in her eyes. "It's gonna be at the Gardens. Our families are all coming down for it, and then there'll be brunch on Sunday at the Guenther House with close friends and family. You're invited to brunch too, of course. It's a wonder we've been able to get everything together so quickly at the last minute!"

"Right? It hasn't even been a week." I glance up at her from the invitation. "How'd you guys manage to get the venue so soon?"

"Turns out Ben's been doing some planning of his own," she says idly. "He had the place booked over a month ago! I'd be shocked at his presumption if I wasn't floating on cloud nine." She chuckles lightly at this and I join her, hoping she doesn't see through the fake sound.

There was a time in college when we were close. She was the first friend I made at freshman orientation and we carried that over into sophomore year. Then she and Ben started dating. Before they became serious, we remained close, but I also felt betrayed on a level I could never convey to her. Ben and I had only been out on a few dates, and we remained close friends afterward. We hung out with our group of friends, night after night, and I never once let it slip that I was still holding out hope that we might try again one day.

I kept it cool at the time, but I also kept my distance from Alice from that point on. Ever since, there's always been a discernible awkwardness that hangs over every conversation we have by ourselves. Even years later, when I should be over it. But I'm not even over her boyfriend—*fiancé*. I can already tell I'll never get used to saying that. The betrayal she doesn't even know she committed still stings, even as the guilt heats my skin and makes me break out in a sweat each time we interact.

"Well, let me know if you need any help setting up," I offer, if only to seem like I'm not slowly dying on the inside. The least I can do is redeem myself by helping ensure the party goes off without a hitch. Not that she needs to know there's an ulterior motive to my kindness. "You can count on me to make any part of the process less stressful."

"Oh, that's such a sweet offer." She puts both hands over her heart, the engagement ring on her finger catching the light like a warning sign. "Actually, since you brought it up, do you think you could pick up Ben's brother from the airport? He's coming back from an away game in Atlanta."

Right. I always forget about Ben's NFL player brother. Why can't I be like the rest of Alice's friends and lust after him instead?

"His flight arrives Friday morning, and I'm having such a hard time getting the day off."

"Of course. Happy to do it." I've met Theo only a handful

of times. He and Ben used to be inseparable when they were younger, but they drifted apart when Theo left home for college. Over the years, I've pieced together that there was some sort of rift between them, but I've never gotten a clear answer from Ben about what happened to cause it. They barely speak now, but of course Theo would still want to celebrate with them. He's family. I'm sure whatever their differences are, he'd still want to congratulate them.

"You're a lifesaver! Thank you so much. He'll be staying with me and Ben. I actually have a spare key on me, hold on." She digs through her purse for a moment before coming up with the shiny silver key. "Here."

"Oh, cool." I force yet another smile I don't feel. "You can count on me."

"Thank you so much, Marcela." She wraps me in a hug, smiling sweetly as we say our goodbyes. "You're too good to us. I'll see you at the party."

"Can't wait!" I lie, my face stretched into the fakest smile of my life.

When I return to my bedroom, I swipe through Tinder for half an hour. Just when I'm about to give up, my phone pings with a match. I wait for him to message first this time, continuously skimming over profiles and swiping until I let out a groan. Needing a distraction from Tinder, I open up the message app and tell Angela about the engagement party. Her reply comes right away.

You need to bring a date.

I groan again, furiously typing that there are no good men left on Tinder. We argue back and forth for a bit before I finally give a half-assed reply that I'll try harder. This is so obviously a lie that she doesn't bother to send more than an eye-roll emoji. I leave her on read and take a shower, hoping to wash off the stench of despair and longing before next weekend arrives.

The first time I met Theo Young, he was drunk off his ass.

It was three months into my sophomore year of college, and until then I'd only encountered fun drunks. Sorority girls dancing on tabletops. Frat bros stripping themselves of all clothing before cannonballing into the pool at the activity center. Even I had been a fun drunk at the few parties I'd been to thus far. Lost my inhibitions as well as myself to the music and talked *way* too much for my own good. But Theo was far from fun that night.

He was…angry, maybe? Not at anyone in particular, except maybe himself. If there's a word to combine rage and sorrow, Theo was that. He drank himself into a stupor in Ben's student apartment, shattered two bottles of tequila and then a mirror with his own hand. When his face was scrunched with incoming tears, I had the oddest feeling it wasn't due to any sort of physical pain. His scream woke half the building, but by the time we got a noise complaint and a visit from campus security, he was already out cold. I'd been scared seeing him like that, but not for myself. Not even for Ben, though he had been backed against a corner the entire night, face sheet white. I wondered what could drive a person to destroy himself like that, and not care who was watching.

It wasn't until he was asleep that Ben tended to his brother's wounded hand. I watched over his shoulder as he cleaned it, my stomach churning at the amount of blood gushing from such a deceptively tiny cut. He looked so small, wincing as he wiped down the cuts with rubbing alcohol wipes, as if scared his brother would wake up from the sting of pain and continue on his rampage. Looking back, that night is what made me fall for Ben even more. We were broken up by then, but my heart ached as I watched the careful way he cared for his brother. Even when I was sure Theo didn't deserve such kindness, after visiting Ben only to act like *that* the entire time. I made my excuses and left soon after, not imagining the morning after could be any better.

Later, Ben told me about Theo's injury. A torn ACL had shot his chances at playing pro football and had been the reason for his drunken furor. "He pushes himself too hard" had been Ben's explanation. "He's had problems with his knee before, but he never lets himself heal properly."

For the meantime, that was that. The end of a career before it could begin. Or so we thought. The sideline turned out to be only temporary, but none of us knew it back then.

The second time I saw Theo I hardly recognized him, and not just because a year and a half had passed in the time between. Not only was he sober, but he was also smiling as wide as his mouth could stretch, genuine happiness shining in his eyes. We were at a brunch date with Alice and Ben the day after they moved in together.

Theo pulled me aside later to apologize for the first time we met. I was struck by his earnestness, so at odds with the thrashing man I'd been faced with before. Even more so that he even remembered I'd been there that night. He was so drunk, I assumed he'd blacked out. He wouldn't let me wave off his apology like it was nothing, my usual gut response when anyone tries to apologize to me for any reason, even a warranted one.

"Truly, Marcela. If I scared or hurt you at all that night, I'm sorry," he said, a gentle hand laid on my shoulder. "I should've controlled myself better. But believe me, it *won't* happen again." I wasn't sure why he bothered making that kind of promise to me when we barely knew each other.

Out of the corner of my eye, I caught Ben watching us closely. His eyes were narrowed in thought, body poised to rise from his seat at the first sign of trouble. Theo's back was to him, so he didn't notice. The conversation didn't last long, but something about it made me uneasy. Like there was a piece missing in this puzzle, but I was the only oblivious one.

As for Theo, I could hardly reconcile the two versions I'd seen of him. I still can't say which one is real.

Now, when I reach the airport, I set my car in park and wait for him to arrive at pickup. It doesn't take long to spot his blond head, mostly because he's at least half a foot taller than the crowd of people around him. I roll down the passenger window and wave him over. He deposits his bags in the trunk before settling into the passenger seat of my tiny Chevrolet.

"Hey." Not much has changed in his appearance since the

last time I saw him. That was a few years ago, maybe? He'd puked in a ficus at brunch, then tipped the waitress a hundred bucks to make up for it. As nice a gesture as that was, I'm still convinced the guy has some serious issues to work through. His hair is shorter than I remember, cropped close to his scalp. He's dressed in gray sweatpants and a hoodie despite the heat, but I imagine beneath all those layers he's still built like a god. At least, that's what Christine, Alice's best friend, says every time he comes down to visit. Every year, it gets harder and harder for Alice to pull her away from the poor guy. It's no surprise she asked me for the favor instead.

"Thanks for picking me up. You didn't need to trouble yourself."

"It's not a problem. I already had the day off and no plans to speak of," I say with an easy laugh. "So, can you believe Ben and Alice are getting married?" I don't actually want to talk about Ben and Alice, but I don't know what else to say around this man I barely know. Since our only commonality is Ben, there really isn't much else to make small talk about. "It still feels like we're too young to be settling down."

He grunts but doesn't reply. Okay? Maybe he doesn't want to talk about their engagement either, though I can't imagine what his reasons are. I go for a new angle.

"How was the game?" Even as the question comes out of my mouth, I brace myself for the answer. My knowledge of football is abysmal at best, and I certainly don't care to change that. The UTSA team was historically bad when I was there, but that didn't stop a concerning amount of students from using home games as a chance to start tailgating at eight in the morning. While all our friends spent the day drinking, Ben and I would skip out in favor of a movie. Though he'd played in high school, Ben seemed to want nothing to do with the sport. Even now, he still changes the channel when a football game comes on.

But surprisingly, all I get from Theo is another grunt. His shoulders sink, head turning away from the windshield. Okay…so no football talk, either. Geez, what else is there to talk about with this guy?

Nothing, apparently. The rest of the car ride is mostly silent, except for when I blaze over a speed bump and Theo's head hits the roof of my car with a loud *thunk*. I apologize profusely and offer him Advil from my purse, already digging through it before he can respond. I end up driving over another bump while I'm distracted. My car veers slightly left before Theo makes a grab for the wheel to straighten it.

"Sorry." My voice goes higher as I take the wheel back, face heating from embarrassment. Thankfully the residential road is deserted, so we don't run the risk of cops being called and mistaking me for a drunk driver. When I shoot a glance at Theo, he's clutching the top of his head with one hand.

"Small car problems." I shoot him a sheepish smile. "I'm *so* sorry. I don't know how to drive with tall people in the passenger seat."

"It's okay," he assures me, an amused quirk to his lips. It's not quite a smile, but it's enough of *something* to put me at ease. "You get used to it in my field. I only wish I brought my helmet."

I laugh half-heartedly at the joke. My smile is cautious,

because even though he's finally loosened up, I'm still wondering what thoughts he's keeping to himself.

When we arrive at Ben and Alice's apartment, it's not a moment too soon. He thanks me for the ride before making his way up the stairs with his bags. I'm still not sure what to make of Theo. Every time I think of him, I see his body sprawled out on the tile floor, shards of glass between his bloodied fingers. Of the pain behind his scratchy throat and the scream that woke half the apartment building. Then I think of him nearly two years later, amiable enough (puke notwithstanding). Smiling like he's never known the pain he displayed the first night we met. Laughing like he's never felt the sting of it.

Years have passed, but I still have a bad feeling about him.

"Are you stalking Ben's brother?"

I snap my laptop shut, and Angela pounces. Bending over my shoulder, she attempts to pry the screen open beneath my splayed hands. I wince but hold on tighter. A few coffee shop patrons turn to stare at us, but she doesn't even blink. Even in public, she's not afraid to act like a child.

That's my best friend, folks.

When I'm finally able to shake her off, she pouts before taking the dark wood chair across from me. "I'm not *stalking* anyone," I tell her. "I'm just trying to prove a theory."

"And what theory would that be?" she asks, raising a brow as she takes a bite of her quiche.

"Doesn't matter. It's kinda stupid, and his profile is private anyway," I say, just as another thought occurs to me. "Unless, he has a Wikipedia page. Football fans care about that kind of shit, right?"

"Well, I suppose this is better than pining over the groom-to-be," Angela notes with a casual tone as she takes another bite. I scowl at her, but she remains unfazed. "Though, I'm not sure if it's the step up it should be, given they're related. But they're not close, *and* Theo doesn't live in town, so maybe he's the perfect rebound candidate for you after all."

"I'm not *into* him." I roll my eyes at the mere suggestion. "I just have…a weird feeling about him."

"Weird how?" she asks. "He's *such* a sweetheart, and not to mention a total babe. You should hear the way Alice's friends talk about him. It's indecent, and that's putting it lightly." I'm well aware. I sat next to Christine the last time Theo was in town, and all she could talk about were the things she wanted to do to him. Then again, since college Angela has always been closer to them than I have, so I can't imagine the kind of intel she's privy to.

"We don't know that he's a 'sweetheart.' We barely know him at all," I argue. "There's a wildcard at every wedding, and something's telling me it's him."

I may not know the reason behind the rift between Theo and Ben, but I know it was intentional on Theo's part. Before he visited Ben the night we met, they hadn't spoken a word to each other in two years. No matter how many times Ben tried reaching out to him, he was met with silence. I may not know much about Theo, but I know enough to be wary.

"The dude covered for Alice's pregnancy scare a few years ago at brunch." My head snaps up from my computer screen. *What?* "He called it 'drinking for two,' and puked in a ficus. There's nothing *not* sweet about that."

But my mind is still stuck on what she said before. *Pregnancy scare?* How come I never knew about that? The thought of Ben and Alice with a baby makes *me* want to puke. Now that they're about to get married, I can only assume they're not that far off from starting a family. But to think, they could've gotten there so much sooner...

"You sure you're not just projecting? Maybe *you're* the wildcard." My mouth falls open in a near-gasp at Angela's suggestion. In the end, the only sound that comes out is a pitiful squeak.

"What? I know what you're capable of with enough alcohol in your system. Open bar is probably a bad call on the happy couple's part."

"*Enough.*" My heart is racing. I have to force myself to take a deep breath. "Maybe I am projecting, but I would never willingly try to ruin their engagement. You know that, right?"

My stomach flips as she swallows another bite of quiche. I'm more anxious than I'd like to be as I wait for her response. Breaking them up is one of my biggest fears should anyone else, especially Alice, find out about my feelings for Ben. I'd never forgive myself for blowing up a committed relationship, least of all one that's been going on for eight years and resulted in an engagement. The fact that Angela seems to think I'm capable of—or even *willing*—to do something like that makes me want to crawl out of my skin and hide under a rock in shame.

"I know." Her eyes soften as she gauges my hurt expression. "But I also know what heartbreak can do to a person. Take care of yourself, Marcela. Even if it means keeping your distance."

"Wait, what do you mean?" I ask her. "Are you saying I shouldn't go to their engagement party?"

"I'm saying"—she leans forward—"be careful. Don't push yourself to a breaking point for the sake of keeping up appearances."

I have no idea what to say to that.

Three

A pathway of paper lanterns leads to the outdoor patio of the Gardens, where white cloth–covered round tables are set up on a raised platform. The surrounding oak trees are wrapped in string lights and, as if that wasn't magical enough, Edison lamps trail down from the highest branches. I reach out and touch one of the bulbs as I make my way up the path, the glass warm in my palm. The venue is like something straight out of my Pinterest wedding board, which only makes this whole ordeal so much worse.

I'm thirty minutes late on purpose, and I plan to leave at least thirty minutes early as well. As much as I value Ben's friendship, there's no way I can stand to be here for the entire party. The tables are mostly filled, large gatherings of people making idle chitchat while sipping from champagne flutes. The breeze lifts my carefully styled hair, blowing it back in my face. I unstick pieces of hair from my lip gloss and smooth the strands behind my ears. At least my lavender dress is fitted, so I don't have to worry about pulling a Marilyn Monroe in front of Alice's grandparents. Talk about awkward.

I sit at a table surrounded by Alice's sorority sisters from college, fingers tapping impatiently as I wait for Angela to arrive. Damn her for running late to everything. Christine is talking animatedly to anyone who will listen about her plan to jump Theo's bones tonight. Nothing I haven't heard from her before. When Alice and I drifted apart, I drifted toward Angela and she drifted toward Christine. Much like my best friend, Christine is beautiful but in a smug sort of way. Her light brown hair falls in a sleek curtain over her shoulders, no frizz or flyaways in sight, almost the same coloring as her golden skin tone, which is straight from a St. Tropez bottle. Her lips are always painted a bold red, the promise of poison no prey can resist. I've seen men and women fall at her feet, and I don't blame them for a second.

When Christine smiles at me, chills run up and down my back. It's a knowing sort of smile, much like Alice's knowing gaze. Piercing. Taunting in the way of a *Bachelor* villain just before they bounce away to tell the lead you're here for the wrong reasons. It doesn't help my case that I've worn guilt as a second skin for years. I shudder at what the two of them must think of me. I'm suddenly conscious of all the ways my dress pinches my skin, the zipper that suddenly feels too tight for me to breathe properly. It's only once Christine returns to her conversation that I'm able to catch my breath.

I'm only half listening to what she's saying as I twirl the straw in my raspberry mojito before slugging it down in three giant gulps. Then I spot Ben and Alice standing together across the grass. Ben smooths back a stray strand of hair from Alice's face, and then his hand cups her cheek. She smiles up at him like he's the only one around them, like they share a secret the rest of us aren't in on.

There's a tug in my chest that feels an awful lot like longing. Sometimes I wonder if I'm only fooling myself when I think about how he used to look at me in that same way. How he still does, sometimes, when we're alone. My stomach is queasy just looking at them. I choke back the taste of vomit, wincing as the sour taste slides down my throat. Then I pick at the ice in my drink for a minute before deciding I'm in desperate need of another. When my phone chimes with three back-to-back messages from Angela, it's settled.

Don't hate me, but I can't make it tonight.

I got a stomach bug from that café.

Stupid, delicious, poisonous quiche.

Yup. Definitely need that drink.

I spot Theo at the open bar, nursing what looks like a Jack and Coke. He leans against a stool, looking out at the crowd of people with his usual, amiable smile. On the surface he almost looks bored, but his leg shakes under the barstool in a nervous gesture. Is he anxious? His face doesn't give him away, but his hand trembles slightly as he takes a sip from his drink.

I call for the bartender's attention and order another

mojito. Theo's head turns at the sound of my voice. He nods in greeting, and I return it with a wave. I take a seat next to him once I have my new drink.

"This place is amazing, isn't it?" I ask. He nods, but when he smiles it looks...off. Angela might think I'm projecting, but I know what that smile feels like on the inside. *Empty.* "So, how long are you in town for?"

"I'm supposed to leave Monday, but..." He shakes his head. "I don't know. It's kinda complicated."

"Oh," I say, puzzled. "Aren't you still with the Cowboys?"

He turns away with a frown and motions the bartender for another drink. It's answer enough. I leave him at the bar and make the rounds, talking with friends from college and family members of Ben's I've never met before. Without Angela I'm left ambling, hopping from person to person with no real direction. All too soon, I'm faced with the happy couple themselves. Ben's arm is wrapped around his fiancée's shoulders, both still laughing at a joke her aunt told them before she left. I stand a few feet from them, eyes assessing the general area (maybe for an escape). But I'm too late when Ben calls out my name.

I step forward to greet them, my voice too high-pitched, but neither of them notices. The party around us is probably too noisy for them to hear properly. Alice is stunning in a gold midi dress with lace and bead detailing on the shoulders. Her sleek black hair is in a half-up, half-down style that looks so much more put together than mine. Ben is equally stunning in an olive-green three-piece suit, smiling ear to ear as his arms envelop me in a warm hug.

"Congratulations," I say near his ear, my voice breathless for no good reason. His eyes are shining when he pulls away from me, and they go soft as he turns back to Alice. She returns his gaze, a shy, soft smile playing on her lips. My heart aches from how good they look together. From how happy they clearly are.

"Thank you for coming, Marcela." Alice takes both my hands in hers. "And for picking up Theo yesterday. You're such a good friend to us." Her voice is gracious, but nothing she says rings true. We haven't been good friends since freshman year, but I recognize the nicety for what it is. I give a half shrug, half smile in some sort of *oh, it was nothing* gesture.

It's a relief when I'm finally allowed to step away. I force myself not to turn back and look at them on my way to the restroom. It will just make me feel worse. The clock on my phone tells me only thirty minutes have passed, and I have to do a double take. That can't be right. It's felt like *hours* already.

When I reach the restroom, I come to a stop in front of the mirror. My hair is a tangled, windswept mess of black curls. Damn whoever thought an outdoor party in early autumn (read: extended summer for Texas folk) was a good idea. The lavender dress squeezes my middle so tight that love handles are clearly visible on my sides. At least my boobs look great, barely restrained from the low neckline. But my face is pink, from drinking or pining over one half of the happy couple, who's to say. I manage to finger-comb my hair into something more manageable, finally taking out the bobby pins and pulling it to one side with the chongo on my wrist. A low ponytail will have to do.

Once I'm outside, a blond head catches my eye. Theo's height gives him away. He's pacing the length of the building's entrance, the moonlight illuminating his large silhouette. His long legs carry him back and forth between the white stone pillars in front of the building I just exited. I consider greeting him with a hello or a quick wave, but he's not even looking in my direction. In fact, his agitated gait almost makes me hesitate to get anywhere near him.

His hands are fists in his hair, mouth moving with words I can't hear. His cheeks are flushed—from pacing or drinking I'm not sure. No one else is around, which seems odd. I assume Christine would've made a move by now. She was just saying earlier how much she wanted to make a move on him. I'm about to ask if he's all right when I catch a bit of what he's saying to himself.

"...loved you ever since we were kids. You can't go through with this wed—"

I halt in my tracks. *He can't possibly be...*

Is he talking about *Alice*?

When he turns around, I quickly duck behind a pillar, clutching my chest with a hand. My heart is beating so fast, it can't possibly be normal. This must be how heart attack victims feel right before they're rushed into an ambulance. My legs can barely hold me upright, but I can't just *leave* him like this.

There's a lot I don't know about Theo, but the same is also true of Alice. We grew distant when she and Ben started dating. What I do know is she grew up in Leon Valley next door to Ben and Theo. From what I've observed, she seemed close with Theo the few times he's come down to visit, but I always assumed it was the kind of closeness born from being neighbors. The same kind of closeness she had with Ben, before their feelings grew into something more.

I shut my eyes as Theo goes on. I stay put, hiding as I listen in on his conversation with himself.

"And I know, okay? I know that I shouldn't do this to you, Alice," he says. I'm not sure how much he's had to drink, but he sounds remarkably sober. "But the what-ifs have been haunting me for years, and once and for all, I have to know if you've ever felt the same about me. If somewhere down the line, I had a chance with you and missed it."

I hold my eyelids closed past the tears threatening to burst free. *Goddammit.* How many times have I spent wide awake at night, wondering the same exact thing about his brother? There's nothing I can do about it now, and there hasn't been for a really long time. Theo has to know that, too.

"I know. Believe me, okay, I know that I must be the biggest asshole on the planet to do this at your engagement party." His voice is a low rumble slowly gaining momentum. "But I…I have to…I have to know."

Theo walks past me with a stumble in his step, his body tilting to one side as he strides forward. Okay, maybe he's not that sober after all. I wait until he's a foot away before calling out his name. He's slow to stop, but when he does, his shoulders tense. He turns his head over his shoulder so fast, I'm surprised he doesn't give himself whiplash. He's unable to disguise the shock in his widened eyes. I step forward cautiously, like I'm approaching a startled deer in headlights.

"How...how long—" He cuts himself off, scrubbing both hands down his face. "Marcela."

"Theo." One step closer and we're half a foot apart, eye to eye. Any closer, and I'll be craning my neck just to look him in the eyes. "You can't. You know you can't do this."

When he takes his hands away from his face, there's a bright sheen to his eyes. I know how he feels. So much more than I'd like to. That's how I know I have to stop him. He turns his head back and forth, looking for any sign of more eavesdroppers, but it's just me. I don't know how long that's been true, though. How could he be so *stupid* to rehearse that big speech of his out in the open, where anyone could hear him?

"You don't understand." He shakes his head, backing away from me.

"Oh no." I throw my body in front of him before he has the chance to get away. The side of my head hits him square in the chest, and we both let out an *oof* as we stumble backward. The scent of whiskey mixes with his cologne, a startlingly intoxicating combination that makes my head spin. Well, that answers the question of how much he's had to drink tonight. I take a few steps back, shaking my head to clear it before facing him.

"Theo, you *can't*. You're drunk and bound to regret everything in the morning. Come on."

I grab him by the arm to drag him away from the party, but he doesn't move an inch. *Of course.* I forgot who I was trying to exert physical force on. His bicep is hard and muscular, warm through the fabric of his white dress shirt. I almost want to keep groping his arm before I remember the urgency of the situation we're in and force myself to focus. Oddly, he's smiling that amused smile again from when I drove over a speed bump and hit his head. I can use that. If my weird antics amuse him, maybe I can distract him from breaking up his brother's relationship.

"Come on, big guy. I'll call you an Uber." I attempt to push him back, which proves yet again to be futile.

"I don't need one." He steps forward as if to walk past me, but I move with him, blocking his path again. This time I splay my hands on his chest, and *holy shit*. But I don't have time to marvel at the feel of his hard abdominal muscles beneath my hands. I quickly remove my hands, before I start getting creepy, although I keep them up high enough to block him from passing me. He heaves a frustrated sigh, no longer amused.

"I think you do," I tell him, pushing up to my tiptoes to whisper in his ear. My head doesn't even come close to his, even in heels, so I end up whispering into his neck. My hand rests at the top of his chest to keep me upright. He shivers under my touch, a low buzz beneath my fingertips.

"Think about what you're about to do. *Really* think about it," I implore him. "This is your brother's engagement party. He'll never forgive you for trying to steal Alice away, no matter the outcome."

That seems to sober him for the moment. He looks past me toward the crowd. I turn around to do the same, and that's when I notice the eyes on us. The number of heads turning our way. The covert whispers. Fucking shit, we have to get out of here *now*.

"How many people know?" I ask under my breath.

He looks back down at me. There's an unreadable quality to his expression. "Just you."

"Are you sure?" I grip his sculpted arm, not daring to let myself become distracted as I meet his dark eyes seriously. "No one else walked past you tonight?"

"No." He starts to shake his head, but then hesitates mid-shake. "Not that I know of, at least…"

"*Fuck.*" I push my hair back from my face. When I drag him backward this time, he gives under my touch and follows after me. "Come on. We have to leave before—" *Before we make any more trouble.*

Because I'm afraid of how tempting the thought in the back of my brain is. *Let him confess. Help Ben pick up the pieces, if it comes to it.* I'm so close to the moment I've dreamed of for years.

But I can't be that person. I just can't.

Not anymore. Theo Young is my reminder.

Four

There's no way he can go back to Alice and Ben's place in his drunken state, so I tell Theo he can spend the night on my couch.

He stumbles into a stack of overdue library books sitting on the entry table, scattering them to the floor. My apartment is cozy (read: tiny), and not at all built for someone Theo's height. He had to bend down to walk through the threshold of my front door, but drunk as he is, he can barely walk straight. He looks down at the fallen books and stifles a laugh by covering his mouth with one hand.

I grab his arm and pull it over my shoulders to steady him. One of mine wraps around his waist. Despite our awkward height difference, thankfully we appear to be more or less the same weight, so I'm able to keep him upright easily.

"Come on, big guy." I step over the books, and after a prolonged beat of Theo's features schooling into deep focus, he puts one foot in front of the other, carefully sidestepping the fallen YA novels. I really do need to return them to work.

After leading him to the couch in the living room, I bend down and return the stack to the table. Then I grab a spare blanket and pillow from my bedroom, but by the time I return to the living room he's already out cold. Long lashes fan the tops of his flushed cheeks. His legs dangle over the end of the couch, like he's a large, cartoon giant. I watch him for a moment as his chest rises and falls in steady breaths. His face looks so innocent when he's asleep, not at all like the face of a mastermind plotting to ruin his brother's engagement.

Maybe, in the morning, I can convince him to keep his feelings for Alice to himself. If anyone's equipped to dole out advice about unrequited love, it's me.

I let out a sigh, unfolding the fluffy, pink blanket and draping it over Theo's body. My mouth quirks up as I watch him sleep. The bright color brings his age down a decade, softening the hard edges of his features. He doesn't look so scary when he's fast asleep, swaddled in a pale pink blanket. His arm moves to drag it over his shoulders, but other than that he doesn't stir. Not even when I ram my foot into the coffee table on my way to my bedroom, or when I let out a whispered, high-pitched curse.

But just as I reach the door to my bedroom, I hear him say something that sounds like my name. I turn around, taking careful steps back toward the couch so as not to wake him in case I'm just hearing things. His eyes are still closed, his facial features relaxed. I linger in the living room for a moment, and just when I'm about to leave again he gives a mumbled "thank you" that barely moves his lips.

At the sight of my warm, inviting bed, the exhaustion of tonight settles in my bones. I take a quick shower and change into an old T-shirt and plaid pajama shorts, before finally throwing back the blue covers of my bedspread and curling myself inside the cocoon of blankets. But as I try to fall asleep, my thoughts won't stop reeling. There's no doubt in my mind that I did the right thing tonight, but I selfishly can't stop thinking about what would've happened if I hadn't intervened and let Theo talk to Alice.

Does she feel the same way he does? Was there ever a time when she did? Is there any chance that if Theo confesses his feelings for her later, she'll leave Ben to run off into the sunset with his brother?

I can't stop imagining the outcomes. There's the most logical one, where Alice rejects Theo and he leaves town, heartbroken. There's possibly the most absurd one where Alice says "I don't" to Ben and marries his brother at the ceremony instead. But with each new scenario in which Alice runs away with Theo, I can't shake the image of Ben's face as he realizes he's losing the love of his life. Of our eyes meeting across the aisle, his shining with unshed tears. I put on my most assuring expression. One that lets him know he *will* get through this. He's devastated now, yes, but—

No.

I shake my head at the thought, not daring to entertain what would happen after that "but." *But nothing.* He'd be devastated, heartbroken, and never trust another woman ever again. That's the last thing he deserves. I was right to stop Theo from ruining the happiest moment of his brother's life before it could even happen. I won't put my own selfish feelings above his.

My sleep is little and fitful, and all too soon my phone alarm wakes me at nine. I'm not sure if I expect Theo to still be here when I step into the living room, but I'm almost surprised to find he is. Then again, where else does he have to go after last night?

He's lying down on his back, hair mussed from sleep, eyes bleary and unfocused. His iPhone hovers an inch over his face as he scrolls. When I knock on the wall to let him know I'm here, his head snaps up from his phone.

"Want any breakfast?" I ask him.

"Sure." He sits up. "I can never say no to food."

"Nice to know we have one thing in common."

Actually, make that two things.

In the kitchen, I bustle around getting coffee ingredients and decide on what to make for breakfast. I spoon grounds into a coffee filter and sprinkle the top with cinnamon. From the fridge, I grab one large potato, four eggs, a jar of my mom's homemade tomato and jalapeño salsa, and a pack of H-E-B Bakery tortillas. I ran out of mom's homemade ones last week. (Note to self: visit Mom soon.) I find vegetable oil and a frying pan in the bottom cabinet beside the oven, then grab a cutting board and knife from the dish rack.

"So," I call out once the coffee's brewing. "Do you wanna talk about it?" There's no need to explain what *it* is. He might've been drunk off his ass, but there's no doubt in my mind we both remember last night with startling clarity.

He grunts from the couch. "Do I have to?"

"You might feel better." I peel off the skin of the potato with the edge of a knife. "Plus, I did save you. The least you can do is offer some sort of explanation." And I have to admit, my curiosity is piqued. When he doesn't say anything for a while, I add, "Whatever you say is safe with me. You don't have to worry about me blabbing to Ben or anyone else. No one needs to know what really happened last night."

He heaves a sigh through the half wall. I let him gather his thoughts for a moment. Finally, he says, "I've loved her since we were kids." I remember him saying that last night, but I don't tell him as much. Maybe having some sort of barrier between us helps him get the story out, because once he starts, he doesn't stop. "She was my first friend in San Antonio, ever since we moved into the house next door to hers. I snuck into her family's tree house and the rest is history."

"What happened?" I ask over the sizzle of browning potatoes. I turn them over in the pan with a blue spatula.

"We lost touch when I left for college," he says. "I was surprised she stayed in town for college. She wanted to be a political journalist. Work for the *New York Times* or something. We talked about it all the time, how I'd play pro football and she'd be a big-shot journalist. I never expected her to stay behind, for her and my brother..." He trails off. "Nothing turned out like I thought it would."

"So, all this time, nothing ever happened between you two?"

"No." Another sigh, followed by a frustrated noise from the back of his throat. "I've never been a big commitment guy, and she was the one girl I wanted to do right by. But she had all these big dreams, and I knew she could really achieve them. I would've gotten in her way, if she actually loved me back." He pauses for so long, I almost think that's the end of it. Then he continues, "I just wanted to know if I ever had a chance. That's all."

My heart aches for him. I know exactly how that feels. My nights have been long with wishes for a different reality, one where Ben and I never break up. Or one where he realizes what a mistake letting me go was. Of him running to my doorstep in the pouring rain. I was never going to be the one who took the initiative, because I knew in my heart of hearts what would happen if I did. He'd turn me down. Say he's happy with Alice, that she's his future, and that I'm such a good friend and beg to just stay that way.

But we wouldn't. Not with my confession laid bare between us, which is why I've kept my mouth shut for as long as I have.

"A lot of shit went down before I left for college. I won't bore you with the details, but safe to say I don't like the way I left things." Theo continues, "I told myself I needed a clean break. From her, from Ben, from my life here. I was only an hour away, but it's easier to avoid people you don't see every day. Unless they're Alice, at least. I never could say no to her, and she'd never let me drift as far as I wanted to. 'We're family,' she'd always say. Once she marries Ben, we really will be."

I step into the living room and hand him a plate of potato and egg tacos and a mug of coffee. He thanks me as I take a seat on the couch beside him. "You must think I'm a terrible brother."

"Not at all," I assure him, meeting his eyes. If he's a terrible brother, I'm a terrible friend. Or at the very least, I'd be a hypocrite to agree with him. But after hearing his story, I can tell he has a good heart. If he could stop himself from pursuing Alice because he didn't want to distract her from her goals, he can stop himself from ruining her engagement.

"But you will be if you get in the way of his happiness. And hers. Wasn't the point of staying out of her way to put her happiness before yours?"

His eyes widen slightly, almost as if in surprise. "Yeah," he says, his voice breathless. He clears his throat and tries again, nodding vigorously. "God, yes. The last thing I want is to get in the way of her happiness. My brother's, too," he adds quickly, almost as an afterthought.

"Then you'll never forgive yourself if you intervene," I say. "Trust me."

Theo nods, not asking me how I know that. I understand how he feels more than anyone can ever know. Not that I plan on telling him as much. Even though he's opened up so much more than I thought he would, there's still a lot I don't know about him. I doubt he'd turn around and tell Alice or anyone else about my feelings for his brother, but what if he tries to confess again and it accidentally comes out? No, I can't take that chance.

It does mean, however, that I'm in the perfect position to help him. I can't possibly judge him for his feelings when I'm no better than he is.

"Yeah. You're absolutely right." He scrubs his face with a hand. "I owe you one, Marcela. Thank you for stopping me."

"No problem." I duck away from his eyes to take a bite from one of the breakfast tacos. We've been talking for so long, they're starting to get cold. I'm about to tell Theo to go ahead and dig in when the weight of his hand falls on my shoulder. I glance up at his solemn expression.

"Seriously," he tells me, his eyes burning with some emotion I can't name. "I could've ruined everything. The last person I should be going after is someone in love with my brother. I can't thank you enough for helping me through this."

"You're welcome," I say hoarsely. For some reason, my throat is dry. Once I clear it, my voice comes out normally. "Now eat up."

He doesn't need telling twice. Theo finishes the potato and egg taco in no less than three bites before washing it down with lukewarm coffee.

"Thanks for breakfast. You're an amazing cook, and now we don't have to go to brunch."

"*Shit.*" I forgot all about brunch with Ben's and Alice's families. "What time is it?"

"Relax, it's not till noon. It's only"—Theo looks down at his phone—"half an hour till. And besides, we just ate."

"Are you kidding? You *have* to go!" I exclaim. "They'll think something's up if you don't show. Not only did you leave the party early, but you never returned to their apartment last night. They'll catch on if you keep avoiding them."

"Then what am I supposed to do?" He bursts up from the couch, eyes widening with panic. "How am I supposed to face them after what I almost did? How do I keep staying with them until I find a place of my own?"

"Wait, what?" I ask. "You're not going back to Dallas?"

"I retired," he tells me. The fact seems to deflate him; his shoulders slump in defeat, and he hangs his head like it's weighing him down. "I don't even want to get into that mess right now. God, what was I thinking? This is a *mess*."

"Hey." I rest a hand on his arm, and he looks back down at me. "You'll get through this, okay? And I'll help you any way I can. I promise."

He meets my eyes, and I notice the color of his for the first time. Dark blue. Twin storms rapidly approaching the shore, right before they wipe out all signs of civilization. Those eyes are twice the destruction—total obliteration.

"You've done more than enough for me, Marcela. More than I deserve."

"No one deserves to go through what you're going through alone," I assure him, even as a twinge in my chest makes my heart ache. At least I have Angela to help me get through all the Ben stuff. Who does Theo have aside from me? Would his friends back in Dallas judge him for going after his brother's fiancée?

"But first things first—"

"Are you sure brunch is really a good idea right now?"

"You can think about it as you get ready." My nose wrinkles as I sniff the air between us. I push him toward the direction of my bathroom. "But maybe start with a shower first."

Five

Once I'm dressed in the first brunch-appropriate dress I can find—a pink floral number I got on sale—I realize everything I need to do my hair and makeup is in the bathroom. All my products are inside the mirror cabinet above the sink, and my curling iron is on the marble countertop. The sound of water rushing from Theo's shower is muffled from behind the bathroom door. I glance down at my phone for the time. *Shit.* We're already late without me having to wait until Theo's out of the shower.

I knock on the door, opening it a smidge in case he can't hear it through the spray of water. "Theo?" I call out, shielding my eyes with a raised hand.

"What's up?" he calls back, voice echoey.

"I need to come in and grab some stuff to do my hair and makeup," I tell him. "Do you mind?"

"Not at all. You can get ready in here, if you want. It's your place."

I only agree because my full-size mirror shattered last

weekend, which is turning out to be a bad omen indeed. Another near-decade of bad luck, here I come. I pull my hair back into a half-up, half-down style and plug in my curling iron to re-curl the tendrils that went flat overnight. A thin layer of condensation begins to fog the mirror, blurring my vision. So maybe sharing a bathroom isn't the wisest idea after all. The fog becomes too thick to see through in a matter of seconds. I wipe it away with my palm, revealing my frizzy bedhead. I could've sworn my hair wasn't this poofy before I walked in. It must be the heat from Theo's shower making it act up.

I let out a sigh as I retrieve a light pink scrunchie from the top drawer. Low bun it is.

"You okay?" I startle at the sound of Theo's voice. I nearly forgot he was in here, despite the ever-present sound of running water.

"Fine," I say, unplugging the curling iron as I rifle through the cabinets for my makeup bag. "Just having some hair trouble."

Sharing a bathroom with Theo is an oddly intimate experience, though that may be because none of my relationships have ever lasted long enough for such a domestic act. I wonder if he's done this before with previous women he's dated. Or, if Ben's stories are to be believed, the mornings after his copious one-night stands. The logistics line up. Now though, as the water abruptly shuts off, I let out an involuntary squeak in my rush out the door. It shuts behind me with a loud boom that makes me flinch. As if I wasn't the one who shut it in the first place.

Yikes. Get a grip, girl.

The sight of his suit from last night laid out on my bedspread does nothing to help the sudden anxiety creeping in my veins. There's a *man* in my bathroom. A *naked* man. He's probably drying off his body with one of my towels this very second. His *naked* body, because all the clothes he came with are lying on my bed.

Oh my god.

I just shared a bathroom with a naked man I know little to nothing about. I can count on one hand the things I know about Theo Young.

Index: He plays (played?) for the Dallas Cowboys. A fact I *barely* know about him, so should it even count?

Middle: He has some sort of feud going on with his brother. Another fact I don't know the details of.

Ring: He's in love with Alice Cho, his brother's fiancée.

Pinkie: He…actually is sweet. I've never once met a man willing to put a woman's goals before his own desire for her. Angela was right about him.

Thumb: Like me, he can't say no to food.

Theo meets me in the living room once he's dressed in last night's clothes, suit jacket tucked awkwardly under one arm and hair slightly damp. Wordlessly, he follows me out to my tiny car. Trapped in the confined space together, I note the smell of my rose-and-amber body wash on him. I'm not sure how to feel about that.

Once we arrive in the parking lot of the restaurant, I send Angela a quick text to check in on how she's feeling. Theo shifts in his seat, eyes roaming the lot as if he can already sense trouble. His head turns right and left so fast he's making me dizzy. When Angela doesn't reply right away, I assume she must be sleeping off the stomach bug. Though I've given Theo a moment to prepare himself for what's to come inside, he looks more anxious than ever.

"Are you ready?" I ask him, already knowing the answer.

"No." His shoulders deflate with a sigh. "Not that it even matters."

The table is full except for two seats by the time we reach our party. Ben sits at the head of the table, Alice by his side. Alice's parents are seated beside her, but Ben's parents are separated by the two empty chairs placed next to each other. A quick reminder of their not-so-amicable divorce. I take the seat next to Mrs. Young, because it's the farthest away from Ben and Alice. With one look at Theo's face, however, I immediately regret the decision. He hesitates as he steps forward, reluctantly taking the seat beside his father, diagonally across from Alice.

His eyes lock on her face, even when she glances away from us. She's the only one who does, though. At every turn, all eyes are directly on me. Christine in particular is staring daggers in my direction, brown eyes narrowed to slits. A chill of unease runs down my spine as I realize something. No, it's not me they're all staring at. They're staring at *us*. At me and Theo.

Weird.

"Nice of you to finally show up, boy," Theo's father says, clapping him on the back. "And with a pretty girl on your arm to boot. Is she the reason you ducked out of the party early?" Then his eyes widen as he leans across the table and pins them on me. "Oh, Marcela! What a surprise!"

"Hi, Mr. Young." I give him a shy wave, not quite making eye contact.

"Oh, no, we're not—" Theo is in the middle of correcting his father when Mr. Young cuts him off.

"It's not like my oldest to spend his time with quality women," he says, chuckling hard at his own comment. Next to me, his ex-wife rolls her eyes the way I wish I could. Instead, I glance up at Theo, brows furrowing as I imagine what criteria his father thinks these women have to meet to be considered "quality." I'm sure I'd rather not know. Then he points a pink finger at Theo and says, "Don't blow it with this one, son."

Maybe I should be flattered that Mr. Young thinks so much of me, but the sentiment only makes me uneasy. I've met him a handful of times at family brunches and always considered him decent enough, but never actually knew what he thought of me until now. In fact, we've never spoken more than a few words to each other, so I have no idea how he's basing his opinion of me.

"Noted." Theo's tone is clipped, as if he wishes he could evaporate into the air and be done with this conversation. I know I am, and I'm not even the one being spoken to.

"Are you still at the library, Marcela?" Mrs. Young asks me.

"Yup." I nod. "We're starting up a YA book club," I say, mostly to turn the conversation away from me and Theo, as if there will ever actually be a *me and Theo*. But I'm afraid to contradict what they think, for fear of making a scene out of an already awkward situation. How will it look if we deny anything happened between us? We can't exactly tell them the truth.

Oh no, your son and I didn't hook up. I just stopped him from sabotaging your younger son's engagement party by pulling him into an Uber and letting him sleep (no euphemisms here!) off his heartache at my place. No, it wouldn't be wise to contradict the assumption.

Out of the corner of my eye, I catch sight of Ben's expression. His eyes are trained on me. His cool expression sends chills down my back, the question in his face crystal clear. He's looking at me like he has no idea who I am. Then his eyes flick to his brother and he just shakes his head. My skin heats at the implication, heart racing double speed for no good reason. I've upset him somehow, coming here with Theo.

I sneak a glance at Alice and find the exact opposite in her expression. She seems unfazed, cutting into her spinach-and-egg-white omelet with a sly smile. When she looks up at Theo, her eyes fill with warmth. Her smile is nothing but friendly, but the same can't be said for Theo. His eyes soften as he meets hers across the table. I recognize the look for what it is. Longing.

His hand shakes slightly as he passes her the pepper shaker, his thumb brushing the edge of her fingers as he hands it off. She doesn't seem to feel his touch, just peppers her eggs and takes another bite as if nothing happened. But Theo clears his throat, as if clearing the emotion building there.

How am I the only one who can see it? Is it that everyone around us is genuinely oblivious, or that this new knowledge has changed how I perceive Theo's interactions with her?

My skin feels overheated. I wonder if I'm as obvious as he is.

As soon as I'm finished eating, I excuse myself to use the restroom. I make myself take deep breaths on the way, but it isn't until I lock myself inside a stall that I'm able to steady my breathing. Why did I think forcing Theo to brunch was a good idea? What if he tries to blow up his brother's relationship again? It'll be my fault for not stopping him sooner. The door swings open, momentarily distracting me from my mini freak-out and back into the present moment. I do my business before washing my hands at the sink, where Christine is reapplying her lipstick in front of a mirror.

She's staring at me in the mirror, and for a moment I can't understand why until I remember her plans to jump Theo last night. Good lord, the trouble Mr. Young's loud mouth is putting me through right now.

"So, how'd you do it?"

Her eyes pierce through me in the same way Alice's do, only she has the wrong idea. I'm not sure how I should answer her. Come up with a lie to keep up the assumption? Deflect? When I settle for a dumb look and a shrug, she rolls her eyes and says, "Forget it. I figured you wouldn't tell *me* of all people."

She raises the strap of her purse higher on her shoulder before exiting, the door swinging on its hinges behind her.

We left the party together, and Theo never returned to

Ben and Alice's place. There were so many eyes on us, anyone could've seen us leave together. Anyone could've misconstrued the truth…

Which might work in our favor.

When I leave the bathroom, I spot Theo waiting to use the men's restroom. Except, when he spots me walking out of the women's, he bounces off the wall he was leaning against and grabs my wrist. He pulls me into a hidden alcove, eyes wide as saucers.

"You've *got* to help me," he says, the panic clear in his voice. "Ben keeps looking at me like he knows something's up. We have to leave."

"What, *now*?" I know why Ben keeps looking at him, and it has nothing to do with the truth. He sees us hooking up as a betrayal because of whatever feud he and Theo have going on. *A lot of shit went down before I left for college.* I regret not asking him to bore me with the details now. I've never gotten the full story out of Ben, only hard-won bits and pieces. The blow-out fight they got into before Theo left for college, the regret Ben had over not being able to make things right before he left, the silence on the other line every time he tried to reach out.

"We haven't even done the champagne toast. We can't just—"

"*Right now*, Marcela." He rakes his hair back with a shaky hand. "This was a bad idea. I feel like I'm gonna be sick if we don't get out of here soon." His skin does have a greenish tinge to it. And if the way he's been looking at Alice all afternoon has anything to do with this freak-out, I need to save him. Angela would do the same for me, and I don't really want to stay for much longer anyway.

"Okay, okay, on it. Follow my lead." I drag him away by the hand as patrons turn in their seats to shoot us odd looks. When we return to the table, I announce that unfortunately we have to duck out early. "I don't think that eggs Benedict agreed with me." I make a show of scrunching my face and put a hand to my stomach.

"Oh no! I'm sorry, sweetie," Mrs. Young says, getting up from her seat and walking around the table. "Theo, honey, get her home safe."

"I—I will," Theo stumbles, giving a jerky nod.

"Congratulations, again," I tell Ben and Alice, and though I can't see it, I'm sure the pained expression on my face is realer than my feigned stomachache. Alice stands from her seat to hug me and Theo goodbye. Ben raises himself to do the same. His arms come around my shoulders, mine patting him on the back chastely. Before I can pull away, his hand gently grips my arm to keep me in place.

"Be careful," he whispers in my ear. For a moment I'm startled, but when I look back at his face, his expression is neutral. I try to do the same, but I sense the mask slipping. My mouth turns up into a shaky smile, and then Theo's arm wraps around my waist as he pulls me out of Ben's reach, and out of the restaurant.

"Nice one," he says once we're back in the car. "I think they bought it. They didn't suspect anything weird, did they?"

Just that we hooked up, but I don't bother telling him as much. I don't understand how he didn't see it, but maybe it's because he was too wrapped up in Alice to notice anyone else at the table.

"No, I think we're in the clear," I say as I start the car. "Do you want me to drop you off at Ben and Alice's?"

"Yeah." He heaves a long sigh.

I nod as I pull out of the parking space. The drive is mostly silent, giving me time to think. For the time being, it seems I've convinced Theo not to confess his feelings for Alice. But if that were really true, why is something not sitting right with me? I sneak a few covert glances at Theo, but there's nothing I can read on his expression. His eyes stay trained out the windshield, lips pursed in thought. I dart my eyes away before he can catch me staring at him.

When we arrive outside Ben and Alice's apartment building, Theo thanks me for everything. I wave away his apology and reply that it's nothing.

"It's *far* from nothing." He meets my eyes seriously. "Believe me. I don't know what I would've done without you."

Ruin your chances with the girl of your dreams and your already-screwy relationship with your brother. Instead of any of that, I say, "Anytime. I've got your back."

He leaves the car, and I watch as he retreats into the corridor. I let out a breath of relief before starting my car. At least it doesn't look like he has any more plans to break them up. But if he changes his mind, I'll be able to say it's not my fault. Theo Young is no longer my problem.

Except...

Be careful.

I shake my head to rid myself of thoughts of Ben.

Tomorrow, I'll clear up the misunderstanding and assure him nothing happened between me and his brother. But when I try to think of a logical reason for why he slept over at my place that isn't the truth, I come up blank. The spark of an idea goes off in my brain just as I reach a red light. That has to be a sign, right? A universal sign to *stop* the incredibly bad ideas circling my head. Especially when the burning gaze of Ben's eyes on us is my main source of motivation. The closest thing to jealousy I've ever gotten out of him.

Be careful.

It doesn't matter what he thinks. Whatever *anyone* thinks happened last night, actually. Who am I to correct them when doing so could put Theo's secret in danger of getting out? I made him a promise, and it's one I intend to keep.

And if the consequence of keeping it is that his family and friends think we're hooking up, then that's a sacrifice I'm willing to make.

Six

On Monday morning, I'm fifteen minutes early for work. I shuffle with my purse and tote bag of overflowing books as I unlock the glass doors and walk inside. The sensors blare as I enter the building, but I don't do much more than roll my eyes. I'm not returning to the scene of the crime, I'm merely returning the books I borrowed...without the use of my library card. *Whoops.* It happens sometimes when I get overexcited about new items.

The smell of aging paper usually calms me, but today it has no effect on my nervous system. The weekend's events are still rattling around in my brain, refusing to cease. I'm surprised I still managed to come in early with how preoccupied my mind has been.

The library is two stories, the ground floor for housing our entire collection, and the second balcony floor for business meetings in conference rooms that anyone can reserve ahead of time to use. New nonfiction is displayed on a large, square table in front of the half shelf of new general fiction. I open my tote and begin returning a few of the books to their proper locations.

This is my Monday morning routine—stealthily returning all the books I finished reading the week prior before Erica, the managing librarian, can arrive to judge me. (She's seen my home library and the embarrassing number of unread books I own.) But there's something about a shiny, new book I don't have to spend money on that I just can't resist. Hence, the overflowing bag of books. Most of them belong in the YA section, which resides in its own cozy corner at the back of the first floor.

I run my hands along the wrapped spines, adjusting and tightening the bookends as needed. This is the section I've always felt most at home wandering. After my dad left, my mom had to work an extra job in order to provide for us, which included most weekends. From the ages of eleven to sixteen, I spent every single weekend at the public library, reading the days away in a pleather chair torn down the middle, beside the gigantic glass windows overlooking downtown. My cousin Marissa was a library assistant at Central Public Library at the time, so she was able to watch out for me and take me home after closing.

I didn't just fall in love with books—I fell in love with everything about the library. From talking the youth librarian's ear off about the latest book I read, to sharing book recommendations with parents to get their kids into reading. My cousin even let me display my favorite books in place of her staff picks a few times. For years, I was an honorary member of their staff until an aide position opened up when I turned sixteen. I didn't even need an interview to be hired on the spot.

A year working at the John Peace Library on campus was enough to tell me public libraries were where my heart truly lived. I spent the next three years working as an aide at the Pura Belpré Public Library before becoming a full-time assistant after graduation. And then my dream came true six months ago when Pamela Brown retired, and Erica recommended me to take her place as teen librarian.

Once I've emptied my tote and shelved all the books in their appropriate spots (and refilled my tote all over again with new books), I clock in and get ready for the day. Angela is already seated at her desk, hair up in a tight bun at the top of her head. She's wearing a button-up shirt and perfectly pressed slacks. Meanwhile, I'm a slob in my wrinkled pants and hoodie over a collared shirt. I plop down in a seat across from her, taking a long sip from my Starbucks cup.

"How was the stomach bug?" I ask, only slight bitterness coloring my tone.

"God awful. I puked the entire weekend," she tells me, and I wince in sympathy. I know it wasn't her fault for ditching me, and I need to stop seeing it that way. "How was the party?"

When I shrug, she throws a pen at me. It hits me in the arm, and I flinch, spilling iced coffee down my shirt. At least the hoodie's dark color makes it less noticeable.

"Oof, sorry, girl."

"What is *wrong* with you?" I ask, patting down my chest with a tissue.

"What is wrong with *you* for not telling me who you went home with on Saturday?!" My mouth drops open in shock, coffee stain forgotten. "Don't give me that look! I don't know whether to be proud or concerned. When I said Ben's brother might be a viable rebound for you, I was *joking*. That said, I'm gonna need details."

How the hell did Angela already hear about that? "Wait, wait, wait, no. I don't know who told you, but—"

"Don't you dare tell me the rumor mill is wrong." She points an accusatory finger at me. "This is the best news I've heard all year, and they better be right!"

"I'm confused. Do you actually want it to be true?"

"At this point, I'm rooting for anyone who isn't Ben."

"Sorry to disappoint." I give a wry smile. "I'll tell you all about it at lunch. It's better chisme than you think."

"I doubt it." She scowls, returning to her computer monitor, shoulders slumped in disappointment.

Her desk is, as usual, a giant mess of books and DVD cases. Part of her duties involve mending damaged books and swapping out broken DVD cases for new ones, but I have no idea how she manages to keep up with them in the chaos that is her desk. A copy of *Loveless* by Alice Oseman sits at the top of the pile, the pristine purple cover catching my eye immediately. But when I try to reach for it, Angela slaps my hand away.

"This is Central's copy. I'm not handing it over to the girl who regularly smuggles books home without checking them out first."

I let out a dramatic gasp, but it's a fair point. I'm about to ask her if it's damaged—although it's the only book in the pile that looks brand new—but she continues with the earlier subject before I get the chance to.

"By the way, you should know that everyone at that party thinks you two hooked up. Alice even texted me a couple times to confirm if it was true. Imagine my surprise to hear it from her first, before my supposed best friend."

I roll my eyes at her dramatic tone.

"It's not true...but you can't tell her that." She raises a brow at me. "I'll explain everything, I swear. Just don't tell her anything for now."

"Fine," Angela grumbles. "But you should probably watch out for Christine. You've unlocked a new enemy."

"Maybe she should've made a move earlier," I muse, until I remember Theo pacing all alone that night. Perhaps he was hiding from her group, trying to work out his speech to Alice somewhere secluded. Is that what Christine meant when she asked how I got to him?

"That was mentioned," Angela tells me. "But apparently, he was acting weird all night."

"Weird, how?" I whip around in my desk chair. Did anyone guess the truth? Better yet, did anyone eavesdrop on him before I did? Angela looks up at me in surprise, but before she can reply, the door to Erica Espinoza's office swings open. Her salt-and-pepper hair elegantly pulled back in a high chignon highlights her sparkling brown eyes. Our managing librarian is kind, but in a cut-the-bullshit sort of way.

"Sounds like you two had an exciting weekend." She smooths down her blue skirt. "But what I want to hear is plans for the book club launch. Has that been finalized?"

"Yes." I nod. "The announcement is going live on all our social media accounts later today. We'll also be hosting reading sprints online every week until the in-person event on the third Friday of the month."

"We thought it'd be fun to create some social media polls too, so the teens can have a hand in choosing what book we read next," Angela chimes in. "They chose our first book, and they'll choose the second around the first week of the new month. Marcela and I have already lined up a couple titles for them to choose from."

"Very good." Erica smiles. "Angela, I believe you're assigned to the circulation desk first this morning."

"Right. It's homework time." She flashes our boss a winning smile as she raises herself from a wheelie desk chair.

Before she became a library assistant, Angela was in the teacher certification program at UTSA. It wasn't until her last semester, deep in the throes of classroom management, that she realized she'd made a terrible mistake. I recommended her to Erica to replace me after I took my new position. Now she's taking classes online to receive her master's and become a youth services librarian. It pains me slightly that one day soon we won't be working at the same library anymore.

My entire morning is spent in meetings until lunchtime rolls around, when Angela meets me outside my office and suggests we go out. The Whataburger drive-thru is packed, which leaves plenty of time for me to catch her up.

"Okay, lay it on me," Angela says. "What were you and Theo doing if not hooking up?"

I hesitate for a moment before I tell her. This isn't exactly my secret to tell, and I know how terrible I'd feel if Angela told mine. But she never has, which is how I know I can trust her to keep Theo's secret. "I stopped him from breaking up Ben and Alice."

Angela nearly drives into the car in front of us. I reach for the grab handle above the passenger window, eyes bugging out of my head as she slams on the brakes. I'm about to yell at her to be more careful, but when she turns to face me she doesn't even have the decency to look fazed. She's jumping up and down in her seat with a level of excitement that terrifies me when she has both our lives in her unsteady hands.

"You're kidding!" she shouts. "Tell me everything!"

So I do. Angela gasps in all the right places, clutching at her chest like I'm the most interesting telenovela she's watched in years. But it's her eyes narrowing slightly in contemplation that I really take note of. I wonder what thoughts are churning in her head, even as I continue my story. After retrieving our food, she parks the car in a space off to the side so we can eat and go over all the facts without interruption.

"Wow. You know, I really don't know much about the guy, but I never would've guessed he had feelings for Alice," she says between bites of her chicken strips. "But then again, he doesn't live here. Maybe it was good of him to keep his distance if he felt like that all along."

"Yeah." I sigh, my stomach sinking as I take in her words like a physical blow. "Maybe that's what I should've been doing all along."

She gives me a sympathetic look, placing her hand on my shoulder. "You tried, honey. It's not as if you could just dump him as a friend."

"Maybe." But I'm not so convinced now. Maybe if I'd phased him out after we stopped dating like I'd originally wanted to, I would've gotten over him a long time ago. But if he proved anything, it's that he wouldn't let go of our friendship so easily. Not like the way Alice and I had drifted apart, neither one of us willing to fight to regain the easy friendship we had when we first met. Ben had made it clear he wanted both of us in his life.

"It's partly Ben's fault, too," she tells me. "If my partner ever insisted on staying friends with one of their exes, I'd run out of there so fast there'd be a smoke outline of me floating in the air."

"That's the thing, though. I'm not sure we're really exes."

I can hardly call a handful of dates across three months a relationship. Never mind that we hung out together nearly every day between our simple dinner-and-a-movie dates. Never mind how thoughtful he was to buy my favorite snacks and coffee on campus when we met up to study. Never mind the "good morning" and "sweet dreams" texts that dinged my phone at the beginning and end of each day. Never mind the late-night phone calls that kept me up till two a.m. most nights. Something about the dark allowed me to be more honest than I would normally be, and he'd reward me with truths of his own. An exchanging of pasts. Perhaps an exchanging of futures, too.

Until he said he thought we'd be better off as friends, at least.

It threw me off, how suddenly and confidently he'd steered us into a different lane. It almost didn't feel like a breakup, except of course for the pain in my chest cavity. There were times when I wanted to ask him why he thought we were better as friends, if he wasn't ready for something real, or if it was something I did or said that made him change his mind. But if I'm being honest with myself, I wasn't ready for the closure his answer would've provided.

"I just think he relies on you too much. He might not know how you feel but dangling that ring in front of you was just *cruel*." She shakes her head, taking another bite of her chicken. "Anf da fa—"

"Swallow before you speak, please."

She rolls her eyes but complies, taking a sip from her straw and swallowing. "And the fact that he always finds a way to get involved every time you date someone new—" She cuts herself off, so angry she can't even finish the sentence. Her eyes shudder closed. "Don't even get me started."

"Please, please don't."

Angela found out about my feelings during the second semester of our sophomore year, when I started dating a guy named Chris. He and I never acted like we were dating because I constantly ditched him to hang out at Ben's apartment with the rest of our friend group. Ben never helped the situation either, because he'd constantly talk shit about the poor guy to anyone who would listen. One night when we'd forgotten Angela was still in the bathroom, he told me I should dump him, arguing that Chris didn't like any of my friends and I barely hung out with him anyway.

So I did.

Angela put two and two together faster than any of our

other friends. When she confronted me about it, I thought she was going to tell me how horrible of a person I was. Instead, she let me cry on her lap for two hours and bought me enough pumpkin empanadas to drown us both. To Angela, my feelings aren't entirely unwarranted, no matter how much I disagree with her. Ben has never crossed any physical boundaries, and he's never once tried to.

The problem has always been *me*.

"The point is, it's a completely different situation," Angela says to try to redirect the conversation. "Plus, you're not the one trying to break up an engagement. And don't worry about Alice. I'll handle her if she asks any more questions."

"Thank you."

I give her a grateful smile, hugging her until my arms hurt from the force. When we arrive back at the library, I feel loads better after having told Angela the truth. I have no idea what Theo will do next, but at least I'm not completely alone in this anymore.

Seven

Turns out, I don't have to wait long to find out. I receive a text from an unknown number when I get home from work. I almost delete it until I spot the area code. 469. Dallas.

> What are you up to tonight?

> This is Theo, btw

I reply that I have zero plans for the night, and he suggests we go out for drinks. On him. I'm sure I'm reading too much into the invitation. Angela's right, though. As far as rebounds go, Theo probably isn't the worst viable option. Not that I'm expecting anything remotely romantic to happen between us. If girls like Christine don't stand a chance with him, there's no way I do. And even if I did, he's the last person, apart from Ben, I should want. Just imagining the tagline to this low budget Lifetime film is enough to make me cringe:

*He wants the bride, she wants the groom.
But what if all they really want…is each
other?*

Blegh. I shake my head to clear the thought. Of the *ridic-ulousness* I have no time for.

But then, it wouldn't be such a bad idea if Theo found a rebound of his own, either. I make a mental note to bring up the idea to him tonight as I text my agreement.

Should I drive or Uber?

He replies with a smiling devil emoji and a time and place. Uber it is.

Well, if I'm about to get trashed on a Monday night, I might as well be comfortable. I change into a faded pair of jeans and my favorite cotton blouse, despite the squint-to-see-it coffee stain on the collar. The bar we're headed to is usually dimly lit, and even if it wasn't, I doubt I'd care. I leave my hair down but keep a chongo on my wrist for when I'll inevitably need to pull it up later in the night.

Havana Bar is my usual haunt, though Theo has no way of knowing that. Connected to a hotel right off the River Walk, it looks less like a bar and more like a speakeasy before the sin and debauchery start. Entirely candlelit, the bar is tinged a devilish red to match the furniture's red velvet uphol-stery. Lounge chairs are placed around rickety wooden tables. It's like something straight out of a novel, which is part of the reason it appealed to me in the first place. Angela and I have spent far too many nights here to count. We even befriended some of the staff and trust them enough to guard our smartphones after a certain number of drinks.

I'm the first to arrive even though I'm ten minutes late. Krystal Ramirez is working tonight, which is lucky for me because she's my favorite bartender.

"Haven't seen you in here in a while," she says, smirking. Her dark, curly hair is tinted red from the jarred candles behind the bar. As if that's not a fire hazard. To this day, I still don't understand how the bartenders can reach the alcohol without accidentally setting the place on fire. With her large hoop earrings and black tank top that shows off her tattoos, she fits right in with the atmosphere.

"You meeting up with Angela?"

"Nope. It's a new friend this time." She raises a brow, intrigued. "Can you get me a raspberry mojito?"

"New friend, old drink. You got it."

Theo arrives the same moment my drink does, dressed in dark-wash jeans and a blue hoodie. His hair is damp, from a shower maybe. When he spots me, he lifts his hand in a wave and makes his way toward me.

"Hey." He envelops me into a side hug, and I get a whiff of his shower gel. I inhale the woodsy musk of his scent, hoping he doesn't notice. He smells dizzyingly good, and I can't decide if this is better or worse for my common sense than when he smelled like my amber-and-rose body wash.

"You surprised me tonight," I say. "What's the occasion?"

"I wanted to say thanks for this weekend." Theo orders

two shots of tequila from Krystal, and when she looks back at me, her eyes glitter knowingly. My face heats at the assumption on her face.

"*Really*, I can't thank you enough," Theo says, calling me back to the moment. "When I got back to my brother's place, I realized what a dick move that would've been had I gone through with it. I can't do that to my own brother. So, thank you." He puts his hand over mine and squeezes. His grip is firm, warm, and it evokes something in me I haven't felt in a long time. Or rather, something I haven't allowed myself to feel. The heat of Krystal's gaze warms the side of my face, but I don't dare turn around to check.

But mostly, I can't bear to make myself look away from Theo. I think of the muscles pressed up against my body during my numerous attempts to drag him away from the party. His rumpled clothes on my bed. The way he smelled like my body wash at brunch. The steady weight of his eyes, pulling me in with the force of a rising tide.

Oh, shit. I'm attracted to him, aren't I?

"Just looking out." My voice wavers slightly. We haven't even been here ten minutes, and I don't like the thoughts circling my head. "Listen, I'm not one to judge. We all make mistakes in the heat of the moment, but that moment has to pass eventually," I say, not only to convince him. I muster all the determination I can to add "And it will."

He looks away from me, brows creased. Then he nods. "I know. You're right. Which is why I have to thank you properly." When Krystal sets two shots down in front of us, he takes one and hands me the other.

"To the moment passing."

"Cheers." We clink glasses and shoot them back. The liquor burns going down my throat, but it's just what I need to get the Lifetime movie tagline out of my brain.

Don't be stupid, Marcela.

But what would be more stupid? Pining over a taken man for the rest of my life, or getting over said taken man by hooking up with his brother?

"What's your plan now?" I ask Theo, if only to stop myself from digging an even deeper hole than the one I'm already in.

"I have enough in savings to get an apartment in town until I can find a job," he says. "Plus, a couple interviews lined up this week. Turns out, a lot of high schools like the idea of a former NFL player coaching their football team." The side of his mouth turns up in a wry grin. "It's not exactly the career I had in mind, but something's gotta pay the bills."

"What happened, by the way?" I ask. "Why'd you retire?"

He lets out a groan. "It's my stupid knee again."

"The one that cost you getting signed the first time?" His eyes widen, mouth falling open slightly. Judging by his stricken expression, this was a bad question to ask. Before he can reply, I attempt to walk it back. "You don't have to answer that. I didn't mean to be so invasive. If you're not comfortable…"

"No, it's not that," he says. "It's just that it was such a long time ago. I didn't think you'd remember."

Of course I remember. The smell of tequila calls it all back—the shouting, the shattered glass, the crying himself to sleep. But he was so hammered, maybe he hardly remembers that night himself. It's on the tip of my tongue to remind him, but I can't find any good way to do so.

When he finally speaks up, I no longer have to.

"Tequila always had a habit of bringing out my bad side." He shakes his head. "Football was everything to me. Still is, in some ways. I got good grades in high school just so I could play, went to college to get drafted to the NFL. It wasn't just that I loved it, but that I wasn't good at anything else. There was nothing else I felt that passionately about."

"A job doesn't have to be a career, Theo. There are plenty of other things you can do." His eyes train on me. "But maybe I'm not the best person to look to. My whole career basically revolves around books."

"Librarian, right?" So maybe he was paying attention to someone other than Alice at brunch.

"Yup. Although, my job isn't without its bad days. Sometimes I just wanna shake the parents who complain about the quote-unquote *inappropriate material* in the YA books their kids are reading. Like there's anything *inappropriate* about a transgender lead or mildly sexual themes. They're *teenagers.* If a bit of light petting offends them so much, they would've keeled over to learn what I was reading when I was a teenager."

"Oh, yeah?" The corner of Theo's mouth lifts suggestively. "Do tell."

There's no way I'm talking to Theo of all people about my sexual awakening through romance novels.

"Shut up." I slap lightly at his arm. "We got off topic. Please, continue."

When we return to the topic at hand, his grin falls a bit. "I don't know," Theo starts. "It all felt more…urgent, back then. Like if I never got drafted, it was all for nothing. All that work, all the long nights spent practicing, all the sacrifices I made to get there. I'd never make something of myself otherwise."

"That's why you were in so much pain." His smile drops all the way suddenly. I hate that I'm the reason. "I didn't know you at all back then, so I…didn't really know what to think, I guess. It makes sense now." I'm almost surprised by how honest he's being with me. Before this weekend, we were strangers. Now he's opening up like we're old friends. Or… like we're *becoming* friends.

Are Theo and I friends?

"I'm sorry, again," he says, his eyes going soft. "You shouldn't have had to see me like that. There's not a lot about that night I remember, and I'm counting my blessings for that." He lets out a nervous laugh.

I can hardly remember why I was there in the first place. Did Ben ask me over, or was I already there when Theo arrived? I'll ask Ben one of these days, whenever I see him next. Even though I definitely shouldn't see him soon.

"It's all in the past." I take a sip from my drink. "By the way, how'd you get my number?"

"I asked Ben first, but he refused and told me to stay away from you." There's an odd look in his eyes. My heart stutters in my chest, but I keep a neutral expression. Ben must hate that we're out together right now, if he was unwilling to give his brother my number. The thought shouldn't thrill me, but in an odd way I want him to disapprove. It's the closest I can ever get to making him jealous.

Bad idea all around, Marcela.

"So I asked Alice instead."

"He really said that?" I ask, though I'm not entirely surprised. Ben's always been protective of me, especially whenever a new guy comes into my life. And given Theo's reputation, I can understand why Ben would be worried if he actually thinks we're hooking up.

I'm about to ask Theo if he corrected his brother (secretly, I hope he didn't) when the door chimes, and a group of familiar women enter the bar. Alice, Christine, and the rest of their crew. I spot Angela behind a blond girl in their group, eyes scanning the bar like she's looking for someone.

From the corner of my eye, I spot Krystal as she smiles to herself and walks out from behind the bar to head toward them. Probably to say hi to Angela, I think. She likes giving Angela grief about the time she drunkenly stroked her cheek and gushed over her "beautiful face." Angela still counts it as the most mortifying thing she's ever done while under the influence.

But all of Alice's friends going out on a Monday night, at the same bar as Theo and me? This has the unsettling feeling of a bad omen. A sneaking suspicion grows in the back of my mind.

"Incoming." Theo's head turns when I gesture toward the entrance. Alice spots us and waves, that same knowing glint in her eyes. We wave back, watching as she sinks into a plush, upholstered lounge chair big enough to seat Christine and Angela on either side of her. I study Theo's face, but he barely reacts. He sits up a little straighter, a wall closing over his easy expression.

"Hey." I almost reach out for his hand but hesitate at the last second. "Are you okay?"

"Sure," he says, but his voice is toneless. His silence is making me antsy, but I'm not sure what I can say to comfort him. My phone lights up with a notification, and since Theo's attention is directed glumly at draining his drink, I check it.

A slew of messages from Angela confirms my suspicions.

> I'm so sorry

> Christine convinced everyone to come and spy on your date with Theo. I couldn't convince Alice to stop them.

> Btw is this a real date??? If so, I need DETAILS, girl!

I thank her for letting me know and assure her that this is far beyond the realm of a date. She texts back three sobbing emojis, and I roll my eyes before sending her a digital one. I'm about to remind her, in great detail, why dating Theo would be a monumentally bad idea when a warm presence beside me makes me turn my head. Theo is glancing down at the screen from over my shoulder.

I lock my phone and turn it over, cheeks reddening.

"Isn't it rude to check your phone during a date?" Theo asks, smirking as my face heats further. I count my blessings he can't see how red my cheeks are in the dim, artificial red lighting. His tone takes on a teasing quality that makes me want to cover my face with both hands. I barely manage to resist as it is.

"Come on, Marcela. Give me a fair chance. We're supposed to be getting to know each other, here." He knocks the tip of his shoe with mine and smirks. Is he *teasing* me?

"According to everyone at the engagement party, we already got to know each other plenty." *Oh god.* Did those words actually come out of my mouth? Theo coughs, eyes shifting away from mine in embarrassment. Is he being sheepish, or does the thought of us together disgust him? Just as a bucket of shame washes over me, his face turns back to me.

His eyes are shining beneath the red light's glow, mouth spread in a ridiculously large grin. I'm pretty sure it's the first genuine smile I've seen on him. He lets out a deep, rumbling laugh, straight from his diaphragm. The tension in my shoulders from accidentally letting slip such a risqué remark dissipates, and I find myself laughing with him.

"This is so much worse than brunch," he says, still laughing. "They actually came here to spy on us, didn't they?"

"Yeah. That's all your fault, by the way." He has the audacity to crease his brows in confusion. I roll my eyes, not buying it. "Christine wants you. It's all she can talk about whenever you're in town."

"Oh."

There's something like disappointment in his slumped shoulders, in the way the corners of his mouth turn down suddenly. I recognize the expression for what it is. It was only a few minutes ago that I was reveling in Ben's possible jealousy that I was going out with his brother. I've inadvertently burst

Theo's bubble that Alice was jealous of us, and that that's the reason she summoned her troops to the bar to do her recon.

"She'd make a good rebound, you know. Christine."

He looks back at me, eyes cloudy. "Right," he says, distracted. "Maybe. If she can get over that I chose you first."

And just like that, the flash of vulnerability is replaced with something sharper. His mouth pulls up in a flirtatious grin, eyes scanning me up and down with the subtlety of a beacon. My heart thumps, and I'm sure my cheeks redden all over again as his eyes slowly trail down my body.

He's Ben's brother.

Ben's older, sexier, NFL player brother. Up until we met up today, I'd been comfortable around him knowing there was no chance he'd want me, and because he's eons out of my league, his attractiveness was a blip on my radar. Maybe it's the atmosphere making me see him this way. Or maybe it's the way he's looking at me now, one brow arched, full mouth curved up on one side in the hint of a grin, blue eyes glittering. Is my attraction to him...reciprocated?

Before I dare find out, I turn my head away from him to catch my breath. The longer I'm around him, the faster common sense seems to leak out of my brain. Only, in my attempt to regain some of it back, I end up meeting three pairs of eyes from Alice's table. They all dart away as soon as we make eye contact, and I turn back to Theo with a knowing look. He's far too amused for my liking.

"You didn't correct anyone after brunch, did you?"

"No," he says, eyes glancing away from mine in an apologetic look I don't believe for a second. Maybe I'm not the only one who wants to piss his brother off. "I thought it'd work in my favor if everyone just assumed. Sorry."

I don't say anything. It might work in my favor, too.

A hand on my shoulder makes me flinch, and when I turn around Alice is standing in front of me. She maneuvers between Theo and me, not bothering to face him as she says, "Theo, could you give me a minute with Marcela?"

He looks down at his feet with a mumbled "Sure" before seating himself three spots down from us. I glance across the bar at him before returning my attention to Alice, gulping down the sudden fear.

"Alice, hey." She takes Theo's vacant spot. "What's up?"

She meets my eyes for so long, I start to squirm. The silence between us grows, awkward and uncomfortable. Nothing in her expression gives her away, but my heart is pounding fast. Dread builds in the pit of my stomach, and I'm seconds away from shouting "WHAT DO YOU WANT?" before she finally says something.

"I hope you know what you're doing."

Eight

There's something ominous about her words. As if she actually *can* see through me, like I've suspected for all these years. *I hope you know what you're doing.*

"About what?" I ask, feigning nonchalance and failing miserably. About sleeping with Theo when I'm in love with his brother? About *pretending* I'm sleeping with Theo to make it look like I don't, in fact, have feelings for a man I can't have? It's comfortably cool inside the bar but sweat starts to bead on my forehead. There are too many ways this line of questioning can go, and I'm far too afraid to guess which direction she'll take it.

She tilts her head, brown eyes narrowed slightly in that inquisitive way of hers.

"You and Theo." *Me and Theo.* Up until this weekend, I never thought there could be such a thing. "Look, you're a grown woman and I respect whatever choice you make. But his reputation precedes him."

I want to laugh, for *so many* reasons, but somehow manage to keep a straight face.

"Ben's worried you're getting yourself into a bad situation. You've never been big on hookups, and Theo's never spent longer than two weeks with the same girl." I flinch again. I knew Theo was bad, but I didn't think he was *that* bad.

"I'm good," I assure her, or at least try to, but she doesn't look convinced. "I wanna try out something casual for once. See how the other half lives, and all that." It's not exactly a lie, but a misdirection. Because while that might be true, I already know that a casual relationship with Theo will only end in disaster.

You hear that, common sense? Now return to my brain, please.

"Really?" Her eyes widen. "I didn't think that was your style."

"Not usually." I play with the straw in my drink to have something to do with my hands, even though nothing but dregs remain inside the glass. "But I don't know. Maybe I'm missing out on all the fun." And I am in desperate need of some fun. Not that Theo would truly make himself an option. But if he did...

Okay, looks like I'm saying goodbye to common sense for the night.

Alice won't be any help either, because she's smiling. Actually *smiling* at the thought of Theo and me hooking up. Maybe I'm a better actress than I give myself credit for.

"Then I hope you have some. Just be careful. Guard your heart around that one."

"I will," I say, and it's the first true thing I've said to her tonight.

When she turns back to her table, Theo fills her vacant spot carrying a second round of tequila shots. Wordlessly, we clink glasses and down them. It burns less the second time around.

"What was that about?" Theo asks.

"Just a friendly warning to guard my heart around you," I say with a faux-dramatic flair. "Did you know your reputation precedes you? I should start calling you Taylor Swift." He bursts into another laugh, clapping his hands. "It's too bad we got caught up in this situation. You could be out finding a real hookup instead of hanging with me."

"Aw, but I like hanging out with you." He reaches out a hand to touch my arm. His skin is warm, heating me from the inside out. *What is wrong with me?* Goosebumps break out on my arms from the simple touch. I only hope he doesn't notice. "Plus, it's kinda fun messing with everyone. Let's enjoy it now, and fake break up later."

"The sooner the better, before this whole thing gets away from us." But inside, I'm surprised by the bloom of disappointment that heats my chest. *Don't be stupid.* How many times do I have to tell myself that before I finally listen? Theo Young is a bad idea. But is he worse than Ben? I still can't decide. Though the more time we spend together, the more I begin to forget all about Ben.

And that can only be a good thing, right?

"It's kinda funny, though."

"What's funny?"

"I was just talking to my best friend earlier today about finding a fling." I'm treading dangerous water here. "I didn't get that far, though. Tinder is a cesspool that I'm too chicken to wade through."

"Is that so?" But he's only half listening as his eyes fall on something past my shoulder. "They're still staring. And *giggling*." His voice pitches higher than normal. He sounds aggrieved by this, but I don't know why. If they're laughing, it's at my expense. Christine is probably (loudly) wondering what he's doing with someone like me, when he could be with her instead.

"Ignore them." My gaze stays trained on him. "They just wish they were in my pretend-place. Except Angela. And Alice."

He winces, and I bite my tongue. Damn my tipsy brain for having no filter. "I'm sorry."

"Don't apologize," he says, his breath hot on my skin. It's only now that I notice how close our faces are. Mere inches separate us. A dangerous proximity, considering the kind of thoughts I've been having about him all night. But it *has* to be better than having them about Ben. I've practically convinced myself of this by now.

"Maybe it was a bad idea to move back here. I thought I wanted to be closer to family, but this…" He shakes his head, unable to finish his thought.

"San Antonio's a big city. You can still keep your distance from her when you need to." I almost reach out and touch his arm, like he touched mine, but hesitate at the last moment and let it fall on the bar. "Don't let her affect your life and how you choose to move forward."

I lean in closer, in what's meant to be a conspiratorial

manner, but the musky scent of him is intoxicating. One whiff of him, and I'm starting to think I understand how addicts feel. His eyes are so blue, deep indigo pools I could drown in. Nothing like his brother's hazel ones.

"You know what you need, Theo?"

"What?" He finally looks at me straight on. The weight of his gaze is almost too much to take.

"A rebound!" I announce, index finger poking at his chest until he moves back a few inches. Already, I can breathe easier now that he's not so close. Maybe if I can convince him to hook up with someone else, I'll stop thinking about him this way. "Get under a few girls. Or over them. Behind them. Whichever position suits your sensibilities. I'm sure you can manage a few."

I nudge him with an elbow, as I imagine a wingman would. His eyes widen in surprise, mouth wobbling like he's holding in a laugh.

"Right." A smile breaks through, wide and almost comical, if he wasn't so damn attractive. But then, a distant scream makes him look past my shoulder again. I turn around too. Alice is clapping, head thrown back as a laugh takes over her body. Christine is frowning, eyes narrowing as she looks up at Angela, who is standing up from the table and shouldering her purse. She waves at the group, and when we make eye contact across the bar, she waggles her brows at me.

I don't have to know the context to know that Angela will always have my back. Whatever she said to Christine had to have been in my defense.

But Theo doesn't know what I know. He's agitated all over

again, leg shaking against the barstool. His eyes are trained on Alice, her glossy black hair and flushed cheeks. Finally, he turns away with a scowl. "Are they bothering you as much as they're bothering me right now?"

I shake my head. I'm completely unbothered, but if he is, there might be a way I can help...no matter how bad of an idea it is. But if I can distract him from Alice, even momentarily, I should take one for the team, right? My eyes fall to his full lips, pursed in a frown I suddenly want so badly to undo.

Talk about tequila bringing out bad sides. And we're not even drunk yet.

"We could always give them what they came here for."

He looks back down at me. "And what would that be?"

The heat in his gaze tells me he already knows. Or maybe he's just matching the heat in mine. His eyes flick down, and now we're both staring at each other's mouths. My skin flushes, fever hot. He hesitates a beat, and when I flick my eyes back up to his, I find indecision there. It lasts only a moment before heat replaces logic, and then he's closing the space between us.

He leans forward until our lips crash together, sudden and collapsing. I taste the salt and lime on his tongue as it slides between my teeth, and I wonder distantly if I taste like raspberries. My fingers curl in his hair, soft and fine to the touch. Oh god, this is the best bad idea I've had in years.

His big hands wrap around my waist, pulling me flush against his chest, between his spread legs. I tug on his hair, and am rewarded with a low, throaty groan against my lips. The scruff of his cheeks scratches against mine, but it's not an altogether bad feeling. Our tongues slide together, and the feeling is almost too much. Pleasure pools low in my stomach, so intense I have to squeeze my legs together to keep from pouncing on him this moment, in front of Alice and her friends and everyone else in the bar.

I didn't expect this. He wasn't supposed to feel this *good*. The kiss was supposed to satisfy my curiosity—a one-time kiss to inspire me to move on to other one-time activities. Preferably, with men whose surnames aren't Young. But now that I know what it's like to kiss him, it's all I want to keep doing. It should scare me, but I just want more of him.

He breaks away, eyes hazy, pupils blown so wide I can't see a single trace of blue. I wonder if I look as wrecked as I feel, as wrecked as he looks right now. If this is all it takes to forget about Ben, why didn't I start doing this years ago?

I clear my throat, backing away onto my stool. Theo's hands fall away from my back, the warmth of him immediately cooling with his absence. We're both breathing hard and staring harder. I don't think I'm the only one surprised by the intensity between us.

"Well." I clear my throat again. "That was…" I put a fist to my mouth, laughing at myself. At *us*. Never mind that nothing about what just happened is funny. Except maybe my audacity.

"Yeah," he agrees, mouth spreading into a wide grin. His eyes trail past my shoulder, and then he throws back his head and laughs.

"What?" I turn around, and then turn back to him with wide eyes. "Oh my god. They *left*."

We burst into hysterics, laughing like complete idiots. He orders another round of shots, and the rest of the night settles into a pattern of order, clink, drink. It's the distraction I need after the kiss because *wow*. I have never been kissed like that before. I'm apparently so quick to dive into literally anything else to get my mind off it that I lose count of how many shots we've downed, and my vision is far too blurry to count the shot glasses on our side of the bar.

"All right, Ortiz, you know what I have to do." Krystal holds out her blurry hand expectantly. "Hand it over."

"If I have to, then so does he." I throw an arm around Theo's shoulders. He squints at me as I hold out my other hand. "Phone. You're as much in danger of drunk dialing as I am."

"I'm not gonna drunk dial Alice," he says past a drunken hiccup. When I don't budge, he heaves a sigh and shoves his iPhone into my hand. Before I hand mine to Krystal, I notice two missed texts from Angela on the lock screen.

> Urgh, Christine had the nerve to say she has no idea what Theo sees in you. Y'all might not really be dating, but I set her straight!

> You should've SEEN the look on her face when I said maybe she should give it up after ten straight years of rejection.

I let out a hard laugh, shaking my head before turning off my iPhone and handing it to Krystal. When Theo asks what's so funny, I shrug and shake my head again. To think Angela missed out on the show Theo and I put on for them. I'll have to tell her all about it later, when my skin isn't still humming from his touch.

"Y'know..." Theo covers his mouth over a burp. The stench could rival a dragon's in terms of flammability. "I hate living with Ben. Like, haaaaate it. This weekend alone is triggering all sorts of bad memories from our childhood."

"But I thought you guys used to be close?" I ask, leaning forward in interest.

"We were. But I didn't mind his bad living habits when I actually liked him. It's like"—his words start to slur together and I have to work extra hard to pay attention to what he's saying—"you leave one sock on the floor in the hallway and it's the end of the world."

"Right." I nod, already losing interest. This isn't the chisme I was hoping for. "Hey, how drunk do you think you are right now?"

His brows crease, lines forming on his forehead as he thinks over his answer. I burst out a laugh, shoving his shoulder so hard he wobbles off the stool. He barely manages to catch himself, and scowls as he situates himself back in his seat. "What'd you do that for? I wasn't done thinking."

"If you have to think about it, the answer is 'not enough.'"

He nods solemnly and orders a final round of shots when Krystal announces last call. Theo isn't the least bit fazed by the bartender's announcement, but he does rush me into downing the shot before paying the tab and retrieving our phones. Krystal calls us an Uber, ensuring we take one together to keep an eye on each other. I'm glad I can always count on her to keep me safe, which I drunkenly gush to her as we leave the bar.

"Do you wanna stay over again?" I ask Theo as he holds the door open for me. Inside the bar, the lights flick off as employees start packing it in for the night. I haven't moved the blanket and pillow he used from my couch, and since he seems to hate staying with his brother so much—and because it's two in the morning—it seems like the kind thing to offer.

Then, because I already sound like I'm propositioning him, I add in a teasing voice, "We've already done the walk of shame once. What's one more time?"

The look he gives me could melt steel. His eyes fall to my lips, and heat pools in my most sensitive places. I try to force my drunk brain not to think about that kiss, but it plays in my mind on repeat. When I lick my lips, I still taste him. All warm heat and lime and salt. He lets out a groan, leaning his head back against the brick building.

Then a flicker of emotion I can't name clouds his eyes. He shakes his head as if he's changing his mind about something. "We can't, Marcela."

I'm surprised by the disappointment that floods me. That's not even what I was asking him. At least, not really.

"You're drunk," Theo says, as if I don't already know this. "And I'm drunk. So, we sh-shouldn't." He stumbles over his words, overemphasizing his point. "We shouldn't do this. Not right now."

My brain catches on that last part, because what in the ever-living fuck does he mean by that?

Not right now.

"Theo." I have no idea why I'm smiling. "That's not what I—"

"It's not that I don't want—" he continues, until a blue Honda pulls up to the curb. The passenger window rolls down, and the driver gives Theo's name. He nods at the driver as he steps forward and holds the back door open for me.

"Milady."

Our eyes meet across the open door. His mouth pulls up in a smile that's not at all wolfish or devious, but something far more genuine. He follows in after me, closing the door behind him.

It's not that I don't want— What?

Me?

There's no way he means me, but I'm not sure how to bring the conversation back to before the Uber pulled up.

"Is Ben gonna be mad at you for coming home so late?" Theo shrugs at my question. His eyes are half closed; I suspect because he's already asleep. "You're welcome to crash on my couch again."

"Cool. Thanks."

Nine

I don't want to be awake right now.

My bed is too comfortable to leave, so I shut my eyes and try to fall back asleep. But something is off, only I can't tell what. Memories from last night come back in a blur. Alice's keen eyes, Angela's flurry of text messages, Theo's face outlined in red candlelight. His eyes growing hooded, right before he bent forward, and our lips met...

Be careful.

I throw back the duvet from my face, eyes wide open. Near-blinding light pours into the room from the window. I almost hiss and pull the covers back over my face, but there's no way I can possibly go back to sleep now. Did last night actually happen, or was it just some sort of bizarre fever dream? When the space on the bed beside me shifts, I freeze.

I fear I may already have my answer.

Slowly, I attempt to sit up but find myself stuck. I'm barely breathing when I catch sight of the arm thrown over my middle, casually, as if he's done it a thousand times.

Theo.

I burst up, the force knocking his arm askew as I furiously inspect myself. I'm still wearing my jeans and blouse from last night, and the sigh of relief I breathe is so huge, it could have its own bedroom. I'm even still wearing the shoes I went out in. My bright blue Keds stare up at me from the white sheets they rest on. Well. That can't possibly be sanitary, but better this than the alternative.

When Theo lets out a loud groan, I turn my head back to him. He's sitting up against the headboard, stretching his thick, muscular arms over his head. My breath catches as my stare lingers on his golden skin. The faint tan lines on his upper arms, where the golden hue of his skin becomes pink. The even fainter traces of blond hair on his chest. His shoulders are so wide-set, his arms look almost long enough to wrap around my body twice. With his height and build, he takes up more space on the bed than I do.

He's so...*burly.*

The duvet creeps down his chest, and I get my first glimpse of Theo without a shirt on. *Holy mother of—*

"What the hell happened last night?" Theo asks before I can finish my train of thought. My eyes snap up to his immediately.

"Shots." My voice is dry and hoarse, for no reason whatsoever. *Because I'm hungover, and not any other word that starts with h.* I clear my throat and try again. "Lots of shots."

He runs a hand through his hair, heaving another groan before he slides himself back down on the bed. "God, my head is pounding. Did we drink the entire bar last night?"

"I wouldn't doubt it." Now that he mentions it, there's a pounding ache at the back of my own head as well. "I have some Advil in the bathroom. Give me a second."

I stand up and walk toward the adjoining bathroom. When I flick on the lights, I let out a startled gasp at my own reflection in the mirror above the sink.

My hair is a tangled mess of knots and god knows what else. Black mascara runs down my cheeks, dried flecks dotted around the circles of my eyes. I don't even remember putting on makeup before meeting up with Theo. What I do remember is distinctly trying not to impress him. I even wore my favorite ratty blouse, though now the brown coffee stain on the collar is so much starker in the light of day. The makeup was from before I left for work, then.

Work. I almost forgot it's Tuesday. Good god, who is Theo turning me into!?

"Hey, can you check the time for me?" I call through the closed door, failing to hide the note of anxiety in my voice. Erica's going to kill me if I'm late. *I'm* going to kill me if I'm late, because it's never happened before. I quickly dab the crusted makeup from my face and grab a bottle from the medicine cabinet.

"Seven thirty-five."

I breathe a sigh of relief as I pick up my toothbrush. *Thank god.* I have two free hours until I'm due at work. Theo leans a shoulder against the doorway, clutching his head. I hand him the pill bottle before squeezing a dab of toothpaste onto my brush. Out of the corner of my eye, I spot Theo covertly checking his breath with both hands raised to his mouth.

"I have a spare toothbrush if you need one."

He nods before stepping into the bathroom. Such a tiny action, but my heart is racing all of a sudden. Maybe it's seeing the two of us standing side by side in the mirror's reflection. The domesticity of it is somehow even more intimate after last night's kiss. How is it that in the little time I've known him, we've already shared a bathroom twice?

I hand him the spare and watch as he twists open the cap of toothpaste. He catches me staring in the mirror, and the side of his mouth lifts in a smirk. I train my eyes back to my reflection, brushing furiously and avoiding his gaze altogether. He beats me to the sink, rinsing out his mouth and washing down two pills with water. When the bottle slips from his hand, he shuts off the water and bends over. My eyes immediately fall to his jeans-clad ass before I force my eyes shut.

Stop gawking at him, for fuck's sake.

Luckily, I make it to the sink before he can get an eyeful of the toothpaste waterfall dripping from the side of my mouth. This whole situation is awkward enough without him catching me quite literally drooling all over him.

"Thanks for letting me crash here again," he says as he leaves the bathroom. His smile is dazzling, indigo eyes glittering. My stomach does somersaults inside my body. If he can sense the internal freak-out, he's too polite to say as much. "I really appreciate it. Even if neither of us has any recollection of how we ended up...you know."

Is it just me, or has his smile turned devilish? I'm not sure if he means the kiss, or the ending up in bed together. Both, perhaps. My pulse stutters with the flash of his teeth.

"Yeah." I hate how breathy my voice comes out. "No problem."

He finds his hoodie discarded on the living room floor. I follow him into the room, my mind reeling with all sorts of inappropriate thoughts. Last night's kiss replays in my head, over and over. The taste of salt and lime and *him* on my tongue, the feel of his big hands on my body. Awakening a side of me that's been dormant for so long, I wasn't sure it still existed.

Still exists, all right.

"So," I start, my pulse drumming a hard beat beneath my flesh when his eyes train on me again. "Last night was...fun?" It comes out as a question. "Is that the right word? *Fun?*" I'm not sure if I'm asking for confirmation or his opinion.

"Definitely fun." There's that wicked grin again. "We should do it again soon."

"Which part?" I'm about to say something stupid, but I can't stop the question from slipping out anyway. "The drinking, the kissing, or the waking up in the same bed part?"

His smile drops.

The mirth in his eyes is replaced with something headier. Something...darker. Two feet of space separates us, but the temperature in my apartment ratchets up.

He clears his throat, but his voice is thick when he answers. "Asker's choice."

I blink once, twice. I'm sure I heard wrong.

"Anyway." His smile is sheepish as he changes the subject before I can even think to ask him what he means by that. "We should probably talk about what happened. I..."

He takes a steadying breath. "Look, I'm grateful to you for you going along with the lie from brunch, but I don't want you to feel like I'm using you. We can tell everyone it was just a miscommunication if you want."

"I think we're past that." I smile wryly, though I'm more grateful than I can say that he's willing to walk back the lie. There's no explaining away that kiss to Alice and her friends, not in a way that wouldn't humiliate us both, but the fact that he's willing to come clean so I don't feel used is…unexpected. "I don't mind."

"Are you sure?"

"Positive." I nod.

"Okay." His brows furrow. "Why is that?"

Why is that, indeed.

If I tell him the truth, would he understand? We're in the same predicament, after all. He's not nearly as intimidating as I first thought. There's a softness I hadn't expected to see in him. A vulnerability I never knew he was capable of. He wouldn't tell anyone if I shared my secret. He'd hold it close, next to his own secrets. My mouth opens to confess the truth, but the explanation tangles and chokes at the back of my throat.

"I haven't been kissed like that in a long time," I admit instead, which is somehow even more embarrassing than my feelings for his brother. I shudder and close my eyes, face heating. "Oh god, that's—"

"No." His hand closes over my shoulder. The warmth of it seeps through my shirt and into my skin. "I haven't either, truthfully."

I look up at him in disbelief. *"Really?"*

He laughs at the surprise in my tone. "I've been too distracted lately. With leaving the team and figuring out what to do with my life next. With Alice…" He heaves a sigh. "I don't regret that kiss, but I wouldn't blame you if you did."

"I don't," I assure him. "Seriously. You just…reminded me what I've been missing." A flush of heat washes over me. "I've never really done the casual thing before. Angela keeps telling me I need to give it a try. She even made me redownload all my old dating apps," I add quickly.

"Angela." His eyes narrow in thought. "She's the one who texted you last night."

"Yeah." I nod. "The really skinny one with big, curly hair that looks like it weighs more than she does."

"Ah." His eyes light up with recognition. "I remember her now." He looks at me again, something inexplicable in his eyes. "So…you're just looking for something casual."

The way he says it almost makes it a question. An understanding, of sorts.

"It wouldn't be the worst thing in the world. Right?" I shrug, ducking away from his eyes.

When I chance a glance at him, he's much closer than he was before. His body hovers over me, head bent until our faces are inches apart. He nearly has to crouch to manage it. My body is very aware of his, still gloriously shirtless, his forgotten hoodie dangling from a closed fist. When his eyes flick down to my lips, something in the air shifts and becomes supercharged, until we're two electric currents about to clash together in a burst of sparks.

"Raspberries." His lips move, but I barely hear the word

that crosses them. A hand comes up to smooth my left brow, to smooth the tension formed from furrowing my brows. "You tasted like raspberries last night."

A gasp, a slow intake of breath, leaves my throat. Has he been thinking about last night as much as I have? A part of me was starting to wonder if I was the only one affected by it. If I'm the only one who wants a repeat of last night. Behind closed doors, without this thing between us being about putting on a show. To almost believe it's real.

"Marcela." His hand migrates to the edge of my mouth, thumb trailing below my bottom lip. The nerve endings there buzz to life, until it's the only inch of skin on my body I'm conscious of. "You need to tell me what to do here. I'm not the one who should start this…for a lot of reasons."

He's right, a warning from the back of my mind says. I always thought I wasn't cut out for casual, based on past failed attempts. But there's no denying the pull between us. There's no denying how badly we both want this.

My eyes flick down to his mouth, memories of his pillow-soft lips on mine. "Why? Because you want me to be sure I know what I'm getting into?" It's a miracle I'm able to keep my voice steady. His eyes close as he nods. I lift myself to my tiptoes, mouth close enough for my lips to graze his ear. "I don't expect anything from you, Theo. I know what this is."

He shudders beneath my touch, goosebumps rising on his shoulders. Because of me? Is that the effect I have on him?

"Are you sure?" His voice is a breathy rasp, warm against my flushed cheeks. "Because I'm trying to be a good guy here, Marcela. But you're making it incredibly difficult for me."

If this is his way of volleying the power back to me, it's working. It's *intoxicating*. We're barely touching, but I've never been this turned on in my life. Maybe it's the proof of my effect on him, maybe it's the anticipation buzzing beneath my skin, but whatever it is, it gives me the courage I need to keep going.

I take a chance and kiss his neck, reveling in the way his body shakes beneath my touch. In the throaty groan he emits in my ear. His hands cup my hips, but they don't move. They lock in place, one last barrier of hesitation to break through. I kiss up his jaw, stopping right before I reach his lips. Our eyes meet and lock. Just like last night, his pupils are blown wide.

"I want this, Theo—"

I barely get his name out before his mouth is on mine. Neither one of us holds back this time as we pull at each other. His hands search over my blouse, and mine brush over bare skin. I push him until the back of his legs reach the couch. He breaks the kiss momentarily to sit, pulling me down onto his lap.

My knees straddle either side of his waist as his big hand cups the back of my neck. His fingers trail the tiny hairs on my nape, making a shiver run down my back. He kisses down my jaw as my hands roam his bare chest, warm on my already overheated skin. We're as close as our bodies can possibly be, but it doesn't feel close enough. There are still too many layers between us. His hands pull on my waist, grinding me into his lap. I feel the bulge in his pants and let out an embarrassingly loud moan.

Bad idea bad idea bad— I shut off my thoughts as if slamming a door shut, bolting the locks for good measure. No thinking, just *this*. Just his hands in my hair, his lips on my skin, his limbs tangling with mine until I lose track of where I end and he begins.

We shift until my back hits the sofa cushions and his body hovers over mine, legs tangled together, hands roaming of their own will. It's only been hours, but I don't know how I made it through an entire night with him *in my bed* without his mouth on mine.

"God, I missed this," he mumbles against my skin, taking the words right out of my brain.

"I didn't think guys like you went through dry spells."

He chuckles against my lips. "What does that even mean? Guys like me?"

"Have you seen what you look like?"

He counters with "Have you seen what *you* look like?" and pulls me into his chest. His hands play with the hem of my blouse, his fingers skating my bare skin. I'm still reveling in his words—*have you seen what* you *look like*—when his mouth moves up and kisses my lips, hard and fast. We've only just begun, but the way he kisses is like we're running out of time. Our hands intertwine as my hips find a rhythm to grind against his jeans-clad erection, right where I need him.

"God, Marcela." He groans, his hands pulling at my hair in the most delicious way. "This is gonna be over before it starts if you don't slow down."

"I don't wanna slow down," I admit, surprised at how husky my voice comes out. "But we should probably move this to the bedroom soon."

Neither one of us moves an inch. His lips scorch as they

form a path down my neck. My sweaty hands slip down his chest, until I find the button of his jeans. He moves my hand away before I can pop it open, and disappointment and frustration flood my chest. But I'm revitalized again when he says, "Bedroom, Marcela. Now."

Right. Yes.

Reluctantly, we leave the couch and I lead him back to the bedroom. He leans down to kiss me but before he can, the silence is broken by the alarm on my phone. The sudden blaring sound startles us both so much, we bump our heads together instead. White hot pain burns the front of my skull.

"Ow! Goddammit!"

He clutches at his head with a pained expression, but his lips are holding back what looks like an amused grin. I grab my phone from the nightstand and shut off the alarm with a heavy sigh. Now that the mood is officially killed, I plop down on the bed with a groan.

"I have work soon." It comes out as a sexually frustrated grumble.

"So I gathered..." His eyes sparkle with amusement. "Guess I should probably go, then."

"Or"—I lift myself from the bed, prowling toward him—"you can stay until the third alarm goes off. That gives us about thirty more minutes."

"Third alarm?" he asks, even as he kisses my lips. Even as the back of my knees hit the edge of the bed. But I can't answer him when I'm pushed down and my back hits the mattress, Theo hovering over me. "I'm sure we can find time for a few things."

That smile is going to be the death of me.

Ten

Theo has a superpower: he can make time pass five times faster than normal. That's the only logical explanation I can think of when my third alarm goes off just when I've gotten his jeans unbuttoned. We're both breathing hard, eyes locked, even as my phone chimes it's incessant noise.

"Are you sure that's your alarm?" Theo asks as if coming out of a trance, the haziness in his eyes clearing. He shakes his head as if to regain his equilibrium. "The sound is different."

He's right, I belatedly notice. My alarm is set to the sound of blaring bell chimes, but my ringtone is much softer. I glance down at it, breath catching as Ben's picture fills the screen.

"I'm so sorry." Theo's eyes crease in concern as I hastily back away from him. "I have to take this."

Before he can react, I dart across the bedroom and into the bathroom. Once the door shuts behind me with a soft click, I hit answer and bring the phone to my ear.

"Hello?"

"Hey." There's a hesitancy I rarely hear in Ben's voice. Or maybe I'm projecting. Apparently I do that a lot. He's said only one word and I'm coiled tight, bracing for impact.

"I feel like it's been awhile since we talked," he continues.

"Yeah," I say. "I didn't want to take up too much of your time at the party and brunch. They were both great, by the way. It looked like everyone had a great time."

"I heard you did, too." His tone turns sarcastic, but I can't tell if it's meant to be teasing or cutting. "Which is sort of why I wanted to talk to you. Do you think we can meet up after work? I'll bring a six-pack of Angry Orchards, just like old times."

I should say no, just to keep the distance between us. But would he suspect anything weird if I declined? And what does he mean that that's what he wants to talk about? Does he not like me seeing Theo because of their feud?

"Sure," I say, hating myself for the answer as soon as it's out of my mouth. I have no idea how I'll respond if he asks me how this happened.

Well, you see, it started somewhere between wrenching him away from your fiancée and the morning after we consumed the entire bar. Now we're dating, and sorry not sorry if you don't like it. Never mind that "dating" is so far beyond a stretch of the imagination, it might as well be in outer space.

This is going to end in disaster.

"How's seven o'clock?"

"Perfect," he says. "I'll see you then."

When I return to the bedroom Theo turns over on his side, propping himself up with a raised elbow. His blond hair is mussed in the most adorable way, sticking up like a child's. I'd rest his head on my lap and run my fingers through it for an entire day if I could. I kneel on the mattress, about to reach a hand to do just that when he asks, "What was that about?"

I blink. "What do you mean?"

"Rushing to the bathroom just to answer a phone call. Ben's not that interesting." His fingers trace the line of my neck until they curl into my hair. Even though he's only teasing, his words still bristle. I'm about to push him away when he says, "If you want to get rid of me, you can just say so."

The thought of him leaving bristles even more.

"That's not what I want." I shake my head. When he breathes a sigh against my shoulder, it sounds like relief. "But you should probably go anyway. The real world awaits."

"Fine." He lets out a dramatic groan as he pulls himself away. "Do you have plans after work?"

Suddenly, I wish I didn't.

"Um, Ben's coming over." I avoid looking directly at his face. "We'll probably catch up for a little while. It won't be long."

"Oh. Cool." His mouth turns up into that devilish grin that threatens to be my undoing. "Text me when he leaves?"

"Sure." I laugh softly. That smile has no right turning me on this early in the day. "Bye."

But neither one of us makes a move. We stare at each other for so long, the air grows hot. Until after a brief moment of hesitation, he bows his head to kiss me goodbye. Only, the moment our lips meet, there's nothing chaste about it at all.

I let out a groan when his tongue slides between my lips, my hands curling into his hair.

I could get used to this.

The warmth of his body is helping make all thoughts of his brother dissipate. Angela was right about that—rebounds really can work wonders.

When we pull away, his mouth spreads into a surprised grin. His eyes shut tight, as if embarrassed we almost got carried away all over again. I hide my face in the crook of his neck to disguise the laugh that burbles up from the back of my throat. His shoulders shake with a laugh of his own, one of his hands coming up to pat my head.

"I should go," he says as he pulls away from me. "Before I get you fired for not showing up."

"Right." The thought does the same trick a bucket of ice water would. I quickly glance down at my phone for the time. I need to start getting ready, and *fast*. "I'll walk you out."

We find his hoodie on the living room floor. When he pulls it over his head, it tousles his blond hair even further. I reach up to pat it down, unable to resist touching his hair any longer. He lets me, lips vibrating with a soft *hmm* noise in approval. "I've got an interview in an hour."

"Oh, good luck!" I throw my arms around him in a crushing hug. After a beat of surprise, he returns it. There's no heat in it this time, as if we're somehow able to cycle through unbridled lust and platonic touching seamlessly. "You got this."

"Thanks." He smiles down at me, almost like he still can't believe last night happened. I can't really either. "See you tonight."

After work, my mom stops by to drop off a collection of home-made goods. Tortillas, jars of salsa, and freshly ripened fruits and vegetables from her garden litter my kitchen counter. As soon as I turn my back to put everything away, the sound of rushing water meets my ears. I heave a sigh, but don't say a word. There isn't anything my mom can't stand more than dishes in the sink. Even if it's not *her* sink.

Despite her small frame, my mother is anything but frail. It remains a wonder how she possesses so much energy to keep up with household chores, taking care of her garden, socializing with the neighbors, *and* multiple volunteer gigs. Even when she was working, she still found ways to keep busy. Now that she's retired, that much hasn't changed.

"Wow. You didn't hold back." I gather a handful of limes in my hands to deposit into my empty fruit bowl. At least it won't be empty for much longer.

"I figured this should keep you stocked for a while since you said you were running low," she says. "The tomatoes should be ripe in a day or two. Don't let them rot—you're not gonna want to miss out on those. I won't be able to grow them for much longer." Homegrown tomatoes cannot be beat. During the summers growing up, I'd eat them by themselves with a dash of salt. They truly put those watery grocery store tomatoes to shame.

"Believe me, I won't."

"Bueno." She nods as she shuts off the water. Her black hair is cut short, but still long enough for thick, shiny curls to form. There isn't a trace of gray, which means she must've gone to the salon recently. I follow her into the living room, where she begins folding a pink blanket thrown haphazardly on the couch. "Was Angela over last night?"

My face heats as I studiously avoid her gaze. I may be a grown woman, but my mother will never see me as anything other than her little girl. The urge to reach out and grab the blanket Theo used not too long ago from her hands is overwhelming, but I curl my fingers into loose fists to quell it.

"Mm-hmm." I give a noncommittal nod. "And Ben's coming over a little later to catch up."

"Ah." She sets the neatly folded blanket down. "How's he been?"

"Good," I say. "He's engaged now, so…there's that." Good lord. *So. There's that.* Could I sound any more monotone?

Thankfully, my mom doesn't pick up on it. She exclaims in excitement and asks me to pass on her well wishes. I tell her I will, nodding mechanically until we've moved on from the subject. Unfortunately for me, she moves the conversation into dangerous territory.

"You haven't told me about anyone new in a while. Are you still on those apps?" she asks idly, but I'm not buying her nonchalant tone. Though she's never pressured me into settling down with the next available man now that I have an established career, I still get twitchy talking about my dating life with her. The pink blanket is neatly folded beside her, a guilty pastel reminder of this morning.

"I am, but they're kinda useless." I try for a shrug, but my shoulders are tense. "I'm taking a break from dating. Possibly indefinitely."

She bursts out in a laugh that puts me on the defensive.

"Why is that funny?" I ask. "You didn't date anyone after dad and you're perfectly happy, right?"

"You're too young to be giving up so soon." She shakes her head fondly, ignoring my question. It was rhetorical, anyway. I know how happy she is now, and what it took for her to get here. "The last boy you were really excited about was Ben, and that was years ago."

I still cringe over the memory of telling her all about him when we first started going out. She was the first person I called after he asked me out, excited about my first official date. Of course, that excitement quickly ebbed when she lectured me to focus more on school and less on boys. Now I wish she'd keep that up and tell me to focus more on work and less on dating. Plus, it's embarrassing that she knows how much I liked him back then when we didn't work out.

"I wish you felt like you could be honest with me." For a moment, it feels like the air in my apartment stills. I hold in a breath and stare at her, waiting for the bomb to drop. "It's okay for relationships to fail. You can talk to me. I want to know about your life. Don't wait until you're engaged to tell me you've been seeing someone. Okay?"

I breathe a sigh of relief that she didn't say what I thought she would, though I'm not sure I like how close to the truth she is. This isn't the first time she's brought up Ben as the last guy I told her about by name. Maybe she's right and I should've told her about the ones who came after him, even if they all flopped right at the start. At least then, Ben wouldn't be the only guy she knows I've dated.

"That doesn't sound like a bad idea, actually." I tap a finger on my chin. "Though maybe I'll wait until after the wedding, just to be safe."

"Don't be mensa!" She slaps my hand, *tsk*ing under her breath at me. A wave of nostalgia washes over me at her favorite nickname for me when I was younger. Still, *mensa* is loads better in my book than *gorda*. It took a lot for my mom to finally let go of that one, even more to convince her she was being more demeaning than affectionate. "I'm serious."

"I know you are." I let out a sigh. "There's just not much to say. I haven't been in anything close to a serious relationship in years. Ever, maybe."

She gives me a disbelieving look at first, but when my expression doesn't change, she looks at me as if in a new light. She stares for a beat, and then finally asks, "Why not?"

I'm not sure how to answer her. Between unrequited feelings for Ben and my ambivalence toward dating, I don't have a good answer. But I know those are just excuses. The truth—that I'm terrified of having a relationship end the same way hers did—is too painful to admit. The last thing I want to do is hurt her, so instead, I dodge the question by glancing at the clock and proclaiming the time. She bursts up from the couch when she realizes she's late for meeting one of her neighbors.

She leaves thirty minutes before Ben is due to show up. I spend the time to myself practicing ways to share the news in a way that conveys the excitement I should feel, just in case.

Ben's engaged! Isn't that swell?

Yup, he's voluntarily shackling the ol' ball and chain to himself. I'm just as unsurprised as you are.

I always knew Ben and Alice would make it.

Always? No. It was more of a gradual knowledge that came with each passing year. With each monumental new step forward in their relationship. If I'm being honest with myself, an engagement was inevitable. The final step forward before tying themselves together forever. They may not have *always* been headed to marriage, but it's always been the final stop. It's only now that the final stop is within sight.

Ben arrives outside my door at seven on the dot. He's got a six-pack of Angry Orchard under one arm, which I take from him when he crosses the threshold. We settle down on the couch, and I try to think of the last time Ben came over to my place. Almost a year ago, maybe? We watched a movie on Netflix, and he gave me relationship advice after I caught a guy I was dating texting his ex. Funny how, to Ben, it was a definite red flag, but when we eventually did break up, it wasn't because of his ex. It was because of *mine*. The irony wasn't lost on me, but it's always been lost on Ben.

"So, Alice told me she saw you yesterday," he says. "At Havana Bar with my brother."

"Yup. It was nice," I say, because I'm not sure how to play this. There isn't much about my dating life I've held back from him, but this feels different, and not just because of the lie Theo and I are perpetuating. There are so many levels of awkward I'm treading here: dating his brother years after dating *him*, their silent feud, that he's the reason why I need this rebound in the first place. More importantly, that he can't know how much I need this rebound to work to stay friends with him. I don't want to lose him. He can't see it, but this is the only way I can save our friendship in the long run.

"He's a sweet guy," I continue, needing to fill the stark silence between us. "He said he's looking for coaching positions in town. And if that means he's staying, then maybe…" I trail off, because the look in Ben's eyes catches me off guard.

"Marcela, we've been friends for years so I'm just going to say it." He reaches out for my hand, and all my feelings come rushing to the forefront. Our fingers intertwine in that way that feels like cheating, but I've never had the heart to tell him so. He'd probably just tell me I'm overthinking it. And maybe I am.

"My brother is not the guy for you."

I resist the urge to roll my eyes. Is that meant to be some sort of revelation?

"Believe me, I know. His reputation, blah, blah, blah." I pull my hand from his to take a sip of my cider. "And that's not really what I'm looking for with him. You have to admit, if I'm gonna have a fling with anyone, your brother is kind of perfect."

"Sure, yeah, for any other random girl at a bar on a Monday night, but we're talking about *you*," he bursts out, frustration coloring his tone. "You don't know him the way I do. I don't want to see you get hurt."

I figured his protective side might come out tonight, but I didn't expect this kind of reaction from him. Even considering their feud, I never expected him to be so against me hooking up with his brother that he'd outright say so.

"I know you guys have your issues, but do you really think he's that bad?" I ask him. "Is that what this is about?"

"No, Marcela. This isn't about that." He takes my hand again and squeezes it, looking into my eyes. I try not to lose myself in the hazel glow of his. "I just know how he is with women. Please don't do this, Marcela. I'm worried about you."

"You don't need to be. I can take care of myself." I get up from the couch to put some much-needed distance between us. I don't like the way his touch makes me feel, when those feelings should be reserved for literally anyone else. When he thinks they're reserved for Theo now, because he's completely oblivious to the truth I've hid from him for years. "Whatever you're worried about, you shouldn't be. No one's getting hurt here."

He's about to say something when his phone rings. His brows furrow when he looks down at the screen. "It's Alice. Give me a minute."

He walks into the kitchen to take the call, his head disappearing behind the half wall. Because I have no shame, I cross my arms over my chest and lean my head back, prime eavesdropping position. I pull out my phone and pretend to scroll down the home screen.

"No, yeah, I'm sorry, babe. I'm still at work." My brows crease together. Why is he lying to Alice? "I'll be home as soon as I can. Love you, too."

I rush back to the end of the couch, a neutral expression settling on my face. When he returns, he grabs his jacket from the armrest. "Sorry, I have to go. But please." He meets my eyes with a grave expression. "Think about what I said."

"Okay." I nod. It should concern me that every lie out of my mouth comes out easier than the last. "I will."

"Good." He walks out the door. The guilt is overwhelming and intrusive, but even more intrusive is the gratification of seeing him so on edge because I'm seeing someone else. I don't fool myself into believing it's actually jealousy, but my imagination can twist almost nothing into a whole relationship. He even lied to Alice about where he was.

I *knew* I shouldn't have said he could come over.

This is bad. We haven't crossed a line physically, but I'm not sure I can say that's true when my hand still feels warm from where he touched it. The concern in his eyes made me want to fess up to the whole ruse in its entirety, assure him that I'd never do anything to hurt him. I know how much his brother affects him. If I wanted to hurt Ben in any way, test the limitations of his protectiveness that feels a bit too much like jealousy, making him think I'm dating his brother is the perfect way. But is that really what I want?

Theo. Think of Theo.

My perfect distraction. When my eyes close, I imagine looking into his. Twin storms. Glittering cerulean when he's showing off his genuine smile. Near black when my hands travel down his body. His warm hands on my waist, locking me in place before teasing the hem of my shirt. Mouths clashing together, the taste of him still on my lips.

Then I remember what he said this morning, his mouth curled up in that wicked grin of his.

Text me when he leaves.

Eleven

'm at CVS when Theo texts back, asking me to meet him at the Northside Football Stadium. I frown down at the message, not exactly picturing the night outside my bedroom. The box of condoms in my other hand stares up at me accusingly, as if to ask *What's the holdup, lady?* I shake my head and buy them at self-checkout anyway. The night could still take us back to my apartment.

At the stadium, I find him sitting at the top of the bleachers. Thank god the stadium lights are still on, or I'd be looking for him all night. The wide field is deserted, as are the stands when I arrive. He's staring out at the turf, blue eyes glittering with longing. I wonder if he has any regrets about the way his life turned out. If he wishes he could go back and do any of it differently.

He spots me when I'm halfway up the bleachers, mouth turned up in a grin. He has an assortment of smiles depending on the occasion, I've come to realize. This one reaches his eyes; they crinkle at the corners and brighten with affection.

His friendly smile, foil to the toe-curling one he showed me this morning.

I settle next to him, and he wraps an arm around my shoulders. His warmth seeps into me, combating the early autumn chill in the air. It's that time of year when the days are still scorching, but the nights are beginning to cool. My head leans against his chest as I look out at the vast football field.

"How 'bout that view?"

"Yeah." He chuckles softly, his breath warm on the top of my head. "You never forget your first stadium game. The lights, the crowd. It was a whole new world. Ben and I used to sneak in here all the time in middle school. We couldn't even run one lap around the field without getting out of breath."

I laugh. "I can't imagine you getting out of breath."

"Well, I came pretty close this morning." I smack his chest, and he grabs my hand with his strong one. He intertwines our fingers, and I shiver. *No guilt.* This is how it should feel. "For someone so small, you can be so violent."

"Don't test me," I warn, and he flashes an amused smile. "So, how'd the interview go?"

"I'll find out Friday," he says. "But my chances look pretty good. Now I just need to find an apartment and bring my car down here. My dad's gonna need his back eventually."

"What about your stuff? Don't you still need to pack?"

"I've been packed for over a month actually," he tells me. "Did you know your entire life can fit neatly into a ten-by-ten storage unit?" I shake my head, and he blows a breath of air between his teeth. "It's actually kind of depressing."

"So you never actually told me the full story of what happened," I remind him. "Do you want to talk about it now?"

"My knee never healed right," he explains. "From an old injury in high school. Ben told me to take it easy after it happened, but I didn't listen. I kept pushing myself, because if I stopped I'd have nothing." He takes a moment to clear his throat. "But during my last appointment with the team's physical trainer, he told me that if I kept playing I could permanently damage my knee down the line. Then I was given a choice. I could keep playing and risk endangering myself at any given moment, or I could walk away."

"Doesn't sound like you had much of a choice to me."

"Maybe," he says. "But that wasn't the only reason I chose to retire. I made a lot of bad choices to get to where I was. Made a lot of sacrifices I shouldn't have. My life could've turned out differently, if I…"

"Confessed sooner?" I ask tentatively. "To Alice?"

He shrugs, but I know better than to believe his nonchalance.

"No sense trying to change the past," he finally says. "I wasn't sure it was a good idea to move back home, but now it feels right." He glances over his shoulder to meet my eyes.

"Really? Dallas is so much cooler than San Antonio. I'm sure you could've easily gotten a coaching position up there."

"Nah," he says easily. "I've always missed it here, to be honest. My mom most of all."

"You're a momma's boy?" I ask, and even though my voice takes on a teasing tone, inside my heart swells with the new information. His cheeks flush scarlet, but I let him off the hook. "I love that. I'm a momma's girl myself."

"Yeah?" he asks. "Not a daddy's girl?"

I roll my eyes. "Oh, fuck him."

He barks out a laugh, and I shove at his arm. "Fuck mine, too," he says.

"They can go fuck each other." I hold out my hand to high-five, and after his palm connects with mine, he intertwines our fingers again. Funny how a week ago we barely knew each other, but now touching him has become second nature. "Who would've known we'd have daddy issues in common?"

Among other things.

"I'm pretty sure there's a club for that," he says. "How bad was yours?"

"Well, he left when I was twelve and I haven't heard from him since." It's funny how many ways you can explain the worst day of your life, how many ways it can evolve over the years. Back when it first happened, when all those raging emotions were still fresh, I let other people do the talking while silently fuming in my mind. After a couple of years it came out curt, with no shortage of resentment. When it comes up now, I like to keep it simple and to the point. Try not to let it show how much it still hurts, even after all these years.

For an entire moment, he's stunned silent. Then he says, "Okay, you win."

He seems surprised when I let out a laugh. I'm a little surprised at myself, if I'm being honest. Of all the ways I've explained my dad leaving, I've never laughed about it before. But I have to admit, it feels good to laugh at something that once caused me so much grief.

"What about your dad?" I ask, because even though I'm laughing now it doesn't mean I'm ready to go into detail. "He doesn't seem...that bad." Aside from weirdly commenting on the kind of girls Theo dates.

"I hated the way he treated my mom before they divorced," he says. "Don't get me wrong, both of them made plenty of mistakes. But they disagreed on how to move forward. He...called her a lot of names." He shakes his head. "We'd get into a lot of fights when I tried to stand up for her."

"That's awful." I try not to let on how much I know about his parents' divorce. When we first met, Ben and I initially connected over our abandonment issues. We used to spend hours talking about all the complicated feelings we harbored over our parents. I know their mom left because she felt stifled by her marriage to their father, even after the fight he put up to work on their relationship. But she'd already made up her mind, leaving Ben to be raised by his dad his last three years of high school.

And then there was the fight. Because it wasn't just his mom at the root of all his abandonment issues. Theo was there, too.

"And he had the nerve to say football is what tore our family apart, when he's the one who cheated with his assistant. What a fucking joke." Theo scrubs a hand down his face.

"What does football have to do with it?" I ask. When he doesn't answer, I try again. "Because of the way you left?"

I'm prying, but I can't help myself. Between Alice and this new nugget of information, I'm more curious than I've ever been about what happened between them. But if Ben's never told me the full story, what are the chances Theo will?

"Never mind," I backtrack. "You don't need to answer that."

"It's okay," he says. "That's part of it. My family is…a lot. I needed space from them, but I took it in unhealthy ways. Ignored them for longer than I should have, aside from my mom. She understood why I needed to get away from them more than anyone."

You ran. It's on the tip of my tongue to say, but I swallow the words and any judgment they might reveal. I can't fault him for a past I wasn't a part of, no matter what Ben has or hasn't told me about it. His issues with his brother are his and his alone to deal with.

"Great. And I just remembered my dad needs his car back by Friday. Alice was supposed to drive me up to Dallas this weekend, but now…"

"I got you," I say, resting a reassuring hand on his arm. "Don't worry about it."

"Thank you." He breathes a sigh of relief. "That's one thing off my plate. It's all really happening now." He looks out at the field again, and when I ask him if it's all right for us to be here by ourselves, he says, "The stadium manager's a good friend of mine. He lent me the keys so I could have a moment alone up here. Get some perspective on where I started."

"And did you? Get some perspective?"

He's silent for a moment, eyes contemplative. "I'm not sure yet."

I wonder if he's thinking of Alice, of the friendship they had in high school. Of the moment he knew, undoubtedly, that she was the only one for him. Of the moment he knew he'd lost her forever.

"You can talk about her to me, you know. Alice. There are no feelings between us, so you don't have to be scared I'll get jealous or anything. I'm a good listener if you need one."

"How'd you know I was thinking about her?" He looks vaguely surprised.

"You said you guys grew up together. I assume that includes high school," I remind him. "She was a cheerleader, wasn't she? You must've seen her a lot on this field."

I remember her saying as much, because Ben was also on the football team. It's easy for me to imagine the three of them here in their assigned roles, completely oblivious to how their lives would turn out in the years to come. What a chaotic, jumbled mess it would be.

"Yeah." He laughs humorlessly. "Yeah, we saw a lot of each other on this field. Spent every lunch of junior year together. She was my best friend, for a time."

"Who's your best friend now?" I ask, knowing I'd be nowhere without Angela. When he shrugs, my heart breaks a little for him. He doesn't meet my eyes. His shoulders slump forward in exhaustion. "Is that why you seem so lonely?"

"Let's talk about you," he says suddenly, pulling away from me and shifting until his body is turned toward me. I turn too, until we're sitting cross-legged in front of each other. "We spend *way* more time talking about me when we're together, and I don't like it." His voice is teasing, but there's a noticeable edge to it. He still can't quite meet my eyes.

"Okay," I say, playing along if only to appease him,

though I am a little scared now that the attention is being turned on me. "What do you want to know?"

"Why the sudden need for a fling? Is there someone you're trying to get over, too?" I immediately look away from him. When I chance a glance back, he's smirking to himself. "Not so fun being the vulnerable one, is it?"

"Touché," I say, relenting, but there's a hint of bitterness in my voice. Because he's just given me the perfect opening to confess my feelings for Ben, and I don't want it. Maybe it's unfair of me to keep it from him when he's shared so much with me, but...

The last person I should be going after is someone in love with my brother.

Would he call the whole thing off if he knew the truth?

It doesn't mean anything, I tell myself. We're just casual. There's no trust between us, no loyalty. He's not going after me the same way he was going after Alice when he nearly confessed his love for her. It's not the same thing, so what does it matter if he knows the truth or not?

Omitting a name isn't lying, and that's all I'm really doing. "Okay, fine. You're right. There is someone." I take in a breath. "He's...a friend from college. We went on a couple dates before deciding we were better as friends. Maybe I thought that was true at the time, but after breaking up we spent virtually every day together. I fell for him without even realizing it. Not until he started going out with other girls and talking to *me* about them. That was a gut punch I never expected."

What I don't say is there was only one girl after me. Alice. But everything else is completely true.

"Yeah, I know how much that can hurt," he says. "It's even worse when the person they like better is related to you. Believe me."

"I'm sure you're right. But…I don't know." I take another breath to gather my thoughts, thinking of every time Ben inserted himself into my relationships. No guy was ever good enough for me, and every mistake they made was a deal-breaker. He said he wished I could see what he saw in me, so I'd know exactly what kind of person I deserved. But as time went on, the more impossible that standard became. I've dated my share of shitty guys, but I can also admit there are plenty I never gave a fair shot.

"I was so blindsided by the breakup. I thought we were on the same page, but maybe I just misinterpreted our whole relationship."

"Or maybe he led you on the entire time," he says. "Guys are idiots. We do that sometimes, when we don't know what we really want. Or when we realize it too late."

"Maybe," I say, but I'm not sure I quite believe it.

"So, do you still talk to him?"

I hesitate a beat before lying through my teeth. "No. He's in a serious relationship now, so I thought it was better to keep my distance."

I only pray I find the strength to actually do this one day, if I never truly get over him. I'd be a much better person, to Ben and to myself. But that's what this whole rebound is for: to get over Ben, so I don't end up damaging our friendship later.

"Maybe you need to do the same with Alice. Keep some

distance." I'm a hypocrite for suggesting it, but he's worse off than me, isn't he? He's the one who just tried to ruin their engagement after all.

"Yeah." He nods, resigned. I'm a bit surprised he doesn't try to put up more of a fight. "You're probably right."

"And you know what a good start would be?" His brows crease in question. I bend down and pull out the box of condoms from my tote bag. His jaw drops as he looks between me and the box. "Wanna get out of here?" I give him my best teasing smile.

"Are you kidding?" His arms close around my waist, spinning me off the bleachers. I let out a loud squeal, grasping his arms for dear life. "Let's get a move on, woman!"

Twelve

We rush back to my apartment, arriving in the parking lot outside my building at the same exact time. He pulls in next to me, jumps from his car, and immediately runs around the vehicle to open my door. His hands cup my face as he kisses me, and he tastes like relief. Like I've been holding my breath all day, and he's finally allowing me the air I'm craving. Each time feels covert and brand new, as if at any second this could all fall away from us.

When we finally manage to make it inside my apartment, he pushes me against the door and pins my hands over my head. He kisses me until my mind turns fuzzy, and I'm aching to feel his hard body against mine. My hands slip from his grasp to touch his hair, and his move up my shirt. I let out an involuntary moan in his mouth, tugging him closer against me.

"This isn't moving too fast for you, is it?" he asks, lips moving down my neck. I shake my head, and he smirks against my skin. "Thank god."

He raises the hem of my shirt, and my arms go up of their own accord. My shirt is off and tossed to the floor in one fell swoop before we're desperately grasping for each other in the dark. Our lips meet again, tongues clashing in the most addicting way. My hands are roaming under his shirt next, inching the fabric upward when the buzz of my phone vibrating in my pocket threatens to undo the moment. I pay it no mind as his shirt is peeled off and we're skin to skin. My hands roam up his sculpted chest, fingers running through the indentations of muscle.

"Bedroom?" I ask, my voice raspy.

He nods vigorously, his head outlined by the dim glow through the blinds. My fingers curl in the belt loops of his jeans to pull him forward, but when my phone vibrates again, I let out a frustrated groan. I pull it out of my jeans pocket and throw it across the living room. Theo huffs a laugh against the side of my head before our lips meet again.

We don't get very far across the room before Theo says, "Dammit," and pulls his own phone out of his pocket. A picture of his brother fills the screen, and my heart jumps.

Damn him.

"Was he calling you, too?" he asks, holding out his phone.

"I don't know. I didn't bother checking," I admit, biting my lip.

"Should I…?" He trails off.

The moment is officially killed. *Good god*, why does this keep happening to us? I nod, stepping away from him for my discarded shirt. It's a miracle I'm able to find it through the darkness, the only trace of light coming from my Blu-ray player displaying the time. Once my shirt is back on, I flick on the hall light and step into the living room. Theo is seated on the couch, looking rumpled and annoyed. As he talks to his brother, I search for where my phone landed and find it wedged under the coffee table. Sure enough, there are two missed calls from Ben on my notification screen.

"Why do you wanna know?" Theo asks his brother. He rolls his eyes at whatever Ben's reply is. "Because it's none of your business." Another pause. "Ben, let her make her own decisions. This has nothing to do with—" He lets out a frustrated noise before hanging up the phone. Dread creeps up my spine when he looks up at me and says, "*Jesus.*"

"What?" I ask. "What did he say?"

My heart races at the sight of Theo's sunken form. He rubs a rough hand down his face, chest rising and falling fast with his breaths. I'm still breathing fast, but for a very different reason now.

"Did he talk to you about me?" When he looks up at me, his eyes pin me in place. "Before you came to see me?"

I mash my lips together, my eyes searching for any clue on his face that shows me what he's thinking. But he might as well be carved from stone for how much he gives away. When I finally nod, he lets out a breath. His body deflates as he leans back on the couch.

"It's not just because of you, though," I say quickly. "Ben's always been like this when I start dating someone. It's protective, macho bullshit, but he just wants to make sure I don't get hurt."

"Believe me. It has *everything* to do with me." He rakes

his hair back from his face with a scowl. I clutch my stomach with both hands. This outright interference is a line I never expected Ben to cross, but I don't feel good about it. Not at all. What would Alice think? And why is he so dead set against us?

"What did he say exactly?"

"He just...*really* doesn't want me around you," he says, a hand resting under his jaw. "Look, I'm not close with my brother. Alice has wanted us to change that for years. Ben thinks that I'm going to hurt you if we keep seeing each other. And apparently, he'd go as far as calling both of us past midnight to prevent that from happening."

I frown. "Sounds sane."

He laughs dryly. "He must really care about you to go that far." But his eyes are narrowed in a way that says he's entirely unconvinced of that.

I don't say anything because I don't trust myself to. But I feel his eyes on me, contemplating.

"You don't have to leave." I step forward, something like conviction drawing me closer. My hand braces his shoulder as I crawl on top of him. His eyes widen slightly as he realizes what's happening, and then they go hazy with want. My knees straddle either side of his body as I deposit myself onto his lap. His eyes stay trained on my face as his hands settle on my waist. I lean into him, kissing his neck. He lets out a throaty groan, the motion vibrating against my lips.

"Stay," I say. "I don't have to do everything he tells me, you know."

"He told you to stay away from me?"

He pulls away slightly, eyes creased as he looks up at me. I rub a thumb over his brow, as if to smooth out the worry from his face. I shake my head, even though that's exactly what he said if you read between the lines. Our foreheads touch when I lean toward him again, my hands roaming over his broad chest. His heart is racing beneath my palm, a hard drumbeat that makes my own thump wildly. Is this nerves, or something more?

He says my name inside a sigh. I'm hardly able to make it out, even though we're sharing the same breath. Even though I can't stop staring at his mouth. Or wishing it were on mine. His hands move up to my hair, sinking into the curls as he brings our faces even closer.

Our lips graze, ever so slightly, when he says, "Don't lie to me, Marcela."

My heart stutters as I rear back from him. I've already lied to him once tonight, but the guilt of it hasn't sunken in until now. How would he feel if he knew the guy I'm pining over is his brother? Part of me thinks he'd understand, given his situation with Alice. But even the thought of telling him the truth makes my stomach clench.

Theo senses my hesitation right away. His hands move down to cup my cheeks, pushing me just far enough that I'm able to breathe properly. I gulp in a shaky breath of air.

"We don't have to do this, Marcela," he says. "I'm not expecting anything from you. And if my brother's warning got to you…we can stop. I don't want you to…"

"Theo—"

"Marcela, it's okay." He raises himself from his spot on

the couch, lifting me off him in one swift motion before plopping me back down on the sofa cushion. The movement doesn't even wind him.

For a moment, I'm stunned. Freshman year of college, I was with Ben when I sprained my ankle outside the main building after class one day. He sprang to life, got a passerby to get a bag of ice from the food court and something to wrap my foot with. But when he tried to lift me, his face lost color. He's lanky, and he was even skinnier back then, which was why I'd tried to stop him. The moment was mortifying for both of us, for very different reasons.

Ben liked to be the hero, I realized later. When the passerby returned with the campus medic and all the works—bandages, cotton balls and rubbing alcohol for the scrape, a pair of crutches—I studied Ben's face when he thought I wasn't watching. At the time I thought he was worried about me, but I realize now that something had clicked into place for him. That medic fussed over me the way Ben had moments before he called for help. Before he tried to lift me off the ground with the physical strength he didn't have.

Two days later, he laid that "better off as friends" line on me. For years, I'd tried so hard not to connect the two moments to each other. But—

I shake my head clear of the intrusion in my brain. This is the last thing I want to be thinking about right now, when his brother is in my living room already talking about him.

"I get it," Theo is saying, trying to be understanding. "You've known him longer than you have me. Of course you'd trust he knows what's best for you over me."

Trust has nothing to do with us. Theo and I don't need it for what we're doing. There are no strings, no feelings, and nothing close to a real attachment between us.

As for Ben, well, I trusted him once. Maybe too much, when I should've known better. Every time he rebuilds that trust with me, it's always followed by stark reality knocking it back down. Breaking up with me, but proving I'm still a priority in his life. Getting together with Alice, but assuring me I deserve so much more than what the guys I'm dating have to offer. Proposing to Alice was the final blow.

I don't trust Theo to not try something stupid again, but I also don't share the distrust Ben has in him. Nothing Theo has done warrants the amount of disdain his brother seems to have toward him.

My heart sinks when Theo stands up. *He's leaving.* I get up, walking him to the door as my mind races with ways to make him stay.

"This doesn't have to change anything," I tell him. "I'm a grown woman for fuck's sake. I'm perfectly capable of taking care of myself. Ben doesn't know this is just a…" My mind spins for the right word.

"Fling?" Theo offers. "Rebound?"

"Either or." I shrug. "We'll figure it out. But besides all that, we're friends, aren't we?"

He melts a little at that. "I hope so."

It's a relief to hear him say that.

"Of course we are." Despite the exhaustion settling in my shoulders, my lips pull up into a smile.

Physical stuff aside, it really does feel like we've become

fast friends since the engagement party. I'm surprised at how much I've grown to care for his well-being since Saturday. I don't want to lose our friendship when it's only just begun. I ignore the intrusive thought at the back of my mind, *that's not the only thing you don't want to lose*, and step forward.

"Ben thinks I'm expecting something more from you. He doesn't know what this is. That's why he's going through all this trouble."

Theo squints in thought. He nods suddenly, as if realizing what I'm saying makes sense. Perhaps it is the truth, and not the jealousy I selfishly want it to be. But I'm also not ready for Ben to know the truth, or at least, a glimmer of the truth of my relationship with Theo.

"Let's figure out what this is first," I say, thinking on my feet. "And then we can decide what to tell people about us. Okay?"

"That sounds good." He nods, mouth curling up in a smile. I'm relieved just at the sight of it.

Thirteen

This isn't the first time Ben turned into someone I hate. I'm sure it won't be the last either, but he always manages to make up for it. He's somehow able to sense when I'm mad at him, even when I don't say a word. To him, perhaps it's my silence that speaks volumes.

When he first got together with Alice, I dodged all his texts until he tracked me down outside my last class of the day. "Are you avoiding me?" He'd asked in that wry way of his, with a half smile to ease the sting. I'd made up some excuse about being busy, but instead of calling me on it he escorted me to the food court and bought me an early dinner. We spent hours talking and he didn't mention Alice's name once, almost like he knew it was a sore point for me. When he walked me to my car, he made me laugh until I forgot why I was mad at him in the first place.

It wasn't that he'd started dating other people that made me angry, not really. That was inevitable. I think I just wanted a reason to hate him—*needed* one, more like—to start the process of moving on. To escape him, not that he's ever once let me.

On Friday afternoon, I get a text from Ben that threatens to freeze me over. I'm stationed at the circulation desk at work and unable to freak out the way I want to, not that there are many people inside the library to see me. Just plenty of security cameras. I type out a reply, and then erase every word. Choking down a groan, I reread his message and rack my brain for any possible way out of this.

> Talked Theo into letting me go to Dallas with
> y'all. Hope that's okay.

It is most certainly *not* okay, but I can't think of a way to tell him as much without raising his suspicion. If I'm anywhere near as obvious as Theo was at brunch, there's no way he won't find out I have feelings for Ben. I'm bound to give *something* away during a four-and-a-half-hour drive in cramped quarters. I don't even know what my tells are.

Do I laugh too hard at his jokes? Are they even funny and I just can't tell because my feelings blind me to the truth of his awful sense of humor? Does my stare linger for a little too long? Do my hands tremble in his presence?

When I'm freed from desk duty by one of the library assistants, I walk into the back and plop down onto a seat in front of Angela's workstation. She looks up from her computer monitor with a raised brow.

"Can you tell when I lie?"

"Talk about a loaded question." She laughs, a great *guffaw* straight from her diaphragm. When I scowl, her expression turns sheepish. "Can we talk about this brilliant idea I got for the book club first?"

My brows raise of their own accord, even as my mind is still spinning from Ben's latest text. But I relent, hoping work will be a good distraction for the moment.

"Go on. And then return to my last question when you're done."

"Okay." She turns around in her chair, the wheels rattling with her movement. "The day we meet for the book club discussion, we should cosplay as our favorite YA characters."

I let out a gasp, and then reach out and grip her shoulders. "Angela, you are *brilliant*." She squeals her excitement. "Should we tell readers to dress up, too?" I ask. "The event is in two weeks, do you think that's enough time?"

"I was actually thinking it should just be us this first time," Angela says. "And then we encourage them to dress up next time, that way they have plenty of time to plan and prepare."

"Good point." I nod thoughtfully. "Now I have to come up with a costume."

"Right, yes. Think about that, instead of—" She cuts off as I narrow my eyes at her, suddenly remembering why I came to her in the first place. "Goddammit."

I tell her about Ben's plan to join Theo and me on our trip to Dallas, and she winces in sympathy. Then I almost tell her about the bar kiss that led to...*more* kissing. I'm not sure what holds me back since she's the one who told me I needed a rebound in the first place. She's the person I go to for all my boy problems. Despite never having been in a relationship (or perhaps *because* of it), she gives excellent advice. There's something about getting your dating advice from an impartial source that puts things into perspective.

Only, Theo isn't some random guy off the street. He's *Ben's brother.* I'm in the middle of the CW's most overused subplot—a familial love triangle. At the very least, I can count my blessings I don't have a sibling of my own to add to the plot. Although my best friend would undoubtedly know what I should do in this situation, she also won't hold back her opinion. Angela is my best friend, and I know she cares about me. But I'm terrified of the shame that'll come with the admission of what I'm doing with Theo.

So, for now, I hold out on her.

When she's sufficiently brought up to speed, give or take a few minor details, I return to the question at hand. "What do I give away when I'm around Ben?"

"Does it really matter if Theo finds out you like his brother? He's in the same situation, just reversed, after all." My expression doesn't change. When I don't answer, she heaves a sigh and relents. "Well, sometimes you fidget a lot. Especially if Alice is around. You get this guilty look on your face every time she looks you in the eye."

"Great. Love that my feelings are always written on my face." I shake my head. "Anything else?"

"Well…" Her lips purse, eyes shifting away from my face. I straighten in my chair at her expression, leaning forward as if to shake the hesitation out of her.

"What?" I ask her. "It has to be bad if you're looking at me like that."

"Don't hate me." My back is ramrod straight at attention. "It's maybe not a tell, more of an observation, but I've noticed that you're more likely to do something if Ben tells you to do it."

My mouth opens as if to speak. When nothing comes out, I force myself to close it.

"You dumped Chris the day after he said you should," she reminds me. "You go to every restaurant he recommends and watch everything he says is good on Netflix. Yeah, yeah, you can say it's because you guys have the same taste," she adds when I open my mouth to interrupt, defenses kicking into overdrive. Every word out of her mouth is a direct punch to the gut. "But what about the time you took him to Biryani Pot and he complained that the food was too spicy? You *love* that restaurant, but you haven't eaten Indian food since."

I cross my arms over my chest. She's got me there. "Okay, I agree with him too much. Noted."

But I didn't agree with him at all last night, when he warned me about his brother. I may jump to answer his every request, but I threw my phone across the room when he called last night.

"Has it ever been…obvious?" As much as it pains me to ask this question, it's one I should've asked Angela a long time ago. But I've never been able to face the shame that comes with asking that question, because it's almost worse than admitting I have feelings for a taken man. "You know, that I…" I wince before the question can fully form in my mind. But Angela's eyes soften at my expression.

"No one else knows, if that's what you're worried about,"

she tells me. "I've talked to Alice and Christine loads of times, together and apart. They've never shown signs of knowing, or even so much as brought it up as a joke. You're in the clear."

I give a jerky nod. "Thanks."

"Anytime. You know I've got your back."

We take Ben's car.

He pulls up outside my apartment building and gets out to greet me. I try not to linger when he hugs me, pulling away from him quickly. Ben leads me to the passenger side with a hand on the small of my back. Goosebumps break out on my skin, and I rub my arms hoping no one notices. After my conversation with Angela, even though she told me no one suspects a thing, I'm more paranoid than ever about other people finding out about my feelings. Ben crosses in front of me to hold the door open. I'm well aware that sitting in the front seat beside him probably isn't the greatest idea, but I panic at the last second and go where I'm led.

We're all silent as Ben turns onto the road—the only sound comes from the radio blaring some top-forty hit I don't recognize. I won't be able to take four and a half hours of this, so to break the tension I ask, "What was it like growing up together?"

Ben is very different from his brother. Nothing really fazes him, which is part of the reason I'm still so surprised that he's trying so hard to keep me away from his brother. He doesn't open up to most people, but he's open with me. Or at least, he used to be. We both used to be.

Theo, for all his scary height and physical muscle, is much more of an open book. I never would've guessed, after the first time we met in Ben's old apartment. Those two versions I saw of him couldn't be further apart, but so far, I've found that I don't have to work hard to get the answers I want from him. I just have to ask.

"A lot of competition," Ben says with a strained smile. "But I always lost, didn't I, bro?"

"Only cuz I got dad's genes. You never had a chance." I laugh at this. Ben is a good half foot shorter than his brother, and much leaner in build. Their father is on the stockier side, and an imposing six feet tall.

The words are light enough, but they clearly land like a physical blow on Ben's chest. His face falls as he looks out at the road. I almost feel bad for him, but something stops me from fully empathizing with him. I know what it's like to be overlooked. To continuously stand in the shadow of a better choice. Despite knowing what that feels like too, Ben did it to me anyway. Maybe he didn't realize that's what he did, but it doesn't matter.

"So," Ben finally says. "How did *this* happen?" He gestures between the two of us with a pointer finger. "You guys are like, the least likely pairing I could've imagined."

I resist rolling my eyes *hard*, but Theo gulps from behind me. His leg shakes against the back of my seat so hard I start to feel queasy. "Um." Ben looks over at me, hazel eyes assessing as I work to get our story straight.

"That was all me," I finally say, turning to Theo with a googly-eyed expression that I make sure his brother catches. "I pounced on him at the engagement party."

"*You?*" Ben asks, the surprise clear in his tone. "Really?" Surprise quickly bleeds into disbelief, his eyes narrowing as he looks over at me again.

"Yup." I twist in my seat to place a hand on Theo's thigh, looking back at Ben as if daring him to contradict me. My brows raise in challenge, and I smirk slightly when his mouth falls open. A rush of satisfaction floods over me at having surprised Ben. "I may have had a few too many mojitos. Can't imagine I would've had the audacity to think I stood a chance with him otherwise." I force a self-deprecating giggle into my hand. "Plus, have you even *seen* your brother?" I sigh dreamily as I turn to Theo, googly eyes on level one thousand.

Part of me fears I'm overselling it, but if I am, it's only because Theo is frozen with panic. But the panic in his eyes softens at whatever lovestruck expression must be on my face. His hand closes over mine, squeezing.

"You're not too bad yourself," he finally says, cheeks reddening. He can't quite meet my eyes.

"Come on, you can do better than that," I tease, with the confidence I've never had around a guy I was actually dating. When I slap at his leg, he takes my hand again and intertwines our fingers. I resist a shiver when his thumb slides up my palm, stroking.

This doesn't feel like pretending.

His lashes lower until he's looking at me through hooded eyes, the corner of his mouth lifting into a wicked grin. He leans in until his lips hover right over my ear, his breath warm on my already-flushed skin.

"You're *beautiful.*" The words are a whisper, but I catch

Ben's expression from the corner of my eye as soon as they're uttered. His eyes dart away from us immediately, like he just walked in on an intimate moment he'd rather not have seen. His hands grip the steering wheel so tightly his knuckles turn white. He heard his brother loud and clear.

I plant a kiss on Theo's mouth, and even though Ben doesn't see it, there's no mistaking the loud *muah* our lips make for anything else. Before I can pull away, Theo's hand settles on the back of my neck, pinning me in place. When he kisses me again, it's so indecent I forget where we are entirely. His tongue slides against mine, stroking in a way that makes me shiver. Ben has to clear his throat three times before we finally pull away from each other.

After a quick lunch at a fast-food joint, we arrive at Theo's old apartment, where he takes one final sweep of the place. When he steps into his bedroom, Ben pulls on my arm. I have no choice but to follow him forward as he opens the door to the balcony.

"Ow." I rub my arm where he grabbed me. What the hell has gotten into him?

"Sorry, I didn't mean to hurt you," he says, placing a gentle hand over the red spot on my upper arm. "But I need to talk to you."

"About what?" I feign innocence, crossing my arms over my chest.

The look he gives me sends chills down my back.

"You and Theo?" His voice is cutting. "*Really?*"

I roll my eyes, looking away from him. "Get over it, Ben."

"I can't. Marcela, he's my brother. I've known him my whole life, and things never end well for the women he dates."

Maybe if Theo and I were actually dating, I'd be more attentive to Ben's warning. After all, that's what Angela seems to think I always do. And as much as I hate to admit it, she's right. I'm always quick to listen to him before anyone else. Before myself, even. While I have to own up to my part, he's also part of the reason most of my relationships have failed. I'm starting to see that more clearly now, maybe because there are no romantic feelings whatsoever between Theo and me. We both know what we are, so there's no reason I need to be worried about him.

Of course, I can't tell Ben any of that.

"You know I've always had your best interests at heart. Don't you trust me?" There's that soft tone I've never been able to deny. "You have to stop seeing him."

I look up, gauging his seriousness. He has his hands on his hips, head hanging like a disappointed father. When he looks at me, his eyes are narrowed to angry slits. My mouth hangs open as I realize he's more than serious. He actually thinks he has a right to tell me to do such a thing, and even worse, that I'll listen to him.

Because I always have.

"You can't be serious." I shake my head. Then I scoff. How have I never seen it before? "*Ben.* You can't—"

Theo opens the door suddenly, interrupting me before I can tell Ben off. I already had the perfect response ready in my head. *You can't order me around like I'm yours to control. You can't tell me who to date if you won't date me yourself.* My mouth snaps shut. Maybe it's better that Theo interrupted when he did. He looks between us with furrowed brows, until his eyes land on me and stay there. His eyes travel over my face for some sign of what's wrong. I try to put on a neutral expression, but I'm not sure it works. Theo's eyes seem to ask me what's wrong, but all I give is a tired shrug.

"Everything okay out here?" Theo asks us, finally facing his brother.

Ben doesn't say anything. He shoves past his brother, letting out a grunt as he passes. My eyes shutter closed. The back of my head throbs suddenly with an incoming headache. When I tell Theo I'm fine, he doesn't look convinced but he also doesn't press me on it.

Luckily, it doesn't take much longer for Theo to finish packing up. When he does, I follow him out to the parking lot, where Ben is waiting for us, looking sulky with his arms crossed. We decide that Ben will drive back by himself and I'll ride with Theo. I take it he's had enough of our overt displays of affection for one day.

His car pulls out of the lot with rushed, jerky movements, like he can't get out of here fast enough. Theo's gaze warms my back, but I can't stop replaying his brother's words in my head.

Stop seeing him. Stop seeing him. Stop seeing him.

When Theo asks me if I'm ready to go, I have to shut my eyes against the concern brimming in his.

"Yeah," I finally say. "Let's get out of here."

Fourteen

The air between us is taut and uncomfortable. Concern radiates off Theo in waves, and it only annoys me more. But as mad as I am at Ben, I'm pissed at myself even more. For waiting on him for as long as I have, only for him to show the least bit of interest when he's no longer my top priority. For the years I've wasted on him.

"You think he bought it?" Theo asks when we're safely tucked away in his silver BMW. I'm surprised he even has to ask, but maybe he's just not good at reading his brother. Or maybe he's too scared to voice the question he really wants to ask.

"Definitely," I tell him. "He couldn't even look us in the eye afterwards."

"Sorry I clammed up on you at first," he says as he pulls out of the parking lot. "Guess we should've worked on our backstory earlier. You're a surprisingly good liar." His mouth lifts into an amused smirk. I just manage to return it, but I feel a bit hollow inside. "First at brunch, and now with my brother. You're *fantastic* in a bind."

"Glad you think so." I salute him, keeping the smile plastered to my face.

He might seem amused now, but just wait until he finds out the real reason I'm using him as a rebound. Hopefully he never does, but who am I kidding? If this lasts for much longer, I'll give myself away at some point.

"What were you and Ben talking about?" There's a hesitant quality to his voice. "It sounded like you guys were fighting. Are you okay?"

"Yeah, we were fighting," I admit, ignoring the last question and hunching lower in my seat with a grumble. "Just Ben on his overprotective bullshit again. Nothing I can't handle."

The setting sun has reached the end of the horizon, erupting in the sky with a burst of color. Pink and orange and lilac. Darkness will cover us in no time, but until then, I keep my eyes trained out the passenger window so Theo can't read anything from my face.

"Overprotective?" When I don't say anything, he adds, "Was this about me again?"

I let out a long sigh. Theo has been nothing but honest with me so far. I may not be willing to tell him about my feelings for his brother, but the least I can do is be honest with him about everything else, right? My mind turns over for the right words. Theo doesn't say anything else as he waits.

Finally, I turn my head back to face him. The corners of his eyes are creased in concern as his glance darts away from the windshield to look at me. Then they turn back. I'm not sure what he caught in my expression, but whatever it was is enough for him to reach out and clasp my knee. The warmth of his hand seeps through the fabric, his touch solid and grounding. I take a breath and prepare to tell him half the truth.

"This isn't the first time Ben's gotten involved in a relationship of mine," I say. "Granted, he thinks we're more serious than we are, but still."

"Hmm." Theo's eyes stay trained out the windshield, but they narrow the slightest bit. I'm scared to ask what he's thinking, but instead he asks for clarification. "And by 'gotten involved,' you mean…?"

"I mean, he gives his opinion freely. No guy I've ever dated was good enough for me, according to him. Which I guess means you're the worst I could do." I try out a light laugh, but Theo doesn't so much as crack a grin. If anything, his mouth sets into a grim line. I don't like the look of it whatsoever.

"Hey, are you getting hungry?" I ask mostly to change the subject, but also because my stomach grumbles so loud there's no doubt he also heard it.

"We can stop somewhere in town." We're quiet for a moment, and I start to think maybe we've dropped the Ben subject entirely. I breathe a sigh of relief to myself. I'm about to ask if I can turn on the radio when he says, "So, did he give you any reason in particular?" His eyes dart back to me, something unreadable in his expression. "Why you shouldn't date me?"

"Um…" I rack my mind for something concrete but come up short. "Just the same thing Alice said, that you have a reputation for breaking hearts." Which reminds me of something else she said that night at the bar. "Is it true you've never been in a relationship?"

His cheeks redden slightly as he looks back out the

windshield. When he finally answers, he sounds exhausted. "Yes. But not for a lack of trying."

"Really?" Alice and Ben make him sound like a lady killer because of the way he goes through women.

"I've tried all the sites," he says. "Tinder, Bumble, et cetera. It's not that there was anything wrong with any of the women, but"—his Adam's apple bobs with a hard swallow—"I kept comparing how I felt about them to how I feel about Alice. Believe me, I know how unfair that is. No one had a chance of measuring up to her because I never gave them the chance to."

Suddenly, I've lost my appetite. My stomach flips so hard, I can almost taste vomit at the back of my throat. I swallow hard, not liking the sinking sensation that makes dread crawl down my back. While in some ways we're complete opposites, in others we might as well be the same person.

What makes a real relationship? I've been in two short relationships following Ben, but he's the only man I've ever loved. Even though I hesitate to call what we had a relationship, there was a time when he was it for me. I didn't need anyone else. But as the years passed and his relationship with Alice got more serious, it feels wrong to call what I feel for him "love." It's tainting what should be a pure and honest emotion into something messy and awful. Something unspeakable.

"Not that I ever should've been comparing them in the first place, but old habits and all that," Theo finishes.

He's always more honest than I expect him to be. More honest than I've been with him so far.

"You've known her your whole life. I can see how that habit would be hard to break."

"Yeah." He shakes his head. "Now, how 'bout we quit turning the conversation back to me for a change?" He smiles wryly. I only realize my mouth is hanging open when he pokes my cheek. "I know exactly what you're doing, Marcela. You really don't like talking about yourself, do you?"

My face heats. We're under the cover of semi-darkness now, purple clouds and indigo sky. But if I can still make out the stubble on his cheeks from the headlights of oncoming cars, I'm sure he can see my pink face perfectly. His thumb brushes one flushed cheek, the rest of his fingers curling beneath my chin. My body reacts of its own accord, breath coming in short pants, thighs clenching.

No one's ever noticed me enough to realize I hate talking about myself. I don't know what it means that Theo does, or why my heart stutters and stops in my chest.

"I guess not," I tell him, biting down on my lip. "Ask me whatever you want."

The statement surprises me, but I find I'm not scared at the prospect of answering any of his questions truthfully. His hand reaches for mine, intertwining our fingers and making goosebumps rise on my skin from the contact. He sets the car on cruise control but keeps one hand on the wheel. Then he turns his head and meets my eyes. I turn my body slightly to the left to better face him.

"Okay." He nods idly, but his tone doesn't fool me for a second. "How often does my brother insert himself into your love life?" There's no lead-up to this question, making me believe it's something that's been on his mind for a while.

I groan into the leather seat, but Theo just laughs. "Quite

a bit." My words are clipped, but that doesn't stop Theo from asking more intrusive questions.

"And you let him?"

"He's one of my closest friends. It wouldn't be any different from Angela telling me what she thinks of the guys I'm dating." Though to be fair, Angela's never been quite as judgmental about any of them as much as Ben.

"Angela, the best friend?"

"Yup." I nod, pouncing on the diversion. "We met in college, the only two English majors who hate Shakespeare. We caused quite a stir, the two of us." He laughs at that. "You've actually met her before. She was at brunch a few years ago when Ben and Alice first moved in together."

"Oh!" He exclaims. "Is she the one who flirted with the waiter for free mimosas?"

"That's the one." I smile at the memory. "And no, she hasn't changed at all since."

"I think I'd like to meet this girl again. See you two in your element." He squeezes my hand. I'm about to respond with a "sure" and a shrug, but a sudden thought stops me. A few days ago, I told him we'd figure out what this thing between us is before we decide what to tell people. But if we're nothing more than casual, meeting my friends feels like crossing a boundary into exclusive territory. Besides, what would be the point if we're not going to be in each other's lives for very long?

"We'll see," I finally say.

"That means no," Theo says, letting out a puff of air. I'm about to tell him otherwise, since I'm still not sure if it's a lie, when he says, "Why don't you want me to meet your best friend, Marce?"

I nearly choke on nothing but air. "Marce?" I repeat, covering my mouth.

"Yeah, why not?" he asks, voice light. "You don't like it?"

First, he asks to meet my best friend, and now he's giving me cute nicknames. *No.* I shake my head. *Not cute.*

He's being way too casual about serious relationship milestones. If this non-relationship is going to work the way we want it to, we need to set some boundaries. The last thing either of us needs is another person to pine after.

I drop his hand and turn forward in my seat. I can't make out his expression in the dark, but concern radiates off him.

"I think we should come up with a couple of ground rules," I say, sitting up straighter in my seat. "You know, for the whole rebound-fling thing."

"Okay, sure." He sits up straight as well, and then takes the car off cruise control. His gaze refocuses out the windshield, and I'm able to breathe easier with his eyes off me. "Like what?"

"We keep our relationship separate from our regular life," I say. "No meeting each other's friends or family. I feel like that could blur some lines."

"I can see that," he says with a shrug. "Except you already know my family. How does that work for your friendship with my brother?"

This rule works out perfectly, because it'll force me to keep much-needed distance from Ben. I thought if I could get over him, with a rebound or otherwise, I'd be able to stay friends with him. But as each day with Theo passes, the less I believe that's actually possible. I need to keep my distance from Ben if I have any hope of getting over him. And after our fight, now I have a reason to avoid him.

"He told me to stop seeing you." I look down at my hands, because if I look at him now, even his shadowed expression might make me hesitate to get this out. "There wasn't a question anywhere in his phrasing, or even a shadow of a doubt that I would fight him. It's unfair that he thinks he can have a say in my love life. That stops right now. I'll have a talk with him tomorrow about it, and then there will be no more Ben interfering in our rebound-ship."

He nods at this, mouth pulling up slightly at my made-up word. "Glad to hear it."

"Great. Now, the nickname…"

"What? I can't even get a nickname in?" He puts a hand to his chest, pouting. "I'm hurt, Marce."

"It feels too…relationship-y." I shake my head. "Next thing you know, I'll be calling you my Theo-bear, and who wants that?"

He blinks twice. "I think we can both come up with something a little better than 'Theo-bear.'"

I throw out my hands. "*So not* the point!"

"Hey, I get it!" He holds up one of his in surrender. "I can see why you'd want to put up some boundaries. You don't want to get hurt, or for any feelings to creep in. But isn't the whole point of a rebound to prove you're still capable of having those feelings for someone else?"

"Yeah, but…" Try as I might, I don't have an argument for that. But that doesn't mean I like the idea of it.

Outside the passenger window, we drive past the San Antonio city limits sign. I can make out the glowing lights of the Hemisfair Tower in the distance, always the first sign of home. Twenty minutes later, Theo drives into the parking lot of the Whataburger two streets down from my apartment. I order a Double Meat, too hungry to be any kind of self-conscious. He doesn't even bat an eye at my order, but he does make a hassle about who gets to pay, handing over his card before I can pull out my wallet from my purse.

"Consider it a thank-you for today," he says as we sit down at a table. "You saved my ass. And...I like spending time with you." His smile is shy, and something cold inside me starts to thaw.

"I do, too," I confess, though I can't quite meet his eyes. "Listen. We're both dealing with our own stuff, so why don't we keep this simple?" He rests his chin in his hand, leaning forward in interest. "You could call us...I don't know. Damaged friends with benefits."

He chokes on his drink, an ill-timed laugh that makes him snort up his Dr Pepper. I laugh way harder than necessary as he wipes his nose with a napkin.

"Unqualified therapy sessions on the couch that lead to *other kind of sessions* in the sheets," I continue when he's finished wiping his nose of soda and snot. I waggle my brows suggestively.

"You're a dork," he says thickly. "And I don't get to be your unqualified therapist nearly enough for that label to apply."

"We also haven't had a proper *other-kind-of* session yet." I bite down on my bottom lip. His eyes flick down to them, heat flooding his gaze like he wants to change that fact. He's not the only one. "But there's always time to change that."

"Yeah, cuz there's nothing sexier than when your damaged friend with benefits snorts up his soda." He smiles wryly, covering his face with a hand.

"Or when she scarfs down a Double Meat cheeseburger in record time," I add. "We're both far beyond modesty at this point, but maybe that's the point. We'll have to do something to kill the attraction later."

"What's so bad about eating?" he asks without a single hint of sarcasm. His brows crease like he's genuinely confused. I can't contain my smile. When I shake my head, he lets it go and returns to the topic at hand. "You do know there's nothing simple about our situation, don't you? Forcing it to be simple isn't a solution."

"I know. But—"

"I can't promise to never have feelings for you." Whatever I was about to say dies in my throat as he continues. "All I can promise is to always be honest with you. So, here's something I haven't told you yet."

Our eyes meet and lock across the table. I'm pulled into those indigo depths, frozen still.

"I like you. I like getting to know you, no matter how hard you make it. I like the way you force me to open up and that you still offered your friendship after witnessing two of the lowest points of my life. You're a good person—a much better person than I can ever hope to be. You deserve so much better than a man who's still pining over someone else, and when the day comes that you walk away from me for good, I'll be cheering you on. There isn't a doubt in my mind that you'll find someone just as amazing as you one day. So, if all I am is a stop to you finding him, then I'm okay with that."

I open my mouth, but no sound comes out. My heart is full to the brim, bursting at the seams with what can only end in heartbreak. I don't feel like the person he's describing. Not even close. Me, a better person than *him*? When I'm pining for his brother and lying to him by withholding the truth? I shake my head and look away from his eyes. In what world could that possibly be true? When I look back at him, he wears a soft smile, just for me. I return it, but I'm sure it comes out watery.

"You're gonna find someone great, too," I tell him, and no words I say to him could be truer than these. "Alice has no idea what she missed out on."

He smiles sadly, looking down at his empty burger wrapper. There isn't much left to say, so we head out. When he drops me off at my apartment, the air is thick with our silence. As much as I want to invite him inside and get a start on our other kind of sessions, I'm exhausted and gross feeling from spending the full day inside a car. My muscles are stiff, and my clothes are undoubtedly sweaty despite the blast of the air conditioner.

"Tomorrow?" I ask, heat in my gaze.

"Crap." His eyes shut, and disappointment slumps both our shoulders. "I'm meeting with the movers tomorrow. Did I tell you I finally found an apartment here?"

"You did not. That's amazing!" I jump up to hug him. "Next weekend?" I ask, raising a suggestive brow.

"Maybe sooner, if we can manage it." His voice is low and husky.

He crosses the space between us, kissing me slowly. His hand rests at the nape of my neck, warming my skin chilled by the night air. When we pull apart, we linger in the space between our breaths.

"Goodnight, Marcela."

Fifteen

On Tuesday morning, Ben texts asking if I've thought any more about what we discussed. It takes me a moment to remember what he's talking about, and when I do, I roll my eyes. I stare at his message on my lock screen as I think about how to respond. No, I clearly haven't thought much at all about what Ben said. And no, I don't plan to stop seeing his brother just because he told me to. I end up leaving the notification on my phone in favor of getting ready for the day.

I'm stuck in the fiction shelves for most of the day, shelving books I through L. It's work I haven't done since I was an aide, but I don't mind it. I need the solitary time to get my thoughts in order. Protective Ben is the closest I've ever gotten to a Jealous Ben. And for years, I've let him insert himself into my love life. All in hopes that one day, he'd tell me the real reason he thought those guys weren't good enough was because *he* was the only one for me.

I always thought I walked a fine line between wishful thinking and delusional, but now I'm starting to think I was just straight-up delusional the entire time. I'm glad I've chosen to mostly keep my feelings for Ben to myself. I'd die of embarrassment if anyone, other than Angela, knew he was an actual, honest-to-God desire of mine.

But it's good that I'm finally seeing these baseless desires for what they are. I'm on the verge of a turning point, and I suppose I have Theo's magnetism to thank. There's no thrill in Ben's sudden agitation over me dating his brother, no rush of satisfaction to see him so on edge over who I'm seeing. It's not an attractive look, and I can't believe I ever thought differently.

On my lunch break, I catch Angela up on the Dallas trip in the uber-long Whataburger drive-thru line, leaving out a few minor details she doesn't need to know. It's not that she would judge me if I slept with Theo, but I'd rather she not know my most recent method for coping with my feelings for an engaged man. Feelings that are slowly but surely fading into dust.

She's not surprised that Ben blatantly asked me to stop seeing his brother, but I'm still rattled by it. It's clear to me now that I've always been quick to listen to Ben over myself, for better or worse. Now I wonder if my response would be any different if Theo and I actually were dating. Because I in no way plan on ending what Theo and I have before it can even begin.

Our conversation is interrupted by a call on my car's Bluetooth screen. Alice's name flashes like a warning sign. I'm tempted to hit ignore, but Angela says, "Go ahead." She's leaning eagerly in her seat, eyes locked on me in a way I don't like at all. But I don't have much of a choice.

"Hello?"

"Marcela, hey!" Alice's voice chirps an octave higher than

usual. I've been with her to enough sorority functions to recognize her damage-control voice. "Ben told me about this weekend. Seems like you and Theo are getting serious."

I freeze for a moment, unsure what to say. Angela lifts a perfectly arched brow at me, as if wondering how deep a hole I've dug for myself.

Deep enough.

"Um, yeah, I guess?" I shake my head before finding my grounding. "Not sure how serious a week and a half constitutes, but we're still going strong, if that's what you're asking." My reply is vague enough, but I'm not sure how far I should be taking this facade. Although Theo never seems to mind when I take control of our narrative.

"For Theo, it's as serious as he gets," she says with a laugh. I wince, reminded all over again of Theo's past with women. A part of me still can't believe he's never been serious about anyone other than Alice, and that to him no one will ever be able to measure up. Not that I have a right to have any sort of feelings about that. There are no promises between us.

"But anyway, since you two are still together, I think we should all go out next Saturday," Alice continues.

My mouth opens, but not a single sound comes out.

"And before you think of a way out of it—because I know that's exactly what you're doing right now—please think about it." It's such a deeply Alice thing to say. Freshman year, she was always quick to spot my avoidant tendencies. "Theo and Ben have some serious mending to do in their relationship. See if you can get through to Theo, and I'll see about getting through to Ben."

I don't know what makes her think I'd be able to do that. "I-I'm not sure I'm the right person to do that. You've known them both for years—"

"That's part of the problem," Alice admits, and my curiosity is piqued. I'm almost on the brink of a breakthrough, but the pieces I have don't quite fit yet. Does she know about Theo's feelings for her, even though I didn't let him confess them at her engagement party? But instead of confirming my brand-new suspicions, she says, "They know all my tricks. Consequences of knowing someone for practically your entire life. But he trusts you. You can get through to Theo."

I highly doubt that, not that I can tell her as much. In the end, I agree to try even though I already know Theo's not going to like this.

I *definitely* don't like this.

Theo is more than eager to come over after work, but I'm sure he won't feel that way for long once I tell him about my phone call with Alice. He's wearing a jean jacket with black pants and a tight-fitting gray T-shirt, blond hair perfectly swept back from his face. A white takeout bag hangs from one hand, which he hands to me as he walks through the door. He kisses my cheek as he passes me, a sweet gesture that has no business making my heart race.

"Hope you're hungry," he tells me. "I got Indian food, hope that's okay."

I open the plastic bag in the kitchen, the smell of curry and fresh naan wafting from the containers. My stomach grumbles in approval. "It's perfect." I smile at the irony. Theo can't read my thoughts, but he grins back anyway.

As he rummages through my cabinets for plates and I turn on the TV, I can't help but note the domestic picture the two of us make. Boyfriend picks up takeout and visits girlfriend at her place after work. Boyfriend searches girlfriend's apartment for kitchen utensils as girlfriend browses for something good to watch on Netflix. Boyfriend and girlfriend sit side by side on the couch in front of the TV, spooning basmati rice and chicken tikka masala into their mouths. Repeat once a week, strategically swapping the type of takeout depending on general mood of the apartment (Thai for rainy days, pizza for lazy days, Mexican for celebratory events), until the end of time. Or until, you know, they break up or get married.

I can even picture how the night ends. Girlfriend spooks boyfriend by making him go out on a double date with his brother and the girl they're both in love with. Boyfriend-shaped hole in the wall is all that remains of him now.

"By the way," he says after a thick swallow. "I got the coaching job."

"You did?" I turn until my whole body faces him. He nods, smiling shyly. "Theo, that's amazing!"

I go for a hug when he sets his food down, but end up jumping him in my excitement. He lets out a surprised laugh as we both end up sprawled in a diagonal position on the couch, legs tangling. A bloom of insecurity fills my chest at having knocked over a former NFL player so easily, but he puts me at ease by kissing the top of my head. His hands tangle in my hair, fingers brushing the nape of my neck. When my skin heats, it's for a totally different reason.

"Are you excited?" I prop myself up with an elbow, looking down at him. "I know you weren't sure this was the route you wanted to go down."

"I don't know." He plays with my hair, the waterfall of dark curls that trail down his chest. "The head coach told me a little about the group of guys, and that got me excited. I forgot what that kind of passion for the game felt like. When it wasn't a dream I fought everything to chase, or a job that was easily swept away from me at the first injury."

"Would it pain you to know I never got much into football?"

His eyes whip up to meet mine. When he raises himself, I'm forced to sit up away from him. "How is that possible? You live in Texas!" The accusation doesn't land. I just stare up at him blankly.

"Is that supposed to mean something?"

He heaves a sigh, shaking his head. "We'll have to do something to remedy this." When my face twists into something like distaste, his mouth falls open in shock. "Marcela!"

"Do we have to?" I remember that I haven't even told him about Alice yet and decide to relent before I'm forced to break his heart all over again. "Okay, fine." It comes out as a grumble, but he pumps his fist in victory.

"So, Alice called today," I say once we've finished eating, because I have to start somewhere. He looks over with a neutral expression I don't buy for a second. Funny how he's only good at lying when he wants to be. "She wants us to go on a double date with her and Ben next weekend."

Theo's entire demeanor changes in an instant. "Absolutely not." His shoulders tense and his jaw locks so tight he could crack walnuts with his teeth. He looks away from me, but not before I catch how his brows pinch together.

"I know it'll probably be awkward." He rolls his eyes in a way that seems to say, *awkward doesn't begin to cover it.*

"Isn't this against one of your rules?" he asks, reminding me of the conversation we had on our way back from Dallas. "We agreed not to get involved with each other's friends and families. Or is it only okay as long as it's not *your* family?"

Ouch.

He's not wrong about that, no matter how much the truth stings. I'm tempted to fold the way he wants me to, to text Alice that I tried but it's not happening, to salvage the night I've nearly ruined. But I have that same twitchy, guilty feeling that tells me I owe Alice anything she asks of me, which makes me push harder.

"Hey, I don't like this either. We're supposed to finally have all the sex everyone thinks we're having." His expression softens a bit at that, the edge of his mouth curling slightly upward. "Look, I know you and Ben aren't exactly speaking, but don't you want to change that? Don't you want to have a relationship with your brother again?"

He attempts a shrug, but his shoulders barely move. Theo still won't look at me, and I'm getting the sense that there's something much deeper going on.

"Is there something else you're not telling me?" I ask. "Is there some other reason why you don't want to do this?"

He heaves a sigh, head turning to face me. His eyes have lost their hardness, but I can still sense him hesitating. Choosing his words carefully in his mind before he speaks them. The same way I do, right before I lie through my teeth.

"No," he finally says. "Just petty rivalries we never apologized for."

"Well." I push a strand of hair back from my face. "You've gotta bury those hatchets at some point. Why not now?"

Another sigh escapes him. "If it's that important to you, then fine."

I'm not sure I'd describe it that way, especially when I have as much reason to dread going as him. Not that he knows that. Would fessing up make things better or worse for him? On the one hand, maybe he'll feel less alone to know I'm in the exact same position as him. We can lean on each other even more. Talk through our feelings in an honest way. Support each other when our damned emotions knock us down to our lowest moments.

But on the other hand, I've already kept my feelings secret from him for this long. If I tell him now, would he see it as a betrayal? Maybe he never would've agreed to this stunt in the first place if he knew how I felt about Ben. How I *still* feel. Will he think differently of me if he knows? See me for the hypocrite I undoubtedly am?

I've most likely landed myself a first-class ticket to hell for not telling him sooner. So, why start now?

There's a palpable tension in the air for the rest of the night. We don't touch, not even our knees, as we watch the TV in silence. I hold my breath for what feels like hours, as if afraid to make any sudden movements. Until the credits roll, and he rises from his seat. When he reaches for his jacket, everything in me deflates.

He's leaving.

"Do you have to go so soon?" I ask, hoping I don't sound as hurt as I feel. "We've still got a whole queue of bad movies to talk through." And an entire box of unopened condoms sitting in my nightstand drawer, but I'm trying not to come off too strong. Maybe enough time has passed that he's changed his mind on our whole arrangement, but he did kiss my cheek when he entered my apartment. But was it a friendly cheek kiss or a friends-with-benefits cheek kiss?

"I just need to clear my head." His hand reaches the door-knob, but he hesitates and takes one last look at me. He lets out a sigh with his entire body. "Don't pout. You're making it harder for me to leave."

Then don't.

"I'm not pouting." I'm *definitely* pouting.

"I don't want to disappoint you." The teasing tone is gone from his voice. "I just need some time to think about all this."

"I hear you." I nod. "Tonight's not a good night." I force myself to sound understanding, but inside I'm hollowed out. I've ruined our night before it could even really begin. And now, as I watch his back as he leaves my apartment, I can't help but wonder if he's rethinking our arrangement, too.

Sixteen

haven't heard from Theo in ten days.

I'm somewhere between panicked and pissed, because while this isn't like him, it's exactly like the Theo Ben warned me about in the first place. After two unanswered phone calls and five messages left on read, I stopped trying to reach him. I learned a long time ago how useless it is to try to keep people in your life who'd rather not be there. After everything we'd been through the past couple of weeks, I only wish he had a better way of telling me as much.

Maybe I pushed him too far by asking him to go on that double date. I wouldn't blame him if he wanted to call off the whole thing. *So stupid.* Why did I let Alice talk me into trying to convince him?

I have no reason to be mad when I knew exactly what we'd be getting into when we started this. But any teeny trace of abandonment brings me right back to sixth grade. The careful way my mother approached me with the note my father left behind, her arm around my shoulders as my eyes scanned the crinkled paper. The way I lashed out at her afterward, like it was her fault he didn't want to be a father. My tías crowding the table, the sympathy swimming in their eyes, the unsolicited advice I couldn't stand.

In the end, my neighbor Miss Yolanda told me something that has always stuck with me. It was on a rare day when I found a chance to sneak out of the crowded house, an opening I took whenever I could. She was tending to her rosebush when I came outside, wearing her outdoor attire: straw sun hat and neon yellow gloves. I don't remember much of what was said, since she often had a habit of talking *at* me. I do remember the acute disappointment I felt when I realized I wouldn't be able to take a walk around the block without her telling my mom I'd snuck out.

"Where do you think you're going?" Her voice froze me in my tracks on the steps of my house. "Don't be so hard on her all the time. I know you're going through a rough time right now, but so is she. Easier to love the parent who stays than hate the one who walked out. Don't waste your energy on things you can't change." She paused once she said her piece. "Go on." I'd looked up at her with surprise. "I'll give you a ten-minute head start."

I thought a lot about what she said, and decided she was right. It was useless to hate my dad for walking out on us when he wasn't here to take my anger out on. I still had someone left who cared about me.

Love the person who stays.

That was never going to be Theo. We don't owe each other anything. I'm a means to an end to him, the same way he is to me. For all his talk about not wanting to use me and inability to promise not to catch feelings for me, we're not in a relationship. I had no right to push him into something he was clearly uncomfortable with. Maybe it's better that we call it quits now, before we hurt each other later down the line. But the least he can do is be man enough to tell me it's over to my face.

Friday afternoon, Angela and I spend the day setting up chairs and tables in the YA section, which proves to be a helpful distraction from my ever-consuming thoughts of Theo. Funny how almost an entire month has passed, and now I need a distraction from my distraction. We block off the entrance with shelving carts to set up for tonight's event. Erica thought balloons would be over the top, but I insisted they give a festive look to the YA shelves. Now I have to wade through a sea of them to find Angela's whereabouts.

"You good over there?" she asks, not bothering to mask her laughter for my sake.

"Never better." I readjust my French braids to fall over my shoulders. "How does my hair look? I think the static is making me frizz up."

"A little bit." Angela comes over to my side of the table, walking through the bright pink death traps. She looks cozy in a gray cardigan and white capris. The only pops of color in her ensemble are the teal tank top and bejeweled sandals. Only Angela could convince everyone to dress up just to turn around and come up with the most casual costume possible for herself.

She smooths her hands over my scalp, and when that

doesn't work, she retrieves a small bottle of hair serum from her purse. "This ought to do the trick."

"Not too much. Don't make me greasy."

She works her hands over the top of my head with the serum, readjusts my gold folklórico earrings, and then fixes the red poms hanging at the ends of my braids. "That blouse is really cute."

"Thank you." I smooth down the ruffles cinching at my waist. The white peasant blouse is detailed with cerulean thread at the neck and sleeves. "You should see the poncho I found at a shop downtown. It matches the preorder art *perfectly*."

Unsurprisingly, we didn't just dress up as our favorite YA characters—we dressed up as our favorite Latina YA characters. Angela's outfit, casual as it may be, is an identical match to the one Lila Reyes is wearing on the cover of *A Cuban Girl's Guide to Tea and Tomorrow*. Once I put on my poncho, I'll be dressed as Sofia from *Before the Dawn*, the book we'll be discussing tonight. It's a YA fantasy with a Latinx-inspired setting featuring a corrupt political system and a star-crossed romance between two foes on opposing sides. Sofia hates Enrique from the very beginning, but her situation forces her to gain his trust to avenge her family. In the advanced reader's copy I received of the sequel, *As Dusk Breaks*, the duology ends with them teaming up to overthrow the corrupt government that killed Sofia's family and living happily ever after as the kingdom's new rulers.

We chose our next lineup of books from across a wide range of authors from different backgrounds. San Antonio has a large Mexican American community, but we also serve people from many different communities. We get lots of kids from the neighboring high school who know exactly which books they're looking for, and the disappointment on their faces when we don't have what they want sticks in my brain more than the excitement when we do. I've made it my mission to buy as many of these books as possible for our collections. I don't just want more kids to read—I want them to see themselves in the books they're reading. If I can do anything to help influence that, I'll fight in any way I can to make it happen.

"Nice." Angela nods. "So, what do you think? Will the teenagers think we're total dorks?"

"I'm pretty sure they know we're total dorks."

My smile is wide in the reflection in the window behind her. This is my night. In a few hours, the library will fill up with teens excited to read, and extra excited to talk about what they read. I've been writing a list in my phone all month of book recommendations to check out before the second book club pick is announced. When I told Angela about it, she said I should publish it on our library's blog and include the link in the bio of all of our library's social media accounts. The link went live this morning and we're going to announce it to the teens at the start of the meeting.

This is my night. I push all thoughts of Theo and his brother out of my mind and focus on making the YA book club go off without a hitch.

The library begins to fill at ten till seven, and seats are already filling faster than we expected. Erica nods approvingly at the table, and then sends me a pleased smile when our eyes meet. Even she decided to dress up with us. Erica is wearing Noemí's bold red evening gown from the cover of *Mexican Gothic*. Her hair is pinned into a bob and she's wearing maroon lipstick to match. The book may not be YA, but I couldn't be more ecstatic that she decided to dress up.

Angela kicks off the book club by introducing me, Erica, and herself. Then she sits down and opens up her copy of *Before the Dawn* as I take over leading the discussion questions. I ask everyone to go around the table and share their favorite part of the book. Most answer things like the atmosphere, the magic, and the characters until Andy Sanchez, my favorite library patron, steals my answer.

"I loved the romance," she says. The fourteen-year-old is tiny, but her personality more than makes up for her prepubescent build. Her brown hair is pulled up in a high bun at the very top of her head, and black square-framed glasses highlight her dark eyes. "Enrique and Sofia? And that kiss at the end— *Swoon*." The table erupts into laughter as she fans herself and pretends to faint in her chair.

"That was also my favorite part," Angela agrees, nodding vigorously. "Love me a good slow-burn romance."

"Love me a good *enemies-to-lovers*, slow-burn romance," I correct to a chorus of murmured agreement. Angela chimes in with something else, but I barely hear her when I catch sight of a blond head over the row of teenagers. A gasp strangles the back of my throat.

Theo is leaning against a wooden bookshelf, hands in the pockets of his jeans. A small smile tugs his lips upward, but his glittering blue eyes are trained on me.

Ignoring him is impossible, but we continue the discussion until it's time for the small-group activity. I check my phone under the table to see if he tried to get a hold of me. I find two missed calls and one eerily vague text message on my lock screen.

Can we talk?

My stomach drops at the sight of it. Nothing good ever comes after that question. Especially considering he spent over a week avoiding my messages *trying to talk*. Now he's tracked me down on a night that was supposed to be special.

Angela tells everyone to break into groups of two to four people, and to find a scene they want to reenact from the book. I can't prolong the inevitable for much longer.

"I'll be right back."

Angela's eyes catch on Theo's form hovering over the table of YA staff picks. "Mm-hmm." There's a knowing glint in her expression, the edge of her lips forming a smirk. I don't like the look of it whatsoever, but I choose to ignore it for now as I rise from my seat. Her suspicions are about to be too little too late if my instinct is right.

"What are you doing here?" I try to push him out of view, but he doesn't budge. When I narrow my eyes at him, he lets me steer him away from the group.

He's dressed casually in jeans and a plain blue hoodie, hands buried in his pockets. His eyes light up as he looks over my shoulder at the groups of teens dramatically reenacting dialogue from the book, as if preparing for the audition of a lifetime.

"What's all this?"

"You're about ten days too late, so I think I'll be asking the questions here."

He rubs a hand at the nape of his neck, expression suddenly sheepish. As much as I'd love to give him a piece of my mind, now is not the time. I glance over my shoulder, locking eyes with Angela. I tap my wrist in a silent question, and she holds up the timer on her phone. The groups have three more minutes to practice. I tell myself that's the only reason why I'm letting Theo off the hook.

"You're interrupting book club." I cross my arms over my chest, daring him to judge me. But that seems to be the last thing on his mind as his smile spreads wider. When his eyes return to me, all my resolve melts under his gaze. I can't be mad at him for being curious about a night I've been planning for weeks. "Why—" I'm about to ask him why he's here but he interrupts before I can, feet bouncing up and down with...excitement?

"Is dressing up a requirement?" He reaches out to touch the red pom tied to the end of my braid. He's far too smiley for the doomed thoughts roiling around in my brain. "Who are you supposed to be? You look cute."

Cute. The word explodes into a burst of butterflies that take flight in my stomach. My shoulders deflate with the last of my paranoid thoughts. He wouldn't call me cute if he was here to fake-dump me, right? Then why avoid me for over a week? I'm still mad at him, but I hand him a copy of *Before the Dawn* and point to the illustration of the protagonist on the cover. He takes the book from my hand to inspect it, brows furrowing as he turns it over for the synopsis. When he doesn't find it, his eyes narrow in confusion. I take it back from him and open the book to the taped-in flap on the inside.

"The descriptions are on the inside for hardcovers," I tell him.

"Sounds cool," he says once he's read what the book is about. "Is this the book club pick?"

I nod as an idea for a punishment suddenly occurs to me. If he came all this way just to dump me, he might as well make himself useful first. *This ought to be good.*

"Since you came all this way, you might as well help." I take his hand and drag him back to the table. He complies easier than I expected him to, even under the curious stares of no less than fifteen teenagers.

"Angela, can you be our narrator?"

She looks Theo up and down as I pick up my copy of *Before the Dawn*. "Is the big guy joining us?"

"What exactly are we—"

"Found it!" I exclaim over Theo's question. I'm flipped to page three hundred in the book, the first page of chapter fifty-seven. Andy's favorite scene, and mine. I hand Theo a spare copy and tell him what page to turn to.

"You're playing the part of Enrique," I tell him. "And be dramatic. I've spent months gaining your trust, so you're shocked and betrayed when I pull a knife on you."

His eyes widen in alarm, but even so there's a hint of amusement glittering in them. "Et tu, Brute?"

I can't help the laugh that escapes from my diaphragm.

"Are we going to practice first?" Theo asks.

"What fun would that be?" I flash my most devious smile. "Besides, we're out of time."

We call the small groups' attention back to the front, and then we're the first group to reenact the scene. Theo's voice is wobbly at first, but gains momentum as he mirrors my dramatic performance. He tries to take a step back when I hold up Angela's bottle of hair serum in place of a dagger, eyes widening in alarm, but a chair blocks him from going any farther. I stand on the tips of my toes as I hold the fake dagger to his throat, not quite touching his skin.

"The rumors were true, I see," he says, eyes scanning me warily. "I was a fool to trust you wouldn't turn on me."

"Not so fun playing the fool, is it?" The final scene in *Before the Dawn* is a reversal for Sofia, whose parents were killed by Enrique's soldiers when they were promised protection. This is the moment she's spent the whole book planning, but in the end she can't do it. She cares about Enrique too much to kill him.

It's a reversal for Theo and me too, except I feel more like Enrique in this scene. I let myself believe I was safe from him, nearly trusted him not to hurt me. But I can't blame him, no matter how easy he made it to forget what we really are. That's not a mistake I'm going to make again. If we're not already over, that is.

I dig the bottle into his neck, and he feigns a pained wince. His glittering eyes tell me he's enjoying this far more than I expected him to. He turns his head slightly down to check for his next line.

"You're no fool, Sofia." His free arm wraps around my waist, pulling me closer to his body, but not crushing me to him like he would if he were alone. "We both know what you're really afraid of."

A whoosh of air, and then the book drops from Theo's hand as he dips my body, his large hands on my back securing me in place. His face hovers over mine before it closes the distance, his lips landing on my cheek in a chaste kiss, because the book kiss isn't exactly what I'd call safe-for-work material.

There's a distinct cry from the audience I recognize as Andy's voice, and then everyone else joins in cheering and clapping. Once I'm upright, Theo and I hold hands as we bow to the crowd.

As the first group of teens rise for their performance, Erica finds a chair for Theo to sit in. He scrapes the chair next to mine, so close I can barely breathe. Angela eyes us a few times between performances with a raised brow. I shake my head each time we lock eyes.

After the meeting, we announce next month's choices and remind them to vote in our social media polls each week. I also let them know about the library blog to check out in case they want to read something else in the meantime.

"Oh, and don't forget to come dressed as your favorite book character next month!" I say.

"If enough people participate, we might even have a prize for the best costume!" Angela adds. I look at her sideways, crossing my arms over my chest.

"Oh, really?" I ask as the teens bustle around, packing up

as they prepare to leave. "I don't remember deciding that. Do you remember deciding that, Erica?"

My boss looks between us with twinkling eyes, but she doesn't say a word.

"It's a good idea though, isn't it?" Angela jumps up from her seat. "Especially if we want to get more of them to dress up."

"And just what prize are we going to use as an incentive?" Erica asks, resting her chin in a raised hand.

Before I hear Angela's answer, a tug at my shirt makes me turn around. Andy links her arm with mine, pulling me away from my boss and friend with surprising strength for a skinny fourteen-year-old.

"What's up, kid?"

"You holdin' out on me, Miss Ortiz?" Her brown eyes glance covertly over my shoulder, but when I try to turn around, she stops me with a hand on my shoulder. I meet her alarmed eyes with concern, but it dies away as soon as she asks, "Is he your *boyfriend*?"

Oh god.

I shake off her hand and turn around. Theo meets my gaze with an easy grin. His hands are in the pockets of his jeans, but he raises one to wave at us. I turn back to Andy with what's sure to be a goofy smile on my face.

"You're too young," I say. "I can't have this conversation with you, yet."

"Are you kidding? I've had ten boyfriends already!" I let out a gasp at this announcement, failing to hide the shock behind it. Even *teenagers* are better at dating than I am. "It's about time you had *one*. I was starting to worry about you, ya know."

"Okay, where's your mom?" I pick up my pace as I lead her out the glass double doors with a hand on her back. "It's time for you to go home."

"You can't get rid of me that easily," she says. "My mom works a lot of odd hours. I'll be right back here tomorrow, and I'll be expecting an answer."

"Then I guess it's a good thing I'm off tomorrow."

"There's always the next day," she says cheerily. "And the day after that, and the day after that! I *will* get an answer from you!"

I don't bother entertaining her antics, only shake my head as we reach the parking lot. Outside, we're met with the silver headlights of a navy Honda Civic. Andy's mother emerges from the driver's side, waving us over. I walk Andy to her mother's car.

"How was the book club?" Andy's mom reminds me a lot of my own. Her curly black hair is beginning to streak through with white, and its cut in a bob that stops right at her shoulders. She looks impossibly young for the mother of a teenager. That is, until she smiles and the lines around her crinkled eyes and mouth show her true age.

"Amazing!" Andy exclaims. "Marcela brought her boyfriend to help reenact the most dramatic part of the book."

I take a deep breath. One day, when she's old enough, I'm going to kill this girl.

"Boyfriend?" Her mom raises a perfectly arched brow, the hint of a smile playing on her lips.

"This is how rumors get started, Andy!" I shake my head before turning back to her mom. In a lower tone, I say, "It's complicated. Neither one of us really knows what we're doing."

"Ah, I see." She smiles wistfully. "I remember those early days all too well."

I'm not exactly sure what she means by that, but I don't get the chance to ask. Once Andy is inside the car, they both wave goodbye. I watch them leave before heading back inside. Most of the kids have left already, until it's just Erica and Angela.

With Theo.

"Code blue," Angela says as I reach the table. At my furrowed brows, she exclaims, "We've got a *non-reader* in the library!"

"I'm signing him up for a library card," Erica says, nodding at Theo seated across from her. He's bent over the table filling out a form. "I know it's what you would've wanted."

"Done." Theo drops the pen and holds out the sheet of paper to my boss. "Can I pick out the design for my card?"

He almost sounds…*excited*.

"You sure can." She hands the form to me. "Marcela, you remember where they are?"

"Not sure why I'm being paid if I don't." I grab Theo's hand and lead him to the circulation desk.

Now that the buzz of book club night is over, I'm left with a peculiar feeling. Theo is *here*, in my place of work, talking with my best friend and boss like it's the most casual thing in the world. Erica signed him up for a *library card* for fuck's sake. A couple of hours ago, I thought we were over. What kind of upside-down world are we living in?

This is breaking all sorts of boundaries, but I get the feeling he doesn't mind so much this time. Not now that they're *my* boundaries.

When I've got him set up in our system and he's equipped with a bright purple library card, I walk him out to the parking lot. We stop under a streetlamp, the light casting him in a golden halo. Now that the chaos has died down, I remember why he came here in the first place. *Can we talk?*

I'm not mad at him anymore, only at myself for not seeing this coming. But more than that, I'm crushed. So much more than I thought I'd be to let him go so soon.

"Are you okay?" he asks, eyes creased with concern.

"Yeah." I clear my throat, deciding to get this over with as quickly as possible. "What did you want to talk about?" His brows furrow. "You texted earlier...asking if we could talk?"

"Oh," he says, something shifting in his expression as he remembers. "Right. I...wanted to apologize for not getting back to you sooner. It wasn't cool of me to keep you hanging for so long. I just had a lot on my mind."

"We can get out of dinner," I blurt, because that's what started all this trouble to begin with. If that's all that's holding him back from continuing our arrangement, maybe we can go back to the way things were between us. "I'll tell Alice I got sick, and we'll never reschedule. It'll be fine."

"No." He shakes his head, though his expression looks pained. As if getting out the one word is harder than it should be. "Thank you, but I'll be okay. I promise."

"Are you sure?" Something isn't sitting right with me. Why avoid me for ten days if he's not backing out of dinner? Why is he giving in so easily after nearly two weeks of nothing?

He nods, kissing my forehead. "I'm sure. I can't keep running away from them forever."

"You could've talked to me." It shouldn't hurt so much that he felt like he couldn't. Not when I've kept my own secrets from him, too. I stare down at the pavement, arms crossed over my chest. "What were you thinking about?" When he doesn't answer, I rephrase. "Who is it you're more worried about? Alice or Ben?"

"Both." He heaves a sigh. "But if I had to pick...Ben." I'm about to follow up with one of the many questions dancing around my head, but before I can, he adds, "Don't worry about me. I didn't mean to leave you out of the blue like that, but I realized that if I'm ever going to move on, I have to accept that this is happening." His chest falls as he lets out a breath. "They're getting married. I should congratulate them face-to-face, at least once."

I nod, but I don't say anything more.

"I won't do that to you again." His hand cups my cheek when I look up at him. "Disappear without a trace. You deserve better than that."

The back of my throat clogs up with some emotion I'm too afraid to name. I clear it and nod, hoping he can't sense how much that means to me. Even if a part of me doesn't believe him.

Seventeen

A purple jumpsuit hugs my curves in a way I wish every article of clothing I own would, the ruffled sleeves falling over my shoulders and exposing much more of my arms than I'm used to. The material is light and breathable against my skin, which is all I ask for of any fabric. However, there's no hiding my broadly set shoulders or the thickness of my upper arms, but for the first time in years, I don't care.

My relationship with my body varies daily. There's what I begrudgingly accept, what I thank God for blessing me with, and what I wish enough glaring could make go away. But I can't pick and choose which parts of myself are worthy and which aren't, not the way other people feel like they can when they comment on my body. And why should I? Why should I be expected to carry the weight of other people's disdain for the body I live in?

On our most recent trip to La Cantera mall, Angela convinced me to buy the jumpsuit because she thought I looked like an Instagram model in it. I didn't buy it because I believed her, but because I'm tired of punishing myself for all the ways my body will never be perfect.

Now I'm glad to have finally gotten over myself. In addition to my arms, much of my back is exposed, showing an expanse of golden-brown skin. The neckline dips into a heart shape between my cleavage—high enough to leave most to the imagination, but just low enough to inspire some illicit daydreams. My eyes are lined with a precisely drawn, dramatic wing courtesy of a fine-tipped pen. My lips are painted bright red, a second pop of color that looks spectacular against the shade of purple. My hair is down and swept over one shoulder in a side part. Even I can't deny how amazing I look tonight.

Theo is surprisingly punctual, considering this double date is the last place he wants to be. I've just finished getting ready—slipping my feet into a pair of low, chunky heels that are easy to walk in—when the doorbell rings. Theo crowds the doorway in a simple white button-down tucked into navy dress pants. When I step aside to let him in, he doesn't move an inch except for his eyes. They scan me from head to toe, lingering in places that make my entire body shiver. I resist the urge to cover myself with my arms, letting him look his fill.

"Enjoying the view?" My voice comes out more low and breathy than the wry amusement I was going for. His eyes snap up to mine, more black pupil than blue iris.

"You always look good, but *fuck*, Marcela." He shakes his head as if to clear it, and I'm flooded with a rush of confidence from having affected him this way. I don't need him to tell me what I already know, but damn if that doesn't stop his praise from sinking into my veins anyway. His hands wrap around my waist, pulling me into him. "You might've just made this dinner worth going to."

"That so?" My hands fist in his shirt, tugging him in for a kiss that will definitely ruin my lipstick. I revel in the feel of him, in the scratchy stubble of his cheeks against mine, in the warmth of his mouth, in the addicting taste of him. Suddenly, as desire pools low in my belly, I wish we didn't have to leave the apartment. We pull away too soon, both of us breathing hard.

"We should probably go, before we're tempted to cancel for a very different reason," I tell him. My eyes catch on his red-smeared mouth, and I cover mine with a hand. "But we should clean up first."

"I've never been allowed to kiss off red lipstick before." Theo's warm breath is in my ear, one hand closing over mine so his other can trace the outline of my lips. His mouth turns up into a smug grin, rimmed a devilish red.

After reapplying my lipstick and handing Theo a makeup wipe to clean his mouth with, we settle into his car ten minutes after we should've been on our way. Ben and Alice are already seated by the time we arrive, menus and water glasses placed in front of them.

"Sorry we're late," Theo says, pulling out a chair for me. My heart melts at the simple gesture, even if he's just being polite. "Guess the time got ahead of us."

"You've got a little something right here." Alice gestures at the corner of her mouth, and Theo's hand comes up to his.

When I look over at him, I see a red stain from my lipstick. His cheeks go pink as he realizes what it must be. I take the cloth napkin from my side and make a show of scrubbing the edge of his mouth.

"*Busted*. You guys can see exactly how the time got away from us." My tone is overly suggestive, but my laugh is genuine.

Once I've gotten all the lipstick off his face, we settle back into our seats with ease. Theo's arm wraps around the back of my chair in that possesive-guy way Ben won't like, and I lean my back against his arm. Alice eyes us with amusement, a tilt to her lips that makes me think she might be happy for us. Ben, however, is looking at everything inside the restaurant but us.

"*Wow*," Alice marvels at Theo and me. "You know, when Christine told me you guys left the engagement party together, I had no idea what to think." She shakes her head, as if she still doesn't. "But you guys actually look really cute together."

"Thank you." My voice is steady, but the gratitude is entirely fake. I can feel Theo's eyes on me like a question, but I don't turn to look at him. "No one's more surprised than me, believe me."

"Oh, I doubt that," Ben says, eyes trained down on his menu. Alice nudges him with an elbow, but he doesn't seem to register it.

"Can't you just be supportive for once in your life?" The entire table looks up at Theo. Ben finally meets his brother's glance, his widened eyes the only show of surprise. "Why is that so hard for you?"

But Ben is stopped from answering his brother's loaded question when our waiter comes to take our order. I'm the only one ready to order, but we tell him we need more time to decide. Instead of opening their menus to make that decision, Ben and Theo continue as if nothing happened.

"Don't kid yourself. We both know this isn't gonna last." Even though he's speaking to Theo, the words land on me like a physical blow, despite knowing what Theo and I have is far from real. But maybe that's why they sting: because he's so much closer to the truth than he even realizes. "You don't have the first clue about what real relationships are like."

"Ben, don't—"

"You, of all people, can't possibly tell me I'm wrong." Ben turns to Alice, using a tone I've never heard him use with her. It's cutting and sarcastic and not at all like him. But Alice doesn't even seem fazed. Her shoulders slump in a resigned way, and her eyes roll just before they shut closed. She shakes her head to herself, almost like this is a conversation she's had before. Like it's one she's tired of hearing.

"You're the one who knows him better than anyone else at this table. Do you really think—"

"Ben, *stop.*" Heads turn around to eye us at Theo's raised voice. Some wear startled expressions, others openly glare, and some even ogle us like we're dinner entertainment. His eyes are hard as they stare his brother down, the two locked in a silent battle. My stomach drops, replaced with a sinking dread. I'm missing something key here, something staring at me straight in the face. I just don't know what it is.

When the waiter stops by a second time, I order two

plates of chicken parmesan for myself and Theo. Then I take his hand and intertwine our fingers. He looks down at me, expression softening immediately.

"We can leave," I tell him, because suddenly this table is the last place I want to be. "I didn't know—" I take in a breath, shaking my head. Ben's eyes are on us, and it's making me over-warm. *I didn't know it would be this bad.* "You don't have to do this if you don't want to. I shouldn't have made you."

"Marcela, don't go," Ben tells me. "There's something you need to know about my brother. If you're going to keep seeing him, which I've already told you multiple times is a bad idea."

"And telling her who she can and can't date *isn't?*" Alice says suddenly, the question posed more as a statement. Her voice is calm and carefully measured, eyes cutting on her fiancé. Another conversation they've had before.

"This is different, and you know it." But he's not looking at her. His eyes are trained on his brother's. "She deserves to know what she's getting herself into, don't you think?"

"Theo?" I squeeze his hand, trying to anchor him to me, but he's not looking at any of us. His chest rises and falls with quick breaths, his other hand clenched into a white-knuckled fist beneath the table. He rises from his seat, breaking contact with me. Before anyone can say anything else, he walks straight out of the restaurant. Ben has the nerve to look smug as he watches Theo's back. I narrow my eyes on him, hating myself for how stupid I've been. Is this really the same guy I've been pining over for almost a decade?

"What the hell was that about?" It takes everything in me

not to scream at him. As it is, we've already made an audience for the other dinner guests.

"He's in love with my fiancée." For a moment, all I can do is stare at him, dumbfounded. *They know.* Alice is pinching the bridge of her nose, eyes shut. "He has been for years. That's what I've been trying to warn you about."

My mouth opens, but I can't think of a single thing to say, aside from the question ringing in my head I can't ask either of them. *You knew all along?*

"There was no reason for you to be a dick about it," I say instead, then leave the table to catch up to Theo.

There's no sign of him outside the restaurant, or any of the surrounding shops. The straps of my low heels are digging into my skin the longer I walk, until I'm forced to shuck them. Theo is nowhere to be seen. The cobbled courtyard is speckled with a few pedestrians ambling around and chatting on benches. I duck my head as I take a seat at the edge of a fountain and pull out my phone. When the call goes straight to voice mail, I curse under my breath. I know he wouldn't leave me behind, not after what he said yesterday, but I wish I knew how to help him.

The edge of a shadow crosses my vision, but when I look up, it's only Alice. I place a hand over my chest as she takes the spot next to me. "You scared me."

"He'll be back," she says. "He's not the abandoning type. He probably just needs to clear his head."

"If you say so," I say, hating suddenly how well she knows him. He said once he's never been able to deny her anything.

That's why he's never abandoned her, but the same can't be said for me.

But that's not what I'm worried about right now, even though I should know better after last week. I'm more worried about how Theo's feeling. I should never have let Alice push me into this, and I never should've pushed Theo further than he was willing to go. Clearly, he was right to be worried.

"Why did you ask me to bring him tonight?" I snap at her, even though part of me knows she doesn't deserve it. "You had to have known something like this would happen."

"Believe me, I didn't think it'd get this out of hand," she says calmly. "You don't know how hard I've worked to get Theo and Ben to repair their relationship. It's exhausting enough without Ben making things worse."

"Yeah," I say with a scoff, shaking my head. "You know it's not your job to fix them, right? Especially not if they don't want to do the work themselves."

She doesn't say anything, but her face almost looks like she wants to. I recognize the way her eyes shift away from me for what it is. Guilt. "It is when I'm the reason they're barely on speaking terms."

That's why she feels responsible. Why she's never let Theo cut himself off from either of them for long. She wants to bring them back together because she's the one who tore them apart to begin with.

"Theo's a great guy. I can't remember the last time I've seen him so happy." She must see the surprise on my face because she adds, "Ben drama aside, that is."

I'm tempted to tell her that none of it is real. That the

only reason we became friends was to stop him from ruining her engagement, and that we haven't even hooked up in the way everyone thinks we have.

"I told Ben not to tell you," she says. I glance back at her in surprise. "I was afraid you wouldn't give him a chance if you knew, even if you guys only started as a hookup. He deserves someone great, and I thought you could be that for him. Maybe that was selfish of me."

I can't tell her the full truth, but I can give her this much. "He told me." She tilts her head at me. I heave a deep breath. "He was honest with me from the beginning. I knew what I was getting into."

"You did?" she asks curiously. She looks like she wants to say something else, but then I catch a large, shadowed silhouette over her shoulder, stepping into the light of the streetlamp. I make out Theo's blond head, his dark eyes piercing even from feet away. His hands are in his pockets, shoulders slumped in defeat.

I'm not sure what Alice sees. He doesn't seem very happy, hovering just a few feet away from us, like he's too afraid to move. I say a quick goodnight to Alice before rising to cross the cobbled pathway. He looks grateful he doesn't have to interrupt my conversation with Alice or interact with her any more than he has to. The pain is clear in his expression, in the unmasked longing in his eyes. I'm unsure how to comfort him, but I desperately want to do *something*.

"Hey." He won't look at me, even when I take his hands. I fold my arms tentatively around his neck instead, and he finally responds by wrapping his around my back.

"I'm sorry for leaving you." He takes in a deep breath. "I just had to get out of there."

My hands sink into his hair. He sighs into my skin. "I don't blame you. I didn't think it'd be that bad. How naive of me."

When we return to the car, Theo doesn't start the engine right away. There are too many questions buzzing between us, even though I'm sure I know some of the answers by now.

"You probably want some kind of explanation," Theo says rather than asks. I tilt my head as I look up at him. Before now, I thought he'd told me everything I needed to know about his relationship with Alice. Or, at the very least, that he would willingly tell me what I wanted to know. But even if that's true, I didn't know the right questions to ask.

"Alice knows you love her," I say. He nods, but he still won't look at me. "And your brother knows it, too."

"Yeah." His voice isn't much more than a puff of air.

"How long have they known?"

"I never made my feelings for her a secret, even if I never acted on them." The words come steadily as he looks forward, out at the near-empty shops. "I'm not the type of person to pine in secret."

Not like me.

I don't know how I didn't put two and two together sooner. He's a terrible liar, which would make him an even worse secret-keeper. If he's loved her his entire life, there's no way he would've been able to keep that to himself. Definitely not for this long. It makes sense that Ben and Alice would already know. But what doesn't make sense is what he tried to do the night of the engagement party.

"She always knew how I felt about her, but I never really knew how she felt," he continues. "It never bothered me, though. We both had different goals in high school. She was still my best friend, and neither of us wanted anything to get in the way of that. But when she got with my brother…"

"What?" I prompt.

His eyes shudder closed. "He knew how I felt about her, too. Everyone did, except maybe our dad. Ben knew I'd take it as a betrayal, but it still didn't stop him."

There it is. Now their feud makes perfect sense.

"That was just the cherry on top of a shitty year," he says. "From my knee injury to the NFL rejection, to finding out my little brother was dating the love of my life. And instead of talking about it like grown adults, he used you as a buffer."

Another puzzle piece clicks firmly into place. My eyes snap up to him in realization. "That was the first night we met."

He nods slowly. "I was a mess. *We* were a mess, and he never should've dragged you into it."

I remember how small Ben looked that night, crowding himself into a corner as he watched his brother fall apart. I never would've guessed it was partly Ben's doing in the first place.

"He knew how you felt about her, and he went after her anyway," I repeat, almost unable to believe it. But I do, because it's the only thing that makes sense. Even though it's a side of Ben I've never seen, vindictive and undermining. Or maybe just a side of him I never wanted to see. "If Alice already knew, why were you planning to confess at her engagement party?"

"Because I wasn't sure if she still knew," he says. "Our friendship was never the same after I graduated. We had different obligations, even if she always made it a point to reach out to me. I wanted her to know those feelings never went away, and I wanted to know, once and for all, how she felt about me. If we could've changed our history, not that I can do anything about it now. Not without hurting a whole bunch of people."

A beat of silence follows his explanation. His eyes fall away from my face, as if realizing he's said too much. I can't look him in the face either, not when I realize he's including me in that list. But the scariest revelation of all is he might be right.

"Ben most of all," I say to break the tension, my mind racing. "Is that why you hate him?"

"He hates me more," Theo says, expression turning icy. "Believe me."

"What reason could he possibly have?" I ask, but he just shakes his head.

"I don't know. Petty shit from our childhood," he says, but there has to be more to it than that. He confirms my theory when he says, "There was a lot of unhealthy competition between us growing up, and a lot of half-buried resentment between us now. So, when he started dating Alice..." He trails off, but I get his meaning loud and clear. I wonder if that's really the way Ben sees her. As nothing more than a prize to be won.

"I'm sorry you're getting pulled into it again now." Theo finally meets my eyes. "I get it if it's too much for you."

"Too late for that," I say, mouth pulling up slightly. He doesn't return my wry grin, and instead manages to look grimmer than before. "Hey. I'm not going anywhere," I assure him, reaching over for his hand. "I knew what I was getting into. Nothing's changed."

"Really?" he asks hesitantly.

"We're in too deep to go back now," I tell him. "And...I wouldn't want to."

I'm not sure why confessing this feels like I'm giving part of myself away, but the way his eyes sear through me sends heat throughout my entire body. When he kisses me, his mouth is scorching against mine. My hands curl into his hair as he fists the fabric at my sides, pulling me in closer.

"Let's get out of here."

I sit back in my seat as he puts the car in drive, laughing when he guns the engine. He's not the only one in a hurry.

Eighteen

T here's no rush this time, our kisses long and lingering and exploratory.

He has me pinned to the front door of my apartment, in full view of the front-facing windows of the next building over. I'm not sure how much the shadows cover us, but surprisingly, I just *don't care*. We've never kissed like this before, his mouth warm and languid on mine. Like we've done this for years. Like we could do it for a couple more. My fingers trace the stubble on his cheeks, reveling in the scratchiness. Our movements have always been frantic up until this point, afraid of running out the invisible clock above our heads. Two teenagers past curfew, ensuring every minute alone counts before we're due back home.

It's different with us this time, but I can hardly mark the change.

"We should probably head inside soon," he says between kisses, but he doesn't stop. I don't either.

"You're probably right," I say against his lips, pressing my body against his.

This.

This is exactly the distraction I need, but we've almost become more than that. I should need him to get my mind off his brother, to forget the ache in my chest every time I see him with Alice, but Ben is the last person on my mind.

When Theo's tongue slides between my lips, all thoughts outside of this moment evaporate. We shift until his back hits the door. One hand slides down his chest as my other reaches for the keys clipped to the strap of my purse. I try for a cool move—unlocking the door while still kissing him, inching us inside while we stay connected—but alas, I am solidly uncool. My steps falter until I fumble against his body. To make matters worse, I accidentally bite down on his lip in an unsexy way as I jam my key into the lock.

"Ow!" He pulls away, a hand raising to his mouth.

"Oh, shit!" I exclaim. "Are you bleeding? I'm so sor—"

"It's fine, just a little sore." He drops his hand, revealing the teeth marks on his bottom lip. Even still, he prowls closer, closing the space between us as his hands rest at my waist. "I've handled worse."

An image of his torn hand comes to mind, rivulets of blood trailing down his fingers. The frown marring his mouth and the wrinkle of skin above the space where his brows met, as if he could feel the pain even in his sleep. Yes, I suppose a bite that didn't even pierce the skin wouldn't be worse than *that*.

I unlock the front door, pull him inside, and flick on the hall light. Theo brushes past me to the couch, patting the space next to him with a smoldering look. His brows furrow when I shake my head as I walk backward from the living room. My back hits the door to my bedroom, even as my eyes stay trained on him.

"No couch," I tell him as the door swings open. "Bed. Now."

His smolder turns dark. "Can't argue with that."

We collide under the threshold, his arms wrapping around my back and molding me to him. Hands spread down my back, moving heat. Chest to chest, lips to lips, legs tangling as I walk him into the room. My hands slip from the scruff on his cheeks to his dress shirt, pulling at the fabric tucked into his slacks. Searching for skin.

His own glide under the ruffled straps of my jumpsuit, igniting every inch of skin he touches. "Is there a zipper or something on this thing?"

There isn't, and that's when I realize we're about to see each other naked. A sliver of light pours in from the living room, lighting the entrance of my bedroom. Not a single shadow covers his face, and I can only assume the same is true for me. There's no way I'm taking the jumpsuit off in front of him or letting him bear witness to any kind of awkward shuffling right before we have sex. I should've worn something easy. Nothing with an absurd amount of buttons down one side I have to wriggle my way out of.

Not sexy.

I'm about to say I'll be right back, opting to change in the bathroom, when he begins unbuttoning his shirt. Slowly, with a confidence in what he has to offer that I've never once possessed. He takes a seat at the edge of the bed and kicks off his shoes. When the shirt is finally off, I'm rewarded with a stunning view of his upper body. Curved arm muscles, hard abdominals, defined pecs. My breath comes in pants, until I'm practically salivating. *Built like a god, indeed.* If I were an artist, I'd immortalize him in marble. The plaque would read, *Viewers, be wary. They say even the eyes of angels burn from gazing at this glorious physique.*

Theo's eyes stay trained on mine, an evil, knowing smirk on his lips as one hand settles on the zipper of his slacks and the other rests at the top button. He stands up and in one fluid motion, the pants fall from his body and pool at his feet.

"Wow." Desire flushes my cheeks, even as a wave of shame and embarrassment crashes over me. "Okay. Wow."

I'm out of words. His eyes go black and hooded as he prowls toward me, the last fully dressed person in the room. And then, the thought I've been pushing to the back of my brain for weeks comes raging forward.

How could a guy who looks like that possibly want me?

My vision goes blurry. I've held off for this long, telling myself that none of it was real. Just a distraction to get us through what we need to get through, and a show we put on for the world to project the place we want to be. Once he's done using me to get over Alice, we'll go our separate ways. Of course I'd never be able to pull a guy like him. I know that. He doesn't really want me, but the escape I can provide him. It almost doesn't matter that he'd never date a girl my size otherwise.

"Hey." His voice has gone soft, hands gently cupping my cheeks. My eyes sting with tears I'm desperately trying to blink away. "What's wrong? What did I do?"

"Nothing." God, even my voice gives me away. I can barely get out the one word over the lump in my throat. I shake my head, forcing myself to clear the thoughts away. "Hold on a second. I'll just go change in the bathroom—"

"Marcela." He tugs on my arm as I try to turn away, his hands gripping my shoulders to hold me in place. "We're not gonna do this when you're upset. Talk to me."

I blink a few more times until I can see clearly, as if that'll prove him wrong. Finally, I sit down at the edge of my bed with a sigh. He fills the space next to me, an arm wrapping around my shoulders.

"I'm not...like you." I choke on the explanation, trying to force the words out before I lose my nerve. "I mean, *look* at you. There's not an inch of fat on your body, is there?"

"Thanks to the rigid diet and exercise routines courtesy of the team manager. The day I quit, I had my first piece of cheesecake in years. *Years.*" He emphasizes this fact with a groan.

"Listen, this is the most nerve-racking part of dating for me," I tell him. "I don't want you to...get your hopes up for what my body will look like."

Oh, god.

I sound like my fourteen-year-old self, furiously going through each article of clothing in my closet the night before high school. Pinching at the baby fat in my cheeks and the handles at my sides. Of course, when I look back at pictures of myself from back then, I wonder how I could have ever thought I was ugly.

"Get my hopes up," he repeats, expression stormy.

"Because other guys have gotten their hopes up and been let down? Is that what you're saying?"

I nod, unable to look at him. There have been people who cringed when they got their first glimpse of my body, and then played it off so they could still get some. Part of me is glad Ben and I broke up before we could cross that point, even if I still wonder what his reaction would've been. Maybe it's better I don't know.

"I guess I've just always had a hard time feeling sexy." It's easier talking to him like this, looking down at our feet instead of at him. Even still, the side of my face is warm from the weight of his eyes. "I'm probably a downgrade compared to the other women you've been with."

"Marcela…" His voice raises in alarm.

"I promise I'm not always this insecure," I say in a rush, heart racing from the sudden note in his voice. *A downgrade?* God, what a crappy way to feel about myself. It's not even necessarily how I feel about myself, but what I expect someone like Theo to feel about me. On my best day, like the one I was having until it came time to undress, I know my worth. I know what I deserve. But I've been with too many guys who never came close.

"You're the most conventionally attractive guy I've ever been with, casual or otherwise, and I just got scared that this was about to become…real."

"Look at me." His voice is as soft as I've ever heard it, but I still hesitate a beat before I do so. He smooths back the curls from my face, and I can't help but lean into the touch. "Did you already forget the way I looked at you before we left your apartment tonight?"

A flush of warmth, sudden and all consuming, heats my skin at the memory. It's a lot like the way he's looking at me right now, but it's also a softer expression. His thumb brushes the side of my mouth before his eyes settle there.

"I wouldn't be here if I didn't find you *unbelievably* sexy." His voice is a low growl, and my insides coil with anticipation. And then his mouth is on mine, rough and wild with need.

"If you need me..." His kisses move down my jaw...

"To show you..." My throat.

"How much..." My neck.

"I want you..."

I let out a gasp.

"That can be arranged." His smirk turns devilish. "Starting with getting you out of this jumpsuit."

He motions for me to stand up, and after a slight bit of hesitation, I do. The way he leans back on his elbows, giving me a view of his sculpted body, is all the encouragement I need to get out of this contraption as fast as humanly possible. I undo the buttons under my right armpit, sliding the ruffled sleeves off my arms. The fabric is a bit tight over my stomach, so I do some sucking in as I slide it down my torso. I wince slightly as it comes down my hips, forcing myself not to imagine how my awkward shuffling must look in Theo's eyes. But when I chance a look at his face, my eyes don't make it past the noticeable bulge in his boxer briefs.

My mouth lifts in a smirk of my own. Once the jumpsuit is off, his hands are on me, pulling me back down onto the bed. His body covers mine as he pins my wrists on either side of my head. He kisses down my neck again, then travels to the curve of my shoulder and my heaving chest. My hand tangles in his hair as I try to calm my breathing. One of his trails the space between the cups of my bra, his lips feather-light on the top of my cleavage.

"Front clasp," he notes, flashing teeth. He unhooks it with a quick flick of his wrist, my breasts filling his hands in no time. "God bless."

I let out an embarrassingly loud moan when his thumbs circle my peaked nipples. The motion sends hot signals straight to my core, desire pooling in my most sensitive places. My hands tug on his hair, and I'm rewarded with a sound of his own leaving his lips. I lift my knees up to his sides, inching myself closer. But he's too tall, and there are too many inches of space between our bodies for my liking.

I lose my train of thought when his tongue is added to the mix, circling one nipple before sucking. A shaky breath is dragged from my lungs, more of a pant than a moan. His other hand pinches my other nipple in time with his mouth, and this time I do moan. Loudly. And then again when his mouth replaces his hand. Perfect, head-spinning symmetry. Then his head moves lower, kisses trailing down my torso, until he rests between my spread legs.

"Condoms?"

"Nightstand. First drawer," I tell him, motioning my head to the left. He pulls open the drawer, retrieving the wrapped foil. My brows crease when he sets it down on the bed beside me, but when his hand dips low inside my panties, I let out another involuntary moan.

"Shit, babe." His voice is raspy, lips hovering just below my ear. "I thought it was gonna take you longer to get this wet."

I don't say a word, because I'm physically incapable of speaking. His fingers work in slow circles over my clit, teasing in the most excruciating way possible. My next groan is one of utter sexual frustration. His hand either needs to go faster, or I need *him* inside me for this ache to ease. He lets out a chuckle, as if torturing me amuses him.

"Theo," I breathe as his fingers work faster, but not nearly as fast as I need him. "God, you're such a tease."

He lets out a breathy laugh at that, leaning down to kiss me. His tongue slides against mine before immediately dipping out and leaving me high and dry. I let out another frustrated groan, burying my face in the pillow to resist a full-blown scream. He only laughs harder at my suffering.

"So needy, Marcela," he chides. "What am I gonna do with you?"

"Fuck me so hard I forget my own name and yours, I hope."

I had no idea I could be so crass, but until now, I never knew I could be this sexually frustrated, either.

"I must not be doing this properly if you're still capable of complete sentences," he says, and it's my turn to laugh this time. His hand leaves my center, dragging my soaking panties down my legs until they're completely off. He eases himself between my spread legs, his body inching down until his face is *right there*, and every muscle in my body coils with wild anticipation.

Is he going to…?

"Let's rectify that, shall we?"

"Oh god!" The words leave my mouth of their own accord when he kisses the folds of my pussy, spreading them open with his tongue. Another flick of his tongue, and I'm seeing stars. I close my eyes, the image of him between my legs too much to bear. But he's not going to let me off the hook that easy.

"Open your eyes, Marcela."

I do, and it's too much. His smirk is cocky, eyes shining with mischief as he licks up my clit, holding my gaze. I moan again, rocking my hips into his face for more. Good god, when did I become this person? It's embarrassing how much I need this. He reaches up to hold my hips in place, his tongue working in fast circles right where I'm aching for him most. My hands clutch at the sheets for purchase, knuckles turning white until the orgasm crashes over me, leaving me shaking.

I doubt I'll ever be able to look him in the face properly again. My bones are liquefied. My limbs have turned to jelly, and I'm quite sure my body temperature will never regulate with him around. And we haven't even had sex yet.

But that's about to change—*thank god*—very soon. He reaches for the condom beside my head, ripping through the foil and covering himself in one smooth motion. "Are you comfortable like this? I don't wanna smother you."

I feel as though he might in this position, but I've also never been confident in my body enough to be on top. He's made it clear, in no uncertain terms, that he wants me, and not despite or because of my size. Ever since we started this whole arrangement, he's made me feel desired in a way I never have before. As if sensing my hesitation, he adds, "We can just try it out. If you're uncomfortable in any way, we'll stop."

Maybe it's the softness of his eyes or the caring in his expression, but I nod. He rolls us over until I'm on top of him, and he helps guide our bodies together. Once I settle over him, I let out a moan at the feel of him. I didn't think I'd be able to start up again so soon, but the new position allows for more control, to feel him more deeply inside me. My hands settle on his hips as I sink myself down, painstakingly slow, until we're both wincing.

Slowly, I begin to move my hips up and down. He lets out a groan, hands gripping my ass to help my movements quicken. *Oh god*, the friction is almost enough to drive me over the edge, but his hand reaches down to circle my clit in fast, unforgiving movements.

I can't take it. The orgasm hits fast and hard, my shaking legs unable to hold me upright anymore. His hand settles at the small of my back to roll us over, and Theo takes control. He uses his elbow to hold himself up so he's not completely crushing me, and his hips resume movement. Did I...there's no way I could've possibly finished before him. Did I just have my first multiple orgasm moment?

I'm still reeling from this revelation when the pressure starts to build all over again. My hands grip his shoulders, nails digging into the tender flesh. He lets out a hiss, but I can't tell if it's from pleasure or pain. Then I look up at his face as his body starts to shake, as his eyes roll to the back of his head. *Definitely pleasure.* But even though he just finished, he also started something again I'm aching to complete.

"Tell me what you want, Marcela." I shiver at his lips on my ear, his hot breath on my skin awakening my senses. Maybe he felt me squirming against him, but however he can tell without me having to say, I'm grateful. "My hand or my mouth again?"

"Let's see if your hand can redeem itself," I say, because I'm not sure I can take the sight of his head between my legs twice in one night. He complies, pulling out of me as his fingers find my clit.

I'm right at the edge when his voice is in my ear again. "I love watching you come apart."

"Yeah?" I've never heard my voice this ragged before.

"*Yes.*" His hand works faster. "God, Marcela. How has no one snatched you up yet?" His breathing is heavy, voice shaky. "How are you all mine?"

I freeze up. The question douses me in ice water until I'm close to drowning.

How has no one snatched you up yet?

Ben's face is branded in my mind, and then behind my eyelids as I squeeze my eyes shut. Those warm hazel eyes, that shy smile reserved for me. And then, the face morphs into one that's become even more familiar to me. Hazel to dark blue, shy to devilish. Strong jaw, ash blond hair, until it's Theo's face I can't shake from my mind.

How are you all mine?

"Marcela?" His voice is a question, and it's only now that I notice he's stopped moving. My eyes flutter open, his face filling my vision. Closer than I remember. "Are you okay?"

"Sorry." I start to sit up. "I just got caught up in my thoughts."

"Don't apologize," he says, shifting away to give me room to breathe. "Do you…wanna talk about it?"

"What?" I croak.

"What you were thinking about," he clarifies. "Do you wanna talk about it?"

I shake my head.

"Okay," he says. I turn the word over in my head for traces of emotion. Is he mad? Is he disappointed?

"Do you want me to leave?"

I hesitate a beat, and then I shake my head again. His chest falls as he exhales, like he was holding his breath. "I want you to stay," I say, not sure if I'm being fair to him. Not when I just realized something that might change things between us from here on.

"Good." He pulls me into his arms and runs a hand through my hair. I close my eyes, lulled by the soothing strokes as his fingers work through my curls. "I'm not going anywhere."

He throws the wrinkled duvet over our bodies. My head rests in the crook of his shoulder. I count his breaths in my head, marking the times his chest rises and falls beneath my hand. Children count sheep. Adults count their lover's breathing. One…two…three…

How are you all mine?

How, indeed.

Nineteen

The next morning, I wake up to an odd sound. I rub my bleary eyes and try to sit up, but I am prevented from doing so by the cage of Theo's arms. I turn over to face him, but his eyes are still closed, his chest rising and falling with slow breaths. My lips turn up of their own accord, and a swell of happiness fills my chest just from looking at him. But it's edged with something else, a bitterness that makes me ache for more time. To rewire the clock above our heads like a cheat and ensure that this—*we*—never expire.

That's not the way I should feel about a rebound.

I stare at him until his eyes blink open, hazy from sleep.

"Morning," he says, voice raspy, mouth lifting into a soft smile. He pulls me in until my head rests against his chest, right below his shoulder.

"Morning, sleepyhead," I say.

"How'd you sleep?" His arms tighten around my body, pulling me flush against his. There's a tentative quality to his voice, and at first, I'm not sure where it's coming from. Then I remember how we left off last night, and the awkward tension that surrounded us.

How has no one snatched you up yet? Because you see, I've been in love with your brother for nearly a decade.

No, that definitely wouldn't go over well.

His body is warm, and I'm dimly aware of the fact that we're both still very much naked. It's too late for more boundaries, but now I'm wondering if we should've set more clear-cut ones. No sleepovers, no cuddling, no anything that will attach us like superglue, that will rip us both down the middle once this rebound ends.

"Good," I lie. Truth is, I hardly slept from all the thoughts reeling in my head. I kept thinking back on what he said at Whataburger, about not being able to promise that he'll never develop feelings for me. *All I can promise is to always be honest with you*, he'd said. I only wish I could promise the same. Or that the person I'm still pining over isn't his brother.

I snap out of my thoughts from the sound of creaking floorboards outside. I turn my head before remembering what woke me. It was the creak of the front door opening.

Shit. Angela.

I sit up suddenly as I hear her voice, and then I remember what day it is. Sunday mornings are when we walk the Leon Valley trail together. She must've used her spare key to come in. *Double shit.*

"Who is—" Theo starts to ask when I cut him off.

"You have to go." I'm about to jump off the bed in search of our clothes discarded on the floor, but before I can, the door bursts open as Angela walks in. Her eyes bug out of her skull. She lets out a shocked squeal, hazel eyes bulging as she covers her mouth with two hands before darting back out the door just as quickly.

I cover my face with a hand, as if that'll hide my mortification. Theo remains unfazed, resting his chin on my bare shoulder. "You think she likes me?"

I have absolutely no answer to that.

"I *knew it*!"

How Angela can jog and talk at the same time, I will never know. My breaths come out in huffs as we crest the top of the hill. I have to put my hands on my hips to keep my torso upright because the second I bend over, I'm done for. But Angela, energized by this new revelation, shows no signs of slowing down.

It was hard to miss the way her eyes followed Theo's every move when we met her in the living room after rushing to get dressed. I all but shoved him out the door before either of them could say a word. Still, that didn't stop her eyes from sparkling knowingly when he kissed the side of my forehead before he left.

"I *knew* you guys were hooking up." She has the audacity to look proud of herself. Until we lock eyes, that is. "But what I don't get is why you kept it from me for so long."

"We weren't," I say, which is only technically true if you don't count making out as hooking up. "Last night was the first time anything happened." This is a more blatant lie, and one she sees through right away. Her brow raises expectantly as she waits for me to cough up the truth. "Okay, *fine*. Last night was the first time we had sex. We did other stuff the morning after we got drinks together, and then again every time we met up after."

"'Other stuff' as in what, exactly?" she asks. When I don't respond, she lets out a dramatic sigh and says, "Okay, fine. You're not the only one with a secret. Confession time? I can go first."

I tilt my head at her, interest piqued. When I nod, she says, "All right, I'm turning around."

Sometimes it's easier to admit what we'd rather ignore with our backs turned, without the pressure of another face staring right at you. Angela turns her back until it touches mine. I grab both her hands and lead her down the path.

"So, you know how I give stellar relationship advice despite the fact that I've never really dated?"

"Oh, you mean like the advice you gave me to rebound from Ben?"

"Bad example from an even worse listener." I scoff, but she has the gall to chuckle. "Anyway, I think I finally realized why I've been ambivalent for so long about dating." A whoosh of air sounds as she takes in a deep breath. "I'm asexual."

"Okay." I'm careful to keep my reaction neutral as we continue up the path. "What made you realize this?"

"Well, you're the only one who knows I've never been kissed." That was the first secret Angela ever told me. She confessed after finding out I still had feelings for Ben in order to make me feel better. *You keep my secret and I'll keep yours*, she'd said afterward.

She puts up a good cover when she needs to, but she's always feared that people would find out and judge her for it.

"My cousins have always said I'm too picky for my own good. And for a long time, I believed them. That's the only logical explanation for why no one seems to be good enough for me, right? Why I reject literally every guy who asks me out? But..." She takes another deep breath. "The truth is, I could never quite picture myself being with them. Intimately, I mean. I went on one date the summer after high school and *freaked out* when the guy tried to kiss me. I had no idea why, and to say he didn't take it well was an understatement." My heart hurts for her at that admission. She never told me about that. "It's like, I never realized I didn't want to kiss him until his face was centimeters from mine. But when I tried explaining that to him, it only made things worse."

"Oh, Angela."

"It's not like I don't want to date anyone, or fall in love one day. I want that so much I ache, sometimes. But I think I've been holding myself back from dating because I always believed sex and love were intrinsically tied. Now that I know they don't have to be, everything's been clicking into place for me. Ever since I read *Loveless*, I finally have an explanation for all this stuff. I have an identity."

The purple book on her desk weeks ago immediately pops into my mind.

"That probably explains why you never believe anyone who tells you you're a good flirt, either." I'm smiling so big, I hate that she can't see it. "And who says books don't have the power to change lives?"

"No one literate." Angela chuckles, gripping my hands so tight. "I'm still sort of figuring out what exactly my identity is. I don't think I'm romantically attracted to men at all, which would explain why I freaked out the first time a guy tried to kiss me. I might've been more amenable if—"

"If it had been Krystal of the 'beautiful face' variety trying to kiss you?"

She lets out a groan as the back of her head falls on my shoulder.

"I'll never tell. Now it's your turn." She lets go of one of my hands to walk beside me, still holding on to the other.

I nod, even as my heart starts beating faster.

We've both been keeping secrets from each other, and that can't do. She's been there for me through everything. Even though I fear I'm making one mistake after another, I know she'll never judge me as harshly as I'm judging myself.

"Why didn't you tell me about Theo?"

I'm not completely sure, to be honest. I keep so many truths from so many people. But most of all, the person I lie to the most is myself. There's this image inside my head of the person I wish I was, and then there's *me*. The one in love with an engaged man and fucking his brother to cope.

I don't keep secrets from Angela because I don't trust her. Hell, with my host of trust issues she's probably the person I trust more than anyone else in my life. *I'm* the problem here. I hesitated to tell Ben I didn't want to be just friends until it was too late. I refused to tell anyone I still had those feelings because I was scared of their judgment. And now, because Angela is the only one who knows the truth about what happened at the engagement party, I didn't tell her when Theo and I started hooking up because she's the only one who knows I'm still hung up on his brother.

I don't want her to know what a mess I've become. No matter how much I trust her, I didn't want her to see how low I could sink.

"I have no idea what I'm doing." Tears sting my eyes suddenly. "I thought Ben was the bulk of my problems. But then, I tried to get over him…by hooking up with his *brother*." I shake my head. "What the hell kind of a person does that?"

"You got caught between siblings. I can't say it's happened to anyone not starring in a CW show, but I also can't say I'm surprised." I bark out a sardonic laugh, a humorless sound. "Do you like him?" she asks suddenly. "Theo?"

"We're friends." She keeps staring at me, as if expecting something more. "What?"

"I've seen you guys together." She shakes her head. "I don't buy it."

I don't have anything good to say to that.

We take a break at a nearby bench overlooking the hilly terrain. My feet settle in a crumpled leaf pile, kicking them to the side as I sit down. The trees are only just beginning to change color in late October, from vibrant reds to a range of orange and yellow and brown. It doesn't start cooling down in Texas until this time of year, and our surroundings reflect that. A late autumn blooms as the rest of the country is already starting to get snow.

Angela's expression turns contemplative suddenly, and when I ask her what's wrong she says, "I've been debating if I should tell you this or not, because I thought it'd just make things worse for you. But since you and Theo are actually hooking up now…" She trails off.

"What?" I ask her. "What's going on?"

"Ben keeps asking me about you," she says. "At first, I didn't listen when he said he was worried about you being with his brother, but then…" She blows out a breath between her teeth. *Oh no.* Angela has never been a big fan of Ben's, even before he started going out with Alice and she found out about my feelings. Alice got so sick of their constant bickering that she sat us all down and had them hash it out in front of everyone. Even though Angela was undeterred by the entire thing, she didn't have much to say other than she didn't "vibe well" with Ben.

But she's always stood firm against him, which is why I'm surprised she looks so torn now.

"He's worried Theo is using you to get back at him," Angela finally says. "And considering he still has feelings for Alice, it's not a far-fetched theory."

"'Using me' how?" I ask. "We're rebounds. We both knew we were into other people when we started this."

"This seemed different." She shakes her head. "Does Theo know you used to date Ben? He made it sound like Theo knew he could get back at him by dating you. Because of your history." *Because of our history?* Is Ben actually saying what I think he is? But then, Angela bursts that thought by saying, "He's convinced Theo's going to hurt you on purpose. I'd think he was acting like a jealous ex, if he wasn't engaged to Alice. That's how much he's been calling me."

I wince, not expecting that *at all*. "He's been calling you?"

"And texting," she adds. "It could just be that he's trying to get inside my head, but I can't risk you getting hurt over something I could've warned you about."

I take a sip from my water bottle so I don't have to respond right away. Is there more that Theo's been keeping from me? I thought we'd settled everything on his end last night.

"I haven't told him about Ben," I say. "If Theo knows, it's not because I told him. But Ben knew how he felt about Alice before they got together."

"Wait, *what*?"

"Yeah." I nod. "He knew all along and went after her anyway. That would give Theo a reason to get back at him. Alice basically admitted she's the reason they stopped talking to each other for so long. And she told me she's been trying to change that, ever since she moved in with Ben. She feels guilty for tearing them apart."

"Does Theo seem like he wants to make amends with Ben?"

Theo came to town to blow up their engagement. Every time he interacts with his brother, it ends in simmering tension or a complete blow up. He didn't talk to me for over a week when I told him about the double date and admitted later his brother was the reason. Not Alice.

"No." I shake my head finally. "No, it doesn't seem like that's what he wants." To be fair, it doesn't seem like Ben wants to work on their relationship either.

"Look, I don't know who to trust here," Angela says. "You

know both of them better than I do, so I guess it comes down to who you trust more. Ben or Theo?"

A month ago, this would've been the easiest question to answer. I would've stood by Ben a hundred percent. Now I have no idea who to believe between the two of them.

"If Theo doesn't want to make amends, do you think he wants…something else?" Angela asks carefully. "Do you think he's beyond getting back at Ben for hurting him?"

"I…I don't know." Theo's image comes to mind. Those wide blue eyes. His kind smile. His promise to always be honest with me. It's hard to imagine him ever doing something so malicious on purpose. *To me.*

"Well, maybe you should think about it," Angela says. "Think of all the warnings you've gotten about him. Even Alice was worried about your relationship. What if there's more to him than we think? And you just can't see it because he's told you enough of the truth to mask his true motivation?"

I frown, considering her point from all angles, but it just doesn't make sense. He always seems so open around me, so earnest in his intentions.

All I can promise is to always be honest with you.

Could that really have been a lie? Has hooking up with him clouded my judgment?

"I've gotta go," I say suddenly.

"Be careful," Angela tells me. I've lost count of how many times people have told me this exact same thing about Theo. "And don't keep any more secrets from me."

Twenty

haven't been on my phone at work this much since…never, maybe.

While Theo is in the process of decorating his new apartment, it doesn't leave us a whole lot of time to meet up during the week. To make up for it, we've been texting nonstop. I'm smiling at the message under the picture Theo just sent me of his newly set up bedroom. The bed is centered against the wall, the morning light distilled against his navy-blue comforter, nearly the same shade as his eyes. A black nightstand sits beside it.

> **Theo:** We have a new bed to christen 😊
>
> **Me:** 🏃‍♀️🏃‍♀️🏃‍♀️
> **Me:** Hurry up already so I can see you!
>
> **Theo:** Patience, woman. Everything needs to be perfect before you can visit.

Me: Perfect schmerfect. I miss you

I stare down at the message before sending it. We're long past boundaries, but something about telling him I miss him, even if it is via text message, doesn't quite sit right. Like I'm showing him a side I haven't allowed him to see yet. *Be careful.* Angela's warning comes unbidden, but I fear it's far too late for that now.

I shake my head. I'm just being paranoid. There's no way Theo can possibly be that guy. And besides, it's perfectly fine to miss someone in a friendly way, and that's all this is. *Friendly.*

"Your cheeks are red."

Andy is standing over me from the other side of the circulation desk, a stack of YA books under one arm. I quickly throw my phone inside a drawer and motion for her to hand me the pile. "I have no idea what you're talking about."

"Were you texting your boyfriend?" Her brown eyes are sparkling mischief. "Did he send you something *dirty?*"

The photo of his new bed immediately pops into my brain.

"Fourteen." I shake my head as she hands me her library card. "You are *fourteen.* Do I need to have another conversation with your mother?"

"No, ma'am." She immediately shrinks. A smug smile tugs my lips up. "Does he make you happy?"

Her expression is sheepish, but there's no hiding the hope shining in her eyes. The question is a simple one, but it twists up my insides until I can barely breathe.

"Yeah." The admission makes me queasy, but I owe her

the truth. I owe *myself* the truth, even if it won't be true for very long. "He makes me happy."

A grin takes up her entire face.

"None of my boyfriends ever made me look like *that* just thinking about them, Miss Ortiz." I resist an eye roll, though I doubt she'd even register it. "You gonna tell him?"

"Shut up and read your books."

"You should tell him." She smiles cheerily. "Live that happily ever after we love to read about so much in books."

I don't have the energy for Ben right now, especially since it's past ten at night, and I'm settling down for bed. But that doesn't stop him from sapping it from me.

Are you avoiding me?

The message comes via Instagram DM after I left four of his most recently sent memes on read. I'm three episodes behind on *The Undoing* and don't have the motivation to catch up, so the memes are gibberish to me. Leaving him on read was just me being petty for the way he treated Theo on our double date. Yes, I am avoiding him as a matter of fact. Though I am surprised he noticed in less than a week.

I leave him on read again, and he must decide our friendship is in need of damage control because thirty minutes later, my phone lights up with his picture. It's a selfie of the two of us from a few years ago at the Austin City Limits

GABRIELLA GAMEZ

Music Festival. His arm is thrown around my shoulders, our cheeks almost touching as we smile into the camera. It's my favorite picture of us, but now I'm mortified that I kept it as his contact photo for so long. We look so much like a couple, my stomach bottoms out just staring at it. At...*us*.

Before I can pick up the call the screen goes black, plunging my bedroom in darkness. *Tomorrow*. I'll deal with him tomorrow.

The next morning, I wake up to a knock on my door. I flip over my phone for the time. It's not even nine yet. A knock sounds again, and I groan as I lift myself up from the bed. My warm, comfortable bed that I already miss as I throw on a robe and pad down the hallway.

I almost expect Theo to be behind the door, surprising me with coffee and breakfast on my morning off. But he told me yesterday he'd be spending a majority of the week unpacking and buying furniture. He turned down multiple offers to help, reasoning that he's asked too much of me already. I know he was trying to be a gentleman, but it's been a couple days since I've seen him and I...I'm starting to ache from missing him. Way more than I should miss a rebound.

It could be Angela at the door, perhaps, since she still has an hour before she's scheduled to go into work. But she would've texted first after the fiasco of catching me in bed with Theo last Sunday. In the end, it's neither one of them.

It's Ben.

My entire body deflates at the sight of him, probably for the first time. It's not that I'm suddenly not attracted to him anymore. No, he still looks good, with his light brown hair swept back from his face and a hand buried in the pocket of his light-wash jeans. His hazel eyes are downcast, and I breathe a quiet sigh of relief that I'm not immediately pulled into them. I've forgiven far too many mistakes looking deep into those light brown eyes flecked with green. He's carrying a carton of Starbucks drinks in his other hand, held out in front of his body like an offering.

"What's all this?"

"A peace offering. Can I come in?" Finally, I'm met with those eyes in danger of blinding me to reality.

I let him pass through the threshold, if only because the caramel macchiato he brought smells heavenly. Even after the shit he pulled at dinner, I'd be a fool to turn away free coffee, right?

He hands me the paper cup, and I take a careful sip of the hot beverage. Then he takes a seat at my couch, and I flick on the lights so he's not cast in the gray light dimly filtered through the darkening clouds outside my window. If it rains, I could spend my day reading through the new stack of books I brought home from work.

After Ben leaves, that is.

"I'm sorry about the double date. You were right. I was a dick," he says when I take a seat next to him. "I just hate seeing you with my brother."

A few weeks ago, I would've reveled in this admission. His words would've played in my head for days after, over and over, my heart full and my head drunk on those sweet, nothing words. Because that's what they are, ultimately. *Nothing.* And now my first thought is Alice. How could he say something like that to me, when he's with someone else? How *dare* he put the idea of jealousy in my head when he knows good and well he doesn't mean it. He wouldn't be with someone else if he did.

"You shouldn't say things like that." I don't register the anger creeping up on me until after I've spoken. My tone is hard-edged, sharp enough to cut.

He has the good grace to look chastened, placing a hand on the back of his neck as he looks down at his shoes.

"You know I'm only trying to look out for you, right?" he asks quietly. "You're my best friend, Marcela. I feel like I'm losing you."

Guilt settles like a stone in the pit of my stomach. Maybe I was naive to think a rebound with Theo would help me stay friends with Ben in the long run. It only drove an even deeper wedge between us, but if Ben's behavior has shown me anything, it's one that was needed.

"I wanted to tell you sooner, but Alice convinced me not to." He shakes his head, scoffing to himself. "I don't know why I listened to her. You needed to know the truth."

"As much as I appreciate you looking out for me, it's not necessary," I tell him. "He already told me everything."

"You knew?" His brows crease in confusion. "And you're still…" He shakes his head at me. "*Why?*" There's so much accusation laced in that one tiny word.

"He's been open with me from the very beginning."

"You deserve so much better than what he can give you. I don't understand how you can't see that." I have to look away from the concern brimming his eyes.

"We're not serious." But that doesn't feel true anymore.

The longer we go through with this, the more time we spend together, the easier it is to pretend we could actually be something real. Even when I should know better.

"Come on, Marcela." His hand falls on my shoulder. "You know he's just going to end up hurting you if you keep this up."

It makes sense why he believes what he's saying. He knew what I knew about his brother all along. Of all the red flags real and imagined in the men I've dated previously, Theo's is probably the worst offense. But so is mine, and he doesn't even know about my feelings for Ben. I knew what I was walking into when we started this. He didn't.

Ben has a point, though. What Theo and I have won't end well, for either of us.

But I'm also not giving in so easily this time.

"Look, Ben." Our eyes meet. "I get that you have your own stuff with Theo. I even understand that you think you're coming from a protective place, but you need to respect my choices, even if you think they're the wrong ones. You don't get to tell me who to date. So, you either have to be cool with my relationship, or…"

"Or what?" There's something dangerous lacing his tone. I don't answer, because I'm not sure I'm ready to lay such a huge ultimatum on him. He belongs to Alice. I don't have a right to put this on him. *Or we stop being friends.*

But at this point, would that be so terrible? What good are we to each other when I can hardly stand to be around him without pushing a host of feelings down deep?

"Or what, Marcela?" His eyes narrow on me.

My mouth opens, but I can't say the words. Not yet. Not when I've only just realized what I should have done a long time ago. If I have half a chance of moving on from him for good, I can't keep spending all my spare moments with him. Thinking about him. Wishing our lives had turned out differently. I won't allow myself to waste any more time appeasing him or following my own damned feelings for him.

When my father left, the greatest lesson to come out of it was to love the person who stays. Even though I was crushed when Ben broke up with me all those years ago, he still stayed. He said I was too important to leave behind, and in nine years, he became one of the most important fixtures in my life. He wanted to stay, and I didn't want him to leave. Even if we couldn't be together the way I wanted us to be.

But what good has his staying done for me, if for nearly a decade, I've been stuck in the same place he left me, waiting for him to change his mind? I should never have held on to the secret hope that when he said *no guy is good enough for you*, he really meant *I've finally realized I'm the only one for you*.

Like that was ever gonna happen.

"Maybe we need some space from each other," I finally work up the nerve to say.

The anger fades from his expression. His brows smooth out and then raise into his hairline, eyes wide as saucers. His mouth falls open in shock. He blinks once. Twice.

"My relationship with Theo is clearly a problem for you," I say. "I understand you think you're only looking out for me, I do, but it's like you don't trust that I know what's best for me. I know the risks. I walked into this...relationship willingly." I slip over the word *relationship*. "So, until you can find it in yourself to be supportive, I think we need to take a break from each other."

He's silent for a long time, eyes shifting away from me. I'm a second away from asking him to leave when he says, "You're really choosing him over me?" His voice is so small, tentative in a way I haven't heard it in years.

"No," I say, already hating how easily I'm giving in. "Ben, I just—"

"Need space." His voice goes hard all of a sudden, a wall closing over his features. "Yeah, I got it."

I take a breath and hold it. "Please try to understand where I'm coming from. I'm just trying to have a normal relationship with—"

"You're deluded if you think what you have with my brother is a relationship." His response knocks the wind out of me. He's closer to the truth than he realizes. But his tone calls up the anger building in my gut, and it takes everything I have to hold on to it. I won't be able to get through this if I don't.

"Okay, if you're gonna be like this we might as well call it now." Something in my voice makes him look up. I cross the room to the front door, whipping it open so hard it bangs against the wall with a loud *crash*. I cross my arms over my chest, eyes pinned on Ben. His eyes widen again in that deer-in-the-headlights way.

"Go on," I say, not buying his expression for a second. "You don't want to support me? The person you've called a friend for nearly ten years? Get out."

"Of course I support you." His voice is softer as he crosses the living room to me. He reaches for my hands, but I step away from him. "You're right. Of course, you're absolutely right. I haven't been supporting you the way I should be, but it's only because I don't want to see you get hurt. Not when he's just using you."

Angela said something similar just a few days ago. "I know what we are, Ben. You don't." But I still have the strangest feeling I don't know everything. There's still something missing.

"Maybe you do. Or at least, maybe you know more than I think," he says. "But what scares me is that he's only using you to get back at me."

"Get back at you for what?"

It can't just be Alice.

He takes in a breath. Exhales. "We were shitty brothers to each other. I know that. He knows that. There are things I did that I'm not proud of." He looks away from me. "The point is, he knows how much I care about you. He knows what turning you against me would do to me. And look at us"—he raises a hand at the space between us—"it's working."

I'm not sure how much is truth and how much is manipulation. Theo isn't the reason I'm pushing Ben away. It's something I should've done a long time ago.

"I need time."

"How much?" he asks, resigned.

"I don't know." I let out a breath. "But I'll let you know when I'm ready to talk to you again."

He nods. Rakes his brown hair back from his face. "Okay. Just please don't make me wait forever for you. I will, but don't make me." His mouth lifts in a sad smile. Something about his phrasing strikes a chord with me.

Don't make me wait forever for you.

Isn't that what I've been doing since the moment we broke up?

"I can't lose you, Marcela," he says, and I melt all over again. "I can't."

My smile is tired, and probably a bit hollow. When his arms wrap around me, I can't help but sink into his familiar warmth. That love for him is still inside me, but it's dimmer than I remember. There's still a pull between us, one I've tried to convince myself is only in my head. Or something friendly I confuse for romantic.

His chest brushes against mine, his hand closing over mine for one brief moment. One brief, supercharged moment where our eyes meet and lock. His lips part slightly as his eyes flick down to mine.

What the hell is happening?

A surge of energy floods my veins when his head bends closer to mine. My heart thumps wildly beneath my rib cage as I snatch my hand back and take two quick, leaping steps backward. It isn't until I've escaped his range that I'm able to breathe properly again.

"Sorry," I blurt, though I'm not entirely sure what I'm apologizing for. Or that I'm even interpreting what happened correctly. What would've happened if I hadn't…

"Go ahead." Awkwardly, I motion him toward the open door.

He hangs his head, unable to meet my eyes. I can't quite make myself meet his, either. He leaves with a rushed goodbye. When I close the door behind him, I'm more confused than ever.

What the hell was *that*?

Twenty-One

Ben just tried to kiss me.

I think.

And I can't sleep, turning over the moment in my head, analyzing it from all angles. I toss and turn, hitting the pillows with my fist as if that'll help knock out the stupid thought from my brain. He wouldn't do that. Not when he's with Alice. Besides, he's the one who said we were better off as friends and has never once given any indication that he's changed his mind. He wouldn't try to kiss me.

But if he did…

If he really did try to kiss me, well, isn't that what I've always wanted? For him to show some kind of interest? I thought I would've jumped at the chance if it ever arrived. Lord knows I've fantasized about it enough times to lose count.

Sometimes in my fantasies we kissed after he announced he was leaving Alice. Because he realized I was the only one for him. I'd admit that I never really got over him either, and he'd interrupt me midsentence to plant his mouth on mine. I'd kiss him back until desire pooled low in my belly and made me dizzy with want. Other times the moment would sneak up on us, like it did today. All it would take is one longing look before he crossed the room in quick strides and closed his mouth over mine.

But instead of reliving my fantasy, I jumped away. I stepped out of his range, stuttering like a tongue-tied fool and apologized over nothing. *Absolutely nothing.* He *totally* tried to kiss me, and I backed away from him. Because I didn't want to kiss him.

I didn't want to kiss him.

This is monumental progress, isn't it? Even if that wasn't what he was doing, it's what I *thought* he was. And I did the right thing, not for any sort of moral reason but because he isn't—

The new, sudden realization hits me with the force of a brick wall. *Theo.* I didn't want to kiss him because he isn't Theo, the only person I *want* to kiss. I blow out a breath between my teeth.

What have I done?

When Theo's apartment is finally perfected to his standards, he texts asking if I want to come over on Saturday to see it.

I haven't told him about the conversation I had with Ben, and I'm not sure if I should. There are so many things I want to ask him, like what Ben meant when he said Theo was only with me to get back at him. But I can't think of a good way to broach the subject with Theo without revealing my feelings for his brother.

They're not nearly as strong as they were before Theo and I became rebounds. Clearly, since I jumped away from Ben the first time he tried to kiss me since we broke up. But I'm not sure if it's enough. I could still backslide, if I'm not careful.

It's dishonest that I've kept this secret from him for so long, but I figure if none of this is real, then it doesn't matter. Theo and I aren't really dating, so he doesn't need to know that Ben is the reason I need a rebound. But the longer we keep hooking up, the less convinced I am that that's true.

Theo's apartment building is tucked away beside a tall oak tree with changing-colored leaves. I'm wearing a thick black turtleneck and skinny jeans tucked into combat boots. The weather has finally cooled to a chilly forty degrees, and my severely underused winter wardrobe couldn't be happier.

On my way over, I stopped by Target for an assortment of cookies as a housewarming present. I carry the bag with me as I walk up to his apartment, but before I have the chance to knock, I freeze at the sudden sound of raised voices.

"*I don't care!*" I immediately recognize the deep baritone as Theo's voice. "I don't insert myself into whatever weird, codependent relationship you have with her. And I *surely* don't try to convince Alice she's making the biggest mistake of her life by marrying you, so you don't have a right to—"

My lungs stop working. I don't hear the rest of what Theo says, or Ben's reply, because Theo's words stick in my brain.

Biggest mistake of her life. Does he really love her that much to believe that? I try to take in a shaky breath, but I don't quite manage it. Not even when I try a second time.

He doesn't owe you anything, I try to remind myself. But the words are a gut punch. A much-needed wake-up call to the reality of what it is we're doing.

"…just doing this to get back at me!" I catch the tail end of Ben's yelled reply. "She doesn't deserve to get dragged into our mess! Whatever you have to say to me, just go ahead and say it."

"Fine. You were wrong to go after Alice, and she was wrong to let you. You're gonna tie her down to this town, and she's going to resent you for it."

If he says anything else, I don't catch it. I'm so invested in eavesdropping that I flinch when the door flies open, a red-faced Ben emerging from the other side. The wind whips his hair back, a large vein bulging in the middle of his forehead visible from outer space.

"Ben, wait!"

I'm not sure why I bother calling out to him. It's almost a reflex at this point to make sure he's okay. When he turns around, he doesn't even seem surprised at my presence.

"I'm done. You can do whatever you want, okay? You wanna let him destroy your life? Fine. Just don't come crying to me in the fallout." And with that, he escapes into his car and peels out of the parking lot. I watch as he leaves, hollow and useless.

Theo's eyes are trained on my face when I turn around. His expression isn't welcoming in the slightest, blue eyes narrowed and mouth open slightly. His eyes bore into me, analyzing in a way that makes me antsy. I try to blink away the tears filling my eyes. How could this day have gone so wrong already?

My arms cross over my chest, a guard against the wind and Theo's penetrating gaze. He looks from me to Ben's car pulling out of the lot.

As if he's just realized something.

"It's him, isn't it?"

"Is what him?" I can't look him in the eyes. I try to hand him the gift in my hands, but he doesn't take it.

"The guy you're using me to get over." He lets out a scoff. "He told me you guys used to date in college. He's the ex you're trying to get over, right?"

I should be angry he's putting it that way—*the guy you're using me to get over*—like he's not doing the exact same thing to me, but all I feel is shame. My face heats despite the cutting, cold air, my whole body growing warm under his stare.

I knew about Alice from the very beginning. He promised he'd always be honest with me, and I kept the biggest secret from him. And this whole rebound relationship was my idea in the first place. Alice and I haven't been friends in years, but Ben is his *brother*. And they already have one girl between them.

His voice is as harsh as I've ever heard it as he continues. "I tried to ignore this feeling for weeks that there was something you weren't telling me about him. Something that felt like an awful lot more than friendship. But I ignored it." He makes a sound between a scoff and a humorless laugh. "I told myself it was nothing, and even if it wasn't nothing, that it wasn't any of my business. We all have our pasts."

"I guess they're not so past after all," I mumble, half hoping he can't hear me over the wind. I'm talking about myself as much as him, but I still can't get past what he told his brother. Still can't stop wondering if this arrangement of ours worked better on me than it did on him.

"Guess not," he says dryly, pointedly. His eyes have gone black, piercing me in a way they never have before. I'm reminded of the knowing glint in Alice's eye in our every encounter, only this is so much worse.

"I told you *everything*. I know it shouldn't hurt that you chose not to, since we're not..." He scrubs a hand down his face. "Look, I know what we are. But please, Marcela. Just tell me this much. Is he the guy?"

When I dare to face him again, I can't tell if he's more hurt or angry. Either way, I know one thing. There's no coming back from this. Once I tell him the truth, it's over. I wouldn't want anything to do with me, either.

"You're right," I say. "Ben's the guy, and I should have told you sooner."

He's the one who won't look at me now. "We all make quite the love square, don't we?"

I expect him to turn me away. Slam the door in my face and announce good riddance. Instead, he holds the door open and motions me inside. I don't move an inch, brows furrowed as I look between him and the front door, confused.

"What kind of person do you think I am?" He shakes his head, rubbing a hand down his face. "I'm *beyond* pissed at you for lying to me, but I'm not a saint, either." He takes in a giant breath, and when he speaks again, there's a measure of calm in his tone. "Come in. Let's talk about this."

I still don't move, eyes blurred again as I realize he's offering me the same grace I gave him the night of the engagement party. A hand comes up to cover my mouth. I choke down an incoming sob. I've spent so much time hiding my true feelings, the awful person I really am, but he's not turning me away. Is this how he felt when I discovered him about to confess everything to Alice? Like his whole life was unraveling at the seams?

He doesn't move from the door to comfort me, and part of me is grateful. I don't deserve his kindness. But another part of me desperately wants his arms wrapped around me like a cocoon of warmth I never have to leave.

"Marcela."

I walk past him through the door before he can finish, dropping my bags as I rush to find his bathroom. The first door I walk through is a hall closet, but I don't even care. I slide down the wall until my butt hits the floor and finally allow the sobs to rip through me.

Twenty-Two

Theo doesn't interrupt until the emotion has passed through my system, leaving me drained and exhausted. I spend a few silent minutes in the darkness before the door cracks open. He's standing over me in the sliver of golden light, taking in my puffy eyes and smeared mascara. I'm not ready to leave the closet, but I can't stay in here forever. With a resigned sigh, I force myself to stand.

"Don't hug me." His brows crease in question. "Don't try to comfort me in any way. I don't deserve it, and it'll just make me feel worse for everything I did. I lied to you, and it got between whatever tense relationship you and Ben already have. I'll answer any questions you have, and then if you never want to see me again, I'll understand."

His mouth sets in a frown. He shakes his head before completely ignoring everything I just said. He pulls me into his chest, holding me even tighter than his usual hugs. The tears threaten to come up all over again, but I'm crushed too far into his chest for them to fall. I hold on to him as tightly as I can, sudden and instant relief flooding through me in a way I can't begin to describe. We're not two people casually hooking up in this moment. We're two people who understand each other.

"Don't cry, Marce." He wipes the tears from my cheeks with his thumbs. "You think I don't get how you feel?"

Of course I don't think that. He's the only person who could possibly understand what I'm feeling right now. I wonder if he's berated himself as much as I have over the years. If he hated himself for attempting to break up his brother's relationship the same way I hate myself for keeping this big a secret from him.

I'm worse between the two of us, too concerned over what other people think of me to tell the truth for once in my life.

"I'm awful." My voice comes out choked. I try to look away from him, wipe away the fresh onset of tears, but a hand on my chin locks me in place.

"You're not awful." His fingers brush my hair away from my tear-stained face. "We're in the same boat. And it's gonna sink no matter who knows."

As odd an analogy as that is, it does just the trick. I let out a surprised laugh, and the side of his mouth quirks slightly in a sad smile. "Boy, do you have a point there," I say, wiping my nose of snot with the end of my sweater.

"Come over here." He takes my hand and leads me to his couch. "Do you want anything? Water, coffee..."

"Got anything harder?" I ask mostly as a joke, but when he shakes his head I can't help but be a little disappointed. "Shame. Guess I'll take coffee instead."

He starts a pot, and when he returns there's a hesitant look in his eyes. "Listen. I can't be mad at you for not trusting me, but can I ask why you didn't? I mean, I'm probably the last person you know who could possibly judge you for it."

"Trust had nothing to do with it," I say. "I didn't want you to think differently of me. I was thinking of myself more than I was thinking of you. It was stupid and selfish, and I'm sorry."

"I forgive you," he says, and that easy absolution does so much to relieve my conscience. Is it really that easy? "But I wouldn't say trust doesn't have anything to do with this."

"What do you mean?"

"I promised to be honest with you because I trust you." His eyes are steady on me. "Not because I expected the same from you, but because you held me accountable to do what was right without ever judging me for wanting the opposite."

And now I've broken his trust by lying to him. I shouldn't be sad to lose something I never knew I had in the first place, but it's another reminder of how I've disappointed him. If I really only saw him as a rebound, I wouldn't care, would I?

"I want you to trust me, Marcela." My heart slams in my chest, the sound filling my eardrums as I look at him. "Can you do that?"

"I don't know," I admit, and it's not just because of Angela's warning from last week, or Ben's reiteration. *He's just using you to get back at me.* I'm not sure who to believe anymore, but that's not what matters right now. That's not what's making my heart race unsteadily right now.

"That's fair"—he blows out a hard breath—"no matter

how much I hate hearing it. We knew what this was when it started. It doesn't leave much room for trust to be built."

The trouble is, there were so many times when I let my guard slip with him. When I let myself pretend what we were doing meant something. So many times I almost let myself trust him with everything, until reality pulled me back. Ten days of silence. Warnings from friends that never cease.

And I surely *don't try to convince Alice she's making the biggest mistake of her life by marrying you.*

I have no claim on him—no reason for all my long-buried abandonment issues to resurface. I have no right to be devasted by his opinion of Alice and Ben's relationship. But damn if it didn't cut me to the quick anyway. I was so stupid to believe this man wouldn't have an effect on me, that we'd both come out of this unscathed.

"It's probably not smart for us to trust each other, to be honest." I try to shrug, but I'm too tense. His sudden, thunderous expression isn't helping either.

"I wouldn't say that," he says quietly, but the intensity in his stare tells me he's holding back. He clears his throat. Rakes his hair back with a rough hand. Lets out a groan so loud, I nearly flinch off the couch. "God, I hate this."

"Not your average casual relationship, huh?" I chuckle to myself at the look of absolute outrage on his face. Then, more seriously, I say, "Listen, I don't know if trust is something I can promise. Not right away, at least. But I will promise to be honest with you from here on out."

He nods. "I'd like that."

"Okay." I take in a bracing deep breath. "The real reason

I kept this secret from you? It's the same reason I haven't told anyone. The only reason Angela knows is because she figured it out years ago. I don't like admitting it because it shouldn't be true," I explain. "I wish it wasn't. I wish I could control my own feelings and see Ben as nothing more than a friend. Not only because it would make things so much easier for everyone, but because I'm sick of being this person." Tears sting my eyes again at the confession I haven't even had the courage to tell anyone. Not even Angela.

"I'm not a good person. I lie all the time, every day, just to keep up with this image of the person I wish I was. I thought that I could still be friends with Ben despite my feelings for him, and that was a lie. I thought if I could get over him by hooking up with someone else, I could keep my friendship with him.

"But the reason I keep making up excuses to hold on to him, to keep him in my life is because I'm hoping one day, he'll…that he'll leave Alice for me or something. Which just sounds *incredibly* messed up now that I've said it out loud." I shake my head, even as a humorless laugh burbles from the back of my throat. "That's probably why I never have until now. And I can't tell him. I can't confess any of these feelings when he's engaged to someone else, but I can't keep pretending I'm okay with being just friends. I can't do it. Not when it chips away at me each day. When I have to make up new lies just to appease myself."

Theo doesn't say a word, letting me get out years' worth of baggage. "But if I've learned anything the last couple of weeks, it's that I can't…I can't be his friend anymore. It's not good for me, or for his relationship with Alice. I caught him lying to her once about where he was when he was with me. And it felt *good*." I shake my head, hating myself as soon as the words are out. "If I can feel that way about breaking up a relationship…"

"Then that makes me just as bad," he says. "You stopped me, remember? You easily could've let me do that exact same thing and reap any benefits that came with it. But you didn't. You're not nearly as bad a person as you think you are. I would know."

"How can you be so sure?" I ask him. "Maybe I picked you out of all the guys I could possibly rebound with because I knew it'd hurt your brother the most."

"And maybe I went along with it because I wanted to hurt him just as badly," he counters.

I sit up, assessing him as if seeing him for the first time.

"You hid something from me, too," I remind him, not accusingly. As far as the secrets we've kept from each other go, his have been far smaller than mine. "You didn't tell me they already knew."

"You're right." His chest rises with an inhale. "I didn't."

"Why didn't you tell me?" I ask him.

"Honestly? I didn't think I'd need to," he says. "Not until you told me about the double date. And then I didn't tell you because I didn't want you to think I was using you to prove something to them. That's not what this was about. Not at all."

At his admission, I know Angela and Ben are wrong. There was nothing purposeful in the way we came together.

We were just two lovesick fiends with feelings for people we shouldn't have, making the best and worst of a complicated situation.

"We could argue this in circles all night, because love is *weird*, and not at all like we're told it is. We're all capable of the worst depravities just to have a piece of it, but the point is we don't act on them. We don't let our bad sides win, no matter what we think we want. *That's* what being a good person means."

I nod, but I'm not entirely convinced yet. His hands cup my cheeks, forcing me to look up at him. "I don't care how this started, Marcela. If you used me first or I did, but what matters now is that we're moving on. I'm ready to walk away from Alice for good. The question now is"—he wipes my wet cheeks with his thumbs—"are you ready to walk away from Ben?"

I let in a shaky breath, holding it in my lungs. His eyes pierce into mine, questioning. When I nod, I try to muster all my energy into it. "I am." I so desperately want this to be true, but I can't tell if it's just another lie I'm telling myself. Just like all my other lies.

"Good." He nods with finality, looking down at me through half lidded eyes. "That's all I need to know."

He leans toward me, and our mouths collide in a kiss that wrenches at my core.

Theo kisses me hard enough to bruise, and I return the strength right back—hands tugging at his hair, nails digging into his scalp. His hand finds its way down my jeans, pulling my panties aside. I'm already wet, moaning into his mouth as his hand works fast circles against my clit. My hand makes its way down his jeans to his hard cock to return the favor.

There is no playful teasing or dirty talk as we shed the fabric separating us and pleasure each other. Only the sounds of our breathing and heavy pants, avoiding eye contact as we bring each other over the edge. I left the condoms at my place, so we have to come up with other ways to satisfy each other.

He's underneath me on the couch, my knees straddling him. My hand works up and down his length as my lips trail kisses down his neck. His hand reaches up to pull my hair, tugging in a way that would be painful if I wasn't so turned on. I watch his face as he comes undone, biting down on the inside of his hand to hold back his sounds. I kiss him as he comes, lips scorching against mine.

As soon as my hand leaves his jeans, he flips me over until my back hits the cushions. He hovers over me with a devilish glint in his black storm eyes, which are edged with just the hint of blue. Not one to be showed up, I bring the hand that was in his pants up to my mouth and lick my fingers.

He growls, pinning both my wrists over my head and kissing me again, scorching a path down my neck, to my collarbone. I suck in a breath, anticipating what's coming next. His tongue flicks over one nipple as his thumb plays with the other, twisting and circling. My hips rise of their own accord, aching to meet him. *Goddammit.* Why didn't I have the good sense to bring a condom with me?

His mouth closes over the peaked nipple, sucking as his hand pinches the other, causing my insides to jolt. I can't reach his lap to grind against from this position, and I'm in desperate need of more friction. My nails dig into the skin of his shoulders, hard enough to draw blood. But he doesn't make a sound as he switches sides, sucking the other nipple as his hand dips between my legs, anticipating my needs.

His kisses trail lower, down my soft stomach to the skin just above my pubic bone. He's done this before, but I'm aching for his tongue on my pussy all over again. It doesn't take long for him to sweep aside my panties and drive me wild all over again. I throw my head back, not caring about the sounds coming out of my mouth as his tongue delves into me. It also doesn't take long for an orgasm to crash over me in waves, my whole body shaking with the force of it.

I let out a satisfied sigh when we finish, resting in each other's arms. His hands play with my hair, his chin resting at the top of my head. Too many emotions swirl inside me, twisting until I can no longer make heads or tails of them. I shut my eyes, and the next sigh is borne of frustration.

Why did I ever think this was a good idea?

"Do you want to stay?" Theo asks, hands rubbing my bare shoulders in comforting strokes. "We can put a movie on Netflix and talk through the whole thing. That's our usual thing, right?" He lets out a nervous laugh when I don't respond right away. "Or we can not talk. Your choice, Marce."

"Um." I raise myself from his body. "I think I should probably go."

"Oh." He doesn't hide his disappointment, and it almost makes me want to change my mind. But he doesn't push me, just says, "Sure. Do you wanna hang out tomorrow?"

"Yeah." I nod, looking away from his eyes as I search for

my discarded clothes. Whatever rush of emotion this is, I need to untangle it on my own. "I'll call you."

"Marcela." He reaches for my wrist, pulling me back to him as he sits up on the couch. His hands cup my face, looking up at me. We're almost eye to eye this way, him sitting and me standing. "Talk to me. What's wrong?"

"I think I just need a moment. Too many emotions." My eyes shut tight as I shake my head, not believing I actually admitted that to him.

"I get it. You don't want to think about Ben," he says, and for a moment I'm unsure what to say. I wasn't even thinking about his brother, but I don't correct him. "Just please don't disappear on me. Okay?"

I tell him I won't, and he lets me get dressed. He goes into a room I don't recognize as I pull on my jeans and sweater, and I'm putting on my shoes when he comes back out in pajama bottoms and a faded Cowboys T-shirt.

"You sure you're okay?" he asks as we reach the front door, hands circling around my waist like he doesn't want me to go. I nod, but I don't even convince myself.

"I will be," I say instead, my hand cupping his cheek.

When we kiss goodbye, it's the most chaste of all our kisses. I don't know if my heart could take it if there was any trace of heat behind it. As it is, the longer we keep this up, the more confused I get about my own feelings. For him. For Ben. Everything I thought I knew twists and changes into something I never saw coming.

Theo. I never saw *him* coming.

Twenty-Three

The next day doesn't do much to help my confused, muddled thoughts. After our walk, I finally break down and tell Angela everything when we get back to my apartment. I kind of have to, after our last conversation.

"You think Ben's wrong?" she asks after I've caught her up on my conversation with him, conveniently leaving out our almost kiss. Or at least what I *thought* was an almost kiss. No need to tell her what I'm not even quite sure of myself. But she gives me a doubtful look now, and it almost makes me reconsider what I believed was true.

"You don't?"

"To be honest, I don't really know. I've yet to really talk to Theo. You've spent more time with him than I have, which is…your business," she adds slyly, her smirk just as sly. But it falls as she returns to the topic at hand. "I don't mean to take sides, but I'm not convinced."

"Okay. That's fair," I say. "What if you hung out with him? You can see for yourself and tell me what you think."

I'm breaking my own boundary rule by suggesting this. But I don't like that she seems hesitant about Theo's intentions. If she hung out with him, she'd change her mind. The same way he keeps changing my mind about Ben.

I'm treading on dangerous territory, but I need my best friend to like him. But if I examine the why of it, I'll lose my nerve.

Her eyes narrow in thought, until finally she says, "Fine. Go ahead and set it up."

"How 'bout now?" I ask, already putting the phone to my ear. It starts ringing before she can nod. When he answers, I invite him over to meet Angela and he accepts, sounding a bit too excited about the prospect for my liking. "Oh god, this is probably a bad idea after all."

"I'll be the judge of that." She's too smug for her own good.

Theo arrives soon after, eyes searching inside the apartment until he spots Angela. She sits up from the couch and crosses the floor in two strides, holding out her hand. "Angela. We've met a couple times."

"I know," he says. "You're the one who scored us free mimosas at brunch a few years ago. I respect someone who can flirt their way to free booze for the entire table. Props."

"Oh, that's so sweet," she gushes, resting a hand over her heart. "I love that that's what I'm known for!"

"Of course you do." I let out a sigh. She nudges my elbow teasingly. "Well, how 'bout we eat already?"

They follow me into the kitchen, taking seats at the barstools. When I turn my back to prepare the plates, I hear

Angela ask, "So, what exactly are your intentions with my best friend?" I nearly drop the pan, whipping around to point the spatula in her face.

"Don't answer that," I tell Theo. "It's a trap. Just ignore her."

"We're each other's rebound," Theo answers her, completely ignoring *me*. Angela cocks her head, assessing the man sitting beside her. "She knows all about my baggage and I know about hers. I know it sounds kinda unhealthy put that way, but rest assured, we're both being honest with each other. Maybe a little too honest at times."

"Huh," she says, lips quirking up in amusement. Then she turns to me and transitions into Spanish. "I like this guy."

"That didn't take long," I return, switching over. "You sure you don't need more time to be convinced? We haven't even sat down to eat yet."

"I'm staying for breakfast, don't worry." Theo looks back and forth between us with a furrowed brow, no doubt wondering what the hell is going on. "But you have my blessing. I think his brother's wrong about him, and that's what we needed to get to the bottom of."

I roll my eyes, thinking of that almost kiss again. "His brother's full of shit."

Angela laughs, motioning to Theo with a slight tilt of her head. "This one must've really did his job for you to say that."

"That's the fastest I've gotten the best friend's approval in a while." Theo's mouth curls up in a smile. She turns to him, eyes wide with amused surprise.

"And he's picking up the language," Angela says in

English, before switching back to tell me, "You should keep him."

"We'll see," I respond in English, wondering how the fuck Theo managed to understand every word. He offers no answers, only eyes glinting with mischief.

They spend an entire hour talking about me, like I'm not in the same room as them. When Angela brings up the library, Theo's eyes light up.

"When's the next book club, by the way?" Theo asks. "I need to know who to dress up as next time."

"There aren't any set rules. Dress up as whoever you like," Angela says. Then she steps forward and looks over at him with an inquisitive look. "You're giving me Thor vibes."

"Oh yeah?" His eyes cut to me, brows waggling suggestively. "Who's more your type? Thor or Captain America?"

Angela covers her mouth with both hands to stifle a laugh. Theo laughs good-naturedly, his cheeks flushed pink. "I thought you had to dress as a book character?"

"Not necessarily." I shrug. "We told the kids last time to dress up as whoever they want. It's just a matter of preference."

"What's your preference?" Oh, lord he's never going to let this go now. "I'm betting you're more of a Captain America girl."

"You're not wrong," Angela says before I can confirm.

"I should buy a suit," he says thoughtfully before throwing me for a loop all over again. "That reminds me, I need a book recommendation."

I sit up straighter. "Wait...*really*?"

"Oh no. You shouldn't have said that." Angela's voice

takes on an ominous tone. "You're never gonna get her to shut up now."

"Like your favorites aren't my favorites? Don't pretend you don't get just as excited as me." I roll my eyes as I jump out of my seat and grab Theo's hand. It's finally time to show him my pride and joy. Angela trails behind us. I lead him to the door positioned across from my bedroom, throwing it open with a flourish.

What was meant to be a second bedroom has been converted into my very own home office-slash-library. A total of eight floor-to-ceiling bookcases cover every wall. For weeks, I struggled to pick a color before finally settling on white shelves. The only exceptions are the two iron half shelves placed on either side of the door. My desk sits in the middle of the room facing the window, which has a not-at-all stunning view of the apartment's office roof. Theo's eyes scan every inch of space, as if unsure where to begin.

"Top favorites are over here." I point to the low bookcases beside my desk. "Adult favorites are on the left, YA and middle grade on the right."

"There are *way* too many to choose from here." Theo crouches down to inspect the iron shelves, eyes widening. His head turns to where I'm standing behind him, and he raises an accusing finger. "I need a top five list."

"You want me to narrow it down to *five*?" I shake my head at the mere audacity. "I can give you ten, *maybe*, if we're not including series."

"Fine but put them order." He rises from the floor, arms crossed over his chest. My eyes bug out at him. As if I could *possibly* do something like that. "Come on, let's settle this."

"And why are we suddenly playing this terrible game with my feelings?" I clutch at my chest, reluctantly walking toward the bookcases. "This is like choosing a favorite child."

"Humor me."

With meticulous care and great pain, I begin sorting out my favorites on the desk. I change my mind way too many times throughout the process, but Theo is surprisingly patient with me. While I'm stuck making decisions I have no business making, he makes small talk with Angela and inspects the insides of each book I place on the desk. At one point it looks like they exchange social media handles, but mostly I'm too wrapped up in sorting through favorites to tell for sure.

Theo lets me rattle on for longer than I ever thought he would about every book I've chosen for my top ten. He's nodding in the appropriate places and even asking questions about my favorite characters and which books have the best plot twists. I look up at him with narrowed eyes, as if not quite believing this man is real. But I answer them all anyway, never once holding back.

"How come some of these are signed and some aren't?" he asks suddenly, picking up a random book from my haphazard stack. "If they're your favorites, shouldn't all of them be signed? You don't go to any events?"

"Few and far between," Angela tells him from the cheery yellow upholstered armchair. I have two reading chairs placed in the corners on either side of the room, mostly because Angela had a habit of calling dibs back when I had only one. Thank goodness I grew up with a mother who knows how to thrift. "We've been to a couple together, but only the ones in Austin. We don't have the kind of time or money to drop everything for a Dallas or Houston event."

"So, you can only get signed books at these events?" he asks.

"Sometimes you can order signed copies from bookstores or author websites. I've also scoured Depop far too many times looking for them," I tell him. "But if I already own a copy, it's not worth buying a second just for a signature. No matter how many times I've been tempted."

"Except when you donate your favorites and need replacement copies," Angela says.

"What?" Theo's head snaps up to me. "But these are your prized possessions. Why would you donate them?"

"Because before I did, the most recent YA books my high school library had was the Divergent series." The proclamation doesn't land the way it should. Theo tilts his head and shrugs. "Do you know how many years have passed since the dystopian craze died out? No hate to the genre, but you know a library's in trouble when the most recent books they have are over ten years old."

"And you willingly give away your own?" He shakes his head. "How much of a saint are you?"

I wave off the compliment. "I'm no saint, believe me. I was just the chubby girl with no friends her own age. All my friends growing up were teachers, library staff, and fictional characters." I ignore the way his eyes go soft. "I practically grew up in the public library, but not everyone has one within walking distance. It's especially important for kids that age to have a wide selection of reading material, and to be able to see themselves in the books they're reading. They need that more than I do."

I can't fathom the way he's looking at me right now, the storm of emotion flooding his eyes. Angela's staring at him with barely concealed interest. When she glances back at me, her smirk is knowing and teasing at the same time.

"So..." Theo clears his throat, his expression clearing of whatever emotion was previously clogging it. "How many replacement copies do you need currently?"

"Goodreads." Angela snaps her fingers at me.

"Already on it," I say, taking a seat behind my desk and booting up my computer. "I've actually got it tabbed right here." I point out the shelf titled Buy Again to Theo. "Ooh, let's check if Depop has any signed copies."

Theo reaches out and shuts my laptop closed. I look up at him with my best puppy-dog eyes, frowning. However, he is undeterred by my expression. "I need a book recommendation. Remember?"

Oh, right. That was the whole purpose of showing him my library in the first place.

Angela leaves soon after I find a book Theo might like. It's not one from my favorites stack because I'll quite possibly die if he doesn't like it.

"So, did I pass?" Theo asks once she's gone. I turn to look at him, eyebrows furrowing in a look of confusion. "Come on. I know a test when I see one."

"With flying colors," I tell him. "Angela might be more devastated than I'll be when all this is over." His amiable smile drops, setting into a frown. I bite down on my tongue, wincing.

Foot, meet mouth.

"I'm sorry." I shake my head. "I didn't mean for that to come out the way it did."

"Don't apologize. I get it," he says, looking down at his shoes. "We knew what this was from the beginning, right?"

"Yeah." I nod, even though that doesn't feel true. Because I had no idea I would feel this way when I stare into his glittering blue eyes, wishing for more time. It's not like we set a deadline on whatever our relationship is now, but it's going to end, and when it does, I know I'll be a mess. "Think that space from Alice did you some good?"

"Definitely." He nods. "I still think she's making a mistake with my brother, but I'm not going to stand in her way." He takes my hand, and goosebumps rise on the skin of my arms at the touch. "What about you? Think you're any closer to getting over Ben?"

"I think so," I tell him, downplaying the truth for karma's sake. I'm not sure if I'm completely over him yet, but the other day was a huge step in the right direction. "And I think this rebound is working a little too well."

"Really?" His voice is low, husky in a way that's giving me flashbacks to the last couple of days. He pulls me into his arms, hands settling at my waist. Just when I think he's about to take this a step further, he throws me completely off guard when he asks, "Do you wanna go out on a date with me?"

I take a step back from him, head snapping up to look at him properly. "What?"

"It wouldn't be the worst idea in the world, would it?" His expression is vulnerable in a way I haven't seen yet. Which might be the most surprising, since we've both been vulnerable in all sorts of ways in front of each other. "I just thought... forget it." He shakes his head. "Never mind."

"No, what?" I ask, tugging on his hand to turn him back around. "Tell me."

"I just thought it'd be nice if we did something different. Spend some time outside your apartment or mine, for once. Isn't the dating portion equally as important as the sex portion of any good rebound?"

"You may have a point," I concede. "All right. What'd you have in mind?"

His smile is blinding and incredibly contagious. My own lips quirk up just looking at him, even as my heart pounds faster inside my chest. I can't tell if its anticipation or dread of the fallout crawling up my spine. But either way, I know without a doubt that when all this ends, I'm going to be *miserable*.

Twenty-Four

've never met a guy who needed two weeks just to plan a date.

To top it off, Theo won't even tell me where we're going, insisting that everything be a surprise. He, at least, tells me to wear something casual with comfortable shoes, and to change into something fancier for the evening portion of the date. On Saturday afternoon, I decide on jeans and a black T-shirt with white running shoes that haven't lost their color because that's how rarely I wear them.

I'm still not sure that an honest-to-God *date* is a good idea, but I'm also curious about what Theo's idea of romance is. My brain keeps turning over what he said weeks ago, until there's a ringing in my ears like alarm bells.

Isn't the whole point of a rebound to prove to yourself you're still capable of feeling something for someone else?

I have feelings for Theo. Not just sexual feelings, but real, full-blown romantic feelings. There's no denying that any-more. I might finally be getting over Ben, but that left me with a whole set of new problems. Which is why it's better that we end whatever we are sooner rather than later, so that we don't hurt each other worse down the line. That's what I have to tell myself to get through today.

When Theo arrives outside my front door, he's wearing jogging pants and a hoodie, his hair mussed from the cold wind outside. The weather is almost enough to make me back out, but then I look over his outfit again. Now that he's dressed like Rocky during a training montage, I'm not sure jeans were the right call.

"You ready?" He steps inside when I make no move to step outside.

"Not in the slightest," I say, looking him up and down. "Does this involve any amount of running? Because you should know right now: I *don't* run."

"It might involve a little bit of running." He's unconcerned as he wraps a big arm around my shoulders and leads me back to the door. "Come on, you'll be fine. You might even like it."

I highly doubt that.

The car ride lasts about ten minutes before we arrive at our destination. The Northside Football Stadium is completely deserted when we turn up. His eyes are sparkling mischief as he puts the car in park. I let out a loud groan, but he just laughs in my face.

"For the first part of our date, I'll be introducing you to my favorite pastime and everything it entails," he says as we walk toward the iron gate. "Starting with the tailgate."

He stops beside a closed food truck, taking a key from

his pocket to open the back door. The truck is painted cerulean, with lighter shades of blue dotted in an asymmetrical pattern to create the logo directly under the window: *Marco's Taco Truck*. I look back up at Theo, surprised. He shoots me a wicked grin as he opens the door, and I follow after him. Inside, the delicious smell of carnitas wafts under my nostrils. My stomach grumbles in approval as he hands me a red basket with two tacos inside. "We can't play without a pregame snack first."

"Mm-hmm," I mumble in agreement, nodding as I take my first bite. "That's a good rule of thumb."

"And no pregame is complete without alcohol." He reaches down to the mini fridge and pulls out two Angry Orchard ciders. "You like these, right?"

My first thought shouldn't be Ben, but the label calls him to the forefront of my mind. He knows I hate beer, so this has always been our thing when he visits my apartment. A near decade–long tradition. But my second thought is of Theo's thoughtfulness. I've never told him Angry Orchard is my favorite brand. He's just seen them in my kitchen enough times to know. My chest twinges as I realize how much he's really gotten to know me.

I clear my throat as I twist the cap, forcing a smile over my racing pulse. "Cheers."

We clink bottles and sip.

"Actually, I lied. I went to one game freshman year," I say, suddenly remembering. He perks up but rolls his eyes when I emphasize the *one* game fact.

"And what was the verdict?"

"My friend and I got so bored, we left at halftime to get drunk in the parking lot." What I don't tell him is that the friend was Alice, back when we were still close. He lets out an exasperated groan and rubs both hands over his face. "I always imagined the best part of any football game would be tailgate and halftime."

"Oof, I think my soul just died a little." He puts a hand over his heart as if in physical pain. "That's it. Rebound over, you were right. We were doomed from the start."

"Shut up!" I yell, hitting his arm. He catches my fist with one hand and brings it up to his mouth to kiss my knuckles. The gesture is so sweet, it makes my heart twinge even more. "Okay, fine! I take it back."

"Glad to see you come around." He actually winks. How can he make a cheesy move look so sexy? "Okay, come on. Finish your tacos so I can show you what we're doing next."

When we finish eating, he takes my hand and leads me out to the field.

"Please don't tell me we're actually going to play a game." I raise myself to my tiptoes to get a better look at the field. Luckily it seems empty, just a vast space of green turf that goes on forever. An entire stadium reserved for the two of us. "I really don't feel like embarrassing myself in front of other people today."

"Do I count as other people?" Theo asks, raising a perfectly arched brow.

"Nope," I say with a grin up at him. When he starts to pout, I add, "No, this is good! That's how you know you've made it to the inner circle. You don't want to be other people."

"If you say so." He returns my grin as we reach the gate, then walks me over to a rickety wooden bench outside the white painted lines marking the field. "Don't worry, Marcela, it's just us today. I'm going to teach you how to play football."

I stare up at him blankly.

"I think you need to rephrase that."

"To what? Here." He hands me a navy jersey, the number 29 in white on the front. When I turn it over, his last name is splayed above the number. Young. The material is worn, like it's been through a few cycles in the wash.

"Oh my god, wait. Is this your actual jersey?" He nods, meeting my eyes with a vulnerability I'm still surprised to find him capable of. I hold it out over my torso to gauge the fit. "*Wow*. You might be the first guy I've dated I can actually share clothes with."

"Promise you'll still love me when all my muscles turn to flab?" His smile is adorably sheepish, whether from the thought of letting himself go or using the word *love* so casually, I can't say.

I know exactly which part makes my pulse stutter.

I avoid answering him by pulling on the jersey over my head. It is, indeed, a perfect fit. He runs out onto the field backward so he's still facing me, tossing the football between his hands. "We're gonna start you out with something easy."

"Easy for you, or easy for me?"

He ignores my question and points to the line in front of him, a foot away from him. "Stand on that white line." I run out to where he indicates, but not without a grumble. "I want to see how far you can throw."

"You will be sorely disappointed."

"I'm not sure that's true," he says. "Come on."

The first time he throws the football, I lift my arms to cover my face. He shouts something I can't make out as the ball hits my funny bone. The vibration shoots from my elbow to my wrist, until I'm left with a fuzzy feeling up and down my arm. "Ow."

"One more time." He jogs after the rogue football, which landed by my foot. "And this time, try to catch it."

"And what do I get for catching it?" I ask in a suggestive tone.

One brow arches, equally suggestive. "I think we can come to some sort of arrangement."

"Keep talking."

"Can't." He grips the football with two hands, readying a second throw. He almost makes football look sexy. "Don't wanna ruin the surprise." My brow quirks up as he returns to his white line. *Surprise?* Before I can ask what he means, he says, "All right, get ready."

I hold out my hands in preparation for the unexpected.

"Bend your knees a little," Theo tells me. "And keep your arms closer to your body."

"Why don't you come over here and show me?" I bat my eyes innocently. "Let's reenact that part of the rom-com where the guy teaches the girl how to do something sporty, so he has an excuse to put his hands on her, all romantic-like."

"Are you saying I need an excuse to put my hands on you?"

"No," I admit. "But maybe I need an excuse to tell you I want you to put your hands on me."

"You *definitely* don't." But he relents, closing the space between us and coming around behind me. I lean back into his chest with a sigh. His fingers trail up and down my arms, featherlight. Goosebumps rise on my skin as if woken by his touch. He buries his face in the crook of my neck, his hair tickling my nose. I raise a hand to run my fingers through his hair.

"Focus," he admonishes, even as he plants a kiss on my shoulder. "Keep your shoulders straight." I adjust my shoulders, as he instructs. He lowers my arms and brings them closer to my chest. "Now ready your battle stance."

"Come again?" I turn to look over my shoulder. "What is my 'battle stance'?"

"Keep your knees bent," he says, rolling his eyes when I smirk at him. "Be ready to pounce at any given moment." I pout when he moves away from me, running back to the line. "I'll throw the ball straight at you to start, but this will get progressively harder. You ready?"

"If I say no, can we stop?"

He laughs. "Not a chance."

His arm bends back, but he brings it forward slowly. The ball arches perfectly my way, and into my hands. I surprise us both when I spring forward, cradling the ball to my chest as I dash past him. He calls after me, asking where I'm going when I run for the white goalpost. I turn my head to smile at him, but it drops open when he breaks into a sprint after me. When I screech, he lets out a booming laugh from his diaphragm.

"You're never gonna catch me!" I increase my stride, running as fast as I possibly can. But I'm no match for a former

NFL player. I'm breathing hard, sweat dripping down the side of my forehead, when Theo reaches me. But he doesn't try to stop me. He runs beside me, matching my pace until I reach the goal and throw the ball between the poles.

"Touchdown!" I scream at the top of my lungs, dancing in circles over the fallen football. "I made a touchdown!"

Theo howls his approval, and it's such a distinctly primal sound that I can't help but laugh. I jump into his outstretched arms and he spins me around, his arms crushing me to his chest as he lifts me off the ground. We're both laughing and screaming. He kisses me as he settles my feet back on the ground, and I wrap my arms around his neck.

"That was amazing!" he says. "Not technically a touchdown, but amazing nonetheless."

"Yeah?" My cheeks warm. "Am I worthy of a real football player yet?"

"You're a worthy opponent, indeed, Marce." He kisses the top of my head, and I almost melt on the spot. "Come on, let's do it again!"

I'm not sure how many hours pass. We play for so long, we only come to a stop when the sun begins to set, turning the sky a vibrant orange. The afternoon ends when he wraps his giant arms around me in lieu of a tackle, and I force us both to fall onto the grass. Our limbs tangle together in a way that's only unfamiliar thanks to the dirt and turf grass covering our bodies. When Theo plants his mouth on mine, I almost wish we didn't have to leave the field.

Maybe football isn't so bad after all.

Twenty-Five

O nce I've showered off the dirt and grass, I inspect my closet for what to wear next. Theo said the second part of the date requires a more formal attire, so I decide on a pale pink dress with a scalloped collar and fake buttons sewn down the middle. I slip my feet into matching flats just as the doorbell rings. I frown down at my phone. He's early.

My breath catches in my throat when I open the front door. Theo's dressed in black slacks and a pale blue button-up that is loose at the collar, with sleeves rolled to his elbows. The last time I saw him so dressed up was at the engagement party, but that was with an added suit jacket and tie. It's like being thrown back in time to when this whole thing started.

There's one added difference: the bouquet of flowers in his hand and the nervous way his eyes dart around the living room. It must only be a coincidence that the roses are as pink as my dress.

"Are those for me?" My heart beats erratically, and I hardly trust myself to say anything more.

"Of course." He offers me the roses. We both avoid eye contact as he places them in my arms with shaking hands. "I hope you have some kind of vase for them or something, I didn't even think about that."

"I do," I assure him. "I'll go put them in some water."

My own hands shake as I rifle through the cabinets before finding a glass vase big enough to fit the bouquet. I'm not sure what he has planned for tonight to seem so nervous, but it's making my own anxiety ratchet up to the highest setting. I shouldn't want this, and definitely not with Theo. Is it my own fault for letting this thing with him go on as long as it has? Are we just leading each other on by entertaining this date night?

He can't seem to keep his body still when I return to the living room. His long legs pace the length of the couch, head bent as he mumbles something under his breath, but it snaps up when I approach him. I'm taken back to the night of the engagement party all over again, stumbling upon his drunken form, talking himself into confessing to Alice.

Only, he's not drunk and I'm not Alice, so I'm not sure what to make of his nerves.

"You ready?" His voice pitches an octave higher than normal.

I nod and smile, but it has trouble sticking to my face. He seems appeased for the moment, stepping forward to link my arm in his so we can walk through the door. I hope he can't feel how fast my heart is beating.

The car ride is tense with our silence, both of us locked inside our own heads until he pulls into the library parking lot. My brows furrow as I chance a glance at his face. The library closed an hour ago. For the first time tonight, his eyes light up with mischief, lips curling up in that familiar wicked grin. I look back up at the library, but the lights are off inside. Theo comes around the car to open my door, ever the gentleman.

"Are we breaking and entering?" I ask, as we head up the sidewalk.

"It's not breaking and entering if you have a key." He looks down at me expectantly as we reach the glass double doors. When I just stare up at him, dumbfounded, he gestures for me to open the door. Finally, I reach into my purse for the key, my fingers slipping until I find the right one and stick it inside the lock.

Inside, the darkness is almost stifling except for a distant, golden glow coming from deeper inside the shelves. I glance up at Theo again questioningly, but all I can make out is the rise and fall of his shoulders as he shrugs. As if he wasn't the one who planned this entire night to begin with. The start of a self-satisfied smile edges the corners of his mouth as we make our way through the general fiction shelves.

I still can't determine where the light is coming from, let alone the source of the light itself. I swear to god if he actually lit candles in a building made up entirely of kindling, he'll make it easier for me to dump him. Especially if I lose the most important job I've ever had because of an elaborate date gone horribly, horribly wrong. If there are as many candles as it looks like there are, we'll be ending the night at the fire department. Or worse, in an ambulance dying of third-degree burns and smoke inhalation. There's nothing romantic about *that*.

We pass the first candle when we reach the back wall's low shelves, where an entire row is lit up in the shape of an arrow pointing right. I rush forward to blow them out, but the lights won't budge. On closer inspection, where there should be a wick is the artificial shape of a flame. My hand touches the plastic with a sigh of relief that deflates my whole body.

They're not real candles. They're battery operated.

"Did you actually think I'd make a fire hazard at your place of work?" Theo shakes his head in mock disappointment. "Oh, Marce. Ye of little faith."

"You can't blame me." I hit his arm. "You've been full of surprises today."

"Please. You haven't seen the biggest one yet."

The arrows lead to the YA section, where hundreds of tea lights sit on the shelves to light up the space. I let out a gasp when my eyes settle on our dinner setup. In the center of the surrounding shelves, where the YA book club met, the retractable tables and plastic seats have been replaced with a smaller, square wooden table covered by a white tablecloth and two matching wooden chairs. A dinner is set up on place mats, in front of two long-stemmed candles that also turn out to be battery operated.

It's like something ripped out of my wildest dreams. Something my teenage self desired so badly, something I resigned myself to accept would never happen the older I got. The low, golden glow against the wooden bookshelves captures my favorite section of the library in magic.

Theo steps in front of me to hold out a chair, his smile growing at whatever shocked expression must be plastered to my face.

"Milady?" And just when I think I've seen it all, Theo grants me a new kind of smile. Two rows of white teeth glitter, as his mouth spreads as far as it can go into a grin that's nothing short of victorious. A hero's smile, captured in gold.

"You did all this for me?" I can barely get the question out past the emotion choking my voice. When I try to clear my throat, it doesn't quite work.

I glance up at Theo, and then the dancing shadow of his silhouette when looking at him becomes too hard. It's not just the setup that's been ripped out of my wildest dreams, but Theo himself, too. He's something plucked out of a fairy tale, or better yet, one of my favorite romance novels. The glittering eyes of a hero, the determined stance of a man who would topple kingdoms to be with his beloved. The vulnerability of a man about to get down on one knee.

"You planned an elaborate dinner surrounded by my favorite books of all time?"

"Does that mean you like it?" His smile softens as tears begin to sting my eyes. Even still, there's something twitchy about the way he gestures to the table. Like those nerves I first noticed in my apartment haven't gone away yet. "Angela helped me plan it. I wanted the second part of the date to be planned around you, since the first part was all football. She helped me set this up while you were getting ready."

"It's perfect." I try to smile, but I'm sure it comes out watery. "Why would you go through so much trouble for me?"

I don't know why the question comes out now of all times, but I suddenly have to know. We're only supposed to be rebounds, but this entire date is the most romantic thing that's ever happened to me and we're not even together. Not really. This isn't the kind of date rebounds go on with each other, if they even go out on dates at all. Dinner and a movie. A nighttime stroll along the River Walk downtown, at the most. Not something that requires enlisting the help of a best friend to plan.

"Let's sit down," he says, not answering my question as he ducks away. He gestures to the chair he pulled out for me earlier, before walking to the other side and taking a seat himself. "And there's another surprise after dinner, so don't go getting teary-eyed on me yet." He lets out a nervous laugh, and it's all too much. I'm on the brink of a mental breakdown, and we haven't even eaten a single bite.

"*Another* surprise?" His smile turns sheepish as my mouth falls open in shock for the thousandth time tonight. "You're too much." My voice comes out in a rasp. I have to clear my throat twice before I can speak normally again. "The pasta looks good." It's a lame observation, considering the circumstances.

He smiles at me over the tea lights, and then we dig in. "So, what's a day at the library like?" he asks mildly, as if my mind isn't already reeling in a thousand different directions.

"Depends on the day," I say, my thoughts distracting me from really answering. Finally, I shake my head and ask what's really on my mind. "Theo, what is all this for? We could've just gone to dinner *at an actual restaurant* and maybe seen a movie after. You didn't have to do…" I gesture all around me with a sound of disbelief. "You didn't have to do all this."

"Maybe I just wanted to do something special for you." His brows crease as he gauges what exactly I'm asking. His mouth sets in a slight frown, but I can't help but keep questioning why he would do this for me. I'm ruining the moment, but I have to know. "Is that really so hard to believe?"

"Well, yeah!" I burst out. "This is the kind of date you plan for someone right before you get engaged. Hell, Ben didn't even plan something this elaborate for Alice. You don't just do something like this for the girl you're seeing casually."

"Okay, then let's talk about that." He sits up straight in his seat. "I don't want to do casual with you anymore."

For a moment, my heart stops. This is it. The end of whatever we are. But when he opens his mouth to explain, he surprises me all over again.

"Relationships aren't exactly my strong suit. I've never been in one before, not a real relationship anyway, but..." He looks over at me, eyes softening in a way that makes *me* feel like the vulnerable one. "Marcela, I don't feel this way very often about someone, but I want more with you. I don't just want to be the person who helps you get over Ben. And I don't just want to be the guy you stopped from destroying Alice's engagement party and mistakenly hooked up with. Maybe it's naive or hopeless to want something deeper with you, but I do."

I want more with you.

He's not ending this. He's...asking me something. Asking for us to be more than casual. My tongue feels like sandpaper. I don't trust myself to open my mouth, because if I do, I'm not sure what will come out. But my throat is so dry, I'm not sure anything would be able to come out at all.

Those dark blue eyes are rimmed in gold as they watch me carefully, waiting for the impact of his confession to land. But I'm frozen solid, trapped in his gaze.

"Marcela," he says when I've been silent for too long. "Is there any chance you feel the same?"

Twenty-Six

Yes. I do. Of course, I do. But also...no. *No.*
We *can't.*

None of this was supposed to happen.

"How..." I start, shaking my head. "How can this possibly work when we're still getting over other people?"

"I don't have all the answers. All I know is that I never expected to feel the way that I do about you," he tells me. "And I meant what I said the other day. I'm walking away from Alice—for good. I should've done it a long time ago, but until now, I never had a real reason to. Marcela, I—"

"Theo, we can't." His face falls until his eyes shut closed. His shoulders slump in disappointment, but when he opens his eyes again, his expression becomes resolute. I hate how my mind is already spinning with ways to beat him down again, but *we can't do this.* "I can't be the reason you walk away from Alice. What happens if—or *when*, really—this doesn't work out? Are you gonna go running back to her?"

"No," he says, his voice firm as he shakes his head. "No, I—"

"Are you sure?" I press. "You said it the other day…you think their engagement is a huge mistake. Do you still believe that? Even though you're walking away from her?"

"That's different." He reaches for my hands across the table, but I hold them out of reach. "I don't think she's making a mistake because she should be with me. How I feel for her has nothing to do with that." Present tense. How he *feels*, not how he felt. This is part of the problem. If this continues for much longer, he's going to turn me into a jealous, paranoid fool. I'll lose him, and I won't be surprised by it.

"How can you be sure?" I ask him. "That your feelings for her aren't clouding your judgment? I mean, isn't she the reason you and Ben hate each other now?"

He lets out a frustrated breath. "She's only part of the reason, but she's not *the* reason. *Ben* is the reason. If he wasn't such a jackass, maybe we wouldn't be fighting for as long as we have."

"That doesn't tell me anything!" I don't mean for it to come out as a yell, and he startles at my tone. "You've been in love with her for your entire life and your own brother stole her away from you. *Of course* you think he's a jackass. How is Alice only part of the problem when to me, it's clear that she's the source?"

I can't be his second choice. I refuse to be anyone's second choice ever again. Maybe I'd feel different if he were over Alice, but I can't expect him to have changed his mind that quickly. Even if mine did about Ben.

He blows out a breath, looking away from me. Then he says, "You're right. I'm an idiot to ask you for anything. But you should know that there's more than just Alice that came between me and my brother."

"What else is there?"

His mouth opens and closes, until the moment passes, and he hasn't uttered a single word. I'm not sure I believe him, that there's anything other than Alice.

"But don't you see where I'm coming from?" I ask him instead. "There's too much baggage between the two of us to give this a fair shot. Because—"

Because even though you might hate him, Ben is your brother and he's not going anywhere, and I don't trust myself not to fall into old patterns.

Because I don't trust you not to fall into old patterns, either.

Because you almost walked away from this once, and I don't trust you not to try to again.

But it isn't fair of me to put that on him. Any of it. I knew what this was when we started. We both did. Maybe the issue is we weren't supposed to last this long. It was only meant to be temporary, and our rebound is long overdue to end.

"Because what, Marcela?" His voice is soft, coaxing in a way that makes me want to dig deeper. Get to the root of all my fears and lay them bare for him to parse through. Unburden myself by burdening him. But I don't want him to change my mind. And maybe a small part of me isn't ready for his mind to change, either.

Instead, I don't say a thing. Because I'm good at that.

"How do we know if we don't try? Marcela—" He bursts up from his seat, coming around the table to kneel beside me. "Forget about Ben and Alice for a second. Pretend they don't exist," he implores me. "How do you feel about me?"

My eyes shut. If I meet his eyes now, he just might convince me, and that's the last thing I want. "Theo, I can't just forget—"

"Answer the question, please." He cups my cheeks with his big hands. "Marcela, look at me. How do you feel?"

"I care about you." The words come automatically, despite the voice in my head screaming at me to run. "Of course I care about you. How could I not? How could I not have fallen for you after—" I cut myself off, mash my lips together to keep from telling him everything.

I have to shut my eyes at his joyous expression, because he won't be feeling that way for very long. *We can't do this.*

"I promised to be honest with you, but I don't think you want me to be *this* honest." I shake my head, at him, at myself, at this wildly romantic date I'm about to burn to the ground.

His hands fall to mine, intertwining our fingers. "Tell me." His voice is low, bracing. "Tell me everything you're feeling, Marce. Please."

I suck in a deep breath. He's going to hate me for this.

"I meant it when I said it was probably a stupid idea for us to trust each other. We've openly admitted to being in love with other people and using each other to get over them. There are no expectations between us, not really. Real relationships don't work like this."

Not that either of us would know. But what I do know is the second we put a different set of expectations on our shoulders, the more likely we are to disappoint each other. To hurt each other in even worse ways.

"No expectations. That's why I could agree to a physical

relationship with you when I knew how you felt about Alice. It's why I could justify hiding my feelings for Ben from you, and it's why you didn't feel the need to tell me Ben and Alice already knew about yours. It's why I held back my anger at you for disappearing without a trace. We leaned on each other the way friends do, lost ourselves in each other to forget about the people we had no business loving. But we don't have any business thinking we can love each other instead. That's not how this works."

"No expectations," he repeats, his voice as hard and derisive as I've ever heard it. "Is that really what we've been to you this entire time?"

"What else could we have been?" I counter instead. "These were *your* terms from the very beginning. Casual. Nothing more."

"Maybe I changed my mind. Are you telling me you haven't? That you never once considered the possibility of something more with me?"

Of course I have. I let myself pretend we were something real to each other more than I acknowledged the truth. He made it so easy to.

"It doesn't matter," I say. "We can't do this, Theo. We don't know how."

But more than that, I'm so tired of being the one left behind. Physically, emotionally, mentally. There are lots of ways to walk away from someone. I wonder if it was an easy choice for my father to make, to put his wants before my mother's. Before mine. If it was easy for Ben to put me on the back burner when someone better came along, knowing on some unconscious level that I'd take any scrap he offered me as gold.

I don't want to hurt Theo the same way I've been hurt. But I want to save myself from the pain of loving and losing him more than I want to protect him from the pain of losing me now.

"This is what you meant the other day." He's looking at me with a sudden, horrifying realization. "When you said trust had nothing to do with this. You didn't mean that you don't trust me. You don't trust *us*."

"You didn't do anything wrong," I tell him. "You've been everything to me, Theo. So much more than I deserve. I just can't give you what you want."

"You're what I want," he says, steadfast, breaking me all over again. "I trust you. I have *real* feelings for you. I'm not expecting anything more from you than what you've already given me. Despite how we started and everything you might think now, what we have has been more than just sex, more than casual, more than 'no expectations' for a long time now. It has been for me at least. And you can't convince me you don't feel the same."

We're at an impasse, because while he might be right, I know in my bones we can't have a real relationship. I rise from my seat and race into the dark, searching for the exit through muscle memory. Theo calls my name from behind me, but I don't turn around. I find the side entrance and push open the glass, running out into the empty parking lot.

I stop once I reach Theo's car. A moment later, the library door crashes open. Theo's long legs eat up the space as his eyes spot me across the lot. He slows his pace, but his chest is rising and falling fast.

"I thought you were running," he says as he approaches, shoulders slumped in relief.

"I was." He bypasses the driver's side and comes straight to me. I take a step back from him, and he halts immediately.

Those blue eyes turn keen as he searches my face, assessing. He takes a careful step forward, and when I don't move he takes another. I'm prevented from turning away when his hands cup my cheeks, locking me in place. My stomach flips, heart racing so fast I start to feel faint.

"What are you so scared of?" he asks finally, voice so low I barely hear it.

I close my eyes with a sigh. My hands come up to his wrists, gently prying his from my face. "I'm sorry, Theo," I finally say, because it's all I can. "Can you take me home?"

He doesn't respond for the longest time. Finally, he lets out a shaky breath and says, "This isn't how I saw the night going."

I look away from him, guilt burning through me for all sorts of reasons.

"Marcela—"

"Can we just go home, please?" I turn away, place my hand on the door handle. The last thing I want to do is talk. I know I'll have to face him eventually, but not now. Not when my emotions are churning a million different ways.

The car ride is tense with our silence—in his stubborn desire to break it, and my stubborn attempt to keep it. His eyes shift from me to the windshield every few seconds, assessing my mood for any changes. I force my attention away from him, out the passenger window. When we arrive at my apartment, I resist immediately running out of the car like I want to.

That proves to be a mistake when I raise my hand to open the door and Theo locks the doors with a *whoosh*. I glance over at him, stunned. His face is unreadable, as if he locked a part of himself away in addition to the car doors.

"We can't end the night like this," he tells me, scrubbing his face with a large hand. "Talk to me. What is it that's really holding you back?" He reaches for my hand but hesitates to take it. Just hovers in the space between us, as if testing the air.

"We don't have half a chance if we still have feelings for other people," I say, and even though it's true, it's not quite the right answer to his question.

"I know." He nods slowly. "We also don't have a chance if we can't trust each other."

"I don't know how to get there." My voice is a whisper, an admission of failure. "And I don't expect you to get over Alice completely, and especially not this quickly. Not when you've spent most of your life in love with her. And I…I'm still confused. About everything." I shake my head. I'm admitting more of the truth than I want to. "It was different when it was just about sex and stopping each other from breaking up an impending marriage. When there weren't all these…emotions between us."

"What emotions, exactly?" he asks, expression opening just enough to let hope through again. I keep my mouth shut, and he blows out a frustrated breath. "You know, I almost ended this." My head snaps up to look at him. "Before the double date. I didn't want to lie about how we started anymore, and I definitely didn't want to sit through an entire dinner with Ben and Alice. I wanted to end it the moment I'd made up my mind, but you didn't answer your phone. I even passed by your apartment before I came to your work. I thought I might lose my nerve if I waited any longer."

I knew it.

All week, he'd been dodging my messages and I *knew* it had to be for a reason. I was right that he'd almost walked away from this. When that cryptic message lit up my lock screen, can we talk, I'd sensed it.

"Maybe you should've," I say. "That's what I thought you were there for. I tried so hard not to be mad at you for ignoring me, and then you showed up out of the blue to dump me on a night I worked so hard to plan." That's when I caught myself falling for him, despite knowing better. I almost let myself believe we could be something real before he reminded me how dangerous thoughts like that were. Told myself that trusting him would only lead to more heartache, more abandonment issues on top of the ones I already live with.

"Instead, you strong-armed me into acting out a scene in front of all those teenagers." His mouth turns up at the corner, lips forming a sad smile.

"It was the only punishment I could think of on the spot." I shrug. "Except, I think you enjoyed it too much."

"I did." He chuckles softly. "Enough to completely change my mind."

I glance up at him, stunned. "What?"

"One look at you, and I couldn't do it. Maybe this is cheesy, but I felt this *tug* at my chest just from looking at you." He puts a hand over his heart, as if indicating the sensation. "It was shitty and cowardly of me to ignore you for as long as I did, but I knew meeting you face-to-face would test all my resolve. Not just test." He shakes his head. "*Obliterate.* And it did."

My eyes sting. I blink the tears back furiously, but they spill over anyway.

"I'm sorry I hurt you." His hands are clenched on the steering wheel, like it's taking everything he has not to comfort me with his touch. "And I'm sorry I made you feel like you couldn't show it. I want the expectation, dammit. I want you to demand more from me, and I want you to believe I can give it to you."

"Theo, don't—"

"I used to think Alice was the only person for me, or that I wasn't a relationship kind of guy. I thought I knew what real love was, and that no one else could measure up to how I felt about Alice." He shakes his head. "I didn't know a goddamn thing. Not before you. And all I had to do was be open to taking a chance."

He unlocks the passenger door from his side, turning forward in his seat without another word. It's the dismissal I've been waiting for, but I don't like anything about it. Finally, I get out of his car. When I watch him drive away, I'm more confused than ever.

Twenty-Seven

There aren't enough empanadas in the world for this kind of hurt.

I've torn through five of them just this morning, but somehow, I feel even worse. As soon as I woke up, last night's events crashed over me like a tidal wave, choking the breath from me all over again.

He almost ended everything. I keep replaying that night when Theo visited the library during book club over and over. The surprise that bloomed in my chest when I caught sight of him. The dread that seeped into my veins when I read his text.

He'd already made up his mind to end things. My heart races just imagining how different everything would be if he had. I'd mark yet another person who walked out of my life without a second thought, but I'd get over it. I always did, didn't I?

But I did get a second thought. Without even trying, I changed Theo's mind.

What am I supposed to make of that?

I let out a groan and bite into a bright pink concha because I ran out of empanadas. What did I do on my weekends before Theo came into my life? I walk into my home library and scan the bottoms of every bookshelf, where I store all my unread books. Grabbing a small stack, I return to the couch in the living room and read a chapter in each book hoping one hooks me. When none do, I return to the shelves again to repeat the process.

I call Angela when nothing sticks, but when I realize I'll have to tell her about last night, I hang up before she has the chance to answer. I'll recount the tale to her tomorrow when she drags me out for our standing Sunday walk. I'm already dreading what she'll say to me.

I'm still grappling with what to do an hour later, when there's a knock on my door. I freeze, dreading who could be on the other side. If it's Angela, I suppose I'll have to buck up and confess last night's horrendous events. If it's Ben, I'll close the door in his face before he can utter a single word. But if it's Theo...

I sneak a peek through the peephole, and chills run down my back. When I open the door, Theo's standing before me, his hair and clothes as disheveled as my soul feels. Dark circles ring his eyes, like he hasn't slept in days even though only a night has passed.

"I'm not staying for long, I just wanted to give you this," he says before handing me a key. My brows furrow as I look down at it. I immediately recognize the shape—it's a key to the lecture hall of the library. "We never got to the surprise part of the date. It's waiting for you in a box under the table."

"You can return it, if you want," I tell him, my voice hollow. I'd completely forgotten about the surprise he'd mentioned last night. "I can pick it up on Monday and—"

"I don't want it back," he tells me, eyes imploring. "It's yours, okay? It doesn't matter what happens with us. I just want you to have it."

I'm not sure what to say to that, so I don't say anything. When he turns to leave, it takes everything I have to hold myself back from asking him to stay. But we can't go back to the way things were. Not when he's laid himself bare, and I'm holding on to all my fear. Not when everything about our relationship has changed. Just as I'm about to shut the door, he turns back around, something like determination shining in his eyes.

"This isn't over for me," he says, stunning me all over again. I open my mouth to speak, but he doesn't give me the chance. "I'm still in this, Marcela. You might not believe we have a chance, but I do. I wish I could prove that to you with more than words. I wish I knew how to make you trust us."

I don't know what to say to that, so I keep my mouth shut.

"If you don't want to be with me anymore, I won't force you," he says. "I meant what I said to you weeks ago when all this first started. I'm rooting for you to get the happily ever after you deserve, even if it's not with me." He meets my eyes across the hallway. "Tell me what you need from me."

"I—" I take in a breath. Let it out slowly as he steps closer. "I don't know."

He shuts his eyes, his expression pained. "Does that mean this is over?"

Over. That was an inevitability, wasn't it? But I hate that the onus is on me. I hate that I can't meet him where he is, that I can't return his trust. That I can't trust how happy he makes me without waiting for the other shoe to drop.

"Can you try?" His hand is in my hair, beckoning me closer. "Is there any part of you that wants to try?"

"Of course there is," I tell him honestly. "But I'm scared of how much I don't trust this feeling to last." I shake my head, try and fail to blink back the moisture in my eyes. "If we try this and it doesn't work, it'll break me. More than ending it with you now is breaking me."

My eyes search his face like I'm seeing it for the last time. His blond hair sticking up at odd ends, the lines around his mouth as it sets into a frown, the deep, indigo depths of his eyes. I memorize every inch of him—the slumped set of his shoulders, the wrinkles in his T-shirt, those strong arms that feel like home.

There's nothing more to say, so he turns around again. I watch his back as he leaves, wondering if he'll turn around one last time before he makes it to his car. But he doesn't. Of course he doesn't. I'm frozen still as his car shakes to life, watching as he pulls out of the lot and then out of view.

For the last time.

On Monday morning, I'm an hour early for work. I pace the hallway of the lecture hall, spinning the keyring around my fingers, contemplating how much more damage this will do to me. I'm a complete wreck in black leggings that barely pass for pants and a baggy jacket, my poor attempt at a Hail Mary against a dress code violation. Not that I care. My main concern is whatever this "surprise" from Theo could be.

I jump when the front door opens on the ground floor, but when I look down from the balcony, I catch sight of Angela's curly head. She spots me from the foyer, and something in my expression must be pitiful enough for her to grant me some measure of mercy after the onslaught of her interrogation on Sunday. Instead of asking any more questions I can't answer, she asks one I can.

"How ya holdin' up?"

"Bad," I tell her, gesturing at my outfit. "Obviously."

She nods as if this is, in fact, obvious. "Did you find it yet?"

I assume she means the surprise. The knowledge that she was the one who helped Theo plan the date only makes this worse. She might be my best friend and her love might be unconditional, but I'm flooded with shame. Shame that she might think I'm a terrible person for rejecting him, especially after he put in all that hard work to make the night special. I turn back to the lecture hall door, then back to Angela with a shrug. "No, still working up the nerve."

"Want me to come with?" she offers.

I shake my head. "Thanks, but I'm good."

When I reach the door of the lecture hall, I pull it open and flip the lights on inside. I spot the cardboard box immediately, but it's not so easily moved. My knees wobble just from trying to lift it off the floor. *Why is it so heavy?* I want to know, but I also don't. Whatever is inside, I know it's far more than I deserve.

So instead, I give up.

I go about the rest of my day as if there isn't a large box upstairs with my name on it. When Angela asks me about the surprise, I tell her it was too heavy to lift. She promises to help me move it at the end of the day, but by the time her shift ends, we've both forgotten all about it. Or at least, she has. It sits in the back of my mind, haunting every task until the day ends.

Two whole days pass before the damned thing makes it into the trunk of my car, and from there a handful of days before it finds its final home underneath my desk. If I open it now, I'll have an excuse to call Theo and thank him for the gift, but I'll also be one step closer to the end. If I don't open it, the mystery of his last message to me will remain unanswered, but on some level it also means we're not over yet.

This isn't over for me, he'd said.

But it is for me. It was for him at one point, too, until he changed his mind. What will it take, I wonder, for me to change mine?

Twenty-Eight

The next few days pass in a blur of mundane tasks and obsessive thoughts. Ben has texted twice. Theo hasn't reached out at all, not that I expect him to. By the time the weekend arrives, I finally break down and tell Angela everything. The football game and my poor one-on-one skills, the candlelit dinner I ruined, Theo asking for us to be a real couple, up to the bitter end outside my apartment when he asked if we were over.

Angela doesn't say it'll all be okay or that I'll get through this, because she's not a liar. Instead, she opts to comfort me in the only way she knows how.

"Cheap vodka for your problems?" She slides the brown paper bag in her hands off to reveal a bottle of Smirnoff. I make a face. "Should I have gotten the good kind?"

"Let's not fool ourselves. There is no good kind." I let out a long sigh as she plops down next to me on the couch. "I'm not really in a drink-my-feelings kind of mood. It's been a long week."

"Oh, thank god." She lets out a sigh of relief. "I'm too exhausted for shots. I'll probably pass out on the floor after two. God, we're getting old." She sets the bottle down on the coffee table.

"We're maturing," I correct. "Some would even venture to call not drinking away your problems growth."

"Maturing." Her mouth twists like she swallowed a mouthful of the untouched liquor. "I call it the beginning of the end. Today we're too tired to drink. Next weekend we're breaking out the knitting needles and sipping tea we made from a kettle. You know you're the third person I've tried to pass this bottle off to? Even my twenty-two-year-old cousin wouldn't take it."

"That's a good idea, actually," I tease. "I've been meaning to take up a new hobby. And I think I have some peppermint tea bags in a cupboard somewhere."

"Sounds healthy. Is this your starter pack to getting over Theo? Letting liquor bottles gather dust and taking up knitting?" When I don't answer, she continues. "We both knew he was a bad idea from the start, right? You can move on now. From Theo *and* Ben."

"Hmm." Although I'm the one who broke it off with Theo, I inexplicably hate that she seems to think it was a good idea. "That would be the logical first step, but alas, I have not been very logical these past few months."

"What in particular wasn't logical?" Her brows crease at my silence. "Okay. What aren't you telling me?"

"What do you mean?"

"Theo," she says. "How do you really feel about him?"

"Oh, would you look at the time? It's—" I'm bluffing to get her off my back, maybe even out of my apartment, until I notice the time on my phone reads a minute past eight. "Wow, it's still early. Maybe we are getting old."

"Not old. *Maturing.*" She smirks as she crosses her arms, raising a brow in a way that tells me she's not going anywhere. "Answer the question. How do you feel about him?"

I let out a tired sigh, but it doesn't hide the despair in my voice. "It doesn't matter."

"Oh, Marcela. *No.*" Her eyes widen as she realizes something. "You've got it bad for him, don't you?"

"I didn't think I could feel this way for anyone else, you know? For years, it's been all about Ben. And the first time it's not about him, it has to be his brother."

"This is a *good* thing, Marcela." She grips my shoulders. "The whole point of this was to get over Ben!"

"But Theo—"

"Is still in love with Alice?"

And I surely don't try to convince Alice she's making the biggest mistake of her life by marrying you.

I don't think she's making a mistake because she should be with me. How I feel for her has nothing to do with that.

Feel. Present tense.

I shrug. The truth is, after everything we've been through, I still have no idea. He only told me that he was done with her for good, but nothing about whether his feelings have actually changed. If maybe, through some miracle, I made him change his mind about her, too. The same way he's made me change my mind about Ben.

"I don't know," I finally say. "It was easier to be with him when the scales were even. They don't feel even anymore."

"Because you're over Ben, and he may not be over Alice?"

"The closer Theo and I got, the more I started to get over Ben,"

I say. "It wasn't because his true colors started to show. Not really. That only happened when I stopped giving him the attention he was used to. He tried to kiss me once, I think, but all I could think about was Theo. How Theo was the only person I wanted to kiss."

The way Angela's looking at me, you'd think I sprouted a second head.

"What?"

"Nothing." She recovers from her stunned expression, shaking her head. I'm still wondering what she's not telling me when her face turns contemplative. "You don't think Theo experienced the exact same thing when he was with you?"

"I don't know," I repeat. "He hasn't said he has."

"Have you told him?" she counters. "That you're over Ben?"

"No."

"The way I see it, you two are like mirrors." She holds out her palms, has them face each other an inch apart. "You were drawn to each other because you understood each other in a way no one else could. Two wildcards in love with one half of an engaged couple. Hooking up should've been a terrible idea." She slaps her hands for dramatic effect. "I thought it *was* a terrible idea. But maybe it wasn't. You guys helped each other grow, held each other accountable, made each other better people. He's the only one who knew how to do that for you, just like you're the only one who knew how to do that for him."

I turn over everything she said, a flush of warmth filling my chest.

"I was worried about what Ben's engagement would do to you," she says, expression sheepish, embarrassed maybe to admit this to me. "It's not that I thought you'd go as far as

Theo did before you stopped him, but I thought you'd try something similarly stupid. I thought you might capitalize on Ben's jealousy, use it to your advantage, but you never did."

"You really think we made each other better people?" I ask, doubtful. But maybe hopeful too, that she could see us that way.

"It would've been so easy for you guys to enable each other's bad intentions. Instead, you expected him to be better. Not for you, but for himself. And I think that made you want to be better for yourself, too." She holds out her palms again. "Mirrors."

"Oh my god." It finally clicks. "I think you're actually right."

"Of course I'm right. It's a shame you don't listen to me more often," she says with a shrug. I scowl at her, but I can't hold it for long. "I don't think his remaining feelings for Alice, whatever they may be, is the issue here."

"Tell me, o wise one," I say sardonically. "What's my issue, then?"

"Why have you never been in a serious relationship before?" Her eyes pierce through me. "It's not because of Ben. It's not because the dating scene sucks. What's the real reason?"

"The dating scene really fucking sucks, though." She rolls her eyes at my non-answer. I know where she's going with this, but as much as I want to refuse to give her what she wants, I can't. "Fine. Because no one's ever loved me before."

"Ha!" I cross my arms in defense at her sudden outburst. "You should've seen him before *and* after your library date. The man was crushed! You think you have it bad for him?

He's got it *So. Fucking. Bad* for you, Marce." She drops his nickname for me so suddenly, I snap my head back to her. She lets out a loud, maniacal cackle, and only laughs harder at the surprise on my face. "What? You can't honestly tell me you didn't know that."

"You were there?" I gasp. "After?"

"Yeah. Had to help the big guy clean up after you left him hanging." She shrugs. "He was a mess." She halts in her tracks. "Wait, should I be telling you this? Oh, shit. Does knowing that make this better or worse?"

"I'm not sure." I stare at her, gathering the courage to ask her something I'd normally be too chickenshit to. "I fucked this up royally, haven't I?"

"Answer me this first," she says. "What's the real reason you're too scared to try?"

"I don't want to lose him," I admit. "I don't want us to break up in a month or a year down the line when we realize we've made a mistake. I don't want the heartbreak my mom experienced when her marriage fell apart. I don't want the abandonment, the broken trust, or anything else that comes with letting someone in. I don't want to let him into the mess that is my life, have him take one look at it, and decide he's better off without it. Without *me*."

"What makes his mess any better than yours?" she counters. "We all have baggage. He's already seen yours and still decided you were it for him. Why can't you trust him with yours the same way he can trust you with his?"

Is there any part of you that wants to try?

"Maybe we need this after all." I swipe the bottle of vodka

and head into the kitchen. "I should have something in here we can use as a mixer."

Angela follows, looking over my shoulder into the refrigerator. "So much for healthy coping mechanisms. Oh, that bottle of Coke should work fine."

"I'm pretty sure it's flat." I grab it anyway, along with two glasses to fill with ice before setting them down on the counter to mix the drinks. "Might as well use this up since I'm the third person you tried passing this off to. It'd be wasteful not to."

"Wasteful." She nods, smirking. "Right."

"Shut up and drink your flat Coke and vodka."

"Whatever you say."

We clink glasses and sip. In the silence, I can't help but think over everything I just admitted to Angela. *I don't want to lose him.* Before talking to her, I assumed breaking up was an inevitability. But maybe...

"I love him." Angela looks up at me, surprised. Even I'm a little surprised by how easily the words came. "I don't want to be the kind of person who's too afraid to try. Pushing him away isn't doing either of us any good. It's just hurting us both now rather than later, when maybe we can actually make it work and neither of us has to hurt at all."

"Love, huh?" Her smirk is wobbly, masking the fear I'm fighting not to feel. "That's a big word."

"I mean it." As if I'm rewarding myself for saying it out loud, I down the rest of my drink before pouring a second round. "Is it really that crazy? That we could maybe love each other after everything?"

"No." Angela softens, then downs her drink like she's the

one with the big revelation. "Just promise you won't forget about me when it all works out with you and Theo."

"Are you kidding me?" I pull her into a hug and her arms wrap around my shoulders like a vise. "*Never.*"

"You should tell him," she says, excitedly. "Everything you told me. He deserves to know how you really feel."

I suck in a breath, anxiety spiking in my veins at the thought. But it's accompanied by something else, something dizzying and giddy that makes the organ in my chest pump harder. Excitement.

"You're right." I nod, grab the phone from my back pocket. "I'm gonna tell him."

"Yes!" Angela throws an arm around my shoulders. "Tell him how you feel! But maybe wait until the morning, or a more appropriate time of day."

"You're right," I say, but this giddy energy isn't going anywhere. If anything, it turns to anxiety. "But what if I lose my nerve in the morning?"

"It's not possible to schedule texts, is it?" She frowns as I shake my head. "Damn."

"It's not even ten yet." I show her my lock screen, where the time is displayed. "How bad would texting him right now be? I have to tell him, and I have to do it before I lose my nerve."

"Give me that." She snatches the phone from my hand before I can react. "How much vodka are you putting in these? Might be time to lock the phones away."

"I wasn't putting that much." But one glance at the half empty liquor bottle discredits me. I don't feel that drunk. A bit tipsy perhaps. Two minutes and a slow blink away from an unintentional nap on the floor, sure. But not drunk.

In the end, Angela's the one who crashes on the floor while I take the couch. The fact that neither of us makes it to the bed should tell us something about the effect the alcohol has on us. When I open my eyes, I can't tell if any time has passed. The lights are still on. Angela is fast asleep on the floor, her back rising and falling gently with her breaths. Her phone is sitting on the coffee table while mine is tucked in the right back pocket of her jeans. She never made it to the lock case.

I'm just going to check the time, I tell myself as I lean off the couch, pinching the sides of my phone with my thumb and pointer finger, ensuring I'm not touching her before carefully sliding it free. She doesn't stir.

Except, I don't even register the time before I find myself opening the message app. I yawn into my hand as I type out a quick message, hoping I'm not too late. That he hasn't already decided he wants nothing to do with me anymore. I can't let this mistake grow any bigger than I've already allowed it to. He needs to know how I feel, and I need to know if he can forgive me. This can't wait. I won't be able to sleep properly with this weight on my chest.

As soon as I hit send, with nothing weighing me down anymore, my eyes blink closed and I fall back asleep.

My tolerance must not be what it used to be, because when I wake up in the morning my head is pounding. Angela must have turned off the lights in the middle of the night. The living room is dark except for the light coming through the window. She's still fast asleep on the floor, arms wrapped around her shoulders like she's cold. I step over her to get to my room and return with a blanket.

"Mmf." Angela turns over, blinking awake, as I drop the blanket over her. "What time is it?"

"I don't know. I haven't checked yet."

I grab my phone from the couch when last night returns to me: me sneaking my phone from her back pocket, pulling up the message app—

"Oh no."

"What happened?" Angela asks, still half asleep until she looks into my face, at whatever frozen expression must be painted on it. "Marcela, what happened?"

"I texted Theo last night." The memory rushes forword until it's all I can think about. God, I don't even know what time it was when I sent him that text. What must he be thinking? I have no way of knowing from my empty lock screen, clear of notifications.

Her wrinkled brow straightens as she spots the phone in my hand. "You little sneak thief."

"You never made it to the lock case. If there's anyone to blame here, it's you."

"I didn't send your ex-rebound a drunk text in the middle of the night, now did I?" She crosses her arms and pins me with a look.

"I wasn't that drunk." Even so, I deserve every bit of the stern disappointment in her face. "Just...sleepy."

"What time did you send it?"

My thumb hovers over the message app, nerves

overwrought. Why the hell did I think sending that message last night was a good idea? I should've waited for a more reasonable hour at least. I should've asked him to talk in person about how I feel, not whatever hastily thought-out text I ended up sending last night.

Angela rises to her knees for a better look at my screen. I'm almost afraid to let her see whatever catastrophe I may have sent Theo, but for the first time in a while, I don't want to be alone to deal with whatever fallout will come of this. After finally tapping the message icon, it opens immediately to our text chain. The message was sent at approximately 2:48 a.m.

> I changed my mind. I can't walk away from you for good. Please tell me you still feel the same.

> I want to give us a second chance.

Oh god.

Of course I meant every word, but that doesn't mean he had to hear it through text. There's still no resolution between us, or the people we've both attempted to come between. But maybe—if he's willing to forgive me, that is—it'll be worth the risk to try. The thought comforts me more than it makes me anxious, which has to be a momentous step forward.

I want Theo. Maybe I even want him to know how I feel.

Just as I'm beginning to think maybe this is a good thing, I chance a glance at Angela. Except when I do, the blood has drained from her face and I find horror in her widened eyes. She looks back at me, shaking her head furiously. My brows furrow in a silent question until I turn back to the screen. That's when I notice what she must have seen first. Because it's not Theo's name at the top of my screen.

It's Ben's.

"Fuck." I let out a breath, chest heaving. "*Holy fuck!* What am I gonna—" I let out a loud gasp as the status below the message changes to read. Then I let out an ear-piercing screech. Angela flinches before making a grab for the phone and tossing it across the room. It lands with a crash somewhere in the hallway.

"Okay, okay, let's calm down and think." Angela reaches for my shoulders in a hard grip. "This is bad, yes, but we can fix it."

"*How?*" I burst, panic flooding my veins. "How can we possibly fix—"

A loud vibration from the hallway makes both of us jump. He's calling.

Angela meets my eyes imploringly, as if to say, *Don't do this.* But there's no going back. The only way out is through. I spent years avoiding this truth I so desperately wanted to be untrue, and all it bought me was a smokescreen.

I want to be better than this.

Before I talk to Theo, I need to clear things up with Ben for good. The text might not have been meant for him, but at one point it could've been. It's time to face up to the feelings I've been fighting to outrun head-on, once and for all. It's the only way I'll be able to make good on my promise to move on from him.

I rise from the couch, numbness settling over me as I carry myself to where my phone landed, pick it up from the floor, and hit answer.

Twenty-Nine

D o you want me to stay?" Angela whispers as I put the phone to my ear. I shake my head, resolute. This is something I need to do on my own.

Angela leaves my apartment wordlessly, mouthing *Good luck* before the front door shuts behind her. I sit down on the couch with a sigh, Ben's voice on the other line hitting me like a ton of bricks.

"What the hell, Marcela?"

Maybe I shouldn't be, but I'm glad I waited this long to confess—even if confessing to *Ben* wasn't what I'd planned on doing at all in the first place. Thanks a lot, Drunk Marcela. But now that the truth is partially out there, I want to be more like Theo. I want to be honest with other people, but more importantly I want to be honest with myself. "Look, Ben, I'm sor—"

"Why now?"

I freeze, the explanation dying on my tongue. *I'm sorry if I confused you. I was drunk, and that text wasn't meant for you.* He doesn't sound surprised.

Why now?

His voice is lowered, a husky whisper as the creak of a door opening and closing sounds over the speaker. I don't know where he is, but I immediately know he's hiding from Alice. He wouldn't ask that kind of question if she were in the room with him.

He knew. All along, he *knew*.

"I'm *engaged*," he says, as if I could possibly forget. "Is that why you've been so weird, lately? Why you went after my *brother* of all people?"

"I—" I have no idea what to say to that. No idea what we're even talking about anymore. *Is he* admitting *he knew?* I scoff over the line. "I didn't go after Theo. It just sort of... happened," I say, which is mostly true.

"Really?" he asks in a tone that's clear he doesn't believe me. "You hook up with my brother the night of my engagement party. And then turn around and text me what you did last night. Now I'm expected to believe your relationship with Theo had *nothing* to do with me?"

I'm stunned silent, chastened in a way I deserve to be. To him, I'm messing with his head, with whatever his mixed-up emotions are right now. It doesn't matter that I never meant to, that I held my own emotions back and lied for so long that I no longer recognize the truth of them.

"I did have feelings for you," I tell him, and though I cringe as soon as the words are out, I also feel immeasurably relieved. "Past tense. You probably won't believe me, but that message wasn't intended for you. I was never going to tell you how I felt. That was a secret I was content to keep buried for both our sakes. For Alice's, too."

This might be the most honest I've been with him in years. As hard as it is admitting all that to him, I'm glad I finally did.

"Last night was a mistake. You weren't supposed to get that message, it was meant for someone else, and I'm sorry you did. I'm sorry if I hurt you or your relationship with Alice."

His sigh is deep, edged with frustration. "I don't know what I'm supposed to think at this point."

"Just forget it ever happened," I tell him, as if it's that easy. But he *has* to. We both do. "Because it was never supposed to."

"Marcela—"

I hang up before he can finish, because I am. *Finished.* Is this what closure feels like? My hands shake as I set my phone down, every nerve end jittery and wired. It's not the feeling I expected, but it's close. The last chapter before the epilogue. But before I get there, there's a new page I'm ready to start fresh on.

Can we talk?

I hit send before I can overthink it. *I want this.* If he meant what he said and he's still in this…

An hour later, there's a knock at my door. I jump up immediately, imagining Theo behind the door as if summoned by the message I sent.

I take a quick glance at myself in the mirror. My eyes are dark and hollow-looking from lack of sleep, and my hair is a mess of tangled curls. I pull it back with a chongo, making a low bun that will have to do before going to answer the door.

But it's not Theo on the other side of it.

It's *Alice*.

Oh god. *What the hell did I do?*

Her usually pristine hair is flat and greasy, tied at the back of her head in a low ponytail. She's wearing a puffy jacket over black leggings and a UTSA sweatshirt. The roadrunner logo makes me feel queasy (or maybe that's the hangover), a callback to those college days of pining over Ben rushing to the forefront, more raw and visceral.

"Can we talk?"

"Y-yes," I say, stepping away to let her inside.

Her left hand comes to rest on her forehead, like she's staving off a headache. Aside from obvious exhaustion, there's something different about her. I just can't put my finger on it yet. She finally sighs as I take a seat beside her. "I saw the message you sent to Ben."

My stomach drops to the floor, along with some other essential organs, I'm sure. My chest tightens, preventing air from reaching my lungs. All this time, I've been so afraid that she already knew. Or suspected, at least. Her keen eyes bore into me, but this time, it's like she's looking at a stranger.

"I always hated that I ruined our friendship," she says suddenly.

"Alice, you didn't—" I shake my head, but she holds up a hand. I'm the one who lied and said I was completely over him.

"I know you gave me the go-ahead, but it still wasn't cool.

It's girl code, for god's sake." She throws out her arms. "It caused the rift between us. Maybe you pulled away because of residual feelings, but I pulled away because"—she takes a deep breath as if steeling herself—"because I was jealous."

My brows furrow, not believing her for a second. Jealous? Of *me*?

"I hated how close you two were, knowing your history. It didn't matter that you were never exclusive. As if that really matters." She rolls her eyes. "But he insisted on keeping you in his life. He said you were a good person, his best friend. The way he talked about you was the way I wished he talked about me, back when we were first dating."

"Alice, about the message—" I start, but she doesn't let me finish.

"He reminded me of Theo a little, actually," she says over me, and I wince. I can so easily imagine Theo talking about her with the utmost respect, even after all they've been through. His eyes shining from just thinking about her. "The way he used to be around me in high school. I've always admired how unafraid he is to wear his heart on his sleeve, even when it's broken. Ben has never been that way."

"Yeah," I say, because I don't know what else to do.

"You look good together," she says abruptly, her eyes turning to me. "You and Theo. Whatever their differences, these Young men have eerily similar taste in women."

I nearly choke on my own saliva. Alice's eyes light up with humor at whatever expression must be on my face.

"Alice, you have to know that Ben has never felt the same way I did. I never meant to send that message to him, and

I can't apologize enough for whatever trouble I caused you guys. I'm the one who's to blame—"

"Stop." She motions with a tired hand. "Don't fool yourself into thinking you're entirely to blame for what happened with Ben. I've always had good instincts, but my mistake was never listening to them. I tried to tell myself for years that what you two had together was purely friendship."

My eyes catch on her hand, and suddenly, I know what's different about her. I let out a gasp.

No ring.

She catches my line of sight and glances down at her bare hand. "Oh, yeah. We're over. Please don't feel guilty. I don't blame you for it. At least, not entirely."

I gulp, feeling immensely and painfully guilty anyway. "Why not?" I ask. I'd certainly blame me if I were her.

"He shouldn't have kept coming to you for emotional support. Not the way he was, and definitely not when he was with me," she tells me. "Even if physical lines weren't crossed."

She shakes her head, and when she opens her eyes again they're shining with empathy. "But if it's any consolation, Theo is nothing like his brother. He's never hidden a single part of himself from anyone. What you see is exactly what you get."

"Yeah," I agree, eyes filling. "Yeah, he deserves someone great."

Alice's brows furrow. "I thought you two were..." She trails off when I shake my head, understanding dawning in her eyes. "Well, that's a shame. I could tell he cared about you."

"He does," I say. Then, as much as I know I'll probably regret asking, I say, "How come you never returned his feelings? Or did you, at one point?"

She lets out a sigh, looking away from me. "There was a moment, my junior year of high school. He'd just finished a football game, and I stayed after to congratulate him on the win. His eyes seemed to pierce through me, and for a moment…I don't know. My heart jumped, and it was like I was seeing him for the first time."

My own wrenches at her admission. If Theo knew, it would change everything for him, wouldn't it? She shakes her head suddenly. "But then he started talking about the NFL, and how I was gonna be a big-time journalist. We'd Skype every weekend and visit each other every other month. All these plans of staying in touch that fell through the second high school was over.

"This feud with Ben felt like my fault, so I thought I should be the one to fix it. I wanted them to resolve their issues before the wedding. Be real brothers to each other again. But the more and more I reached out, something funny happened." Her lips curl in a smile. "Theo reminded me of all the dreams I'd forgotten about. Leaving Texas behind for some big city. New York. Chicago. DC. It reminded me that somewhere along the way, with Ben, I had settled before my life could really begin."

I look over at her, not entirely comprehending what she's saying.

"We didn't break up because of you," she says, holding up her ringless hand. "It was because of me. I've secretly been applying to jobs out of state for months. Not because I really intended on leaving. I wouldn't have said yes to Ben if I was," she explains quickly. "But last week, I got offered a position at the *Washington Post*. I was all set to turn them down, until I saw your text on Ben's phone this morning."

My eyes widen, emotions spinning in different directions. I give a surprised laugh. "Should I be congratulating you, or…?"

She nods, mouth breaking out into a wide grin. "Yeah, that'd be a start." She laughs. I pull her into a hug, half surprised when she accepts and wraps her arms around my shoulders. "I have no idea how I'll afford rent since it's only an intern position, but it's a starting point."

"That's incredible," I tell her. "Really. I'm so happy for you."

"Thanks," she says, pushing her hair back behind her ear. "And you won't have to worry about me anymore, if I'm part of the reason you and Theo aren't together anymore."

"I…" I start, not sure what to say. Does Alice and Ben's breakup change anything? On my side, I don't think it does. But for Theo? If any part of him still cares about her in a romantic way, there's no way I can see past that.

Finally, I shake my head. "I don't know."

"Well, I hope you get some clarity soon," she tells me, getting up from the couch. "Thank you for talking with me. And don't beat yourself up too much."

When she smiles, I can see what Theo saw in her. Her warmth comes through, eyes sparkling like we're in on a secret from the rest of the world. I see her to the door, and she stands tall as she walks away. She doesn't look back, but I don't expect her to. That bubble of jealousy I'm used to doesn't fill me. I have nothing but respect for her.

I close the door, leaning back on it with a sigh. They're really over. How many times in almost a decade have I waited for this exact moment to transpire? I imagined I'd be thrilled. That I'd run to my car and speed down the highway to where he lives, hesitate before knocking on his door, and then…the fantasy always ended there. I never once imagined that the outcome would fall in my favor.

Only now, I can't imagine wanting anything less.

Thirty

Two days later, I meet Ben at a coffee shop before work.

As far as bad ideas go, this one takes the cake. But he was insistent on meeting in person "to talk." If he hates me, does he hate me enough to want to chew me out in a public setting? I'd hate me if I were him. I'm partially the reason he and Alice are no longer together.

He's seated beside a window, warming his hands with a giant red mug. A latte with two pumps of vanilla and almond milk, most likely. He's wearing a jean jacket over a gray sweatshirt, his right leg shaking underneath the table. His hair is shorter than it was the last time I saw him, and it's styled with product. Of all the times I imagined his breakup with Alice, I never expected the reality. His eyes are clear and bright, no trace of dark circles underneath them. His clothes look perfectly pressed and washed. A smile even tugs the edge of his mouth when he spots me by the entrance.

Maybe he doesn't hate me then. Odd.

Alice, the woman he was about to marry, left him three

days ago. He should be a heartbroken mess of a man who can't bear to leave the house. But there's something about him that seems almost...unbothered.

"Hey." I take the seat across from him. "Listen, Ben. I'm so sorry about Alice."

"It's not your fault." His smile comes off strained even as he waves off my concern. But I don't understand why he'd even bother, after that text. "Really, Marcela. Don't blame yourself."

"I don't know how to do that." I shake my head. "Are you..." I clear my throat to cover the stupid question I was about to ask him. "How are you?"

"Surprisingly, okay," he says, and I'm not sure how I can believe that. "Maybe we just weren't meant to be."

"Meant to be or not doesn't erase the eight years you guys spent together," I say. "You shouldn't be afraid to let yourself feel whatever you're feeling about Alice—"

"Look, I really don't want to talk about her," he says, expression shuttering. *There it is.* A trace of how he really feels, right below the unbothered facade. "But the other day was a wake-up call, to say the least. It's got me thinking about all the choices we made to get here, and I can't—" He shakes his head. "I can't fathom how it came to this."

I don't say anything, but my thoughts turn a hundred different ways.

"Do you ever wonder if we could've made it work?" he asks suddenly. "If we'd given ourselves a real shot?"

What the hell is even happening right now?

Is that the reason he asked to meet me? To ask me the

question I've been asking myself for nearly a decade? Nine years. It took nine years, a drunk text, and his brother to make him ask me that question. It's too late. God, it should've been too late *years* ago.

"Do you?" I ask, because maybe I owe it to my past self to finally have the answer.

"Yeah," he says. "Recently, yeah. I've been thinking about it a lot."

How is it possible that I'm bone-tired and exhausted, but also that years' worth of weight has been lifted off my shoulders at the same time? To be relieved and disappointed at the same time?

"Just recently?" I ask. "You hadn't...thought about it at all before you and Alice broke up?"

"I mean"—he shifts in his seat—"I've never really had to. I thought being with Alice was the right choice. That we were perfect for each other, even if sometimes our relationship wasn't," he goes on, but I've already checked out. I have my answer, and it's the least surprising conclusion.

I'm his second choice.

I'm the girl he sidelined for the better choice. Now that the better choice is gone, he's got me all lined up and ready to go. But this isn't all on him. It's on me for ever giving him the idea that I'd be okay with this. There's nothing left to be guilty over, but the shame remains. And oh, it burns me from the inside out.

"...but you were always there for me." I've missed most of what he's said, but I return my attention at this last part. "Anytime I needed you, you've always been there for me.

No judgment, no complaint. You were always the person who stayed. And I know there were a lot of times when I took that for granted." *No kidding.* "And I'm sorry for that. God, Marcela, I'm so unbelievably sorry for that. But know that words can't express how much I appreciate you." He reaches out his hand as if to grasp mine. He hesitates at the last moment, from whatever expression must be on my face. "What's wrong? Was it—was what I said not okay?"

"I'm such an idiot." The words burst free of their own volition. My eyes shut, because I can't even bear to look at him for a second longer. "*God*, I'm a complete and total idiot. And you have no idea."

"Marcela—"

"You don't know how long I've waited to hear you say that." Or maybe he does. *Why now?* I laugh humorlessly. "*Years*, Ben. Actual years, I've sat and waited for you to change your mind. And it never would've happened if I hadn't fallen in love with your brother."

There's that word again. *Love.* And here I am for the second time, telling someone who isn't Theo how I feel. But I can't focus on that right now, or the utter astonishment on Ben's face.

"That's not the point." I redirect my focus on Ben. On the *anger* brimming just below the surface. "But let's go back in time and think about it. Why did you think we were better off as friends?"

"I don't know," he says, but there's something in his face that makes me not believe him. "It was so long ago. But I knew you were someone I wanted in my life. The emotional connection we had back then, you don't find that anywhere. It's rare."

"But it wasn't enough." At least, it wasn't for him. "Why is that?"

"I guess I just didn't see us that way at the time," he says, and there it is. It almost doesn't matter we were together *that way* for weeks. Why would it, when the whole time he didn't see it? See *me* the same way I saw him? It's the same coded shit I used to get all the time from guys I met on dating apps. I tricked myself into believing he was different from those men, that the connection we'd formed was stronger than that. That it actually meant something to both of us, even if we didn't work out romantically. But the only reason we didn't work is because he *decided* that we didn't.

"You didn't 'see us that way,'" I repeat, practically spitting the words in an effort not to scream. "You mean you didn't see *me* that way. Physically."

"I was stupid," he says. "I didn't appreciate the connection we had at the time. I thought we worked better as friends."

"You thought you could do better, but you wanted me around just in case," I translate.

"You never said anything." His face colors with embarrassment. I know I'm right on the mark because he can't look me in the eyes anymore. "I thought you agreed with me."

No, I never did tell him how I felt. Partly because I was too humiliated to have been so off base, and partly because I thought if I kept him in my life, he'd change his mind. I didn't want closure, but I needed it. Desperately.

"Let me ask you something, then." I straighten my shoulders.

"How could you regret that we didn't give it a fair shot if you were never attracted to me in the first place? Is this some kind of game to you, or are you just that scared to be alone?"

His jaw clenches, but he doesn't answer.

"You kept me on the hook, leaned on me when you couldn't lean on anyone else. And then, you got with Alice." His shoulders lower the longer I keep talking. "You made me your second choice. I am so sick of waiting around for you, Ben. No one is worth waiting ten years for. Absolutely *no one*, and least of all you."

He sits back in his seat, mouth falling open.

"I never meant to make you a second choice," he says.

A wave of frustration crests over me. "Then why am I here?" I'm too mad to feel embarrassed when heads from the table next to us turn to stare. "Alice left you, and suddenly you want to reminisce about the past? What do you think you're making me now? It's too late, Ben."

"Because of Theo." His mouth twists. "Because you think you're in love with him?"

"Yes, I'm in love with him," I say. "He's not at all the person you've been trying so hard to make him out to be. He's kind-hearted, open, and funny, and he's always been up front with me from the very beginning." He opens his mouth to cut me off, but I don't let him. "Which is a hell of a lot more than I can say about you. He told me *everything*. About Alice, and his relationship with you, this weird animosity between you guys. I don't entirely understand it or know if it can be fixed, but it's fucked up."

"If he really told you the truth, you'd know it wasn't just me—it was *both* of us." He stops himself before he can go on. Takes a breath. "I know I have my part of the blame. I never meant to hurt him, and I felt awful about it for months. But he wouldn't even listen to me when I told him to slow it down." My brows crease as he goes on. I thought he was talking about when he started dating Alice at first, but the last part doesn't make any sense. "He wouldn't even listen to the doctors when they warned him he could permanently damage his knee and have to retire a few years into his career."

"Wait—"

"But that didn't stop him from shutting me out and blaming me for it in the first place," he says. "He thought I did it on purpose, to get back at him for all the teasing and shit talk."

Theo's torn ACL. He said it was from an old injury that never healed right—but he never told me that *Ben* was the cause of it. Alice isn't the reason they stopped speaking. It all stems back to the injury. That's the root of the crack in their relationship.

"I'd never do that," Ben says. "It was an accident, but he's never once let me live it down. It doesn't matter how many times I apologize, he doesn't care. Not as long as he can still blame me for taking everything from him at every turn."

I don't think that's what Theo really blames him for. Not anymore, at least.

"I have to go." I don't care if there's still unfinished business between us. *I'm* finished, and that's all that matters. He calls me back when I dash across the coffee shop, but I don't stop.

Ben has been the source of pain for all of us for too long. Theo's NFL dreams, cut short. Alice's career, stalled. My romantic relationships, *a fucking joke*. For the first time, I'm finally seeing him clearly. And I don't like it one bit.

On Wednesday night, Theo is sitting on a bench outside the library. He never answered my text. I've been walking around in a fog all week, checking my phone every time it vibrates, waiting for a reply that never came.

Now he's here, bundled in a brown coat and olive-green beanie, hands buried in his pockets for warmth. I'm so stunned to see him out here, I drop my lunch box. What's dorkier than carrying around a lunch box? Dropping it at the sight of the rebound you're still in love with. Even worse, when I bend down to pick it up, I'm so antsy that I accidentally kick it forward. The poor floral-print bag flies across the sidewalk and hits Theo's leg. Just when I thought I couldn't get any dorkier.

"Here." He picks it up from the cement, then raises himself from the bench, immediately towering over me. I take the bag from his hand, wincing from embarrassment.

"I didn't mean to scare you. I got your text, but I wanted to see you in person." He blows out a breath, eyes shutting. "And to see if you heard—"

"I did," I tell him. "Alice told me they broke up."

I wonder who told him, Alice or Ben. Does he know my rogue text message is the reason? God, I hope not. I want to tell him myself, so it doesn't sound like I betrayed him coming from someone else. But now that he's here, and he knows Alice is single, I can't help but fear he's changed his mind about me.

"Yeah." He nods. "So, I guess I was just wondering if that changes anything." Those blue eyes study me, gauging anything in my expression that could give some sort of clue to the question he's posed. I walk past him to the bench, setting my stuff down on the sidewalk as I take a seat. He returns to me, taking up the space beside me. His thigh touches mine lightly. I don't pull away, but I almost want to. I can't sort out my thoughts properly in his proximity.

It's not Ben and Alice's relationship ending that's changed things for me. I'm partly the reason they're over, and it's because of a text I meant to send to Theo. I don't feel a single thing about their breakup, but I have no idea how he feels.

"I don't know," I say, because I want to hear his answer first. "Does it change anything for you?"

Alice's words keep repeating themselves in my head. *There was a moment.* I can't stop thinking about what Theo would do if he knew. If he'd drop me in a second, just for the chance of re-creating that moment with Alice. He's settled in a new job here, but are his feelings strong enough to follow her across the country? They were strong enough once for him to try to stop her from walking down the aisle, if I hadn't intervened.

"Not really." Theo shrugs. "I meant what I said to you. Alice was never going to see me that way, and even if she does—"

"What?" I interrupt. "Even if she does, what? Would you be with her instead?"

"She's not the one I want." There's something in his tone that gives me pause. A fraught earnestness that makes me want to believe him. I want so *desperately* to believe him. His eyes soften as he looks at me, and I wonder how I look to him. If any trace of hope gives me away.

"I don't know how long it takes to get over someone completely, if that ever really happens. But you've made these past few months…" He clears his throat. "Better than I ever could've imagined, given the circumstance."

I understand what he means. He surprised me. Took my life by storm and tore through everything I thought I knew to be true. He became so much more than a rebound, long before he asked me for more. Now I can hardly imagine what my life would look like without him in it.

And that terrifies me.

"What about you?" he asks again. "If Ben feels the same way you do, would you…" He trails off, unable to complete the question. Maybe he doesn't know about the drunken text after all. When I don't answer right away, he turns away from me. "Right. Of course. I should've known, given how much he tried to keep us apart."

"Theo—"

"No, don't." He whips up from the bench, pacing the length of the sidewalk. His voice doesn't raise in anger. Instead, it's carefully controlled. Resolute. "It was stupid of me to think I could change your mind. He's clearly interested in you, and if you want to give him a shot, I can't stop you. No matter how much I might want to, and *believe* me…" An emotion I can't name bleeds through his tone suddenly. He kneels directly in front of me, the lamplight reflecting in his blue eyes. "I want to. But I don't want to be the only one fighting for us. Especially if I'm not the one you want."

His hands rest on my knees, warming through the fabric of my jeans. I reach out toward him, hands cupping his cold cheeks. I've gone so long without touching him that the second I do, I breathe a sigh of relief. Even now, with all my mixed-up emotions, this just feels right. It's hard to tell who moves first, who kisses who first, only that the second our lips touch I melt into him. His hands move up my back, pulling me closer. I latch on to him, arms curling behind his neck. I lose myself in the warmth of his mouth, in the touch I've spent weeks craving. He's what I want. I can't deny that anymore.

He's right. He shouldn't be the only one fighting for us, but if we do this the fight won't be over yet. Something tells me that nothing will test us more than Alice and Ben's breakup. I want so badly to believe him when he says I'm the one he wants. That he won't go running to Alice now that she's free. That in time, I'll be the only one who owns his heart the same way he's the only one who owns mine.

"Marcela—" He sucks in a breath as I kiss down his neck. My nails graze his nape, fingers curling in the soft hair there. "I don't think this is a— *Fuck*."

His exclamation comes when my warm hand meets the bare skin of his stomach, roaming up his side. "Do you want me to stop?" His stubble tickles my lips as I ask the question against his jawline. We lock eyes for a beat, and I wait for him to take the out. I wouldn't even blame him for it. He's right. We shouldn't be doing this now, not when we have nothing figured out.

He doesn't take the out. He kisses me instead, and this time there's urgency in our movements. His tongue slides against mine, searching, coaxing. My arms wrap around his neck as his hands settle on my waist, pulling me off the bench in one swift motion. I drown in him all over again, never once craving a breath of fresh air.

Thirty-One

W e go back to his place.

   We waste no time stripping each other of winter layers. First our coats, then the second layer of outerwear, until finally, the last layers come off and we're skin to skin. A ridiculous amount of clothing litters the living room floor as Theo walks me backward through the living room, kissing down my neck as his fingers find the top button of my jeans. He pushes me against the door, hands moving up my back as I step out of my pants and kick them to the side. My bra is the next article of clothing to go, and then he twists open the doorknob to his bedroom and leads me inside.

   The back of my knees hit the edge of the mattress, and everything becomes real. We should talk first, maybe, before we do this. He has no idea I'm reconsidering everything, that I've fallen in love with him despite the odds, that even though I'm still not sure if we can make a real relationship work, I'm not ready to lose him for good, either. But where does that leave us, if not the limbo my fear has created for us?

"Wait." He pauses from rifling through the top drawer of his nightstand. I reach for his shoulders, hands curling in his hair as my arms wrap around his head. "Come here."

I kiss him slowly, using my body to convey what my words can't. My fingers hook in the belt loops of his jeans, pulling him into me. I find the button and zipper of his jeans, then push them off him. My hands skirt the top of his boxers, and his body shivers in response. But when I touch him through the thin material...

"*Fuck.*" He buries his head in the crook of my neck. When I inch my hand inside his boxers, he lets out a guttural groan in the form of my name. He bites down on my shoulder, light enough not to break skin, but hard enough for me to let out a hiss. He replaces his teeth with his lips, kissing the spot to ease the slight sting.

His hand closes over mine, easing it away from his cock. When I look up at him, his eyes are hazy. His other hand settles on my lower back as he eases me backward onto the mattress. His knees settle on either side of me on the bed. We never got to christen this bed before I blew up our first date. This is my first time inside his bedroom. Maybe my last.

I shut my eyes, as if that'll help shut off my thoughts.

"Are you okay?"

I don't answer his question. Instead, I wrap my arms around his neck and pull him down. I close my mouth over his, kissing him hard and fast, until all thoughts outside this moment dissipate. His hands travel down my hair, down my back, and then come up around to my chest. My breasts fill his hands, and I let out a groan into his mouth. *Yes.*

His fingers circle my peaked nipples. When his mouth closes over the right one, my nails dig into the skin of his nape. He sucks in a breath, but I'm barely breathing. Not when his other hand keeps circling, or when it dips down inside my panties.

"Marcela." His voice is breathless when he feels how wet I am, two fingers gently moving up to reach my clit. He rests his forehead against mine. Through the dim glow of his window, his face twists into a pained expression. "Don't tell me this is the last time."

He kisses me before I can respond, before I can even think of a proper response. A kiss that slices a gaping hole inside my chest, even as a shot of pleasure surges through my veins. His hand works fast, but his mouth moves faster. So fast I can barely keep up with him, so I let him lead the pace. I nearly whimper when he pulls away, until I realize it's to search through his nightstand for a condom.

Before I can process what's happening, he flips us over until I'm on top of him. He lifts us up until he's pulled himself into a seated position with me in his lap, his head leaning back against the headboard. Our eyes meet and lock for the first time tonight. They're obsidian under the pale moonlight, glittering black rocks cast in a neutral expression. There's no smug smile tugging his lips, no hint of the devious smirks I'm used to. It's disorienting.

He tears through the packaging and sheathes himself in one swift motion. This time, I don't need help guiding myself on top of him. I almost reach for his shoulder, but steady myself with a hand on the headboard instead. Our faces are so close this way, chest to chest. Too close for comfort, when he wears that guarded expression I've never seen on him. When I know it's because of *me* that he has to protect himself in the first place.

Slowly, I move my hips up and down. I grip the headboard tighter to hold myself up, and I shut my eyes to avoid looking into Theo's face. His hands close over my hips and squeeze, helping to quicken my movements. I think I hear him say my name, but I'm too stuck inside my own head to be sure. His lips graze my shoulders, kissing up my neck, my jaw, until finally his mouth closes over mine.

"Theo," I moan his name into his mouth. I let go of the headboard, reaching for him instead. My arms wrap around his body, hands curling inside his hair. I melt into him, until I can almost pretend nothing's changed between us. That this isn't our last night. What an absurd thought. Why would either one of us give this up when it feels *this good*?

He finishes soon before I do, his hand replacing his cock until a wave of pleasure washes over me. We collapse onto each other, breathing fast and shallow.

"Stay." Is that a note of pleading in his voice, or is that my own twisted, wishful thinking? "It's too late for either one of us to be on the road. Please."

"Okay." I can't make out his features anymore. Total darkness swamps his bedroom now. Maybe that's better. "I'll stay."

He pulls me into his body until I'm crushed to his hard chest, burying his head in the crook of my shoulder, one hand settled beneath my hair at the nape of my neck. My heart slams in my chest, emotion choking the back of my throat. There's no way he can't feel my heartbeat through my skin.

I don't know what this was, but I don't want it to be goodbye. The thought of losing him only makes me want all our nights to be like this, curled in his arms, listening to his breath even out as he falls asleep. Maybe that's what finally gives me the courage to take the leap.

"I want to try." I can hardly hear myself speak, my heart is beating so hard. His body stills beside me, waiting. "But this is hard for me. You're the best thing that's happened to me in a long time, and I don't want to fuck this up."

"You won't." Those two little words hold more conviction than I have in my whole body. "I won't, either."

"That's not something you can promise," I say. "I already fucked up. I'm part of the reason they broke up. I sent Ben a text meant for you, and it blew up their relationship."

His body rolls away from mine, and for a moment I think he's changed his mind again. I should've told him the truth sooner, before we slept together. Maybe he's realizing a real relationship together is all too much to deal with, and we were foolish to try. I squint my eyes against the light as he flicks on a lamp. Theo sits up, back against the headboard.

"Explain." His face is carefully controlled neutrality.

I explain the situation as best I can, talking through my feelings with Angela and the drinks that followed, and how that plus sleep deprivation may have contributed to sending that text to the wrong brother.

"Alice saw the message before he did, and then, well. You know the rest."

He's quiet for a beat, contemplative. "It wasn't your fault."

"That text is the reason they're not together anymore." I shake my head. "Of course it's my fault."

"No." There's that conviction again. I only wish he could share some of it with me. "It's not. If their relationship were stronger, they would've been able to handle it. They had deeper issues they needed to work through, but they couldn't do it."

He's right, I suppose. Alice wouldn't have applied to jobs out of the state and kept it from Ben otherwise. She looked happier telling me about her internship than she did telling me about her engagement. Maybe she was looking for a reason to leave. Maybe I gave her one.

"Are you sad that she's leaving?"

"No." He turns off the lamp and returns to his place in bed, arms around my body. His hand moves up my back in gentle strokes. "No, I'm not sad. We talked about this for years when we were in high school. The reason I said their engagement was a mistake is because she boxed away her dreams without even trying. Ben—" He blows out a breath. "I know how he is. Before we stopped talking, he didn't want me to leave after high school."

"What?" I ask. "Really?"

"Yeah, he thought I'd abandon him if I made it into the NFL. Our family was already falling apart. He didn't want to lose me, too. And in a way, I guess he was right." He shakes his head. "I know my brother. He holds on to the people he loves impossibly tight. He knows how to twist your words into something you feel guilty over for years. He turns your ambition into selfishness if it doesn't include him somehow, but especially if it means leaving him behind."

I can't lose you. Yes, I know exactly what Theo means.

"It was exhausting. He was my brother and I loved him. I still do," he explains. "But sometimes, I think I hated him more when we were close."

The realization hits me then. If what he's saying is true, and there's not a doubt in my mind it is, then Ben would've done anything to make sure Theo couldn't leave, that he'd never be able to achieve his dreams and leave Ben.

"Do you think that's why he hurt you?" My heart thumps wildly in my chest. *This is none of my business.* Theo's shoulders tense up under my touch. "I'm sorry. It's just—I saw him a few days ago and he let it slip that he was the reason for your injury in the first place. If it wasn't for him—"

"God, how do you do that?" He sounds like the wind's been kicked out of him.

"Do what?" I shrink, even though he can't see me.

"Find all the worst parts of me." He rolls away from me. "I've never even let myself say it out loud, but it's like you've infiltrated my most selfish thoughts. The injury was an accident. I've come to terms with that over the years, because the alternative…" He trails off, as if afraid to voice it. "The alternative has almost broken me too many times. I've entertained the idea too many times, but it never made me feel any better. I'm through wondering if my own brother would do that to me on purpose. The truth can't do me any good now. It's over."

I nod to myself. Better to drop the subject now, and let bygones be bygones. If that's what will help him heal.

"It doesn't matter. Not if I left anyway and shut him out when I did," Theo says. "I knew it would hurt him, but I still did it. Maybe I am selfish, but I never thought that was the right way to love someone. To hold on to them so tightly, you never gave them room to breathe. It's the same way he loves Alice. And you."

I vaguely remember Alice majoring in journalism, but not any of those dreams Theo's talking about. In fact, when she talked about her future back then, it mostly revolved around Ben.

"I never thought of it that way," I say. "I was probably conditioned not to because of my dad."

He doesn't say anything, waiting for me to go on. I don't plan on saying anything more, but something about his comforting silence, the darkness engulfing us, and my promise to *try* makes me continue.

"I hated him for leaving us. I've never hated anyone like I hate him. My whole body *burns* with it when I think about it for too long, even now. For years, I thought the worst thing you could do to someone you love was leave without a trace." I take in a steadying breath, steeling myself to be as honest with Theo as he's been with me. "That's why I kept hanging on to Ben the way he hung on to me. Because even if I could never have him the way I wanted, I knew he'd never leave me. That's what I thought love was. Never leaving."

A beat of silence. "Do you still think that?"

"No." I shake my head. "He wouldn't have held on to me the way he did if he really loved me. He wouldn't have cast me aside so easily. It wasn't good for us, staying in each other's lives the way we did. It just took me way too long to realize that."

"Okay," he says, my head tucked beneath his chin. "Are you sure you want to do this? Try?"

"Mm-hm." I cover a yawn with my hand. It crosses my mind that we should probably talk about what that means, but I'm too exhausted and the warmth of his body is too comfortable. I sink into him, into the best sleep I've had in weeks.

It's early when his alarm goes off. The curtains are still dark, which is how I know it's way earlier than I need to be up for work. He turns his back as he gets dressed, careful not to make another sound to wake me, even when his lips touch my forehead. I'm still in shock over what I agreed to last night.

I want to try.

Try what, exactly? A relationship? Trusting us?

I turn these thoughts over in my head in the adjoining bathroom. I hop into the shower for a quick rinse, where I revel in the ocean scent of his body wash. I'll smell like him all day. Every time I catch the scent, I'll wonder if I'm making a massive mistake. Maybe I'll have a different answer each time. For now, I choose to move past my reservations and do exactly what I told him I'd do. *Try.*

The smell of coffee and bacon wafts through the hall as I make my way into the kitchen. His back is to me as he fixes two plates with scrambled eggs. When I clear my throat, he turns around. The smile he sends me is tentative, half guarded and half hopeful.

"Morning." He pushes a plate across the counter. His eyes

crinkle at the corners when I don't move. "Why are you so far away?"

I push myself off the wall I'm leaning against, barely registering that I seem to have forgotten how to walk. "Sorry."

"Don't be sorry." He places a fork on my plate. "Eat."

"Okay." I cross the space and plop myself on a barstool. "Can you—"

He's already pouring me a mug of coffee, with cream and sugar just how I like it. I take a bite of bacon, smiling up at him when he places the mug beside my arm.

"So," I start. He glances at me, eyes startlingly blue, and I lose all my nerve. "I didn't know you could cook."

"I know the basics. I don't normally cook this much before work, but I have some extra time before I have to go in today." He's already scarfed down half his plate. "We should talk."

My stomach flips, but I manage a small nod. "We should."

"That wasn't just the heat of the moment talking, was it?" he asks, and part of me is grateful he's making sure this is what I really want. "I don't want to hold you to something you're not ready for."

"I meant what I said," I assure him. "I…" *I love you.* I'm nowhere near ready to tell him that yet, so I change tact. "I don't want to lose you. You're important to me, Theo. If you think this can work—"

"It can." A determined glean enters his eyes. "I know it can."

He's so sure of himself. So sure of *us*, despite knowing how we started. Even without all the baggage we're bringing to the table, relationships are always a gamble. If we do this, we could end up losing each other. It's all or nothing with Theo. And that terrifies me.

"I'm willing to try." I wish I could give him more than that, more than my cautious hope. He deserves someone as all in as he is. But maybe I'll get there if I try hard enough.

"Are you still scared we won't make it?" he asks, his voice quiet.

"Oh yeah." I try to laugh, but it comes out breathless. "That's a given. I don't know how not to be. I've never done this before, Theo. I have no idea what I'm doing."

"Neither do I," he says, reaching for my hands. "This is all new to me, too. We're navigating this together."

I like the sound of that. *Together.*

"That being said"—he takes in a deep breath, and every nerve ending in my body stands on alert—"I don't mean to test your newfound trust so soon, but I agreed to help Alice move out of her apartment tomorrow night."

"Oh."

"I can cancel if you want me to," he says quickly. "If you're not comfortable with that."

The thought of them alone together doesn't make me feel good, even though I trust Theo enough not to do something stupid. He's not the same man who almost ruined her engagement party all those months ago. We've both come a long way since then, but I'm not ready to put our relationship to the test so soon, either.

I open my mouth to ask him to cancel, but what comes out instead is "Can I come with you?"

He seems surprised at my request, but he nods and says, "Sure. She'll probably appreciate the extra help."

"Cool." I nod, feeling anything but. "We're really doing this, huh?"

"We really are." He walks around the counter and takes the stool beside me, turning me until we're facing each other. He breaks out in a smile that rivals the sun. "Does this mean I get to call you my girlfriend?"

"I don't know." I melt into him when his hand lifts to cup my cheek. "Does this mean I get to call you my *boyfriend*?"

"Call me whatever you want," he says against my lips. "As long as I get to call you mine."

Thirty-Two

wish I had a camera.

The look on Alice's face when she opens the door, and then when her eyes fall to Theo's hand in mine, is nothing short of priceless.

"What's this?" Her mouth spreads into a wide grin I'm sure I've never seen on her before. "Are you guys back together?"

I glance up at Theo, letting him take the lead on this. I'm not sure "back together" would be the right way to describe it, but it's not too far off. Besides, Alice doesn't know the truth of why we really started seeing each other, so from her perspective "back together" makes sense.

Theo meets my eyes with a shy smile, brings our clasped hands up to his mouth to kiss my knuckles, and says, "Something like that."

"I'm glad." She claps him on the shoulder, the contact only lasting for a second before her arm falls back against her side. "Come on in. We've got a lot of work to do."

The door is held open by a cardboard box, and her welcome mat is gone. Inside, a stack of boxes block the couch and what appears to be kitchenware wrapped in old newspaper covers every surface of the granite countertops. I get to work helping Alice pack up in the kitchen while Theo loads her car with the boxes that were previously packed. He picks up each one easily, without so much as a grunt except for when he adjusts the wide TV box against his shoulder. Before long, sweat beads his forehead, his skin glistening.

"When are you leaving?"

"Next week," Alice says, grabbing an empty box and a roll of tape. "I'm staying with Christine in the meantime. The goal is to move all my stuff out of here by the end of the day."

"So soon," I say. "You must be excited."

"I'm more stressed at the moment. Aside from Theo, I couldn't get help from anyone last minute, so I'm really glad he brought you. Christine helped for approximately one hour before bailing on me yesterday. But I'm sure excitement will follow once I've gotten everything taken care of." She stares at the stack of boxes taking up her living room. "There's no way all this is going to fit in my car."

"Will you need a second trip?"

"That's what I was trying to avoid." She heaves a sigh. "I *need* to get out of here today."

I stare at her for a long moment. "That bad, huh?"

She sends me a knowing look that speaks for itself. No wonder she took the TV. She's taking almost everything, if the empty cabinets are any indication.

"Car's full," Theo announces, watching us stare at the

stack of remaining boxes. "Are you really taking all of this with you when you move?"

"Of course not." She crosses her arms over her chest. "I'm just taking what's mine."

"Does that mean you're giving away any of this stuff?" he asks. "Can I call dibs on the espresso machine?"

He elbows her side playfully, and she waves him off, shaking her head but smiling with exasperated fondness. There's something about seeing them interact together that clicks something into place for me. This must've been how they were together in high school, teasing each other the way life-long friends do. There are no more longing looks on Theo's end, no visible trace of the feelings he has for her.

Is it possible that he's gotten over her?

She's moving across the country next week, and he's not a wreck the way he was the night of her engagement party. Instead, he's happily helping her pack and calling dibs on whatever she's leaving behind. He did exactly what he told me he would, didn't he? He let her go.

"Maybe I shouldn't, but I kinda feel bad for Ben," he says, eyes sweeping the bare apartment. "You're not leaving him with much, are you?"

She shrugs, but I don't quite buy the careless motion of her shoulders. "He's lucky I'm leaving him the sectional."

"He is lucky," I say. "It's a lot nicer than mine."

"My neck can speak to that." Theo rolls his head in slow circles, startling us both when his neck cracks with a loud, crunching sound. His eyes cut to me in playful accusation. "I couldn't do that before spending one night on your couch."

I'm about to roll my eyes and call him dramatic when Alice's face morphs.

"When did you sleep on her couch?" She glances up at him, confused. He stills, eyes trained on the floor as he realizes the mistake he's made.

"Um." I'm still racking my brain for a way out when headlights beam through the blinds, and the low rumble of a car engine sounds outside. It's just my luck that my way out of this conversation includes *him*. "Is that who I think it is?"

"What?" Alice turns to where I'm looking.

"Someone just pulled up," Theo says.

We wait in silence as the car door slams. A moment later, a key turns the lock and the front door swings open.

His shoulders are slumped as he walks into the living room, eyes downcast. That's why he doesn't see us at first. When his head lifts and his eyes lock squarely on me, he freezes for a moment. He turns toward Alice, and then Theo, and that's when his whole body flinches back.

"Ben—"

He doesn't wait around for his brother's explanation. Ben turns on his heel and walks out the door he just came through. Theo doesn't hesitate before following him outside.

Alice and I exchange a look, both of us wondering if we should follow. This feels like a reckoning. After months of tip-toeing around each other, this is the confrontation that was coming. They need a chance to work out their issues in an honest way. It shouldn't be our responsibility to interfere or help mend their relationship.

I nod once, and we walk outside.

"What the hell are you doing here?" Ben asks. "You can save whatever speech you planned—she's made up her mind. It's your fault she even applied to that internship."

"I don't have a speech this time." Theo's voice is dry as he holds up his hands in surrender. "She asked me to help her move out, and that's all I'm doing."

This time. A callback to how this all started, but Ben can't know that, can he? He doesn't react to Theo's specific phrasing, doesn't seem to notice anything strange in it. But then, he's too angry to notice much of anything.

"That doesn't change the fact that she's leaving *because of you.*" He shoves at Theo's chest, and though Theo doesn't fall over, he nearly loses his balance.

"Ben, *stop!*" He halts at the sound of Alice's voice, head swinging around, eyes bulging with rage. "I…thought you weren't coming back until nine." Alice shifts her weight from one foot to the other. "They're just helping me pack."

"It had to be *them* of all people. It's not like there was anyone else you could call that I'm still on good terms with." He keeps his eyes trained on Alice, maybe because of the three of us, she's the only one he can stand to face. Even if his venomous tone suggests he'd rather have nothing to do with any one of us. In a way, I can't blame him. In his mind, he's sharing oxygen with three enemies. Three ghosts reflecting the mistakes he'd sooner bury than own up to.

"Ending our engagement and moving halfway across the country wasn't enough, now you need to humiliate me in my own home? Haven't you done enough?"

"Don't talk to her like that." I step forward, blocking him from Alice. "You don't have the right. You're just as culpable—"

"*Me*? You think this is *my* fault? What the fuck is even happening—" He lets out a laugh, humorless and wild. Runs his hands through his hair until his face stretches back. It would almost be comical if he wasn't so pissed. "I would still be engaged if it wasn't for you! That fucking text *blew up* my entire life!"

Okay, so we're doing this out in the open then. I'm conscious of every car that passes by, a few even slowing down to stare. Despite the curiosity of strangers, I'm far more scared of the chaos that will be unleashed if we attempt to hash this out inside. There's an entire box labeled BREAKABLES in there—any one of us might be tempted to crack it open for ammo.

"She didn't blow up your life," Alice cuts in. "I did. I chose to end our relationship, and don't you *dare* pretend not to know why."

"You saw the text before I did!" He throws out his arm, raising his voice. "You wouldn't even let me explain—"

"You didn't have to. It opened my eyes to what's been right in front of me this entire time. Every time we had a fight, she's the one you ran to. Do you know how many times I wondered if you were looking for a reason, any reason at all, to break up with me so you could be with her instead?"

A punch in the gut couldn't knock the air from my lungs as much as that question just did.

I never knew about any of their fights. I always thought

Ben and Alice were happy and in love and in it for the long haul. He never once hinted at the cracks in their relationship. I wonder how much I would've latched on to the hope of one day having him for myself if I'd known.

"I've been trying to get through to you for *years* about how unsatisfied I've been with my career, but every time I tried you took it as an attack. You never listened to me, never asked me what I wanted, not once. You can't blame Theo for reminding me of the dreams I left behind, or Marcela for one goddamned text message. They didn't blow up our engagement." She shakes her head. "They saved us from the worst mistake of our lives. Ben, we don't work."

I don't notice the shine of his eyes until tears streak down Ben's face. He tries to hide his face with his hands, but it's too late. Of all the times we've shared our pain in the past, of all the low moments we've experienced together, I've never seen him like this. I've never seen him broken.

We used to understand each other in a way other people didn't. That's why I've always been drawn to him. He was the first guy I ever saw myself in. I latched on to that, believing that was the reason why we should be together. But maybe we're too much alike in the worst ways for us to have ever worked out.

Ben doesn't understand how this happened, but I do. He told me once this was his worst fear. Becoming like his father, abandoned by everyone he loves. Now I'm watching it happen in real time.

"Why is everything always my fault?" His voice comes out garbled from the effort of keeping his voice steady. "Why am I the only one to blame here? If you never saw that message, we'd still be together."

"Maybe." Alice sniffles. She's crying too, now. "But that doesn't change the fact that we had problems we couldn't solve. Getting married wouldn't have fixed them."

"Right. Fine. I'm the problem, once again." He heaves a deep breath, collecting himself. "Never mind that *you* were the one looking for a reason to leave, and you found it in the form of something I had no control over. But sure, I'm the bad guy here."

"I never said that—"

"You didn't have to." He's not looking at her anymore. He needs someone to blame, and his eyes are pinned straight on the only logical source in his brain. His brother.

"This is exactly what you wanted, isn't it?" Ben asks. "Well, congratulations. I ruined your life all those years ago, and now you've successfully ruined mine."

"I never wanted this." Theo shakes his head.

"And I don't believe you," Ben seethes. "You never would've turned the two people I care about most against me otherwise."

"Enough." Theo drags a hand over his face, exhausted. "It's only been a few months, and we're back to the same bullshit. I made my feelings about your relationship with Alice clear from the start, but she made her own decision. I never influenced her. And let me make one more thing clear to you: No part of my relationship with Marcela was to get back at you. You're the one who chose to see it that way. It was never a game, it was a method of survival. For both of us. That's how it started, anyway. Anything after that, quite frankly, is none of your goddamned business."

His chest falls, shoulders sinking in relief. I never realized how much the lie of how we started was weighing on him, but with the truth finally out Theo seems calmer. More assured of himself.

"I came back to San Antonio to be closer to family, but if you're going to continue blaming me for your own actions, we need to get something straight." He steps forward. "I'm not gonna take this abuse from you anymore. Any part of it. At this point, we're only brothers in name. We may as well stay that way."

"You're not the martyr you think you are." Ben grits his teeth. "You can't put this all on me! You said it yourself—you've only been back for a few months, and my life has *imploded* because of you!"

Theo lets out a mirthless laugh. "Of course I know I'm no martyr. But I'm not the one who blew up your life. I almost did try to, once," he admits, looking at his brother head-on. I try to catch his eye, shake my head, anything to silently communicate to him that he doesn't have to go this far, doesn't have to be this honest, but he doesn't so much as spare me a glance. "You don't know what it looks like for me to ruin your life, and you have Marcela to thank for that."

Ben's brows crease, his expression turning wary. He turns to face me. "What is he talking about?"

Alice is looking at me too, the same confusion written on her face as when she asked when Theo slept on my couch. I wonder if she's piecing together the ways they're related, even now, waiting for Theo to confess his greatest shame.

"You don't have to do this." I take his hand, make him meet my eyes. "It's already over. You didn't do anything wrong."

His gaze is steady as he looks down at me. He gives a slight nod, telling me he's okay, silently communicating that this is something he needs to do, and that's when it hits me.

I don't want to lie anymore.

He wasn't talking about the relationship we had before, not really. That's never been a lie, even when I was telling myself it was. *This* is the lie he meant. The secret he kept from both of them for months.

"I almost told you not to marry my brother," he says to Alice. "At your engagement party. I didn't have any right to involve myself in your relationship, and I'm thankful Marcela stopped me. I'm ashamed of myself for the way I acted, but I can't say there's much about that night I regret." He brings our clasped hands to his chest, intertwines our fingers. My chest fills when he looks down at me, eyes soft. "Except for any doubt it made you place in our future. If I could do everything about that night differently and still walk away with you at the end of it, I'd do it this second if it meant being worthy of you."

I don't know who looks more shocked, Alice or Ben. Alice keeps blinking at us like she can't believe what she's seeing. For a moment, Ben just freezes. I'm not sure what Theo thought he would accomplish by coming clean to his brother, if it was to clear his conscience or any doubt I'm still harboring about our relationship, but whatever the reason can't be worth the ammo he just put into Ben's hands.

A derisive clap of his hands and humorless laugh fill the air. He doesn't look angry anymore.

"Well, isn't that romantic?" His smile is brutal, and it's aimed straight at me. "You stopped him from running away with my fiancée, by what? Throwing yourself at him?" Another laugh. "Well, if that isn't love, then I don't know what is."

"Ben, don't—" Alice tries, but it comes out half-hearted. Resigned.

"No, no, they should know what they're getting themselves into," he says over her. "Don't fool yourselves into thinking you can come out of this as something real. You're smarter than that, Marcela." He gives me a knowing look, one that's both familiar and chastising. "He's gonna hurt you the same way he hurt me. I told you all about that once, didn't I?"

He did, but he also left out so much. I can understand why Theo needed a clean break from him, at least for a while. He came back eventually. Maybe his return was influenced by Alice at the time, but I wonder if she's not the only reason after all. If Theo kept coming back, hoping something about his relationship with Ben would change for the better.

"No fiancée, no best friend, no brother. And it all started when he moved back. You really think that's a coincidence? You're willing to take that risk?"

I wonder if Ben knows he's found a way to use my worst fears against me, twist and jab them straight into the center of my chest. But it's the way he's warped them to make himself out as the victim that finally pulls me back. Because it all comes back to what *he* wants.

"No." I shrug. "I don't think it's a coincidence. I just think it makes you a shitty person."

"You're fucking delusional." He's called me that before, hasn't he? He steps backward, grabs his car keys from his jeans pocket, and walks around to the driver's side. "I'm done. With all of you." He looks at each of us in turn before shaking his head and hiding away inside his car.

I take a deep breath as his car pulls out of the parking lot, watching as it turns the corner and disappears. Theo isn't the person his brother thinks he is. I've known that all along. That's not the part of what he's said that bothers me.

Don't fool yourselves into thinking you can come out of this as something real.

I tried telling myself something similar at the start of this, didn't I? It's why I set boundaries in place, never mind all the times we broke them. We weren't supposed to last this long, but we did. We weren't supposed to fall for each other, but we did. We weren't supposed to become something real, but we did.

We've beaten the odds before, so who's to say we can't do it again?

Alice heads back inside, but Theo makes no move to do so.

"Are you okay?" he finally asks. I glance up at him, this man I should've lost a long time ago, and nod.

"I should be asking you that." He's the one who just cut himself off from his brother. As shitty as Ben might be, that still has to hurt. "Are you, Theo? Okay?"

He drags in a deep breath, steadying himself. "I'll be fine, Marcela."

It's true enough, I think. He's not fine now, but he will be with time. I wrap my arms around him, giving him the comfort I know he needs. His arms come around my back, pulling me into him.

"It was a long time coming," he goes on. "Something has to change between us before we mend our relationship. If that's even something either of us wants to do. And right now, it's the last thing I want."

"I don't blame you. Believe me. Our friendship soured when I stopped doing what he wanted. I made plenty of mistakes too, but there's no going back for me. I understand why you can't, either. Why you might not ever be able to."

"As much as I hate him, I can't close the door completely," he says. "He's my brother, but that doesn't mean I have to subject myself to his crap all the time. Unfortunately, that also means I'll always care about him. Even if he never changes."

I want to tell him that that's okay. He can change his mind at any point, give Ben all the chances he's willing to give or none at all.

"He's wrong, you know," he says. "We're not delusional. We walked into this with open eyes from the get-go."

"Not you, though," I remind him. "I didn't tell you—"

"You may not have said his name, but you told me there was a guy," he counters. "You were as honest with me as you were comfortable being. I can't fault you for that." He gusts out a sigh that tickles the top of my head. "What are you thinking?"

I tilt my head up to the dusky sky. Instead of answering, I tell him we should help Alice so she's not stuck here another night. We spend the next two hours boxing up Alice's entire life with Ben until the walls are bare and the living and dining rooms are nearly empty. Since we came in Theo's car, we play the most high-stakes game of Tetris of my life filling it with Alice's remaining belongings.

When we finish unloading everything at Christine's apartment, Theo hugs Alice goodbye and I count all three seconds it lasts for. They speak quietly for a moment, words I can't hear from where I'm standing beside the passenger door. They wave as they walk away from each other, a final send-off before Alice steps inside and Theo climbs into the driver's seat.

On the drive home, Theo takes my hand and asks, "My place or yours?"

I smile at him, at this man I don't have to part from yet.

Thirty-Three

A pparently, being in a "serious" relationship means taking turns shuffling an overnight bag to each other's place every week; keeping extra food in the fridge and toiletries in the bathroom; and playing rock paper scissors to decide what to watch on Netflix, where to go out to eat, and whether to spend the weekend in or out of the apartment.

Theo proves to be the more magnanimous of the two of us, never disappointed on the nights I win the final decision. However, the same can't be said for me after I'm dragged across town to a burger joint that burns our fries and gets both our orders wrong. I stare daggers at him across the table all night until he offers to make it up to me with the takeout of my choice.

"You're too good to me." I bump his shoulder with the side of my head in affection as he starts the car. He smiles down at me, and I almost say it. Three little words I've been holding inside my chest since the night he asked for more.

"Not possible." He chuckles to himself. "We probably should've looked up reviews before we tried somewhere new."

"Probably," I agree, staring out the window as he pulls onto the ramp. "You know, this relationship thing isn't much different from what we were doing before. Although, we probably spent more time at my apartment than anywhere else."

"That's why I always vote to go out more." He glances at me once he's merged onto the middle lane. "We were only real behind closed doors, when there was no one around to prove anything to. Now that we get to be real everywhere, I'm making up for lost time."

His explanation makes my heart melt. "In that case, how can I say no to that?"

My apartment is ice cold when we arrive back. *What the hell?* Theo and I exchange a look before I rush to the thermostat. It's stuck on sixty degrees, but it feels even colder. Theo offers to call the front office right when I realize what happened. I turned it off days ago because I knew I'd be at Theo's apartment.

"No need," I say as I flip the switch back to auto and turn on the heat. "Old conservation habits die hard."

"Guess we should warm up in the meantime." A mischievous glint lights his eyes as his arms pull me into his chest. "I have a few ideas."

"Oh?" My blood heats with anticipation. "Let's grab a couple blankets first." I point him in the direction of the linen closet as I step inside my bedroom to change.

After dressing in my warmest pair of pajamas that won't last a second on my body as soon as Theo comes back, I can't shake the feeling I've lost sight of something. I don't remember what until he returns.

The door swings open. Instead of blankets, Theo's holding a large, unopened box in his arms. His last gift to me on the date I ruined. The one I didn't have the courage to open, just like the three little words I don't have the courage to say to him.

"You never opened it." He sounds more confused than disappointed. "Why?"

"I..." A heavy sigh deflates my chest. "I don't know. I guess I was waiting for the right moment, and then I completely forgot about it when I put it away." It's not quite a lie, but definitely not the whole truth.

"This might actually be better," he says, setting the box on the floor. "We can open it together. That's how I thought this would go anyway. I'll go grab a knife from—"

I wrap a hand around his wrist, halting him. Confusion settles over his features again. He steps closer to me, assessing whatever my face must look like right now.

"Wait." I don't have a good reason to stop him. When I pictured myself opening the box, I was alone. More assured of myself, the way Theo was when he laid his heart out on the table for me. When he was more honest than he needed to be with Ben and Alice. When at the end of it all, he still chose me.

If I could do everything about that night differently and still walk away with you at the end of it, I'd do it this second if it meant being worthy of you.

He's not the unworthy one here. *I* am.

I want to be the person he sees in me, but his gift is a reminder of the person I was when I ran from him. The one who broke his heart and ruined his grand gesture because I was too scared to try. Maybe I'm scared that when I open this box,

I'll realize just how well and truly unworthy of him I am. Of how incapable I am of maintaining something real. He's done so much for me, but what have I ever done but push him away?

But it's also more likely that I'm being dramatic. Letting my fears rule me, despite all my best efforts to set them free. *Easier said than done.* We've been official for weeks, but I still can't shake the feeling that we've both been holding back. The words I won't say and the box I never opened. The tentative way he looks at me sometimes, scared of doing or saying the wrong thing to push me too far. I'm not sure he realizes I'm terrified of messing this up the same way he is.

He's looking at me that same way now, soft eyes and tired smile. Instead of asking, he heaves a sigh and kisses the top of my head. "It's okay," he tells me. "We'll wait. But trust me, you're gonna kick yourself for waiting so long when you finally open it."

"I won't wait much longer," I assure him. When we're both cocooned in my bed, a mix of tangled limbs, I assure myself of it, too.

No more waiting.
No more holding back.

My mother lives alone in the house she raised me in. The cheery yellow paint looks fresh, and so does the vibrant blue of the front door. The wooden fence is wide open, which is odd since she's nowhere to be seen outside. It's not like her to be absent-minded about that sort of thing. I'm about to call her when I finally spot her emerging from the backyard, dressed in her straw sun hat and bright orange gardening gloves. I breathe a sigh of relief.

"Mija, what are you doing here?"

She meets me at the front door near her rosebush, the vines grayed to near white. I'm not sure how she manages it, but no matter how harsh the winter it endures, by late spring, her roses are always in full bloom. Her surprise turns to concern as she inspects my face. Whatever she sees makes her frown, brows furrowing.

"Let's get you inside."

She removes her gloves as we pass through the door, tossing them aside on the porch rather than taking the time to put them away properly. Inside, she says, "Give me a moment to wash up. I've been using the weed killer all morning, which I really need to stop altogether. Yolanda from next door is convinced the stuff gave her cancer last year. She's got a lawsuit going on with the company, you know." I follow as she goes toward the bathroom.

"I remember, you told me about that the last time I visited," I remind her. I've heard all her stories at least three times. "Aside from working with poison, how've you been?"

"Oh, you know nothing much changes around here," she says. "But let me guess, you're here for the salsa and tortillas, ah? You're in luck. I just made some yesterday. I was going to call you when I got through with the garden. To ask if you wanted me to drop them off, but I guess there's no need now." Now that she mentions it, I realize my stockpiles are running low again.

"That's…oh, well, thank you." I shake my head. "Actually, I have some news I thought you might like to hear."

"What news?" She sticks her head out the door. I'm better able to take her in now that she's taken off her gardening garb. Her hair is graying at the roots, as if she hasn't been keeping up with touch-ups as much as she'd like. But even so, it's her eyes that still make her look young. They're big and brown and brimming with excitement as she looks into my eyes. "Good, I hope?"

"Definitely good." I nod at her, trying to contain my nerves for what I'm about to tell her. Last time I told her about a guy I was dating, I was too naive to see past my giddy excitement. Now I wonder if I'm too jaded to recognize what happiness looks like when it's staring me in the face.

Once she finishes up in the bathroom, she leads me to the bright green sectional she bought last year. One touch of the velvet material tells you how comfortable it is, especially compared to the years-old, threadbare couch I grew up with. It's no wonder she raves about all the naps she has on this thing.

"What's his name?" I can't be sure how she immediately knows this is about a guy, or if she's just being hopeful.

"How do you know I'm seeing someone?" I cross my arms over my chest.

"What's his name?" she repeats, eyes twinkling. "How did you meet? And more importantly"—she looks me squarely in the eye—"when do *I* get to meet him?"

"Don't get too ahead of yourself." I haven't told her a single thing yet, but I can already tell my cheeks are turning pink. "His name is Theo."

"Last name?" She pulls out her phone, poised to google him. Good lord, this woman is no better than Angela.

"Mom!" I shake my head at her, resisting the urge to pull the phone away from her. "Put the phone away. This is why I don't tell you anything, geez."

"Excuse me for looking out for you." She scowls but does as I say. "I'll look him up later," she says beneath her breath.

"Theo Young." I watch her face for the first sign of realization. "That's his name. I met him…" We're heading into dangerous territory here.

"Young? Like Ben Young?" Understanding settles behind her eyes when I tell her he's Ben's older brother. When I told her I was dating Ben, she always made it a point to mention how happy I looked. Then when we broke up and I told her we were staying friends, she looked at me with such pity I couldn't stand it. Now the first signs of wariness creep into her eyes. "I see. What does he think of you and his brother?"

I'm done. With all of you.

Of all the people who have come and gone from my life, I've never had the satisfaction of a confrontation before Ben. Getting a clean break, no matter the mess that brought it on in the first place. It feels good to finally know where we stand with each other, even if we're no longer on speaking terms.

"We're not friends anymore," I say. "A lot has happened the past few weeks. You probably don't want the full story."

"Of course I want to know!" Her voice raises, and maybe it's her tone compounded with the four walls of my childhood home around me that suddenly makes me feel like a preteen again. The fights we used to have, the blame I used to put on her for something outside of her control. "You're my daughter. If you're hurting, I need to know about it. Tell me."

So I do. I spill my guts, starting from the very beginning. The engagement party, discovering his feelings for Alice, stopping him from confessing them. I tell her about our friendship, but I hesitate to admit our arrangement. It's not exactly a mom-approved topic of conversation, but I explain around it, and she gets the gist. "I wasn't supposed to fall for him. None of this was supposed to happen."

"Aye, mija. She pulls me into her arms. "There is no 'supposed to.' It doesn't work that way. You don't get to decide who your heart wants."

"Then what *do* I get to decide?" I ask her, voice wobbly. "What do I get to control?"

"Not very much, I'm afraid." She wipes the tears from my cheeks. "Only what to do about it."

What does that mean? I'm about to ask when she continues. "You get to decide if staying is worth the pain you'll endure, the sacrifices you might have to make to keep him, all the good things he brings to your life. You get to decide your limits, and when to walk away should you need to. None of those are easy decisions to make, but they're necessary. For your happiness, as well as his.

"It doesn't mean you failed if things don't work out." She smooths the hair back from my face, wipes away the tears I didn't realize were falling from my cheeks. "Nothing in this life is certain. We know that more than most people."

"I love him," I tell her, and it's the most conviction my voice has ever held. "He's worth staying for. He's worth all of it."

"Then have faith in him, Marcela." Her arms wrap around my back, small but strong. "Have faith in yourself, too."

Faith. That's what I've been missing all along.

When she asks me to tell her about him, I start from the very beginning. I tell her about his mistakes and mine, the ways we helped each other overcome them. I tell her about reenacting the last scene from *Before the Dawn* and the way my heart leapt when he dipped my body and kissed my cheek, and the way the crowd of teens roared afterward, led by Andy. I tell her about the "touchdown" I made during the date he planned, and how I almost ruined everything with my fear later at dinner.

"I hate how much your father leaving hurt you. I wish I could stop it from affecting you this way." Her arm tightens around my shoulders.

"Me, too. But you know what?" I glance at her, and suddenly I can't help the small smile that breaks through. "I'm not afraid anymore."

"So when do I get to meet him?" she asks again, nudging my side with an elbow.

"Hmm, I don't know." I tap my chin in thought. "I'll bring him around when there's a ring on this finger." I hold up my left hand, wiggling my ring finger. She rolls her eyes heavenward and heaves a deep, bone-weary sigh. "Or maybe I'll just invite you to the ceremony and you can meet him afterwards."

"You think you're funny?" Her tone is sarcastic, but her eyes are glittering. She slaps my hand playfully, telling me to be serious, which only makes me take it a step further.

"Or maybe I'll wait until you're a grandma."

She roars her outrage, and I laugh until my stomach hurts.

Thirty-Four

I am a faithless idiot no longer.

All in. I'm all in. The more I tell myself this, the more I believe it.

I take a deep breath before gliding the scissors across the tape, careful not to pierce through the cardboard. I have a half hour to myself before Theo is due home, and just enough courage to face up to one of my last mistakes.

I let go of the cardboard flaps with a gasp. Inside the box, face up, is a hardback edition of *An Ember in the Ashes* with the latest cover. Theo was paying more attention than I thought when he asked about my favorite books. He even remembered when I complained about cover changes, and my disinclination to buy the new covers to match despite how much it bothers me. I find the second book in the series buried beneath other books. In fact, the entire box is filled with books from my Buy Again shelf on Goodreads. There isn't a single book missing from that list. At the very bottom of the box is an envelope addressed with my name in a messy scrawl.

I've never seen his handwriting before now. I pull out the card and open it to reveal the handwritten letter inside.

Marce (no, I'll never stop calling you that),

I haven't told you this yet, but I am endlessly inspired by you. You have the biggest heart of anyone I've ever known, but what's most surprising is that you don't even know it. You're always trying to give more of yourself to people, even if they don't deserve it. Maybe I'm even one of those people, but you'll probably tell me differently. Anyway, I love how easy it is for you to see the good in people, even when they're at their worst.

I've been wanting to pay you back for your kindness for a while, and I finally got the idea a few weeks back, as you can probably tell by the contents of this box. I've never seen anyone as passionate about something the way you are about sharing your love of reading. I was in awe of you the night of your first book club. No one talks about books the way you do. It kills me that a woman with your strength ever felt so isolated growing up, but I suppose I have a lot of books to thank for turning you into the person you are now.

When you said you donate a pile of books from your own collection every month to your high school's library, it reminded me all over again of your endless kindness for others. It's something people take for granted, and it made me want to give you something in return. You should never be without your favorite books.

If you'll let me, I'll make sure each and every one of your all-time favorites are always signed by their author. Because you deserve to have special books in your personal collection.

Theo

This man is far more than I deserve. If I'm lucky, I'll spend the rest of my life learning how to deserve him.

When I look inside, every single copy is signed by the author. Some were personalized to other readers, but others are special editions I could never afford. *He knows me*, I think as I place each book back inside the box and push it beneath my desk. *But I know him, too.*

By the time Theo arrives, my mind is turning over possibilities. More than once, he asks me what the sly smile on my face is all about, and more than once I dodge his barrage of questions. An idea bursts to life fully formed when he tells me about Friday's last game of the season over dinner. It doesn't take much to convince him to spend the night at his place tomorrow, but a silent question remains in his furrowed brows.

"What are you so happy about tonight?" he asks as my thumb reaches up to smooth away the tension between his brows.

I shake my head, resisting the urge to even say *You'll find out soon enough.* Knowing him, there's no way he'd let me get away with it. I distract him for the final time tonight by whispering something dirty in his ear that makes him drop his fork and drag me into the bedroom. Unfortunately for me, it only makes it harder for me not to tell him everything inside my heart.

I love you. I trust you. I have faith in us.

But I force myself to wait, because it'll be all the more special when I do.

In all my wild excitement and grand plans, there's one important fact I failed to consider: half a week is not nearly enough time to plan a grand gesture.

I worried over my own mediocrity for days, and then worried it would all be for nothing when I was almost kicked off Theo's campus on my way to the practice field. No wonder it took him two weeks to pull off his grand gesture. But I've waited far too long to tell him how I feel as it is. I'm not waiting any longer.

The only problem with my impatience to grand gesture him back is there wasn't much I could do in a time crunch. Let alone the fact that I've never grand gestured someone in my life, *and* that I was mistaken for a student right as the practice field came into view when an older teacher patrolling outside asked to see my hall pass. Once I explained the situation, he pointed me in the direction of the front office, where I could sign in. Unfortunately for me, that required doubling back all the way where I started from. *Great.*

The practice field is crowded with rowdy teenagers. No part of me is excited to push through them to get to Theo, who I'm having a hard time spotting as it is. I push myself to the tips of my toes, scanning the crowd for a tall, burly blond man, scowling to myself when I come up short.

Where the hell is he?

Of course. Now that I've gone through the trouble of making it to the field, he's nowhere in sight. I'm the absolute *worst* at this.

"What are you wearing?"

I grab at my chest with a hand as I whip around. There he is, standing right in front of me in sweats and a hoodie, clipboard hanging from one hand as he ruins half a week's worth of mediocre planning.

"No!" I shove at his chest with a pom-pom when he tries to hug me. "Where were you ten minutes ago? Everything is going wrong!"

"I was dropping off attendance," he says, bewildered eyes scanning my outfit from head to toe. "You're wearing my jersey."

I'm not only wearing his jersey, but also face paint with his number on my cheeks. My hair is in pigtails, and the hairstyle alone was enough to age me down ten years. Coupled with the outfit, a backpack with a rolled poster sticking out, and pom-poms, it's no wonder the staff was confused.

"I had this all planned out," I whine. "I was going to wait until all the kids were gone, sneak in through the gate when you were alone, and perform this stupid cheer routine I learned on YouTube."

His eyes grow bigger the longer I talk. "You learned a cheer routine for me?"

"Yes, I did." I cover my face with my hands, careful not to smudge the paint on my cheeks. "I even watched the video again in the car because I was worried about forgetting the moves. Then you went and ruined my plans and now I forgot them again."

I shove at his shoulder when he has the nerve to laugh at me.

"It's not funny!" I come at him with a whirl of pom-pom furry this time. His eyes shut with the force of his grin, his laugh booming louder beneath the clear, open sky. He bats the poms away easily, crushing me to his body and bending to kiss me in a way that can't be described as decent on school grounds.

"I love you." The words come rushing out of me as his arms wrap around my back, pulling me into him. My chest fills with a flood of emotion. I cup his face in my hands and look into those gorgeous blue eyes that doomed me from the start. "It's not too soon to say that, is it?"

"Are you kidding me?" He shakes his head like he's in awe of me. "I would've said it first, and a lot sooner if I thought I wouldn't scare you away."

"Been holding back on me, have you?" I look up at him shyly. "If we both have, I guess it's my fault. This was supposed to be my way of telling you I don't have to try anymore. I'm all in, Theo."

"All in, huh?" He tugs on one of my pigtails, fingers curling around my hair. No one's ever looked at me the way he is now, with such love and affection it feels like my chest could burst at any second.

"All in." I nod up at him. "I'm not holding back anymore. I love you, Theo. I trust you. I'm choosing to have faith in us because there's no one else I'd rather be with than you."

It's a relief to finally get these words out.

I let out a squeal when he picks me off the ground, spinning us in circles. My arms wrap around his neck. I've never felt like this before. I never knew how happy loving another person could make me.

"You still haven't said it yet," I remind him as he sets me down, poking at his chest with a delicate finger. "Not that you have to if you don't mean it, or need more time first—"

He shuts me up with a quick kiss.

"I love you, Marcela." A hand brushes my hair back, grips the back of my neck until I'm looking up at him. "Don't you dare ever think otherwise."

"I won't," I tell him. "I promise."

"Looks like the field is clear." He flashes a wicked grin, the one I love so much. The one that started it all. "Let's see that routine you came up with."

I sit him down on a bench and pull out the poster I made for him. Theo's eyes widen at all the blue and silver glitter. The sign reads GO COACH THEO with about nine exclamation marks after it, the number 29 written on every inch of free space in alternating colors.

"I hate to break this to you, but those aren't our colors," he says, trying to hide his smile behind a hand and failing. "Those are our rival's...and we're playing them tonight."

"But…" I pout at him. "They're the Cowboys' colors."

"I know." He takes the poster from my hand, the edges curling from its time shoved in my backpack, and stares down at it like it's the best gift he's ever been given. When he glances back at me, his smile makes my heart melt all over again. "Thank you for this."

"That's not even the best part." I pull out my phone and put on a cheer mix I found on Spotify. It takes me a moment to remember the moves I learned, but he doesn't seem to mind my fumbling through the dance. Halfway through the routine, he stands up and pulls me onto the bench with him.

"Hey!" I shove at his chest with a blue pom-pom. "This isn't supposed to be dirty."

"Then let's go home and make it dirty." My thighs clench at the heat in his eyes. "Good with you?"

Home. It doesn't matter if he's talking about my place or his. Wherever Theo is feels like home.

"What time does the game start?" I ask. He tells me, and I calculate the amount of free hours that gives us. "Two and a half hours, not counting driving time."

"Then it's a good thing my place is closer." He nips at my ear, and I resist a shudder. "Come on, before you get me fired."

"Says the one who made it dirty." I scoff at him playfully.

I'm giddy with every step we take back to the car, and not even from all the "I love you" sex we're about to have. When we reach his car, he looks at me quizzically as I come to a stop beside the trunk. I knock on the metal twice, stalling.

"You might wanna check this thing before we get back."

He reaches out an arm as I try to back away, make a

quick break for my own car a few paces down the parking lot. "Marcela Ortiz, what did you stow away in my trunk?"

I gesture to the keys in his hand. "Only one way to find out."

He pushes the button that pops his trunk, and all that giddy excitement in my blood turns into pulsing anxiety. What if he hates it? Or worse, what if he ordered one without telling me? He already ruined the first half of my surprise. I'll scream into the sky if he's ruined this one, too.

His face changes from wary confusion to Christmas morning in the span of half a second as he unzips the garment bag, and I know I landed this one. "You *didn't*." He glances over at me, then back down at the costume.

"For the next book club," I tell him as his fingers graze the jacket of the suit. "You can be Captain America. Or would Thor have been better? Maybe I should've asked—"

He shuts me up with another kiss.

"I can't believe you actually did this for me." He can't stop smiling, and it's the most brilliant thing I've ever seen.

"I can't believe you gave me a box of special editions." He pulls me into him, gazing at me with such adoration, I'm surprised I'm not a puddle of goo at his feet. "You really know how to meld our worlds together. I only got the idea for my grand gesture from yours, and it wasn't half as good."

"Sure it was." He kisses my forehead. "I like the way you think. There's no reason for our worlds to be separate. Not when they're made so much better combined."

"Me performing cheers I don't know the moves to, you inspiring dirty daydreams cosplaying at work events." We're grinning like idiots. "Your world and mine."

"Your world and mine," he repeats. "Get in the car. Let's go home so I can show the woman I love how much I *appreciate* her." He says the word suggestively, in a way that has me sprinting for the front seat. When I ask about my car, he says we can go back for it after the game.

Four hours and the same number of orgasms later, I'm sitting on the cold bleachers with a blanket wrapped around my shoulders and my Kindle in my hands. Every so often, Theo turns to send a playful scowl my way. I return the gesture by sticking my tongue out at him each time.

When I finish my chapter, I jump up in my seat and hold up the sign Theo begged me to leave in the car. I don't even care about the odd stares I'm getting from parents and staff or the fact that I have no idea what's happening on the field when I yell Theo's name. He startles at the sound of my voice, but his frustration at whatever's happening in the game morphs at one look at me, curling sign in one hand and pom-pom in the other. His face breaks out in a wide grin that shows off his teeth. He shakes his head slightly at me, but he can't even feign exasperation.

"Don't be sad," I tell him after the game ends, the scoreboard displaying a 21–26 loss. "I'll break out the pom-poms again if it'll make you feel better."

"How can I possibly be sad when the woman I love owns pom-poms?" He's suddenly steering me to the car so fast, it's an effort not to trip over my own feet.

At home, when we finally have the privacy to jump each other again, we take our time. There's no rush, no place to be, no expiration date hanging above our heads. There's only the two of us, and all the time in the world.

Epilogue

ONE MONTH LATER

A re you freaking out?"

Theo rubs his palms on his jeans, I suspect because they're sweaty. He glances away from the blue painted door and down at me with wide, alarmed eyes. His smile is shaky, but when I reach for his (sweaty, indeed) hands, it eases into something more relaxed.

"Maybe a little," he admits.

"Stop worrying! She's going to love you."

"I can't help it." His voice pitches higher than normal. He takes a step back off the doormat, pulling me with him. I stay on the top step so we can talk at eye level. "I've never been in a meet-the-parents situation before. In fact, I'm pretty sure I'm the guy they warn you to stay the hell away from."

"You were never really that guy." I roll my eyes. When he shrugs, I squeeze his hands. "And it's one parent, so that should cut the pressure in half. Come on—" I tug him back toward the front door, succeeding only because his guard is down. His eyes grow comically wide as I ring the doorbell of my mother's house.

"Mija!" My mom pulls me into a bone-crushing hug, and I sink into her warmth. I pat her dark hair before pulling back from her. Her dark brown eyes flick over my shoulder. "And this must be the novio who took you away from me. Come in, come in."

She pulls Theo into a hug next. He towers over her, her head barely reaching his chest. My heart warms as I watch his hands squeeze her shoulders affectionately, the way his eyes crinkle from the smile he greets her with.

We follow her down the hall to the dining table. Theo's eyes roam the pictures hanging on the walls. The home I grew up in hasn't changed much since I left for college. The light blue paint in the living room looks fresh, even though the shade has stayed the same. The cherry wood table near the front door is littered with mail and a ceramic bowl of keys. The smell of my mother's cooking wafts from the kitchen, filling my nostrils with the scent of spiced ground beef and fresh bread. I may not live here anymore, but this house will always be home.

Theo pauses at a gigantic gold picture frame above the living room mantel. Twelve-year-old me is standing in front of a white backdrop, holding up the long skirts of a purple folklórico dress. My face burns as he grins and points at my chubby, adolescent cheeks. I bat his hand away, gripping his wrist and dragging him into the kitchen with all my might.

"I've got conchitas on the stovetop and tortillas fresh off the comal, so you two better be hungry."

"I'm always hungry," Theo tells my mom. She flashes her teeth, and I can tell she likes him already.

We serve ourselves soup and tortillas in my mom's gigantic, mismatching serving bowls and take a seat at the dining table. My mom asks us what we want to drink, and when we tell her, she grabs two cans of Coke from the fridge.

Theo's nerves evaporate as he gushes over my mom's cooking. Her cheeks turn a delightful shade of pink at the compliments, and she even gets up from the table to serve him seconds. He finished his first bowl in record time, considering my own is still piping hot.

"Thank you for the meal, Ms. Ortiz," Theo says, ever polite. Even though he has a good foot and a half on my mother, his voice is that of a terrified ninth grader. I rest a hand on his knee to stop its shaking. He stops, glances at my face, and takes a deep breath.

My mom's smile is kind. I warned her beforehand that he was nervous about lunch. "Of course! Thank you for coming, even though I know you were scared to." He freezes, and she rushes to reassure him. "No, no, that's fine! I was nervous the first time I met Marcela's grandparents. Of course, I was pregnant at the time—"

"We really don't need to rehash the story," I say, but my mother sighs, completely ignoring me.

"My life didn't turn out the way I planned, but I made *damn* sure my daughter could have a good life." She goes on. "I told her to ignore the boys and focus on school. And look at her now—not just one, but *two* degrees!" I blush, even if I am a bit pleased. "And a career! I was worried when she said she wanted to major in English—"

"Mom—"

She ignores me. "Especially because she insisted she didn't want to teach, which is what I wanted her to do. You'll always have job security in that field. They say it all the time on the news, *We need teachers, we don't have enough teachers*—"

"I'm not a teacher," I say, even though she's not listening. Theo is rapt, his attention squarely on my mother. "The point was to become a librarian, which I am now."

"Or nursing!" She brightens, as if just remembering. "There are never enough nurses, either. And I'm sure you'd make much more money, but then, you'd also have to work more hours—"

I don't try to interrupt this time. This is just the way she is, dreaming up big ideas that are never for her. She goes on until she circles all the way back to her first point, which in true fashion, turns out to be mortifying.

"…Which is why I gave her condoms when she went off to college."

I choke on my drink, fizz burning the back of my nostrils. Theo covers his smile with a hand.

"So she wouldn't end up like me." Her eyes soften. She reaches for my hands, which I reluctantly give her. Theo glances over at me, concern furrowing his brows. "You did it *right*. You waited until you finished school and settled into a good job. You put yourself first before finding a man to settle down with. That's the way you should do it."

My skin heats at the implication. "You make it sound like we're getting married or something." I shake my head. All of a sudden, I'm the nervous one.

My mom waves a hand, as if that's another moot point. To her, I guess it is. "You will." I nearly choke on my own saliva. Theo has the nerve to hide a laugh—at *me*—behind his hand. "Maybe to Theo, maybe to someone else. Or maybe you won't marry at all." I tilt my head, wondering if she's about to go off on a second tangent. "The point is I'm proud of you, no matter what you choose to do with your life." She reaches for Theo's hand. Hers is small and bony compared with his giant one. His hand curls around hers gently. "No matter who you choose to spend it with. I trust you, mijita de mi vida."

My eyes sting, even as I try to blink the tears away. *I trust you.* For so long, I haven't even trusted myself to make that decision. But now...

I meet my mother's warm brown eyes, the ones she gave me, crinkled at the corners. Then I look at Theo's. I used to think they were twin storms, but they're the calmest eyes I've ever looked into. A glittering ocean that washes peace over me.

"There. I've said my piece," my mom says with a crooked smile. "Let me go get the photo album. I have so many stories to share."

Theo looks up, an excited gleam in his eyes even as I throw my head back and let out a groan. So many *embarrassing* stories, more like. My mom leaves the table, and Theo gets up to follow. When I slowly rise from the table, he turns back to me.

"What's wrong?" he asks.

"Nothing." I shake my head, and I suspect my smile is watery. "I just didn't know relationships could be like this."

"Like what?"

"I don't know…" I take a moment to form the right words. "Like something you take day by day."

His smile comes easily. "Hey. Come here." I get up from the table and sink into his outstretched arms. "I'm right where I belong. Are you?"

I nod into his chest.

"That's all that matters," he tells me.

As my mother returns from her bedroom with three gigantic, floral-print albums, she calls us into the living room to look through them. With Theo and me on either side of her, she introduces my first boyfriend to my childhood via photographs. I don't care that we started out as rebounds, or if this is only a stop to something bigger. *Nothing* feels bigger than this.

In this moment, there's nowhere else I'd rather be.

DON'T MISS
GABRIELLA'S NEXT BOOK

COMING SUMMER 2025

YOUR BOOK CLUB RESOURCE

Reading Group Guide

THE NEXT BEST FLING PLAYLIST

Dear Reader,

For me, the start of every new writing project also marks the start of a new writing playlist. Music is an integral part of my process in order to get into the headspace of these new characters I'm creating and the world they live in. Some of these descriptions contain spoilers, so you may want to wait to read through this list until you're done with the book. Without further ado, here are some songs that can be found on *The Next Best Fling*'s writing playlist:

1. "Right Where You Left Me" by Taylor Swift: This song is peak Marcela pining over Ben for nearly ten years. He's long moved on, and she's still stuck in the past.

2. "The Other Girl" by Kelsea Ballerini (with Halsey): The dynamic between Marcela and Alice is an interesting one. They're not

exactly friends, but they don't resent each other or wish ill will on the other, either.

3. "Taste" by HUNGER: Anytime I was building sexual tension between Marcela and Theo, this song was on in the background. The entire *Mosaik* album truth be told, but if I had to pick a favorite it'd definitely be this one.

4. "Hotel Room" by Blake Rose: Proving that lyrics don't always have to match up with the actual story if the vibe is immaculate, this song was played so much during drafting that it ended up on my Top 5 on Spotify. To me, this was such a high-intensity sexual tension bop that finding out the song was about catching your partner cheating on you was such a shock to me…but not enough to take it off this list.

5. "Overdrive" by Conan Gray: This song captures everything dangerous and unclear about Marcela and Theo's relationship. They don't know what they can be together other than casual, even when "casual" can no longer contain the emotions they feel for each other.

6. "Hours" by Florrie: There is truly no better song that embodies Marcela and Theo's relationship than this one. Discovering this song felt like serendipity. The singer isn't over a past relationship, and neither is her new lover. They both acknowledge and understand each other's pasts and the ways they hold them back from going all in with each other, despite their growing feelings for each other.

7. "Golden" by Harry Styles: Longtime Swifties know what gold descriptions mean in a Taylor Swift song. I'm just silly enough to take it out of the Swift-verse and apply its meaning everywhere, even a Harry Styles song. When Marcela falls for Theo, she starts seeing him in shades of gold. But just like Harry, she's afraid of getting her heart broken by a sun that shines too bright.

8. "Champagne Problems" by Taylor Swift: This song was on repeat during Marcela and Theo's library date gone wrong. It's not a marriage proposal, but just like Taylor, Marcela knows she's letting down a good man who wants more from her.

9. "Fall In Love" by Caroline Kingsbury: I love a song with big emotion that you can

just blast in your car and scream the lyrics to. I can imagine Marcela having a cathartic moment with this song during the third act, when she's so unsure about whether she and Theo can actually make a real relationship work. Just like Caroline Kingsbury, she never really wanted to fall in love.

10. "Symptom of Your Touch" by Aly & AJ: This song was on repeat during Marcela and Theo's fraught reconciliation. Despite sinking into each other, Marcela still isn't sure if getting back with Theo is the right thing for both of them. But she knows one thing: she's done resisting the pull between them.

DISCUSSION QUESTIONS

1. Marcela's feelings for Ben have been unrequited for nearly a decade. Have you ever experienced unrequited love?

2. Do you think exes can truly be friends after their relationship ends? Why or why not?

3. Marcela and Alice were close friends who slowly grew apart once Alice and Ben started dating. Do you agree with Marcela's choice to phase Alice out but stay close friends with Ben? What do you think her life would be like in the present day if she'd made different choices in her past?

4. If you witnessed someone about to ruin a wedding (by running off with the bride/groom or otherwise), what would you do? Would you interfere like Marcela did, or would you watch the chaos unfold from afar?

5. Marcela holds herself back from love and relationships because she saw her parents' marriage fall apart when she was young. Could you empathize with her choices? Were there any times you were frustrated with her decisions?

6. Rebound relationships are often looked down upon because no one wants to feel like a second choice. Do you think Theo is Marcela's second choice, and/or vice versa? Can rebounds ever last?

7. Theo talks about cutting off communication with his father and brother after a family fight. Have you ever needed space from a family member determined to cross your boundaries? How did you resolve the situation?

8. At one point, Marcela wonders if the strong feelings she has for Ben, despite him being attached to someone else, makes her a bad person. However, she doesn't feel the same way about Theo despite him being in the same predicament with Alice. Why do you think that is?

9. When Theo tells Marcela he wants more from their relationship, she tells him that they don't know how to be in a "real" relationship. Do you believe she's justified in thinking this?

10. Have you ever planned a grand romantic gesture for someone, and/or vice versa? What was the experience like?

ACKNOWLEDGMENTS

Oftentimes I'll arrive at these really big moments in my life and think, *I can't believe I actually got this far.* As long as I can remember, I've dreamed of becoming a published author, and there are moments when I still can't believe I get to be one. Writing this page is a reminder that I couldn't have come nearly as far as I have without the help of so many people. Let me start from the beginning. The hugest of thanks to my parents for always being loving and supportive, and especially for always believing that this was a dream I could achieve, even when I didn't believe. Y'all are the best.

Thank you to my best friends and forever first readers, Asha and Justine. I wouldn't have the courage to put my work out there in the first place if it wasn't for your constant praise and belief that I'm actually kinda good at this writing thing. Special thanks to Natalia Sanchez, CP extraordinaire. I wouldn't be the writer I am today without you, and I can't wait for the day you're published alongside me. You're next. Everyone read it here first. Thanks also to Lexie Bowman and Shannon Bright for early reading and feedback, y'all are the best!

To the agent of my dreams, Samantha Fabien, thank you for cheering me on to greatness, and for being the calming presence I so desperately need in what can be an anxiety-inducing industry. Thank you for believing in me and my stories. Your encouragement and guidance is invaluable to me.

Junessa Viloria, thank you for loving Marcela and Theo as much as I do. But more than anything, the hugest of thanks to you and Sabrina Flemming for helping me mold this story into something I'm so incredibly proud of. This book is so much better now than it was before because of all the hard work and long nights (yes, I read the time stamps on those emails) you guys put into it. I'm so incredibly grateful that you guys believed this book could be something truly special.

Thank you to Mari C. Okuda and Shasta Clinch for spotting all my echoes, timeline errors, and positioning inconsistencies in copyedits. I'm much less embarrassed by these pages now because of you both. Huge thanks to Leni Kauffman for the most beautiful, stunning, gorgeous cover my eyes have ever had the pleasure to look upon. You seriously knocked it out of the park! Thanks to anyone I might've missed at the Forever Pub team. There's so much I don't get to see behind the scenes, so much hard work that may not get recognition from the authors who don't have a peek behind the publishing curtain; so for all the little and big things that went into making this book happen, thank you from the bottom of my heart.

Finally, to you. Yes, *you*, dear reader, for picking this book up. Whether you bought a physical copy from your local bookstore, downloaded the ebook or audiobook, or borrowed a copy from your local library (Marcela would approve). Whatever way, shape, or form this book came into your life, your support is truly invaluable to me.